SHELTER

LOST TOWN : BOOK TWO

NATHAN HYSTAD

Cover art: J Caleb Design
Edited by: Christen Hystad
Edited by: Scarlett R Algee
Proofed and Formatted by: BZ Hercules

ISBN: 9798301761096

PROLOGUE

Ten years ago

Arcadia

The breeze blew against Logan Rutherford's brow, helping ease the unbearable heat. His pants were torn at the ankles, and muck covered his hiking boots, but he was alive after two weeks across the Shift.

The first twenty-four hours, he'd stayed in place, praying Isla or the team at LTC might learn what happened, then find him. But the natural Shifts were rare, and it likely wouldn't strike that same location in Colorado for months.

He'd decided on the direction to take by the sunlight. He opted to have the blaring orb hitting his back rather than his face during the arduous days. Onward Logan walked, constantly checking the gear and inspecting the dark tablet. Without it, Logan couldn't connect to the Shift, stranding him on this world.

While he missed the creature comforts of home, he was proud of his accomplishment. He'd discovered a way to travel to a different planet, though it wouldn't become public knowledge. Logan hadn't started LTC for the glory. He'd done it to cure his insatiable curiosity. As a kid, his mother had told him to question everything, and to make his own decisions about what was real and what wasn't.

Logan pictured his mom receiving the news of his disappearance. She'd assume he'd been lost on a rock-climbing expedition, and would mourn his death with every fiber of her being. Dot's Diner in Carmichael, Indiana would fill with locals, offering a shoulder for her to cry on. All the while, Logan was here, very much not dead.

"For now," he whispered.

There were no signs of humanity, but he'd stopped along the journey to document various animals and bugs. Birds with three eyes; pink butterflies larger than his fist, fluttering through the air, unafraid of his presence. And why should they be?

The sun descended beyond the forest he'd carefully avoided. Out here in the plains, Logan spied the terrain, keeping high ground in case of an ambush. He couldn't imagine what might lurk in the shaded, cooler woodlands.

With the night threatening to envelop the land, Logan called it. His left knee flared from overactivity, and he wished he'd brought stronger painkillers along with his emergency rations. A cold compress too.

Logan chose a spot on the unforgiving ground, away from the rustling waist-high grass and a hundred yards past the looming treeline. The moment the last rays vanished, glowing orange insects revealed themselves. Others sang mournful tunes as they awakened.

He welcomed the sounds and stretched his legs out in a sun-tanner's pose while gazing at the blanket of stars. A constellation directly above reminded him of a cat, and another lower in the horizon passed for a football, if the proper dots connected.

Logan examined his pack, noting it was short on supplies. The water tablets were there in abundance, but he needed to cross a stream in the next while to refill his nearly empty canteen. He'd avoided fires so far, but the increasing darkness threatened to choke him. Logan hurried, jogging to the forest's edge, and gathered as many dry twigs and branches as he could before it was completely shrouded in night.

A fire would give him the solace he required to continue his perilous quest. He was Odysseus, seeking a path home to Ithaca. Logan hoped his journey was simpler than the tragic Greek hero's.

Logan formed the kindling, sparking the base with his lighter. It took a few tries, but it started to burn, and he slowly added fuel until a fire cast a crackling glow over his makeshift camp. He erected the small tent and opened the last of his prepackaged food.

"It was nice while it lasted." Logan bit into the protein bar, knowing he'd have to forage if he wanted to survive beyond a handful of days.

He finished his water, shaking a drop from the canteen, and screwed the cap on.

The land was beautiful, unspoiled by humanity. He imagined the LTC board members' expressions when they found out what he'd uncovered. Logan assumed they'd seek to monetize his incredible breakthrough, and he promised himself he'd never allow them to. He and Isla would work on creating a bridge between Earth and this world for the sake of research. Logan believed the Shift could carry them to countless unique planets. This was step one of his plan.

Logan was dozing when he heard the howling. Initially, he thought it was the wind cutting through the forest, but it quickly became apparent that wasn't the case. He rose, scanning his surroundings, which wasn't simple given the brightness of his fire and the darkness of the terrain.

The noise stopped, and he breathed easier. When it

began again, the creatures were closer. Panicked, he searched his pack for something to fight with, and came up empty.

Logan slowly spun, finding a trio of beings stalking toward his camp. They moved languidly; their flicking tails had…fingers on the ends. "What in the…"

A crack banged from the plains, and it continued, growing louder. Logan braced himself, unsure which threat was more menacing. The beasts were three feet high, probably weighing eighty pounds each.

"Get out of here!" a woman's voice shouted.

Logan froze, then saw the outline of a group coming to his defense. They bashed rocks together, the noise driving the threat from his camp. He watched the howling animals scatter into the forest.

There were six people wearing mismatched clothing. The woman's hair was cut unevenly, like she'd sawn it with a sharp rock. All the men wore beards, and one was missing an arm. The cloth over the stump was cinched tight.

"Thank you," he managed after a silent moment of appraising them.

"You're welcome," the woman said. She stood ahead of the others, indicating she was directing them.

"What's your name?" he asked.

"Ruby."

The men moved to his fire, stomping it out.

"What are you doing?" Logan demanded.

"The light's drawing the Hangers," Ruby said.

"Hangers?"

"That's what we call them. They hide in the treetops, dangling from branches, and drop when you're not expecting it. It's wise of you to be out in the open, not in the woods, but the fire is too interesting to ignore." Ruby narrowed her gaze. "Who are you, stranger?"

"Logan." He offered to shake her hand, and she flinched. She shook it after a brief hesitation, but it didn't seem normal.

"You're from Earth?" he asked.

The men chuckled as they collected his belongings. "Where else?"

"You could be a local…"

"No, there are no people on Arcadia," Ruby said.

"Arcadia." Logan tested the name on his tongue and smiled. "It's perfect." It denoted a virgin wilderness, an unspoiled land, again reminding him of his own personal Greek tragedy. Perhaps he'd died in the mountains, and this was the afterlife.

If that was the case, Ruby, the stunning woman before him, was an angel sent as a guide. She turned and began walking, while the men carried his pack and possessions.

He jogged to catch up. "Where are we going?"

Ruby glanced at him with a crooked smile. "Home. To Shelter."

PART ONE
REALITY

1

Caesar examined the cell phone. 00:00:00. The countdown had ended, but they hadn't Shifted.

The town residents lingered at the border, some openly weeping at the twist of fate. They'd seen a glimmer of Earth, and Summer Dawson had stepped beyond the barrier, rushing toward Harrison. She'd stayed on their planet while the rest of Carmichael remained behind.

"This doesn't change our mission," Anders reminded him.

"I know." Caesar viewed Amelia with Dot and almost reconsidered their plan. This town required solid leadership. "Before we go, we have to talk to the powers that be. Things are different."

Anders nodded and set his gun aside. "I agree."

Ten minutes earlier, they'd been prepared to leave in search of Logan Rutherford, as Isla had wanted. Now their outlook had taken a turn for the worse.

Amelia Miller brushed a strand of hair past her ear and sighed, a deep resounding exhale that he felt to his core. She was tired. They all were.

Caesar hugged her, sensing the woman needed reassurance and strength to guide her in the coming weeks. She melted into the embrace, and he released her, not wanting it to be uncomfortable for Amelia.

"What was that for?" she asked.

Caesar noticed how Dot and Sharon were watching. "You looked like you could use it."

"This is bad."

Caesar nodded. "Anders and I will find Logan, if he's still alive, and bring him to Carmichael."

"Should we go to the Den?" John Paulson had joined along with his sister, Haley.

"We'll have to pivot," Anders suggested. "Carly's pretty shaken up, and I should be there for them."

Caesar had the advantage of being alone, if he could consider that a good thing. Since Christine's death, there was only himself to worry about, and that was how he preferred it. Now that he'd met these individuals, his sense of duty had kicked in.

Caesar addressed the townsfolk, standing on the hood of Vince's truck. "Listen up!"

They continued chattering amongst themselves, and Caesar cleared his throat, talking louder. "Listen *up*!"

Vince stuck two fingers in his mouth and whistled piercingly, nabbing the residents' attention.

"Thanks," Caesar muttered to the gas station owner, who leaned on the cab, smoking a cigarette. "The Shift didn't work. The countdown ended, but we're not on Earth."

"No kidding," someone called from the crowd.

"Why?" Eldon bellowed.

"When will it try again?" Mack asked.

Caesar lifted an arm, silencing the flurry of incoming questions. He let them peter out, then continued. "We're entering phase two. The Shift only took Carmichael at the surface, meaning the wells are dry. Our food supply has to be monitored and accounted for. No more wasteful festivals, okay? I suggest you stay in the storage facility again until we're certain the Repulsor will keep the Howlers at bay. Then return home if you choose." He glanced at Amelia. "We have to name a leader, and I elect Deputy Miller."

She blinked, then frowned at him. "Dot's much more—"

"No, darling," Dot said. "I agree with Caesar. I second the motion."

"All in favor?" Caesar asked, and eighty percent of the locals' arms waved in the air. "Done. Amelia is in charge. She needs deputies for enforcement. Do we have any volunteers?"

Another ten arms rose, and he gestured to Amelia. "It's your team. You choose."

Amelia walked through the area, eyeing the candidates. She tapped Freddy Wickenhouse on the shoulder and strolled to Kong, even though his arm wasn't up. He lowered his chin in agreement, and his pregnant wife held his hand.

"Freddy and Kong, do you accept?" Caesar asked the pair. They were as good as he'd hoped for. Since he and Anders were leaving, Amelia needed backup.

"I do," Freddy said.

Kong rubbed his tattooed knuckles. "Same."

"Let me join you," Haley Paulson said.

Caesar glanced at the young woman, seeing fire in her eyes.

"She can shoot," Kong told them. "I bet she took down more Howlers than anyone else on that rooftop."

Amelia appraised the girl. "Why are you doing this?"

Haley looked embarrassed at the attention. "Because I've wanted to leave this town every day since my parents were killed, and now that I can't, I value it. I've seen what we can do when we work together, and I won't let that change because of our current situation."

John nodded at her, and Caesar noticed the man from the Den remained in the vehicle past the border.

"Okay, you're in, but on a trial basis." Amelia motioned to the others who'd offered. "We'll find uses for everyone."

"Operate as a team, and above all else, protect one another. We're going to locate Logan," Caesar said, and climbed off the hood.

There was no applause as the folks returned to their cars. Even Vince got into his truck, and his son Jimmy joined him. Soon there were only Caesar, Anders, Dot, John, Jamal—the stranger from the Den—and Amelia with her three new recruits.

"It could be worse," Kong said when the rest were gone.

"How?" John asked.

Kong shrugged. "It just could. We have each other. The Repulsor protects us from the Howlers, and there's corn to harvest."

Caesar waved Jamal from his vehicle, and the man limped over, holding a palm to his wrapped stomach. It wasn't bleeding through the bandages, which Caesar took as a good sign. "Tell us about the Den."

Jamal stayed in the shade. "It's not much to look at. We've built shelters with logs. Ben's a wilderness expert, which helps tremendously. He used to live off the grid, then Shifted to Arcadia years ago to our advantage."

"Arcadia?" Dot asked.

"That's this planet. Someone at Shelter, where Logan's

from, came up with it. His wife, perhaps."

Dot paled, and Caesar offered an arm to steady her. "My son is *married?*"

"Yeah, they run Shelter together. I've never been there, but that's what I'm told. Her name's Ruby. She's one of the originals," Jamal said. "They have a guy who's been on Arcadia for twenty-something years."

Jamal was much more talkative now that he was healing, and no longer being threatened by Lillian Carson. Thinking about the rogue agent made Caesar peer into the forest. Where had she gone?

"I have a daughter-in-law," Dot whispered.

"We'll retrieve them, Dot." Anders winced when a single howl carried on the wind. "Your job is to keep everyone alive." He said this to Amelia and her new deputies.

"Not a problem," Freddy confirmed. His father—the local vet, and about as close to a doctor as Carmichael had—had been killed by Lillian last night.

"Watch out for her," Caesar warned, and didn't have to say the name, since they all knew who he meant. "I'll travel to Shelter, and John and Jamal can bring the Den's population to Carmichael. Do you think they'll come willingly?"

"Yes. No." Jamal smiled. "It'll be an issue for some of them."

"What's the Den like?" Amelia asked.

"There are forty-one people at last count. We have log houses, containing up to four residents in each. We've grown food, and use a catchment system for water. The rain's unspoiled in Arcadia, so I suggest leading with that project."

Amelia scrawled in her notepad. "Catchment system," she repeated. "Before you leave, can you describe it to me?"

"Gladly."

Caesar's gaze settled on the military vehicle, almost expecting Lillian to burst from the woods to steal it. "Let's reconvene in town. I don't trust leaving our things out here."

"Good call." Anders climbed into the transport, starting the engine. He drove it along the border, past the alien terrain, and onto the street. John did the same with the second vehicle they'd taken from Isla's base behind the corn maze.

Caesar stared at the unfamiliar world before getting in. Summer's parents had seen Harrison standing in anticipation of their arrival. But the Shift had failed. Why? Lillian claimed there were dark motives for the Shift, with the Senator greedily desiring Arcadia. In that case, what part was Harrison playing? Was he a hostage, or leading the operation? He had to be involved, because Harrison Gregory wasn't a pawn.

They'd observed LTC tents, and someone had seen a woman behind Harrison. Was it his assistant Wanda?

Caesar left the border with far too many unanswered questions.

"What were you thinking?" John asked Haley as they entered their house.

"I can't be a deputy, but you can leave Carmichael with a stranger and travel through Howler-infested lands?" Haley shouted.

"When you put it that way…" John paused in the living room, assessing their home. Haley's salon station was there, and a flat screen faced the worn sofa. The lamps were originally from his parents' wedding, and the wooden floors were scratched and scuffed from years of kids dragging toys on them.

It made him yearn for his old life, if only for a moment. He pictured a birthday cake on the table, his mom singing, his father adding a deep baritone to the song while Haley froze in embarrassment. He imagined the artificial Christmas tree they'd decorated with homemade ornaments from school projects, and a faded angel from his mom's own childhood. It had remained sealed in cardboard boxes since they'd died.

Every inch of the place was filled with memories, more good than bad, though he rarely allowed himself to recall them. He sank onto the couch, and Haley joined him.

"I miss them too," she said.

"This is crazy."

"I know."

"I shouldn't have offered to escort Jamal to the Den. I could ask to stay and—"

"No, go," Haley added.

"I thought we'd be sent home."

"So did I. Why have the countdown if it meant nothing?" Haley asked.

"I've been wondering the same thing. Obviously, it was related to the Shift, but Isla missed something." John wasn't in the loop like Caesar and Mr. Lawrence, but he'd gladly do what he could to help the people of Carmichael.

"What happened to Katie? Weren't you two…"

"It was all a mistake," he said.

"She can hook up with Brent," Haley proclaimed.

John peered at the fireplace, then at the window. Donovan walked down his own driveway, kicking a pebble. The kid looked utterly devastated. "Make sure Don doesn't get into too much trouble."

"Isn't that his parents' job?" Haley asked.

"You didn't hear?"

"What?"

"Donovan's dad was one of the Howler victims from the first night they attacked."

Haley strode to the picture window, her hands on her cheeks. "That's terrible."

John checked on his mom and dad's room, viewing their pristine bed. The drapes were closed, and he entered, tossing them wide. Motes of dust drifted off the fabric. "I'll make you proud."

Haley watched him from the hall. "We both will."

John had left in a hurry a few hours ago, given the countdown's imminent end, but since the Shift had failed, he could be more methodical in his departure. They were going to meet at Isla's base in an hour, and he'd venture off with Jamal from there.

Haley vanished into her room, and John took in the space he'd called home for his whole life. The place was dark, and he flipped the light switch on instinct. With the generator off, nothing happened. So many memories lay within those four walls. He opened the closet, gazing at a box above his clothing, with old sports trophies jutting from the top.

John shut it and returned to the kitchen. He had a gut feeling that he'd never see this house again, and that he needed to make mental notes of all its nuances. He ran a palm over the countertops and stared into the backyard.

"Time to go. Let's stop at the cemetery," Haley said.

"Why?"

"You know why." Haley put on a pair of big black sunglasses and moved to the sidewalk where their ride sat.

John didn't bother to lock up, and followed his sister,

taking the driver's seat of the Gellers' busted SUV. They'd told him to keep it as long as necessary, since they had others in the garage.

He drove to the cemetery where they'd buried the dead two days earlier. The backhoe had discovered alien terrain beneath the dirt, along with strange, colorful rocks. John parked ten yards from the site, facing the graves. The mounds were rounded, each of the deceased marked with a white cross, their names written in black paint. Mr. Tucker was working with Pastor Odell on making more permanent headstones, but it wasn't a priority.

Haley got out before John and walked to one of the newest graves. They'd put Isla on the opposite side of Darcy, not wanting her bones near the man that had killed her. John read Isla's name, then marched to the end of the line and stopped at Darcy's.

"You're an idiot," he said. Haley hung in the shade, leaning on an elm tree. "Of all the stupid things to do...trying to score drugs. Shooting the one woman that knew what was going on. Damn you, Darcy!"

Anger burned through his veins. "You were always smart, but never applied yourself. After one game, you gave up on baseball, quit studying for exams, and—" John made a fist, his nails digging into his palm. "I couldn't convince you there was more to life than partying."

The sun beat on his neck, and John glanced at the sky, finding it completely devoid of clouds. Arcadia was a relentlessly hot world. He joined Haley in the shade. "We're on another planet."

"It's nuts, isn't it?"

"Darcy's dead, but we're not. We can make something of our lives." He extended his pinky.

"You're coming back, right?"

"I promise," he said.

"You know the rules…"

"There's no breaking a Paulson family promise," he finished.

2

*I*sla's base seemed different the second time Amelia entered it. The underground bunker was crowded near the office, but more spacious with the pair of Joint Light Tactical Vehicles missing. The JLTVs were parked outside, waiting for their respective drivers to venture away from Carmichael and deeper into Arcadia.

Dot strode through the base like a ghost, drifting to the monitors, then the supply shelves. "My Isla did this?"

Amelia recognized the pain in her voice. Isla had befriended the woman under false pretenses. She'd been Logan's partner at TCL, and from what Amelia had gathered, possibly more. She wondered how Isla would have reacted to the news that Logan was married, and that he ran Shelter with his wife.

Caesar and Anders climbed down the rungs, and she saw so many similarities in their movements. They could have been brothers, despite their vastly different appearances. Caesar was taller and thicker in the chest. Anders wasn't small, but he was thin and wiry. Yesterday, they'd fended off fifty Howlers in the maze, and looked as if they'd gone twelve rounds with a heavyweight champ. The duo sloughed it off like it was just another day in the office.

Amelia smiled when Freddy and Kong came, their eyes

wide in disbelief.

"When you said she had a base, I figured it was a room in a barn, not"—Kong motioned at the elaborate setup— "a high-tech villain lair."

"Isla's not a villain," Amelia said.

"Really?" Anders asked. "She took our town hostage, tricked Caesar into coming to Indiana, and arranged for weapons to be delivered to the Wests, causing their ultimate deaths. We've buried nearly thirty bodies in the cemetery since Saturday. If that's not a villain, then enlighten me."

"I guess that makes sense when you put it that way." Amelia walked to the desk, moving the mouse to activate the screen.

"Nah, Isla's not bad. Lillian Carson is," Caesar said. "And she's on the loose. Lillian might search for Logan too, but the odds are, she'd rather access this base." He passed a metal device to Amelia. "Keep this place locked up. Maybe post a sentry at the barn until we figure out where our friendly neighborhood DOD agent is."

Amelia hated that the woman had lied to them. She'd worked with Senator Rutherford and Isla to arrange the plan, but the TCL founder hadn't known their true motives. Rutherford didn't just want his nephew home; he wanted control of this unspoiled world. *Let it go*, she told herself. *They've put you in charge, and you can't fail them.*

"We'll do that." Amelia pocketed the key. She powered the map on and paused when Haley and John Paulson arrived. John whistled as he lowered into the room and gazed at Jamal, who sat in the second chair, nodding off. She was about to wake him when the man from the Den blinked his eyes open and rolled to the computer. "The Den is here."

Jamal pointed to the screen, and Amelia dropped a pin

on the location.

"Is Isla's guess at Shelter accurate?" Anders asked.

"We have nothing like this at home, so it's all done with paper and charcoal." Jamal surveyed the map. "It's in that area. They stay clear of the forests for good reason."

"The Howlers," Caesar said.

"That's the reason. The Den is by a lake, and Shelter's in the dusty plains," Jamal said.

"Are there other towns?" Haley asked.

"Sure. We've heard rumors of a big settlement to the north, but no one's ever gone that far. We're guessing the Shifts have occurred for ages, and probably across the globe. There might be entire civilizations hidden on Arcadia." Jamal motioned to the map, which was mostly white space beyond Isla's rendering.

Amelia tried to imagine entire cities of inhabitants, torn from Earth at random and forced to survive on an alien planet. As far as they knew, a whole town like Carmichael had never been Shifted.

"Once we break from the forest, the JLTVs will move a lot faster. We're going to use the plains and get to Shelter as soon as possible," Caesar said.

"There will be issues," Jamal told them.

"Like?" Anders gritted his teeth.

"A hundred miles between the Den and Shelter is a canyon. It's two miles deep."

"We'll go around," Caesar said. "Have you tried to?"

Jamal shook his head. "It's possible. Our scouts and traders cross by foot, because there are no cars on Arcadia. You'd have to go north, since the forest connects to the canyon in the south."

Caesar made notes on his phone. "That shouldn't be a problem. It'll divert us a day or two, tops."

Amelia was grateful she could help at town, but part of

her wished to be going on the adventure with Caesar. She hadn't seen much of the new world, but Arcadia was special.

"And the trip to the Den?" Haley asked Jamal.

"It's fairly easy, as long as the weather holds up."

"What about the weather?" Amelia prompted.

"I keep forgetting you don't know Arcadia. We're so used to the patterns. It's second nature. This is the heart of summer, which only lasts for another few weeks. Usually, the season is capped by a storm."

Dot leaned closer. "What kind of storm?"

"Tornadoes, wind, hail, thunder like you've never heard."

"Seriously?" John asked.

"We had to completely rebuild the Den a couple years ago, but were lucky it missed us last time."

Amelia gestured at the map. "Where is it the worst?"

Jamal glanced at the screen, then at her. His finger ran along the path, arcing between them and his home; then it cut straight through their position. "I'm sorry. Carmichael is directly in its path."

Caesar sighed, and Amelia could tell his pain medication was wearing off. "We have time. Best guess is…"

"Three weeks," Jamal said. "But it might be sooner, or later. Gemma would know better. She's from the Den."

"Then my goal is to have Logan here and working on the Shift by then," Caesar said.

"We'll prepare for the storm if necessary." Amelia had a lot on her list.

"Begin building the catchment, do an inventory on food, and begin planting seeds on every inch of free soil," Anders told Dot. "If a tornado doesn't throw us to Oz, you'll die without sustenance and water."

"Consider it done," the diner owner said. "We'll feed the town like we're a big ol' commune."

"I like it," Haley told them.

Anders poked a toothpick into his mouth. "Is there anything else, or can we expedite this meeting?"

"You can go." Amelia dismissed them. Everyone filed from the room, heading up the ramp to the rear of the barn rather than using the rungs. Caesar waited behind. "Did we miss something?"

He stepped toward her, limping slightly. "We survived the first three days by the skin of our teeth, but it's going to be tougher. Keep them alive, Amelia."

"And bring Logan back," she said.

"I will, or die trying."

Amelia didn't doubt that one bit. She touched his cheek, unsure where the spontaneity came from. He didn't flinch, and leaned his forehead on hers.

"We should—" She stopped when a shadow drifted from the exit. Anders stood with an M4 in his grip, watching them with a grin. They separated, and her body tingled with a foreign sensation.

"I'd better…" Caesar walked away, and Amelia silently prayed to whatever god protected Arcadia for their safe return.

With the press of a button, she sealed the ramp and climbed the metal rungs into the barn, locking the hatch. She had the only key for the digital lock, and was glad that Lillian couldn't access the base.

Once outside, Amelia thought about Summer Dawson, the teenage girl who'd escaped through the Shift only hours earlier. "Tell our story," she whispered to the sky.

"Can you repeat that?" Christine asked.

A fan blew into the tent, ruffling Summer's hair. "Could you shut that off?"

Christine nodded at a soldier, and he pulled the plug. The tent became deadly silent. Harrison sat beside her, which made Summer feel like he was her defense lawyer, and she was being grilled by the prosecution.

"I've told you everything."

"Again." Christine had a recording device on the table, and a red light blinked on the camera. Summer appraised the scar on her cheek. It was slightly puckered and pink, adding an element of danger to her interviewer.

"It was Friday night, and I rode my bike to my friend Carly's house to watch a movie. I lost one of my phones," she said.

"One of them?"

"My mom is super strict and doesn't let me use social media, so I have two," Summer said.

"Go on." Christine made notes on a laptop, even though it was all being recorded, which was a little excessive.

"The Wi-Fi cut out, and the lights flashed on and off or whatever." Summer thought about lying on Carly's bed, with dreams of what their lives could become. It seemed like a lifetime ago, not three days.

"There were power fluctuations?" Harrison interjected, and Christine glared at him.

"I guess so."

"Does that check out?" Harrison asked the representative from LTC.

"Logan's Shift link drew a lot of power for such a small device," the man said. Summer hadn't caught his name. "If Isla figured out how to harness it and make a town vanish, then it would…" He typed quickly on his keyboard and glanced up. "This can't be right."

"What?" Harrison rose and leaned over the guy's shoulder.

"Isla must have built her own grid," he said.

Christine smiled. "She did. It's all in the blueprints."

The lights dimmed, and a projection shone onto the inner side of the tent. Summer had no clue what they were looking at, but Harrison seemed impressed.

"What kind of technology is this?" he asked.

"A new fusion, not on the market," the LTC rep said. "You know how touchy the petroleum and nuclear sectors are about stepping on toes. We designed the systems, but I wasn't advised Isla had taken our designs and turned them into a large-scale Shift connector."

Summer was on Earth. She thought about it while the adults discussed a topic she couldn't comprehend.

They were on the border of Carmichael, where she'd grown up, only the town was no longer there. Instead, alien trees filled the area. Surprisingly, the region wasn't covered with curious reporters. From what she'd concluded, no one missed them yet.

A few miles away, her school continued to exist. Jackson, the nearby city, was beginning another Monday, unaware that a region of its county had vanished.

How could she be on Earth, when everyone she knew and loved was…gone?

"I have to get back," she said. When they didn't pay attention, she rose, slamming a palm to the table. "I have to get back!"

"Where?" Christine asked.

"To my family!"

"There's no Shifting until they bring Logan Rutherford. Isla hoped the Shift would stick, and that everyone would return, but it failed, so we're playing the waiting game," the woman said.

"Who are you?" Summer asked.

"She's a traitor," Harrison stated.

A shiny pistol appeared in the woman's grip a second later, and she kicked a chair over, lunging for Harrison. Summer rushed to the door, then was held by a soldier as the gun smacked Harrison across the temple. He crumpled to the ground, and Christine stared at him before holstering the weapon and fixing her hair.

"Where were we?" She sat at the head of the table, and the LTC employee gaped at her.

Summer allowed the soldier to guide her to the chair, and she sat, unable to keep her hand from shaking. "Is he…?"

"He's fine."

The soldier dragged Harrison from the tent.

"If he wasn't so close to Caesar, he would be dead," she said.

"Wait, you know Caesar?"

"Do you?" Christine asked, and Summer nodded. "Then tell me the story."

Without Caesar's boss' protective energy, Summer had no choice but to concede to her demands. "Carly and I snuck out at around ten to smoke a joint."

"You don't look like the type," Christine said.

"We aren't, but being fifteen is boring."

"I can't remember that far back," the woman said.

Summer eyed Christine, wondering how she and Caesar connected. "Do you know Anders Lawrence?"

"Come again?"

"Sorry, Caesar called him Anders Montrave," Summer corrected, and Christine's expression betrayed her.

"Where did you hear that name?" she hissed.

"Anders is Carly's dad."

Christine pulled her phone out and typed hastily. She stalked to the exit, clutching her cell with white knuckles. "Were you aware that Anders Montrave was… Yes, sir. Okay." She hung up and stared down the row of tents. "Continue."

"So you do know him," Summer said.

"He was there."

"Where?"

"When I died." Christine didn't elaborate, and put the phone away.

After a silent moment, Summer figured it was better to obey the erratic woman across from her. "We saw three trucks speed by, and followed them to the West farm. I guess Lillian murdered the couple."

The information seemed to surprise her too. "Lillian Carson killed two old farmers?"

"That's what I heard."

"This keeps getting worse." Christine lost her hard edge and closed her laptop, then flicked the camera off. She motioned to the soldier. "See if Harrison is awake. I think I made a mistake."

"What about me? I really want to Shift—"

"That's impossible," the LTC rep said.

Summer noticed he wore a nametag, and she read it. "Why…Gunther?"

"Because even if we had the tools to do so, the energy resonance won't be aligned for another week," he said. "Don't even get me started on the TFM connection."

"What's going to happen to me?" Summer asked.

"We'll let you know when we figure that out," Christine said, then left. Gunther trailed after her, leaving Summer alone until the soldier returned.

She sighed and slunk into the seat. Summer had to

escape the camp. With her mind made up, she rose and walked to the sentry. "I have to pee."

He lifted an eyebrow, then stepped aside. "Right this way."

3

*J*ohn glanced in the rearview mirror, watching the sendoff as he drove from Carmichael. Haley waved at him, then turned, his departure already forgotten as the town fought to stay alive for the next few weeks.

"You feeling okay?" he asked Jamal. The guy had been hit with buckshot at the Benyuks', but had somehow survived.

"The pills help." He rattled a bottle and stowed it in his pocket.

"You have to lead me to the Den, so don't overdose." The moment John said it, he thought about Darcy, and shuddered.

Jamal used the computer built into the passenger side of the JLTV, and a light appeared on a radar. "This is worthless without a mapping system." He turned it off.

John had driven a variety of vehicles, even a dump truck on a summer job a few years ago, but nothing as cool as this. He almost clipped a tree, and steered hard to avoid it.

"Careful, these things are worth four hundred large," Jamal said.

"Four hundred grand?"

"Yep."

"That's like… a bunch of my houses," John told him.

"Really? Ouch. Your town of…" Jamal glanced at him. "Carmichael."

"… must be off the beaten path." Jamal settled into his seat, leaning on the window after turning off the mapping display. "What state?"

"You weren't in Indiana before the Shift?"

"Nope. Chicago. Technically, Grundy, but who's counting?"

John wasn't sure what that meant, but assumed it was part of the metropolis' extended reach, like how Carmichael was in Jackson County. Connected, but far removed by a mere twenty miles to the city. "What happened?"

"I was on the L, heading to work. It was Memorial Day, and the car was basically empty because of that."

"What did you do?"

"I worked for a gaming company. We developed those fancy 3D console games, using other people's engines. I wanted to design my own, but the team kept me too busy. I dreamt of starting a company, poaching a couple of talented colleagues, and doing a seriously epic project. I was taking a train to the office on a holiday because some overseas investor asked to see a screenshot. Something shone at the end of the car, so I grabbed my laptop and walked to the anomaly. The Shift showed me Arcadia from ten feet up, speeding by like I was on the L but on a different world. Stupid me. I stepped closer and almost broke my ankle landing in the plains."

John listened with awe, imagining a Shift without others around to help. "That must have been wild."

"Wild doesn't begin to describe it." Jamal groaned and set a hand on his stomach. "It wasn't as bad as being shot, I guess."

"But you were discovered," John said.

"Not right away." Jamal stared at the alien landscape, and John did the same, maneuvering slowly within the forest. He kept an eye out for Howlers in the trees, and thought he spotted a couple hanging from the top branches, tracking the vehicle as it passed through their land. "I'm a scout now, spending most nights alone in the wilderness, but ten years ago, I was a skinny kid with no experience in nature. I grew up in the burbs, devouring fantasy books the size of the Bible, and playing D & D with friends. Outside was filled with bullies, bugs, and humanity. I preferred the comfort of my basement and orcs." Jamal smiled, possibly recalling a particular memory.

John didn't quite relate, since he'd been into sports, and rarely went a day as a kid without practicing one of his skills. "You've made it this far."

"That I have." Jamal clenched his jaw. "Damn me for getting shot. I should have scoped the property out before knocking on a stranger's door. I hadn't seen an actual house in a decade. I got sloppy. Next thing I know, I'm being dragged from the bed, bleeding through the bandages, and there you were at the barn. If I haven't said thank you enough, now's my chance."

John didn't feel like he'd done that much at the Wests'. "You're welcome."

"Where do you think she'll go?"

"Lillian?"

"Yeah."

"Hopefully, she'll be gutted by a Howler on her way to find Logan," John said. "She doesn't have access to Isla's base." Jamal adjusted so John couldn't see his face, and it was a telltale sign he wanted to divulge something important. "What is it?"

"She knows where Shelter is," he whispered.

"How?"

"I told her, okay?" Jamal shouted. "Damn it, she had a gun to my head, and I was in pain…I have a girl at the Den. I can't die."

John reached for the radio, but Jamal snatched it first. "Let me."

He pressed the talk button, but no one responded. "We're already out of range."

"I should turn back," John said.

"Caesar and Anders seem quite capable. I bet they can handle one woman," Jamal said.

John had enough life experience to know that was far from true, but he didn't want to waste light and get stuck in the forest with the Howlers when it became dark. "Fine, but don't do it again."

"I wasn't thinking," he admitted.

"Even if Lillian has the location, how will she get there?"

"Exactly," Jamal said. "What's your story?"

John contemplated the loaded question. "Nothing to tell. I was born in Carmichael, and I work in the city at a hardware store. Or I used to."

"What department?"

"It's a smaller operation, owned by a local. He's a good man, and the customers are decent," John said. "I doubt I have a job when this is over."

"You like it?"

"It almost pays the bills."

"Then who cares?" Jamal laughed lightly. "If I ever Shift back, there's no way I'm going to a normal job."

"What then?"

"I've spent ten years fighting to stay alive. I don't think I could handle being on Earth," he said. "It's why I didn't want to be there when we thought the Shift would occur."

"And the girl back home," John added.

"Maya's gonna be pumped," he said.

"That's her name?"

"Yep. She was the one that found me half dead after a week hiking alone, and is the only reason I didn't die." Jamal fished a lighter from his pocket. It was one of those red plastic types Vince had on display at the Gas-N-Go. He flicked the metal top, but it didn't spark. "I used to…" He mimed smoking. "My parents told me it would kill me, and it ended up saving my life. Maya was on a scouting mission and spied the smoke from miles away, then quickly came to snuff it out before I drew the Hangers' attention."

"Hangers?"

"You call 'em Howlers, we call 'em Hangers." He simulated their tail clasping a branch. "Maya brought me to the Den, and I've been there ever since."

John was excited to visit the town. The Joint Light Tactical Vehicle's suspension absorbed the bumpy ride with efficiency, taking it far better than his old truck would have. John remembered physical possessions were suddenly irrelevant, and tried not to care that he'd damaged it beyond repair. Now his health and well-being took priority. John needed to help them return to Earth: if not for himself, then for Haley. "You still have a laptop?"

"Nah. We had to trade that to Shelter," Jamal said.

"How come?"

"It's part of the deal. Logan takes our electronics and rebuilds stuff to create things like the Repulsor." Jamal patted his pocket, as if searching for the one he'd left with Amelia. "I've had that for three years. You have no idea how much easier it is to sleep with it on."

"The town's grateful for your donation," John said.

"Donation. It's not like I had a choice."

"You'd rather have them attacked every night?"

"No, I wouldn't."

"What else does Logan Rutherford create?" John pried.

"I've heard rumors about a tower, but he's quite secretive about it."

"A tower?"

"Apparently, he spent five years trying to link with home, without any luck," Jamal said. "But this is all hearsay, since I've never gone to Shelter."

"Why not? You're a scout."

"Because that's Ben's job."

"Ben, the wilderness expert?"

"The one and only." Jamal yawned and rested his head. "If our game of twenty questions is finished, I'm gonna get some shut-eye."

"Go for it."

Jamal pointed forward. "Go in a straight line, and wake me if you find anything strange."

John peered around the alien forest, instantly noticing a dozen *strange* things. A .pink butterfly drifted by, and a three-eyed bird swooped in, snatching the insect from the air. He wanted to comment, but Jamal's breathing had already changed.

He kept moving at seven miles an hour, eager to escape the forest.

———————

"You have this under control?" Caesar asked Anders.

"I've said it a dozen times, you make an awful backseat driver," Anders replied.

"That's because I'm in the passenger seat," he joked.

"You're worse than my wife."

Caesar had a million queries for the man beside him,

but wanted to pace himself. They were still recovering after their battle in the maze.

Anders must have been thinking the same thing. "Remember when you shot the plastic Minotaur?"

"My aim was good," Caesar said.

"Damn, that was almost fun."

"Fun?" Caesar rubbed his own shoulder and noticed Anders holding an arm tight to his body where he'd injured it. "I haven't been this beat up since Beirut."

"You were there?" Anders asked.

"Four years ago."

"I heard about that," he said.

"Really? From whom?"

"I have friends in the industry," Anders said.

"Do you miss it?"

Anders glanced at him from the driver's seat. "Every damned day."

"It's better on the outside, I imagine. You have a house and family."

"I guess so." Anders deflated slightly, steering through the forest.

They were moving in the opposite direction from John and Jamal, on their way to the Den. Caesar hoped they arrived at their destination with no delay, and that his mission went smoothly. Something told him that wouldn't happen, since operations rarely happened without a hitch. Or ten.

"I love my wife, I really do. Joe and Carly are incredible children. But how can anyone understand what we've gone through? We served our country, only to be secretly dragged back. People think this kind of work only happens in spy movies or novels. We've lived it. Hell, we're *still* living it." Anders grabbed his coffee cup, taking a sip. "You're lucky you're so free."

"Free?"

"Not tied down by a family. It probably makes you a better agent."

"Or more careless," Caesar admitted.

"I'm sorry I said it like that. I know how you felt about Christine."

"Did she ever…"

"Mention you?" Anders asked. "Sure. She didn't use your name, but it was obvious she'd gotten married on a whim. Christine showed up for a job in Columbia with a ring. I didn't ask until the operation was complete and we were on the way home. After that, I couldn't get her to stop talking."

Hearing the story made Caesar's chest ache, and he told himself it was just the bruised ribs from yesterday. "Istanbul was special," he said, recalling the place they'd met.

"They almost fired her for associating with you," Anders said.

"Where were you for that mission?" Caesar asked.

"Carly had the chicken pox."

Caesar laughed, wondering how things would have been different if Anders was there when he'd met Christine in the field.

"What's funny?" Anders asked.

"I let that part of my life go, and then I came to Carmichael. You were with my wife when she was killed in Chile, and I don't know how to react."

"It was a biotech—"

"No. I spent two years debunking it. The case was a setup. Maybe to kill Christine and to imprison you. Or they wanted to kill you both, but you stayed alive," Caesar said.

Anders Montrave, now Lawrence, winced and sped up, moving between the giant alien tree trunks. "If that's true,

I'll have to seek justice."

"I've already tried. The trail is dead." *Like my wife,* Caesar thought.

"No trail is dead. You didn't have me on the job," Anders said. "I was extradited home and didn't even try to figure out what happened in Chile. I just wanted my family."

Caesar had the plan. Find Logan Rutherford at Shelter and bring him to Carmichael, where he'd use Isla's base to connect to another natural Shift.

"You're going over it again, aren't you?" Anders asked.

"How did you…"

Anders tapped his temple right above a bandaged cut. "Great minds and all that."

"What do you think?"

"I appreciate the simplicity, but there will be obstacles."

"Agreed." Caesar pictured the odd electrical power room beneath the ground near the maze. "Even if Logan is alive, he might not be able to use her device to link and Shift us home."

"He has to," Anders said. "This is daunting, but it's good to be useful."

"Instead of dwelling on our return, let's break it down into steps."

Anders drank more coffee. "First step. Make more of this." He pulled over.

"We're still in the forest."

Anders reached behind him, grabbing his M4. "Then we keep these close by."

"I wish we had a second Repulsor." Caesar exited the JLTV and walked the long way around the military vehicle, confirming the dirt bikes connected to the rear end. He found Anders on the other side, crouching by the gas stove. The coffee percolator had water in it, and he dumped the grounds in, then began boiling it. "Lots of people love those new pods, but there's nothing like coffee brewed over a flame."

Caesar disagreed but didn't comment, and was just glad to have the stuff accessible in their present situation. He'd already taken his maximum medication dosage and didn't want to get dependent. He'd seen too many good people go down that road, and some never returned.

He strode into the woods, gazing up. There weren't any Howlers in the area, and he took a long breath, ingesting the fresh air. The sky was blue, peeking through the canopy above. Arcadia was beautiful, but like most of nature, deadly under the right circumstances. He couldn't be complacent in his surroundings, because that was when he'd be attacked.

"Quite the sight, isn't it?" Anders arrived, clutching the gun near his chest.

"Yeah. Reminds me of the redwoods in Sequoia," Caesar said.

"I've never been."

"How come?"

"Honestly, I wouldn't let us leave Carmichael since I came home. Helen had dreams of seeing Paris, Rome, Malibu…and I refused to step out of the comfort of a small town. Boy, was I wrong."

"Maybe when this is finished, you can—"

Anders smiled at the comment and nodded slowly. "I'll take the family on vacation to Italy. Helen knows what I did, but she never talks about it. She just walks and walks, like she can erase the past with every step. An exercising exorcism."

"Did you make that up?" Caesar asked.

"No, it's a bit of a chestnut between us," he admitted.

"Come on, coffee's done."

They refilled their stainless cups and stored the gas stove. "Want me to drive?" Caesar offered.

"Sure." Anders took the passenger seat, gazing around as he operated the display screen. "How many times did we use similar vehicles?"

"Daily for a while there." Caesar didn't like to think of his deployments in the early weeks of his military career. The memories were too heavy, and he needed absolute clarity.

Anders turned the screen off and pulled out the notepad he'd marked up at Isla's base. "We should have another ten miles of forest before we're on the plains."

"Then a mere two hundred and ninety miles with a giant crevasse between us and Shelter," Caesar added.

"Pretty much." Anders flipped through the pages. "Jamal mentioned another town along the way, so we could stop there."

"Maybe on the return trip with Logan. He's our priority."

"What about the northern place?"

"I thought that was just a rumor," Caesar said.

"Arcadia might be filled with settlements across this continent and beyond. What I wouldn't give to have satellite images."

"From the sounds of it, that's what Lillian's friend, Senator Rutherford, plans to do."

"With our usual technology, we'd get a quick view of the world and could identify every village which is probably his goal," Ander said.

"Under the guise of rescuing his nephew. According to Lillian, she'd been ordered to get Logan by her boss."

"Senator Rutherford?"

"She didn't say, specifically, but it has to be, right?"

Caesar asked.

"I hate being thrown into a mission without seeing the full picture." Anders blew on the steaming coffee while Caesar guided them on, rolling over the uneven ground as fast as he could without jeopardizing the tires.

"Once we have the proper information, everything will become crystal clear. But let's start with finding Logan." Caesar recognized the edge of the forest, ready to exit the Howlers' home, and into the unknown.

4

The line at the grocery store was two blocks long, and Amelia noted how distraught the people appeared. They'd fended off Howlers for two nights straight, and when they believed they'd be Shifted, it faltered, leaving them on Arcadia. Amelia would be dejected herself if she didn't have so much to do. That would be the key. Keeping the population busy.

"Don't forget, when you're finished here, come to the town office for your task assignment!" Amelia called.

The line shuffled on when Sharon and Dot exited Esther's grocery store, each carrying a spotted banana and a couple of bottles.

Amelia gestured at her new deputies: Freddy, Kong, and Haley Paulson. The young woman carried the rifle on her shoulder with more confidence than Amelia had ever felt. "Kong, would you head to the sanctuary and confirm the rotation is set for the week?"

"Done and done." Kong broke from their group, moving in the opposite direction.

"What can we do?" Freddy asked.

"We need to canvass the town, make sure there's no one unaccounted for. Mayor Vivian had the residency list, but it wasn't up to date. Please add any locals that weren't on file. Then cross-reference it with our list of deceased and everyone that's signed up at the storage facility."

"I thought we were deputies," Freddy said. "You know, patrolling the streets for danger, answering calls."

Amelia had dealt with eager vigilantes a hundred times over, but hadn't expected it from the veterinarian's calm son. "There's more to being in law enforcement than that. It's a lot of paperwork and waiting."

"Don't worry about it," Haley said. "Come on, Freddy. This is better than being attacked by Howlers."

"Is it?" Freddy smiled and gave Amelia a nod as they ventured to the mayor's office. Amelia was saddened by the loss of Vivian, and not just because she'd somehow been named her successor. The woman had been a vibrant influence on the town, and her own muted colors and demeanor paled in comparison.

Dot lingered in the shade, with Sharon beside her. They both set their groceries on the sidewalk and looked exhausted as Amelia approached. No one had slept last night, and it was wearing on them all.

"How's the first few hours going in the store?" Amelia asked Dot.

"Esther has it under control. We're giving out vouchers, one per person, and using up the produce before it spoils. The generator almost clunked out, but Mr. Tucker's back there working on it. If the power goes to those freezers, we'll have an issue on our hands."

"What about corn?" Amelia asked. The crops were plentiful, but the stalks had to grow, then be harvested, before it was useful.

"Another month and we might start harvesting the older farms, but some won't be ready until October," Sharon said. "You can't reap what you sow until it's time. Farming is a patient person's game. That's what my father always said." Sharon passed Amelia a few vouchers. "They're dated, so don't forget to use them or they'll expire."

Amelia hadn't even thought about her own stomach, but the moment she did, it growled with hunger. When had she eaten last? "Thanks. Where are you two off to?"

"We've reported everything the town donated from their pantries. Since the groceries are sorted, we'll work on the garden plan," Dot said.

"And that is?"

"Carmichael has its share of private gardens. Nearly all the properties have their own lettuce, peas, carrots, potatoes, et cetera. With everyone staying at the storage sanctuary, we're bringing a team to collect what's yielded so far. I'm assembling a schedule, and in groups of five, will take quadrants, checking on progress twice a week. We're also going to turn the grassy field here into a community garden."

At the comment, Amelia's gaze settled on the park across from Dot's Diner, and she laughed when she spied the bulldozer. "Who's driving it?" She squinted, trying to see.

"Vince."

"You trust him?" Amelia asked.

"No, but he volunteered. He's seeking to make amends for his ill behavior this past weekend," Dot said.

"I love the plan, ladies. See you soon, and good luck." Amelia was proud of how inventive they'd been, even in the wake of such a disastrous weekend. Only five hours ago, the town had awaited their return to Earth, and when it didn't happen, they'd somehow recovered.

Amelia moved to the back of the line and read the voucher. It was hand-written, so it could easily be counterfeited, but she hoped that wouldn't be the case.

"Amelia," Hank said. "Head to the front."

"Uhm…"

Soon, the entire line turned and pointed to the entrance, where Pastor Odell was next up. "Are you sure?"

Mrs. Lemar blinked big eyes wide under her plastic-framed glasses. "Missy, we need you healthy and well-fed."

"Thanks," she said, appreciating their kindness. On Friday afternoon, these people had seen her as a nuisance, an outsider with a badge, and now they treated her like one of them.

Amelia halted behind the pastor, not wanting to cut in front of the man.

"Good afternoon," he said.

"Is it?" Amelia had lost track of time.

"By the grace of God, we're going to be okay, Miss Miller." Pastor Odell smiled brightly, and it was infectious. "I'm having a sermon this evening, if you'd like to come by."

"I might do that." Amelia wasn't sure where to go next, since she'd already delegated the most imperative tasks. With the teams sent off in different directions, heading deeper into Arcadia's wilderness, she was at a loss. If things went according to plan, they'd have Logan activating the Shift in less than a month. If not, they'd have to pray the harvest worked and settle in on Arcadia. Jamal claimed their summer would only last for a couple more weeks, followed by intense storms.

There was so much to do.

"Next," Esther called. She beamed when she spotted the pastor and their newly elected leader. "Come in, both of you." Esther extended her wrinkled hand, accepting their vouchers. "Please take two pieces of produce and two cans. That's all we can spare at the moment. It'll have to last you the full day."

Amelia scanned the fruit, and glanced up when the lights dimmed and cut off. She grabbed an apple and an orange, then went for a can of lentils for protein, and a soup. "Is Mr. Tucker out there?"

"He sure is, bless him. If the generator fails, the frozen section will become perishable."

Amelia walked through the small store, leading into what passed for a warehouse, eyeing the few skids of supplies like canned goods and cereal boxes. She figured there might be enough food to last three weeks, which seemed to coincide with the various timelines.

"Son of a…" Mr. Tucker had his cowboy hat off, and he kicked the machine with his boot.

"Dad, you're getting too worked up. Your heart," Evan warned him, and looked at Amelia approaching. "Hey, Miss Miller."

"Amelia," she said. "Having problems?"

"Nah, I can fix anything, but…" Mr. Tucker gasped, and found a cap on the gravel in the alley. He screwed it on and restarted the machine. It choked and sputtered to life. "Good as new."

"I should be off," she said. "Nice work."

"Miss… Amelia…" Evan scratched at a pimple on his chin.

"Yes, Evan?"

"For goodness' sake, son, just tell her."

"Tell me what?"

"I heard there's an underground operation going on in town," Evan said.

"Is that so?"

"I guess Clive's got a few people stealing food from houses, and he's selling the goods," Evan told her.

Amelia sighed. "Thanks, Evan."

"Any time."

Amelia strolled past the line, struggling to keep her expression from revealing the rage within as she found her squad car. Karl had finally replaced the tire; it didn't visually match, but at least it was the proper size for the rim.

Amelia sat in the driver's seat and touched the blank screen. She had a walkie in the glovebox, and a Jackson County map. She remembered studying it when she'd first started with the department, trying to memorize every side road and pit stop in the region. The county covered the city of Jackson and five towns, each of the remaining four larger than Carmichael. They had outdoor swimming pools, summer parades, and thriving communities.

Amelia bit into the apple, watching the street. She flipped the visor, finding her own reflection startling. Her eyes were dark, her skin pale in contrast. Her hair desperately needed tending to—not that those things mattered now. Survival was everything.

Juice from the fruit dripped onto the car seat, and she grabbed a fast-food napkin in the console, dabbing it. She wouldn't eat another burger from her favorite chain, or drink a milkshake from that ma and pa diner on the interstate. She'd be stuck in Arcadia, never finding her husband, not having a family. The dream was so old, it didn't even feel like hers now.

Amelia set the core into the napkin, placing it in the cupholder, and took a deep breath. Carmichael was functioning, but Caesar had known that wouldn't last. The flames of chaos would spread, and Clive was just the spark it needed.

*S*ummer paced the tent, willing the guard to leave his position. She'd attempted to run hours ago, but he'd caught her within twenty seconds. Since then, no one had visited her. Not Harrison, not the woman with the scar…

She was on Earth, with none of her family or friends, and it was scarier here than on another planet.

The sun beat on the tent relentlessly, and the air felt suffocating.

"I need water!" she told the guard. His posture shifted enough to prove he'd heard her. The man had a radio on his shoulder, and his chin tilted to it. Five minutes later, a woman in fatigues entered, carrying two bottles of water and a brown paper bag. "What time is it?" Summer asked.

"Sixteen hundred," she said, and unceremoniously left.

"Sixteen… It's four." Summer tore the sack open, sitting at the desk. The chair was metal and plastic, reminding her of something she'd used in elementary school. The food was wrapped in tinfoil, and she peeled away the top, digging into a burrito. Nothing had ever tasted so good. Sauce dripped onto her hand, but she didn't rush to clean it up. Summer devoured the wrap within minutes.

She checked the bag, seeing it was from a place in Jackson they'd never visited because of her father's acid reflux. At first, she thought there was a receipt at the bottom, but it had a note scrawled on it instead of prices.

9 P.M. sharp. – H

'H' had to be Harrison, and that meant he planned on doing something in five hours. Could he actually free her? He seemed to be a prisoner in this camp too. The woman, Christine, was clearly in control, even if the senator was involved.

A moment before, she'd felt helpless, but things had

changed. Harrison was Caesar's boss, which meant he had power. He'd help Summer find her family.

Summer drank half of the water and wished there was more food.

"What would Princess Diamond do?" she whispered. She wouldn't have been in this situation in the first place. Thinking about the cartoon hero made Summer picture her friend Carly, and she said a silent prayer for her safety.

"I see someone was hungry." Christine came in from a flap on the rear of the tent.

Summer surveyed the corners, wondering if there was surveillance on her. Hopefully, it hadn't picked up the note's message. Summer reached into the bag and clutched the piece of paper, crumpling it. She shifted in the seat, sticking the balled-up note under her leg.

"What do you want?" she asked.

Christine was tall with wide shoulders, reminding Summer of an Olympic swimmer. "What I want is to bring Logan Rutherford home. And Carmichael."

The town's name was said as an afterthought—for Summer's benefit, no doubt. "Were you aware the town wouldn't be returned?"

Christine smiled gently. "No. That wasn't the plan."

"Why? What were you going to do with all these soldiers?"

"That's not important. Now Carmichael is collateral. Do you know what that means?"

"I'm fifteen, not an idiot," Summer spat.

"You have spirit. You remind me of myself at your age."

"I doubt that," Summer muttered.

"One of life's biggest ironies is that we rarely see beyond our own perception. When we're a teenager, we know everything, and no matter what your parents, teachers, or friends tell you, you're right. Some of us grow out of it, but most never do. Here's what I've learned in my forty years walking this planet, ten of which I've been dead for," Christine said.

Summer didn't understand the last comment, but didn't interrupt.

"Life isn't fair. People suck. Money talks." Christine gazed at Summer.

"That's it?"

"Pretty much."

"That's sad," Summer said.

"Like I said, life isn't fair."

"What about family?"

Christine winced. "Since we're not going anywhere, I may as well tell you."

"I'm waiting."

"I was married to Caesar," she said.

Summer had been trying to play it cool, but that fractured her composure. "You were?"

"Does that surprise you?" Christine asked.

"Yes!"

"Ouch. He *is* quite handsome—"

"Ew, he's like eight hundred," Summer said.

Christine laughed, and the simple act made her seem far younger.

"But Caesar is so…decent," Summer said.

"He's that to a fault."

"And you're…"

"Mean?"

"No, a bitch," Summer finished, surprised at her own bravery.

Christine rose, her cheeks growing slightly red. "I thought we could work together. Clearly, I was mistaken."

Summer fought the urge to keep insulting her.

Harrison had given her a note, and that was all that mattered. She only needed to hang on for four hours and meet Caesar's boss.

She noticed the fluttering insects outside as Christine marched past the stationed soldier. The six pink wings flapped, then it landed on the man's back. If there were bugs from Arcadia on Earth, what else had Shifted?

5

*T*he trek through the woods took longer than John wanted, but they eventually emerged from the treeline into a vastly unfamiliar terrain. He glimpsed the trees in the side mirror, then the grassy plains that stretched out for eternity in the other three directions.

Jamal slept soundly, as he'd done for several hours. John almost stopped to check if he was alive, until the man's chest moved.

He slowed the JLTV and threw it into park, then got out.

John grabbed a rifle from the backseat and observed the landscape with the scope. They were slightly elevated, giving him an incredible panoramic view of Arcadia. Somewhere straight ahead, the Den awaited them. From this position, it was approximately forty miles. The ground was far more forgiving, but with the dense browning grass billowing in the wind, it would be impossible to see any bumps or holes, meaning he'd have to continue taking it slow.

"Quite the sight, isn't it?" Jamal approached silently. John hadn't even heard the vehicle open.

"It's a big change from Chicago," John told him.

"That it is. The first morning, I freaked out when I

realized I couldn't walk down the block to buy a cappuccino."

"I'd been planning on selling my house and leaving Carmichael," John admitted. "I spent years biding my time, and then we finally made a decision, and bam." He slapped the barrel of the rifle into his palm.

"Ain't that the way of life?" Jamal gestured to the left. "There's a freshwater lake with some incredible catches five miles that direction."

"There are fish on Arcadia?"

"Not quite the same as at home, but they're close. Three eyes, like everything else." Jamal stretched his arm just wider than his shoulders. "Usually about five pounds, and taste like chicken more than cod, if you can believe it."

"Let me guess, the chickens taste like onions?"

"Nah, I haven't seen a three-eyed chicken, but the birds are a little gamey."

The reality of their situation took hold, and John imagined how life would look in two years if they couldn't Shift. He pictured Anders Lawrence wearing a leather vest and throwing spears to impale a grazing animal. Every day would be a battle for survival, like Jamal and his people experienced. "Do you tire of it?"

"Living on Arcadia?"

"Yeah."

"Always."

"But you found a partner."

"I'm beyond grateful for Maya, but I think she'd give up on us just for a piece of pecan pie from her mom's kitchen," he said, and John couldn't tell if he was joking.

"Will you show me how to fish here?"

"There's a lake on the way home. It's not as nice, but it'll do the trick." Jamal opened the JLTV and pulled off his shirt. Traces of blood had seeped through the white bandages, but far less than earlier. "Can you…"

John leaned the rifle on the bumper and began unwinding the stomach bindings. The buckshot had spread across Jamal's abdomen, but the vet had removed the pieces of metal before Lillian Carson killed Dr. Wickenhouse. John used the ointment in the first aid kit and wrapped Jamal up again.

"Sorry to make you do that," he said. "I'm kind of useless."

"No problem." John climbed in and started the engine, realizing a big hole in their plan. "Jamal?"

"What's up?" Jamal strapped his seatbelt on, careful to move the shoulder strap behind him.

"How do we transport the people back to Carmichael? We only have one vehicle."

"They'll have to hike," he said.

"In three weeks?"

"Two, because we can't be out in the open when storm season begins," Jamal said.

John felt the seconds ticking down in his mind. "Then we better hurry."

The sky was picturesque, a pure blue he'd never quite seen before. The sun was so large and bright, it seemed impossible that summer might end.

The grassy fields danced in the breeze, sending ripples through the land like waves in the ocean. If his situation wasn't so dire, he'd appreciate it.

"What about you? Have a woman?" Jamal asked.

"Nah."

"No way, dude, I don't buy it."

"We broke up."

"Why do I sense more to the story?"

"Katie moved to Carmichael recently, and we dated for a while. Turns out she was married and going through a divorce, and we ended up…agreeing we weren't a good match."

"That bad, huh?"

"What?"

"The sex."

John glanced at Jamal as he laughed. "Don't mind me. I hear the same gossip every day, so anything new is exciting."

"We both made mistakes."

"But you're stuck on Arcadia together."

"It might have helped my decision to volunteer for this mission."

"Risking your life on the road to avoid a chick. I respect that," Jamal said.

The vehicle bobbed and dipped in the grass, almost sending them toppling sideways.

"I'm used to being on foot. This is brutal with no roads," Jamal told him. "I'm glad to have this killer ride, not a sedan."

John eased his tight grip on the steering wheel and lightened the pressure on the gas pedal. "It'll be a bumpy trip."

"Then it's a good thing I can sleep through anything."

John examined the gauges, which showed his speed at seven miles an hour. At this rate, they'd have to break for the night after only getting a third of the way to the Den. He wouldn't risk upending their vehicle in the dark.

"Tell me more about this place," John said, and Jamal set into his tale, describing his home, the town, and their daily routines.

John listened with interest, relieved to have a distraction as they drove on.

*T*he last of the sunlight fell beyond the horizon, ending their first day on the road. Caesar finished putting up his tent while Anders relieved himself ten yards away. "Could you do that farther?"

"It'll repel rodents and predators while we sleep. I'd suggest you take that section of our camp, and I'll stay on this side." Anders zipped and moved to their stove. Having a fire would add to the risk of attracting unwanted attention from the local wildlife, particularly the Howlers, so they'd elected to use the gas cooktop.

Isla had a great store of supplies on hand, and they'd taken a dozen propane canisters for this purpose. She'd also had months' worth of canned goods, rice, and oats in the facility, but they'd agreed not to advise the population until it was necessary.

Caesar opened the rear of their vehicle and lifted two cans. "Stew or chili?"

"Since we're not sharing a tent, I vote chili. My wife never makes the stuff," Anders said.

"Care to elaborate?" Caesar smiled at his reaction.

"Just cook it." Anders picked up the M4.

"You don't like to be without the gun, do you?"

"I spent the last ten years trying to pretend I wasn't…this. It's good being a soldier again."

Caesar wore a shoulder holster, and understood how one could feel naked in the field without being armed.

He spilled the contents into the saucepan and fired up the burner, which hissed and circled into a flame. Caesar stirred it and lowered the lid. "You do much cooking?"

"I can burn water," Anders said. "Helen always handled that stuff."

"What have you done for the last decade, if you weren't

on the job?"

"Consulting. It's a BS gig given to me by my old boss. I put on a suit and check over various Indiana businesses' finances. Mostly, I meet struggling owners and send the files to a corporate office that handles the minutiae, and I return with a solution, looking like a hero."

"I can't picture you in a suit."

"Neither can I," Anders said.

"Do your children know you were arrested in Chile?"

"Kind of. Joe was slightly older, and he remembers that year without me. Carly, not as much. I've tried making it up to them by being around every day."

Caesar was certain the biotech mission was done to set Anders and Christine up, but what he couldn't understand was why. Anders didn't believe him, so he didn't broach the subject while he monitored their dinner.

Orange bugs lifted from the grass, buzzing as they glowed. Soon the landscape surrounding them was dimly lit by the insects.

"Reminds me of being a kid and catching fireflies," Caesar said. "My brother and I would spend hours out there with these glass jars, trying to gather enough to read by."

"Where's he now?"

"Alaska with his wife and three children."

"Are you close?"

"I haven't seen him in twenty years."

"So closer than me and my sister," Anders said. "I try to tell myself that Carly and Joe will stay tight as they get older, but who knows? We're the only animals on the planet that force relationships past our maturity."

"True story." Caesar tested a spoonful and gave it another minute before doling out equal servings. They chatted about family as they ate, then cleaned up, stowing the dishes and stove. Anders returned a moment later, holding the tablet from Isla's base.

"What's the matter?" Caesar asked.

"It was on." Anders showed him the screen. The light cast shadows behind Caesar, and he reached for it.

"Is something running?" Caesar viewed the main display and saw a notification icon. He hit it, expecting nothing to happen, but a program activated.

Link to device 255889.33 failed

Link to device 255889.33 failed

This went on for half of the screen, the timestamps suggesting the connection had been attempted every thirty minutes since they'd Shifted.

A single message, varying from the others, sat at the bottom.

Link to device 255889.33 successful

Caesar clicked the blue hyperlink attached to the note, and the image changed.

Device 255889.33 LTC (Operator: Logan R)

Device 256615.21 (Operator Isla F)

Caesar stared at it, then at Anders. "He's here...she was right."

"His tablet is, but—"

"It wouldn't be able to connect if it wasn't charged, and for that, he'd have to be alive," Caesar said.

"Or someone else had to keep it charged."

"Do you always play devil's advocate?"

"Pretty much," Anders admitted.

"How does that work out for you?"

"It's wise to consider all angles to a problem."

"I couldn't agree more." Caesar studied the tablet. "Is there a way to communicate?"

"Let me try." Anders took it without Caesar putting up a fight and tapped the small keyboard icon. "Who are we talking with?" He read it aloud, then hit ENTER.

Device 255889.33 LTC (Operator: Logan R)

Logan Rutherford. Is this Isla?

"I'll be damned." Caesar's heart sped up. "How does it transmit messages? There aren't any underground cables, or satellites, or towers to ping off."

"LTC was doing some cutting-edge stuff, from the sounds of it. If they built a Shift device, maybe connecting two devices on the same continent isn't so tough," Anders said.

"Harrison would know better than me."

"Was he a good boss?"

"He *is* a great boss. But we prefer to think of ourselves as partners," Caesar told him.

"Sure, that's what they all say. Let me guess, Harrison says he'd do the job himself, but his heart couldn't take it?" Anders asked.

"You're not far off." Caesar focused when another message came.

If you don't respond, I'll cut the connection.

Anders watched Caesar as if he sought direction.

"We could pretend to be her," Caesar said.

"What good would it do?"

"He might get spooked if we disclose who we really are." Caesar gestured to the tablet. "Tell him we're working for LTC and his uncle."

"Nice idea." Anders typed, this time not speaking the words, so Caesar read them.

Device 256615.21 (Operator Isla F)

We've come through a Shift in Carmichael, Indiana. Isla built the device, and your uncle made the plan.

"That cut it?" Anders asked before sending.

"Sure."

Device 255889.33 LTC (Operator: Logan R)

Where is Isla now?

"We have to come clean," Anders said. "He knows who I am."

"Fine."

Logan, it's Anders M—he corrected the last name—*Lawrence. The municipality of Carmichael is on Arcadia. Your mom is safe, and there are people protecting the town. We're coming to your position.*

They waited for a moment, and a response came.

Anders…what about Isla? How did you get this tablet?

Caesar's new partner sighed. *She's dead, Logan.*

After what felt like several minutes, another message appeared.

The connection is weak, and you might lose it during your trek. I'll keep the beacon on so you can track my location when you're closer.

Anders tried another message of confirmation, but it kicked them out. When he re-entered the program, he saw a familiar note.

Link to device 255889.33 failed

"Guess we have to keep trying," Caesar said.

"This is great news. He's alive. We'll bring him to Carmichael, and he can Shift us home." Anders put the tablet into the truck and closed it up. "We should turn in."

"I will in a minute." Caesar sat on the folding chair, watching the stars when Anders zipped up his tent.

He inhaled, breathing in the fresh, heady scent of the plains surrounding them. Arcadia was flourishing. The glowing insects had dimmed, returning to the grassy surface. The forest lay in the distance, far from their position, but the Howlers' calls echoed from the woods. Caesar grabbed his weapon and settled into the tent.

6

*A*melia watched the Raddison farm from the road, using binoculars to inspect the scene. Clive sat on the front porch with a man she didn't know, both drinking warm beers and rocking on faded wooden chairs.

Clive stood and shone a flashlight at her. She'd stuck to the shadows, but Clive must have spotted the car. She had to decide whether a confrontation was necessary or if she should leave for town.

While Clive strolled down his gravel driveway, she used her radio. "Deputy Wickenhouse, this is Miller."

"What's up, Chief?" They'd all gotten to calling her that, and she didn't dispute them. Amelia had to separate herself from the pack.

"I'm at the Raddison place, and I'm going to talk with Clive. I thought someone should know."

"You want backup?"

Amelia had dealt with men thinking she couldn't handle herself her entire life, and she'd proven every one of them wrong. "Nope. I'll be there in ten."

"The facility is set for the night, and we're heading to the church for the service. Want me to save you a seat?"

"Sure." Amelia flicked it off and climbed out of the squad car, keeping her hand on the holstered gun. "Clive."

He viewed her intently and reached behind him. She nearly pulled her gun when he removed a can of beer from his pocket. "Drink?"

She glanced at the man on the porch, then at Clive. "No, thank you."

Clive downed the first and dropped it to the ground, cracking the next. "What can I do for you?"

"The Repulsor's range doesn't stretch this far out," she said.

"I figured."

"You and your friend should follow me to the sanctuary."

"Why? You wanna throw me in a cage?"

"Listen, Clive—"

"I don't know what they're telling you, but I'm not doing nothin' illegal. My pals were killed. Darcy shot that woman in my home. I'm done with the drugs and the like."

"What about black-market food?" she asked.

"I'm arranging a trading post, is all." Clive pointed to the nearest barn. "People need gear. Guns, ammo, gasoline, propane, you name it. We're building a market to trade supplies, rather than stealing or whatever."

"Is that so? Can I see this market?" Amelia asked.

"I'd rather you didn't."

She glanced at the structure. "No drugs?"

"Nope. They're gone, ma'am." His pupils looked normal, and he seemed surprisingly calm. But that didn't mean he wasn't selling the stuff.

"Okay."

"Okay?" He was clearly surprised.

"I don't have time for this, Clive. If I hear one peep about you selling drugs again, or ripping someone off, I'm shutting you down. And that jail cell is still up, so don't forget what I said." Amelia turned and walked to the car.

"Deal!" he called while she got in.

Amelia didn't look at him while she drove off, glad to have that exchange over with.

She watched the cornfields and noticed movement to her right. When she slowed, the tops of the stalks rustled in the wind. If there were Howlers in the crops, they were well hidden. They weren't sure how far the range was, but she doubted it would cover the outskirts of town.

Amelia rolled the window down, listening for howls, but it was silent.

Five minutes later, she pulled up to the church, parking in the nearly empty lot. The hum of generators carried across the street, where they kept lights on in their temporary shelter. The fence had been fixed, and she waved at Buck Iverson, standing guard near the building entrance with his tall son, Adam. They returned the gesture, and she walked to the building, cheering up with the singing emerging from the pews. Instead of using a generator, Pastor Odell had a hundred candles lit. After the Franklin house incident, she hoped they were being cautious.

The seats were full, and when the hymn ended, the congregation sat. Pastor Odell locked gazes with her, and Freddy lifted a hand from the second row. She gave the pastor an apologetic smile for her tardiness and circled the room, sliding in next to her new deputy and his wife, Belinda, who wore a cream-colored dress and held a clutch on her lap.

Amelia looked around the crowded church, glad to see how many of the residents had dressed up for the occasion. She felt shabby in her work uniform, which needed a good steam.

Pastor Odell slowly traversed the stage, settling in at the lectern. "It's not Sunday, my usual full-service day, so

I wish to thank you for attending. Yesterday, I spoke about trusting in God. That He has a plan for each of us, and today, I'd like to comment further."

Amelia hadn't been there for the previous sermon, but figured she'd catch on quickly. Pastor Odell's voice was deep and melodic, drawing her in.

"*Behold, God is my salvation; I will trust, and will not be afraid; for the Lord God is my strength and my song,*" he said. "Fear can steal our faith, can it not?"

"Amen," Mrs. Henderson said from the other side of the pew, then bowed her head.

"We'd prayed that we'd be sent home yesterday, and technically, we were, if only for a moment. God isn't finished testing us, as he once tested Job. While the future isn't clear, know that God is in our tomorrow, and the day after that. He will never forsake us," Pastor Odell said.

"Why did this happen?" Candice Dawson asked. She wore all black, as if in mourning. Summer had gone through the Shift and become the only resident of Carmichael to escape Arcadia.

"Perhaps your sweet girl going to Earth is a blessing in disguise? She can help bring us home," Odell said.

"Did God create Arcadia?" Faith asked.

"God created all," Odell answered with a smile. "If you'll hold your comments, I'd be happy to discuss your questions after the sermon."

People chatted, then grew silent while the pastor continued.

Amelia watched the congregation as the message went on. This was a community of hard-working, salt-of-the-earth folks, who'd done nothing but try to live their days in relative peace.

Someone moved near the exit, and Amelia glanced to find Haley standing there with her rifle resting on her shoulder.

Odell stopped twenty minutes later and asked Kong to read a passage. The big bartender nodded and left his seated family, taking the podium. He talked softly, nervously wringing his hands while he spoke. When it was finished, he gently closed the Bible and returned to his seat.

"Thank you for coming and remember that you're not alone. God is always present, through every trial and tribulation. Without fail. If anyone needs support, I'll be here for a couple of hours," Odell said, then gave a last prayer.

Amelia shut her eyes along with the rest of the group, and soon they were departing, shaking hands and venturing to the parking lot, then to their provisional home across the road.

"That was lovely," Belinda said. "Do you go to church in Jackson, Amelia?"

Amelia licked her lips. "Not consistently."

"Oh." There was judgment in the woman's tone. "It's not for everyone, but Freddy and I are loyal followers, aren't we, darling?"

Freddy nodded without answering.

"We were married right here two years ago." Her palm went to her stomach. "One day, we'll have our children baptized by the pastor in front of our friends and family, won't we, Fredrick?"

"Yep."

"I better check on your mother." Belinda kissed her husband's cheek and wandered off.

"How is Margaret doing?" Amelia asked. Lillian Carson had killed Freddy's father and the Benyuks, and his mom had been injured.

"She's fine, at least physically. I hope Lillian shows up." Freddy clutched his gun. "She deserves to die."

Pastor Odell turned from his conversation and whispered to Mrs. Henderson before stalking closer. "Freddy, those are not words I like to hear in my church."

"She does," Freddy said.

"Do you know who forgives us?"

"God," he murmured.

"That's right. But more importantly, by you forgiving someone that's done you wrong, you set yourself free. And there is no better feeling than that," Pastor Odell said.

"It's not that simple."

"I'm not suggesting it is, Freddy." Odell squeezed his shoulder. "But your father wouldn't want you walking around armed with vengeance on your mind, would he?"

Amelia saw the flicker of anguish in Freddy's expression as he responded. "No, sir."

"Then, by the grace of God, you will surrender."

"Yes, sir."

Amelia pictured her mother, felt the cool palm slapping her cheek. She sensed the leering gazes of the men coming home with the dreadful woman from a late night at the bar, and unbidden tears fell.

"Deputy, is there something you'd like to release?" Pastor Odell asked.

"I'll leave you two to talk." Freddy marched down the aisle, joining his family at the exit.

Odell motioned for her to sit, and she took the front row.

"My mother wasn't a good person," she said. "I wasn't physically harmed, but I struggle to forgive her."

"Is she around Jackson?"

"My brother died after getting home from a deployment. This was seven years ago, before I became an officer. My mom left Jackson in the middle of the night, and my aunt later said she settled in Florida."

"You're carrying a heavy burden with you."

"What does that matter? We all have baggage, don't we? It's what makes us unique." Amelia didn't enjoy discussing the past, especially in a time of crisis where their survival was far more important than her own mental health.

"Can I pray with you?" Pastor Odell pursed his lips, frowning slightly.

"No, thanks. I'm afraid it might be wasted on me." She rose and patted him on the forearm. "I appreciate the effort, and the sermon was very good. We're lucky to have you in town."

He stepped aside, and she was glad he didn't argue his case. "Have a pleasant night, Amelia."

"You as well."

The church had emptied, and the candles flickered as she walked by them. Pastor Odell moved through the aisles, snuffing the flames while humming a hymn.

She viewed the alien moon, thinking about Caesar and Anders out there in the wild. John had Jamal, who knew the region's layout, but he was also recovering from a grievous injury. She gazed at the steeple, and asked a higher power to watch over her new allies.

"What's it like in winter?" John asked.

Jamal shivered, despite the heat of the fire. "It's not a long season in these parts, but it can be tough."

John added more of the dried leafy branches to the flames. "You're sure we're far enough from the woods to have this?" He continuously peered in the direction they'd come from, worried a pack of Howlers were surrounding their camp.

"Yes. Even if they get close, we have weapons and the military transport to hide in. These are built for worse than the Howlers."

His confidence eased John's trepidation. He assumed each day on the road would become more routine.

"Anyhow, you asked about winter…we're always hit with snow, but it only lasts around the Den for two weeks," Jamal advised. "It may not sound like much, but when you're living in an uninsulated cabin that's used to the sun beating on the exterior, it's dangerous. We've lost a few because of the Wanderers too."

"The Wanderers?" The name stuck to John's tongue, and he sipped from his water bottle.

Jamal watched him as if he'd said he'd never heard of Santa Claus. "It's tough, remembering how it is on Earth." He pointed to the bag beside him. "And these pain meds are making me loopy. Wanderers come in with the snow. They're the size of a fox with a snout like an anteater, only they're not as cute."

"They…" John ran a finger across his throat.

"Not quite. They burrow in the snow, enter our homes, eat the walls, blankets, any food stores we have. They're ferocious when cornered, but they don't attack us directly," he said.

"How do you stop them?"

"We've built stone fortifications, which helps, depending on how high the pack gets. They can't climb well, and since we've made the banks taller than five feet, we've held them at bay for two years now. Then the melt occurs, and the Wanderers vanish with it."

"Where do they go?" John asked.

"I haven't followed them home." Jamal grinned and bit a piece of jerky. "Don't tell Maya I had this food, or she'll be angry I didn't save it for her."

"No problem." John poked the logs with a stick and waved ash off his pants. "What do you miss the most?"

"About home?"

John nodded.

"The noise. The smell of the bakery under my apartment. The hum of the L. TV sitcoms. Comic books." Jamal laughed. "I can keep going."

"Sure."

"Horror books. Basketball playoffs. The first bite of a double pepperoni deep dish." Jamal finished his piece of jerky and sat back in his collapsable chair. "My parents. Thanksgiving dinner. Exchanging Christmas gifts."

John recalled his own childhood, before his mom and dad were stolen from them in the car accident on the interstate outside Carmichael. "You're lucky, then."

"How could you possibly think that?" Jamal asked.

"Because you had so much to live for."

"What do you miss?"

"Nothing."

"I'll ask you again in a year, and you'll have a list."

"A year?"

"Do you really believe this plan your friends concocted will work?" Jamal looked doubtful.

"If you don't, then what are we doing driving to the Den?"

"If there's a chance Logan is the same man they're searching for, and that he can connect a device in Carmichael to Shift us home, my people need to know their options," Jamal said.

"Options? You make it sound like they won't line up for the return trip."

Jamal gazed at the flames, and his dark eyes reflected the flickering orange glow. "Not everyone will leave."

"Why?" John tried to imagine a future where he'd choose Arcadia over Earth.

"Because we've built a home. We've changed too much to abandon this for a world that we barely understand anymore."

John digested the comment. "You won't stay, will you?"

Jamal smiled again and shrugged. "That'll be Maya's call."

"Even ones that could affect both of your lives forever?"

"Especially those. I've learned to be happier with myself and my existence with Maya on Arcadia than I'd ever been in Chicago. I trust her decisions."

John didn't know what time it was, but he was beat after the day's travel. "Mind if I…" He yawned before finishing the sentence.

"I'm doing the same. Let's douse this." Jamal used a shovel from the JLTV and scooped a load of dirt on their dugout. Smoke poured up as the fire was extinguished, and John secured their camp gear into the vehicle. Jamal had elected to sleep in the back seat while John slipped into his tent, checking to ensure his revolver and rifle were nearby.

He thought about their conversation, and wondered what, if anything, waited on Earth for John Paulson.

7

*S*ummer Dawson was a captive.

She envisioned how Mr. Lawrence had dealt with his year of imprisonment in Chile. Carly's dad always had an edge to him, but neither of the girls had suspected he'd been an actual spy for the US government, or an organization connected to them. Summer wasn't told the details.

Without a clock, she had to guess how close she was to reaching nine P.M. The area seemed less hectic beyond her tent's walls, but the guard remained at the exit. Summer had bothered him twice more to escort her to the bathroom, and he'd suggested she take it easy on the beverages.

She hadn't heeded his advice. Summer toyed with the nearest empty water bottle, peeling the label off. She set it by the other labels and moved to the next bottle.

"Excuse me," she said.

When the soldier didn't respond, she spoke louder. "Excuse me!"

"What?" he turned, blocking the exit.

"What time is it?"

"Why?"

"I want to know what TV shows I'm missing."

The guy cracked a smile at that. "My girl won't ever miss an episode of that show with Princess Diamond. She's obsessed. Ever seen it?"

Summer glowered. "I'm not a little kid." *But yes, I have the entire series, and the collectible cards in my desk at home…on another planet.*

"Sounds like something my kid would say," he told her, then looked at his watch. "It's eight forty."

"Thanks." Summer walked around the tent, looking at the small cot with fluffy white bedding. The table had two chairs, but it was empty otherwise. She read the backwards letters, LTC, through the walls, and pondered what the company Isla had worked for did. Summer had already told them Isla was dead, and that Caesar believed Logan may have survived. When she'd Shifted, she'd expected to be welcomed with open arms, only there was no media, no fanfare; just soldiers, LTC employees…and Christine. How did the woman get that scar on her face?

She had fifteen minutes before the deadline.

9 P.M. sharp. – H

What would happen then?

Summer had too much energy, and she wished she could hop on a bicycle and speed down the streets of Carmichael with her headphones on without a care in the world. Would she ever have that freedom again?

She plopped onto the cot, kicking her legs out, and watched the exit. The soldier leaned to his radio, nodded, and glanced into the room. Summer averted her gaze, acting as bored as possible, and when she looked again, he was gone.

The sun was nearly set, and the sky glowed red. It made her think of the adage: *red skies in morning, sailors take warning. Red skies at night, sailor's delight.* The sight gave her confidence that tomorrow would be an improvement on today.

Someone moved outside, and Summer assumed it was the guard returning to his post, but Harrison's assistant, Wanda, entered. She wore a beige pantsuit, and the heels looked uncomfortable on the rough terrain beneath them.

"What—"

Wanda put a finger to her own lips, gazing at the street. "We don't have long."

"Where are we—"

Wanda grabbed her wrist, dragging her from the tent. The area was quiet, with the soldiers and LTC staff focused on something a hundred yards north.

They circled behind the rows of temporary structures and found Harrison waiting with a gun gripped.

"Are we leaving?" Summer asked.

Harrison appeared to be torn as he viewed the cluster of soldiers. "Damn it. Tell me about these Howlers again."

"Why?" Summer's blood turned to ice when she heard the familiar animal cry.

"Everyone outside!" a voice said into a bullhorn. Christine stepped out of their command central, with the LTC representative Gunther.

Harrison stood by Summer. "We have a plan, but I can't show you tonight. Don't worry, we'll get you out of here."

"I don't want to leave. I want to Shift home," she said.

Harrison sighed. "Give me time." He stowed his gun, and Summer was surprised they'd even allowed the man to walk around armed. Was Harrison on Christine's team, and what did any of it matter? They needed to bring Carmichael to Earth. Did they have aligned agendas?

Summer guessed there were forty of them on hand, and she spied a man with the same uniform as Deputy Amelia Miller. He wore a sheriff's hat and walked like he'd just ridden in on a horse.

"Are you the girl from the other side?" he asked.

"Who are you?"

He tapped the star pinned to his shirt. "Sheriff Lyle."

"I'm Summer."

"Did you see Deputy Amelia Miller or Lieutenant Reagen Olds?"

"Reagen's dead."

The sheriff became still. The red horizon darkened, and the moment it dropped, the glowing insects from Arcadia appeared. No one seemed bothered by it, but the howling creatures buried in the forest had a different effect. Inside the border were miles of alien terrain. "How? Was it the monsters?"

"You could say that," Summer told him. "He was a bad man."

Lyle nodded. "I heard that from his girlfriend. I'd hoped she was mistaken. Was Amelia in on it?"

"Deputy Miller?" Summer asked. "No way. She's a superhero."

Lyle smiled at her comment. "Good."

"We wouldn't have made it this long without her."

Harrison listened to their conversation while Wanda typed on her phone, looking distracted.

"We have a problem," Wanda told them.

"Is that news?" Harrison asked.

She showed them the screen, and an image of a Howler traipsing through Jackson. "I guess they've spread out. So far, this is the only sighting."

Christine hurried over, holding her own phone. "Harrison, I can't leave the border. I'm asking Senator Rutherford for more soldiers. We must contain this boundary by any means. Why didn't we think something might have come with the forest?"

"Because you were too busy screwing the people of Carmichael," he mumbled.

"Will you go to Jackson and deal with the Howler?"

"You want me to find a random animal in a city?"

"Do you see the hardware store in the background?" Harrison rolled his eyes. "Yes."

"Then check it. This video was posted five minutes ago."

"I'll get my guys on it," Sheriff Lyle said.

Christine's gaze lingered on the dark woods. "No. The fewer involved, the better. And don't forget, this stays with us."

"Yes, ma'am." Lyle held his hat at his chest.

"What about me?" Summer asked.

Christine glared at her, then softened. "Bring her, but don't let her out of your sight. We can't let the world know what's going on in Indiana."

"Why should I listen to you?" Harrison asked.

"Because you can't stop us. LTC will retrieve Logan Rutherford, then have the ability to Shift to take back what's rightfully ours. And because I've been given permission to offer you a board chair."

Summer swallowed, expecting Harrison to quickly decline.

"Can I think about it?"

"Don't take too long. The senator isn't very patient, and neither am I." Christine walked off while a helicopter's rotors fired on. Drones lifted from near the border, five in total, hovering over the forest.

Soldiers busied themselves by placing more floodlights in the cornfields. A corn harvester rolled up behind them, stopping by the steady stream of parked white vans and trucks.

"What's that for?" Summer asked.

"I assume she wants to cut down the corn along the border so the team can patrol the edge. I'm betting that by the end of tomorrow, there's a fence circling this region, and another two hundred soldiers," he answered. "Wanda, stay here and keep close to someone with a machine gun."

"I wouldn't have it any other way," his assistant said.

"What about us?" Summer flinched when she recognized a Howler's cry in the distance.

"We're going to Jackson." Harrison led her to the end of the vehicles and retrieved the keys for a nondescript sedan from his pocket. He was older, with receding gray hair, but he moved with the same casual intensity as Carly's dad and the fake FBI agent, Caesar.

Summer hopped into the car with a sense of dread, and they left the scene. Her parents and friends were all on Arcadia, and it was wrong for her to be elsewhere. She'd taken this road a million times to the interstate, then to Jackson, but it was totally different now.

They trundled onto the highway in a couple of minutes, and soon sped by the exit to her school, where the bus dropped her off every day. She was on summer break, and it seemed like ages since she'd attended. Next year, she was in the tenth grade, but that life was so distant from her present situation.

"That's your school?" Harrison asked as they passed, speeding on the quiet road toward the nearest city.

"I'd rather not go there."

"What's the problem?"

"You said you'd help."

"I am."

"By taking a seat on some stupid board? I thought we could escape."

"If you want to find your family, trust me. I'm going with you to Arcadia."

"You are?" Summer asked.

"Caesar's only there because Isla cloned my phone. I don't believe a word out of Christine's mouth," he said.

"Why?"

"Because she was supposed to have died years ago, and my friend mourned her for ages." Harrison signaled and merged off the interstate, entering Jackson. "Now she suddenly reappears? It was a setup, and I have to figure out why."

Summer gawked at the city. Jackson seemed huge, with fast-food restaurants still open. The roads weren't very busy at almost ten on a Monday night, but the parking lot at a local bar was packed. They passed the theater, with posters for coming attractions catching her eye. Harrison had his GPS on, and she read the name of the hardware store, believing it was the same one that John Paulson worked at.

"The video's gone," Harrison said when he parked and checked his phone. "Christine and the LTC team move fast."

"Can they really remove stuff from the web?"

"They wiped Carmichael from the face of the Earth," he said. The headlights shone into the alley behind the store. Wooden pallets were stacked high by the garbage, and the recycle bin overflowed with broken-down cardboard boxes. He looked at Summer, and she could tell something was wrong.

"What?"

"They're not bringing Carmichael back," he said.

"What do you mean?"

"Christine won't let this get out. She'll keep a lid on the entire project."

"And how does it end?" Summer whispered.

"We'll deal with that later." Harrison exited the car, and

she hurried after him, wishing she had a shotgun. The world was so different on Arcadia. If she ran around with a gun in Jackson, she'd be thrown in jail.

Summer grabbed his arm. "How does it end?"

Harrison pushed the safety off and stalked the alley. "With no witnesses."

She looked up at the last second and shoved Harrison. The Howler landed hard, dropping from the telephone line. It hissed and lunged at Caesar's boss, but he was faster. Four bullets tore into the animal's flesh, and it fell to the asphalt.

"Thanks," he said, panting his breaths.

"You owe me."

"That I do."

8

*T*he morning air was as refreshing as any Caesar had ever inhaled. He'd slept like a log, only waking when he'd heard Anders preparing breakfast. The tent came down in seconds, and he stored it in the vehicle, then accepted a cup of coffee. He preferred it with a splash of cream, but out here in the wild, he couldn't be picky.

Anders was a man of few words, and Caesar respected the silence as they ate garlic sausage cooked on the stove. Before leaving, Caesar ensured there was no evidence of their stay.

"Is that necessary?" Anders asked, taking the driver's seat.

"Old habits die hard."

"Don't I know it?"

The sun had barely risen, and a mist clung to the prairies. An hour later, it still hadn't broken, and it became thicker as they descended into a dip in the land.

"Should we wait it out?" Anders slowed and came to a stop.

"Probably for the best." Caesar guessed the fog would dissipate with the sun any minute.

Anders cut the engine. "Did you hear that?"

"No."

"There it is again."

Caesar tried to pick up the sound, and finally did. "It's coming from…" He viewed the vehicle's beige hood, barely able to see the end in the dense mist. A giant slug slid forward, leaving a trail of slime in its wake. It made a noise, like a squeegee on the windshield, when it squirmed closer. He gazed at the rear window, finding two of the creatures on it. Then one startled him by ascending his door.

"They're everywhere," Anders said.

"They're probably drawn to the heat." Caesar rolled his window down and used his handgun to flick the foot-long bug off. Goop dripped from the barrel, and he wished he'd thought it through. He grabbed a tissue, wiping it. Before he closed it, another climbed up the glass and fell inside. Caesar pushed the button and it sliced the bug in half, the head dropping onto his lap.

Anders laughed at him until he noticed the windshield. Ten slugs were present, with more coming every second.

"If they get under the hood, we could be screwed." Caesar picked up the beheaded slug, careful not to touch it.

Anders started the JLTV, activating the wipers, which hit the slugs but didn't clear them until he put the wipers on high. The mist began evaporating, and Caesar saw thousands of the things stalking out of the grassy plains. Their tires slid as they squished dozens. Anders pushed the gas, fishtailing before gaining traction. He sped from the low point, slowing after escaping the horde of bugs.

"I hate snails."

"Snails have shells," Caesar said.

"Can you get rid of that?" He gestured at the tissue in Caesar's hand.

"Gladly." He tossed it out the window, and they

continued on their path. The sun was higher, casting warmth throughout the valley.

An hour later, a light appeared on the dash, and Anders tapped the display. "We're overheating."

"Let's check."

After parking in a grassy field, Caesar exited while Anders popped the hood. It hissed up, sticking with hydraulics. Something sizzled beneath it, and Caesar spied the culprit. A half dozen slugs had melted to the engine.

"Great, just great." He spent the next five minutes scraping the guts off, and Anders gestured to a nearby pond.

"We shouldn't use the drinking water." He brought a bucket, and the pair strolled through the waist-high grass, Caesar gripping his M4.

The pond had hundreds of tiny bubbles, making Caesar wonder what was under the surface. Arcadia was teeming with alien life. "What if there are other life forms?"

Anders dunked the bucket, filling it three-quarters of the way. Little fish with four dorsal fins swam by, scattering because of the disruption. "We've seen a bunch of them."

"No. I mean… *life forms.*" Caesar patted himself on the chest.

"Jamal would have mentioned that."

"We're in the wilderness. They could have cities far away." Caesar studied the water, then gazed at the sky.

"I haven't seen any satellites."

"Maybe they don't need them," he said.

"There have been no blinking lights, or light pollution on the horizon. I don't know, Caesar. Arcadia doesn't have little green men wandering around."

"I hope you're right."

Once they returned to the vehicle, Anders doused the steaming engine with pond water, and they waited for the steam to subside. The dash icon was gone when Anders started it up again. "Let's avoid another slug trap."

They were days from reaching Logan, and it seemed like they weren't making enough progress. Caesar had to be patient on this rescue mission, given the harsh terrain and unfamiliar setting. He wished Isla had the foresight to bring a helicopter with her, because it would have cut their time down significantly. That made him wonder why they weren't better prepared. He voiced his concern to Anders.

"Good point. Isla wanted to track Logan, but lacked the resources to get everything on her wish list."

"If Senator Rutherford was helping, why didn't he pull some strings?"

"I think you're giving him too much credit. Do you know how difficult it would be to borrow a couple of these JLTVs and a helicopter? That's why they had to source weapons illegally with Lillian's help," Anders said.

Caesar sat upright when a thought struck him. "What if Logan wasn't really the target? Lillian said it herself. Logan only became a priority when the Shift didn't work."

"Damn it," Anders said.

"What?"

"Whoever is in charge didn't want Carmichael to return."

Caesar blinked slowly, processing the news. "They'll come up with some excuse...probably torch the alien forest and claim Carmichael burned to the ground, while leaving us on Arcadia."

"Why?" Anders asked.

"They secretly want access to the world. And we're a roadblock."

"This organization didn't think of one thing," Anders told him with a smile.

"That two rogue agents would ensure they fail," Caesar said.

Amelia woke with a start. She gasped and sat up, reaching for her gun. Most of the dwellers were asleep, despite the sunlight entering the front doors. A few moved at the sudden noise she'd made, and Amelia gave them an apologetic smile, stowing her weapon.

Dot spoke with Klein in their makeshift kitchen as they worked at the gas cooktops.

Amelia's mouth was sticky, and she desperately needed a shower. She wandered to Dot, inspecting the pot of oatmeal being stirred. "Good morning."

"Howdy, Chief," Dot said smugly. "Want a bite?"

"Sure." Amelia accepted a steaming bowl and plastic spoon. "Could I borrow your house?"

"Of course, dear." Dot pulled a keyring from her pocket, then removed one. "The water tank won't be hot, but take a quick rinse. Use any of my products."

"Thanks again," she said. Many of the folks would head home during the day, when the threat of a Howler attack was far lower, but Amelia didn't live in town and had nowhere to call her own.

"Is it good?" Klein asked.

"What?" Amelia stammered, then understood. "Yes, the food's delicious."

"I found a stash in the cupboards at the diner," he said. "We took oatmeal off the menu earlier in the year. Folks prefer it in the winter months, so we can feed the town breakfast for a week."

"I thought you…" Amelia let Klein dollop a second helping into the bowl.

"Fired him?" Dot crossed her arms. "I did, but Klein's

promised he's done with Clive, and I don't want his talents to go wasted. There are lots of great home cooks in town, mark my word, but they're not used to catering to the masses."

"I'm grateful for the second chance," the big cook said. He wiped his hands on the crusted apron and smiled at another resident as he gave oatmeal to them.

"Ew, is this puke?" a kid asked.

Reese West interjected, crouching at the eight-year-old's side. "That's no way to speak to your elders. Now apologize and take your breakfast, Jack."

"Okay." Jack took the food. "Sorry it looks like puke." He showed a gap in his teeth and ran off.

"Don't mind him," Reese said.

"You don't have to watch them all day," Dot said. "His mom's around here, somewhere."

"I like it, for the most part." Reese had heard her grandparents being murdered days earlier, yet kept positive. What Amelia wouldn't give to have that fourteen-year-old's courage. She supposed the girl was putting on a show, that the effects of the trauma, combined with the Shift, would put her into therapy later in life, but the same could be said of most of Carmichael.

"You're doing a great job," Amelia told her. "If you need anything, ask me."

Reese nodded, rushing away with her own serving.

"We have good kids here," Dot said. "Things are under control this morning, but come by the gardens after if you're able."

"I will," she promised, and with another thanks to Klein, Amelia was off. She stopped at the washroom on the way out, relieving herself, and used sanitizer rather than waste their quickly depleting water stash.

Amelia said hi to some people near the facility, and

almost jogged to the squad car, eager to be alone. She hadn't spent this much time around others, and didn't realize how draining it was to constantly be on.

The instant the car door sealed, her mood improved. As she drove, Amelia went over the list of upcoming tasks.

Amelia parked at Dot's house, recalling dropping the woman off a couple of nights earlier when she'd borrowed her car. At that point, they didn't know about the Shifting, or Howlers, or who Isla truly was.

She used the keys, glad Dot had the common sense to lock up. Amelia expected it to be welcoming and full of old photos, but it was nearly as lifeless as her own place in Jackson. It practically looked staged. The diner had a personality all to itself, and Amelia assumed it would have trickled into Dot's home life, but clearly, that wasn't the case.

She spun the deadbolt and kicked off her boots. The hardwood floors were worn but clean. The fireplace had no ashes, but judging by the tools, Dot utilized it when the days grew cold enough. On the mantel were generic overseas décor pieces, and Amelia spun a golden globe, finding no dust. If she hadn't used a key to get in, she would have thought it was the wrong house.

Amelia examined the kitchen, which had more of the woman's personality. A few small appliances were on the counters, with a dozen others on display near the pantry. The shelves were mostly empty, meaning she'd been good to her word, and donated what she had to the town's supply.

She didn't want to pry, but curiosity won. Amelia opened a cupboard above the fridge and found five bottles of unopened whiskey and a carton of cigarettes. She slid the smokes free and inspected the package. It looked old, the same brand her mother used to light up.

Amelia closed the cupboard and told herself to stop snooping. She proceeded to the bathroom in the hall, discovering a standard layout. The vanity was tidy, with room to spread makeup and accessories. The toilet was dated, and the shower curtain had that new plastic scent, indicating it had been changed recently. She wouldn't have thought much about it if she didn't see the packaging jutting from the cylindrical white garbage can.

"Who replaces the curtain during a crisis?" Amelia asked her reflection.

The window gave light, and she undressed, bringing the t-shirt and her underwear into the bathtub with her. Before dousing herself in cold water, which was in short supply, she rinsed and scrubbed her items, then hung them on the towel rack. Amelia hopped in, using soap, then a little shampoo, all while unsuccessfully trying to trick herself that the water wasn't bone-chilling.

Cognizant of the limited reserve, she finished and dried off. Amelia surveyed her naked reflection, which she usually hated doing, and discovered a half dozen abrasions and cuts. That explained the uncomfortable shower. With an investigation of the medicine cabinet, she used antiseptic and placed bandages on the most grievous wounds.

She found a bathrobe draped onto a hook and slid into it, carrying the wet clothing to the deck. The morning sun was low but hot, and the second she put the articles on the railing, they started to dry.

Amelia spied the stovetop on the outdoor table and decided to use Dot's coffee percolator while she waited. The town needed her alert, and a twenty-year-old habit of beginning her mornings with caffeine wasn't going away.

The gas hissed as the flame filled the burner. It took her a minute to remember how to operate the machine, a distant suppressed memory from her real father bringing her camping as a child. She smiled, recalling the brief time in her life where he'd been around, popping in once a year to check on her, until he vanished forever. Now she was the one that had disappeared, and doubted anyone cared.

The coffee boiled in the aluminum percolator, and she flipped the burner off, pausing when she heard something. Amelia listened, recognizing the sound of shattering glass. "Damn it." Dot's house butted up to a neighbor behind her, and someone was at the back door. Amelia's gun was inside, and it would be smartest to retrieve the weapon before facing the assailant. She also still had Dot's personalized fuzzy robe on.

A man kicked the shards of glass and turned the handle. He gazed backwards, seeing the new chief watching him with an empty cup of coffee in her grip from Dot's. He wore a bandana to block his features.

"Stay where you are!" she shouted.

Amelia sighed when the guy ran, and bolted down the deck steps, scaling the fence. The robe's tie caught on the top, and she managed to unsnap it, cinching the clothing while jogging to the driveway. Whoever had broken into Dot's neighbor's home had escaped.

"It's a good thing you're trained for this," she told herself, taking the long way to Dot's.

Once she had access to her radio, she called it in, requesting Kong and Haley come to Mission Street to investigate what was missing from the homes. She suspected whatever it was would end up for sale in Clive's barn.

Before leaving Dot's, she noticed a brown door, probably leading to the basement. Amelia tried it, but the handle was locked. She tested the main entrance key, finding it didn't work. She shrugged, closed Dot's up, then rolled away from the place in her squad car, with a headache creeping in. Amelia opened the lid to the coffee in the to-go mug sitting in the cupholder, and blew on it, grateful at least one thing had gone according to plan.

9

*F*orty miles didn't sound like much, but the trek was far more arduous on a world without roads. Jamal was livelier today after a long night's rest in the JLTV. They'd taken their time in the morning, making sure to eat and hydrate before venturing onto the 'road,' which was a term John used loosely. In the grassy plains, there were dips and valleys, most hidden from sight until you drove into them. He'd stopped twice to assess damage, but realized the military vehicle was equipped to deal with rough conditions.

Jamal made notes in his journal as they traveled, logging anything that might be a landmark for his homemade map. Each scout returned with their findings, adding to the master 'file' at the Den, which, according to Jamal, was a carving in an old wooden door they'd discovered.

"How many people do you think Shift to Arcadia each year?" John checked the speedometer and pushed up to eight miles an hour, until the ground grew more uneven and he returned to five.

"Who the heck knows?" Jamal asked. "We usually only add one or two at the Den, and Shelter has over a hundred residents."

"Nothing like Carmichael has ever occurred before?"

"Not to my knowledge, though it's been rumored there's the odd vacant building," he said.

"Vacant?"

"I heard it second-hand, but they told Ben of an empty community."

"No one went back?"

"It was up north, across the canyon. Do you have any idea how many resources it takes to send scouts a couple hundred miles? We can't explore on a whim," Jamal said.

John tried to imagine a ghost town in the middle of Arcadia, and hoped that wasn't a precursor to Carmichael's future. Would a scout find his home in a century, wondering what happened to them?

They drove on, conversing like old friends. It was relaxing having Jamal to converse with. He was so different from Darcy. "Have you lost people in Arcadia?" John eventually asked.

"Sure. A bunch."

"What happened?"

"You name it. Howlers. The Wanderers. Storms. Freezing weather and flooding summers. Some seasons, we're a week from starvation; then another, we're flush with food and meat. The problem is, with no power sources or salt, we can't preserve very well, even with Ben's techniques."

John figured that made sense. "You can fish."

"Our lake isn't huge, and we have to be careful not to over-fish, or we'll go hungry the following year."

"How do you keep going on?"

Jamal shifted in his seat and watched John. "You work hard each day, then go to bed too tired to think. But I also lucked out and found Maya, and that is worth waking up for."

"How much farther?"

"The odometer says we've gone twenty-one miles since leaving Carmichael, so about thirty, give or take."

"Then what's that?" John pointed to the right, where the peak of a building rose out of a grassy knoll.

"Hit the brakes!" Jamal was out of the JLTV before he'd put it in park. John drove closer, then hurried after him, running across the unforgiving terrain. "This is incredible!"

The building was composed of white brick, with a spire atop it. A tattered American flag blew in the wind. It had three levels, the second with a sprawling balcony overlooking what would have once been a courtyard. A single car was there, the air released from the tires long ago. The fender had rust, and the black paint was faded.

"Slow down!" John shouted. "You're going to reinjure that wound."

Jamal obeyed, but still walked hastily. "I've never found something like this before."

There was a lot of territory to cover, and if the scouts rarely ventured beyond their allotted trails, it made sense that an object Shifted decades earlier would remain undiscovered.

John paused at the car and tried to open it. The oxidized handle pulled clean off, and he wiped a sleeve on the grimy window, peering into the preserved interior. "It's an old Caddy."

With great effort, Jamal lowered to his knees and revealed the border of the Shifted land. The concrete was sliced, much like the road surrounding Carmichael. Alien weeds grew through cracks of the courtyard, and John spied the now familiar pink butterflies coasting through the air.

"Bring the guns," Jamal said, then let John help him

up.

John returned to their ride and grabbed his rifle and a shotgun for Jamal, which he used like a cane until they reached the building's entrance. From this vantage point, the structure felt even bigger. "What was this place?"

"We'll find out. There could be anything living inside. It's the perfect spot for a nest," he warned.

"I'll keep that in mind," John said. The door was stuck. He put his weight into it, and the hinges fought him every step of the way. Once it cracked open slightly, Jamal shoved his shotgun in and used the barrel for leverage. It relented, and they were in.

Jamal aimed the weapon while John activated the flashlight. He walked to a bronze placard by a desk, reading it aloud. "Western Lake Mental Hospital."

"It's a psychiatric hospital," Jamal said. "And an old one at that."

John strode to the desk, finding an ancient rotary phone. The décor screamed another century, and he picked up the handset, then set it on the cradle. A newspaper sat by the upended chair, and John lifted it carefully. He skimmed an article on the front page about the war. "It's from January 4th, 1942."

"How could a building like this be taken, and no one know?" Jamal asked.

The walls had water stains near the windows, but the glass had miraculously held up over the years. "Maybe they'd already abandoned it. These places often get shut down or lose funding."

"Could be." Jamal limped out of the foyer and encountered a barricade to the rest of the interior. The bars were shut, with a rusted chain dangling from the center. John pushed off the padlock, and it clanged to the floor loudly, before he swung the gate, stepping into the hall.

"You've never seen a building Shift?"

"Not the entire thing, and nothing this big." Jamal's eyes were wide as they walked deeper. He checked the first room, which had a few security uniforms.

John picked up a nametag. *J. Freeman.* "What happened to this place, Mr. Freeman?"

They found a staff breakroom, complete with an old coffee maker and cupboards full of dishes. "I want to take it all for the Den."

"Do you know how much lead is in this stuff?"

Jamal set a floral-patterned plate down and shrugged. "Better than what we have."

Next, they came upon a space with sewing equipment and a handful of rocking chairs. Someone had knitted half a scarf, and Jamal gathered the needles and yarn into a bag.

"What are you doing?"

"We can make things with this and patch up our clothes."

"But you'll have to haul it to Carmichael after," John said.

Jamal kept collecting the gear. "There's no guarantee of a Shift home."

"What else do you need?" John asked.

He wasn't prepared for what they discovered after venturing to the adjacent room. The fireplace had broken pieces of furniture near it, and three skeletons lying at the stone hearth. "They probably froze to death." Fragments of their clothing clung to the bones. From his best guess, it was two men and one woman. Were they workers or patients? Empty tin cans lingered on the floor, along with utensils. "Should we bury them?"

"I don't have the stamina," Jamal admitted. "And we can't delay our trip."

"You're right." John sealed them in.

They spent the next hour combing all three stories, not finding it occupied until they saw evidence of an old bird's nest in the attic. John backed the JLTV to the front steps, and they filled it to the top with handheld mirrors, a few transistor radios, and countless other items Jamal figured would help his town survive.

John imagined the staff huddled in on a frigid winter night, stoking the fire and listening to news of the great war happening overseas. Most would have family enlisted and sent to the frontlines. Then they'd been transported by a natural Shift, changing their futures forever.

"Quite the day," Jamal said.

"We wasted a few hours."

"It won't be a waste when Maya sees this beauty." Jamal gripped a sparkling gold necklace.

"Let's aim for another twenty miles." John wanted to get on with the mission, eager to return home.

The noise was ceaseless. It was an irritating cacophony of trucks backing up and jackhammers pounding into the alien ground. Since they'd returned from Jackson last night, having killed the Howler, they'd been given more freedom around camp. Armed soldiers guarded the roads, so there was just one way in, unless you wanted to risk the cornfields. Summer had done enough of that for a lifetime—not that she had anywhere to go.

Her mom had an older brother in Poughkeepsie, with two grown-up kids she barely knew. Her dad was an only child, and all the grandparents were gone, her Granny passing away a year earlier at a retirement home on the West Coast. Summer recalled the somber affair where she'd told herself she never wanted anyone to give her a funeral.

"Do they think a five-foot fence can really hold a group of Howlers?" Summer asked Wanda.

Harrison's assistant laughed and gestured at the generator connecting to the chain link. "It will when they're zapped with 8000 volts." She mimed being electrocuted.

"You're far less uptight than your boss," Summer said.

"Harry? He's not always like this."

"I can't even picture him smiling." Summer backed out of the way as a pair of soldiers rushed by, hauling a section of fence. "How long have you worked for him?"

"Me?" Wanda squinted beneath her sunglasses. "Twenty years."

"Wow."

"Yeah, I was on his staff when he was still serving his country."

"He's not now?"

"Not what?"

"Serving," Summer said.

"Indirectly, yes. On paper, no." Wanda sent a message on her phone.

"Who's that?"

"We have an operative in the field. She's delivering reports, but Harry's busy, so I'm screening them."

"She?"

"Women make the best operatives," she said. "Harry has a couple on his team, though his missions often lean toward"—Wanda put a hand conspiratorially close to her face and whispered—"blowing things up."

"What about Christine?" Summer sipped from her soda, glad to have a chilled beverage on the scorching afternoon.

"She works for someone else," Wanda said.

"Senator Rutherford?"

"Not officially. In this case, yes."

Summer wasn't sure Wanda would elaborate, but she continued.

"There are five major players in our arena. Two out of the US, one from France, another in Britain, and a fifth from Southern Africa."

"What about China… Russia?"

"They have similar operations, but that's usually who we're up against," Wanda said. "Christine and Anders worked for the other American team, until Chile. Caesar and Christine got married pretty quickly. In this field, you have to seize the day."

"*Carpe diem*, right?" Summer smiled.

"That's correct. You speak Latin?"

"Just a pinch. My mom's forcing me to take all sorts of languages. She says I have to speak at least three proficiently to excel in my college applications," Summer said.

"What's your favorite?"

"I dunno. French, I suppose." She thought about Adam Iverson, and how they'd shared one dreamy afternoon together before she'd so clumsily entered the Shift.

"Why so glum?" Wanda motioned to the construction. "Besides the obvious."

"I met a boy."

"Here?" Wanda sounded concerned.

"No, back home. We'd never talked, mostly because his family doesn't believe in technology or something," she said.

"You can't fight progress." Wanda pulled Summer out of the way as a bulldozer sped by. "These guys are maniacs."

"You try putting up a twenty-mile fence with a hundred soldiers and no time." Harrison's voice startled Summer, but she kept her composure.

"How much have they done?" Wanda asked.

"A third, which is pretty dang good if you ask me. Christine promised them a cash bonus if they're finished by nightfall."

"Think they can do it?" Summer inquired.

Harrison's arms were crossed, and he lowered his sunglasses on his nose, staring at her. "If there's one thing I won't bet against, it's soldiers with an incentive."

Wanda pointed at Harrison's gripped phone. "No more signs of Howlers in Jackson County?"

"Not yet. They've stuck close to their natural habitat, but it won't last for long."

A large truck came in too fast, not realizing the road ended, and the front tires crashed onto the alien land. The trailer carrying more chain-link fell to its side, spilling the contents.

Men shouted at the driver, and Harrison led Wanda and Summer from the spot. Summer figured he wanted them out of harm's way should things get heated, but quickly realized he had underlying motives. While the soldiers were distracted, he slipped into a large white tent at the end of their camp.

"What's this?" Summer entered, gawking at the assortment of computers. A dozen towers blinked and hummed with power, and the main desk sat empty, a screensaver of the LTC logo bouncing across the monitor.

"I've been trying to figure out where the Shift is," Harrison whispered.

Summer barely heard him over the sound of machinery and the beeping devices in the tent.

"And…" Wanda adjusted her pantsuit collar and gazed around.

"Gunther's their lead tech on the Shift program, which means he's the only one that worked on it since the board shut it down. Isla did the rest herself, but they had Logan Rutherford's initial blueprints. He's duplicated it."

Summer tried to follow the logic. "Meaning?"

Harrison glanced at the exit and bolted to the main computer. He removed a keycard from his dress shirt pocket and tapped it on the digital lock. "I still have deft fingers. Trick of the trade." He kept the card and opened the black metal case within the drawer. There was a faded LTC logo on the box, and a series of numbers indicating a nomenclature Summer wasn't familiar with.

Harrison detached the device, which was basically a round tablet with three recessed antennae. When he touched the screen, they all extruded, and the machine powered on. A clock appeared, and it only took Summer an instant to understand what they were looking at. "It's another countdown," she whispered.

It read 130:01:18, and descended with each second.

Wanda had her phone near it, and an app flashed on, duplicating the countdown. Harrison did the same, then hastily returned the Shift device to the case and slammed the drawer closed. "We have five days before the fluctuations are similar enough to travel to Arcadia." He knocked on the desk.

"We?" Summer asked.

"You don't think I'd let you go alone, do you?"

"What about me, Harry?" Wanda fluffed her hair up. "I wouldn't do well—"

"Don't worry, Wanda. You'll stay to tell the story. I'm going to draft up a message in the off chance we end up trapped there," he said. "And you'll have to get Fatina and my daughter to the safehouse."

A soldier walked by, and Summer figured they were caught for sure. Harrison ushered them to the far side of the tent, and she held her breath while they hid.

"Clear," he said, then continued.

Harrison waited a moment before stepping from behind the whiteboard, and squared off with Summer, grabbing her shoulders. "Can you keep it together for five days?"

"That depends."

"On what?"

"Do you have any headphones?"

INTERLUDE

Logan

Shelter

"*T*his is going to work," Ruby said.

Logan clutched the tablet from the top of the barrel, finding the connection lost. "Isla's dead."

Ruby stroked his hair while they lay in bed. "Did you love her?"

Logan rolled over, watching his wife. "I did."

"You're lucky I'm not the jealous type," she purred.

"It wasn't like that with us."

"But it might have been, if you…"

"Didn't leave on a solo mission before my technology was perfected," he finished.

"Do you think you and I would have made it in reality?"

"Reality? Is this not real?" He poked her in the thigh.

"You know what I mean."

"Probably not," he said.

"Logan Rutherford, never one to mince words."

"I'm just being honest. How would we even have met?"

"Sometimes a girl wants to be told she's special on any world," she grumbled, and slipped from the bed.

Logan couldn't help but ogle her. "If it's any

consolation, there's no way you'd have given me the time of day on Earth."

Her laugh was growly. "And why not?"

"Because you're a goddess and I'm a tech dude. Pale. Nerdy. Working late into the night. I wouldn't have taken you dancing, or on romantic beach walks…"

"But you do that now," she said.

"And I'm grateful for it." Logan set the tablet aside. "I haven't thought about Anders Lawrence, or my hometown, for ages."

"Who's the other guy?"

"No idea."

"I finally get to meet your mom." Ruby dressed slowly, and viewed herself in the metal sheet hanging on the wall they used as a mirror.

"My mom is on Arcadia," he said. "How is any of this possible?"

"Isla and your uncle, that's how."

"The senator never gave two craps about me. Why bother?"

"You're still that naïve, aren't you, Logan?"

"I am anything but—"

"They want Arcadia. Even if they backed Isla to Shift an entire town, there's—"

Logan hopped to his feet. "Oh, no."

"What?"

"Isla couldn't have done that on her own. She would have come with an extraction team and found me. She had to know that the tablet might eventually contact one another," he said. "Isla wouldn't risk my mother!"

"But she did."

"Only because she was persuaded."

"By whom?"

"Someone that wanted all the witnesses disposed of,"

Logan said.

"Then they won't be happy when you get to Carmichael and transport the town and its residents to Earth?"

"We'll be gunned down," he declared.

"Then it's a good thing there are guys with guns on our side," she said. "Who is Anders?"

"I always assumed he was a regular joe, but I remember…" Logan recalled the rumors from his mom before he came to Arcadia. "I think he was imprisoned in South America."

"For what?"

"No one knew." Logan exited their home, gazing at the night sky. Stars twinkled in the distance. "How many other alien worlds could we connect the Shift to?"

"None of that matters," she said. "We only have the here and now."

His gaze floated to the tower he'd begun building a decade earlier. It wasn't finished, because he'd run out of parts.

"Our people will be upset when we leave," Logan said.

She shook her head. "No, they'll be happy for the shred of hope."

Logan grabbed his tool kit. "I'll dismantle it. It'll be simpler to transport."

"Do you want a hand?" she asked, yawning.

"Nah. Why don't you finish what you were doing before I interrupted?" he said with a smile.

"Interrupt me anytime, if that's what happens."

Logan hefted the box, filled with an assortment of screwdrivers and wrenches. They were almost as rare as electronics on Arcadia, and some he'd made with parts of other garbage they'd collected.

He walked through Shelter. Most of the population

was in bed, but a few remained up. Some chatted by an outdoor fire, and invited him to join, but he graciously declined and continued to the tower on the village's outskirts. It had taken him years to assemble, but knew it would be much faster to dismantle.

Isla had already built a proper Shift at Carmichael, and if it remained intact, Logan had no doubts he could transport them back to Earth.

INTERLUDE

Christine

Arcadia Forest, Indiana

The floodlights died as Christine strode deeper into the woods. The carbine felt at home in her arms, like she'd been missing a limb since being deemed dead.

The trees were magnificent. She paused and watched the heavens beyond the rustling branches. Keeping this secret for an entire week seemed improbable. A month, impossible.

She lowered the weapon and touched her scarred cheek, being thrown back to the moment she'd escaped the explosion. She'd detonated a bomb, but the hatch had been damaged in the warehouse battle. Anders was in another part of the building, and when she dove, landing in the bay's cold water, she instantly knew she'd been cut.

He'd fought like a banshee trying to find her. She'd listened to his calls from her hiding position under the dock and stayed put when the officials showed and arrested him.

On record, Christine, along with three supposed biotech engineers, had died, their bodies unidentifiable from the chemical fire. Caesar had been notified of her death by email.

"What have I done?" She leaned on the tree trunk,

wishing she could take it all back. She wouldn't be traversing an alien forest at midnight, and her husband wouldn't be driving across another planet. It was possible their relationship could have actually worked, despite her continuous deceit. He didn't deserve that kind of treatment. Christine could forgive a lot about her own past, but this wasn't one of them.

The team had finished the fence an hour earlier, beyond their bonus time, but they'd get the money. She hadn't expected them to pull it off, given the constraints. Only Harrison seemed unsurprised by their ability to complete the job.

Caesar always spoke highly of his boss, and Christine saw why. Sitting in the peaceful woods, she regretted striking him in front of the girl. Christine's orders were to look and act in charge so everyone fell into line, but it wasn't easy.

Her phone buzzed, and she checked it, glad the portable cell tower they'd brought worked this far in. "Hawkstone," she said.

"Do you have them contained?" the man asked.

Christine tried to picture him but couldn't, since they'd never met. When they spoke, she imagined a figure shrouded in darkness. "The Howlers are behind the fence." At the mention of the dangerous beasts, she glanced upwards, glad to find the higher branches clear of the predator.

"Did Harrison accept the position at LTC?"

At this point, she was certain his voice was modified. "Not yet."

"Have him answer by tomorrow."

"Or what?" Harrison Gregory was an important man, with people that would miss him. Politically powerful individuals.

"*Kill him.*"

"Sir, if I may—"

The call ended, and for a moment, she thought they might have lost connection, but the reception was fine.

Christine thrust the phone into her jacket pocket, lugged the gun to her chest, and began the march. Soon the floodlights' glow beamed from beyond the barrier, and a pair of gloved soldiers opened the gate. The electric fence hummed with energy, and she was careful to avoid touching the metal.

Despite the late hour, she noticed Harrison by his sleeping quarters. He met her gaze, and she felt the urge to confide in him. Maybe they could work together, bring Carmichael home, and she'd be reunited with Caesar.

Instead, she breezed past him without a word.

PART TWO
NEW FRIENDS

1

"Someone broke into nineteen houses and four acreages," Freddy said. They leaned over the desk in their makeshift police station at the town office, where Vivian had once presided as Carmichael's mayor. Amelia had left her framed photos up, along with her credentials from an out-of-state community college. She'd graduated with a degree in Fine Arts twenty-five years earlier.

"Are you listening?" Freddy asked.

"Yes." Amelia blinked her gaze to the map. The homes affected had small X's drawn on them. The acreages were all close to Carmichael. "What did they take?"

"It was the darnedest thing," Freddy said. "Only electronics."

Amelia frowned and scanned the list Haley had compiled on her notepad. "CD player. Tablets. Laptops. Old desktops. Televisions. Why?"

"Most of the stuff in these houses is ancient. It's not like Mrs. Henderson had the latest technology," Haley told them.

"The mystery continues." Amelia sat in the chair, spinning slowly to face the window. It was another scorching hot day out, so with a limited water supply and endless tasks to perform, they needed to exercise extreme caution. There were no doctors, and the closest thing they'd had was Freddy's dad, the local vet who'd been killed by Lillian. "Where are we with the tents?"

"Clive's bringing them, but he's demanding something in return," Haley said.

"What?"

"He wants double rations."

Amelia almost wished Gus had finished Clive off when he'd shot Clay and Ron. "No way. What else?"

"Ammunition." Haley read off the list.

"What kind?"

".223."

"For an M4?"

"Not the ideal choice," Freddy said. "But it means he's got some weapons out there."

"They must have missed a crate." Amelia didn't love the notion of confronting the man again and taking the cache of guns. "If he doesn't have ammo for them, we're fine. What else?"

Haley glanced at Freddy, then at her. "He'd give us the tents for dinner with you."

Amelia felt heat rising in her chest, but it wasn't embarrassment. It was anger. "I'll wring his tattooed neck."

"There's another option," Freddy said.

"What?"

He stood taller. "We take the tents."

Amelia knew there would be tough decisions to be made. "Let me talk to him."

"At dinner?" Haley nudged Freddy's arm.

"This isn't funny." But even Amelia cracked a grin. "Have you finished the registered resident list?"

"We're done." Haley showed her the paperwork. "There are only two unaccounted for from the fire."

"And no one's come forward to say who they were?" she asked.

"Not yet," Freddy said.

"Nice work. Can you run a border patrol again and check in with me?"

"Yes, Chief." Freddy bowed his head and folded their map. "Where are you going?"

"To Kong at the catchment system, and then off to see how the gardens are progressing."

"You can't grow food without water," Haley reminded her.

"We're aware of that." Amelia gazed at the sky through the glass. "Let's pray there's rain once we're done with the catchment."

"See you later, Chief." Haley paused at the door. "Thanks for bringing me on board."

"You're doing very well," she said honestly. Amelia hadn't been sure about the young woman, but she'd already proven to be a valuable asset to the team. When they were gone, Amelia took a moment to herself. Who was breaking into the houses, and why take antiquated electronics? She'd figure it out eventually. There weren't that many people in town, and most of them had loose lips. Amelia assumed Clive was involved, so she'd deal with that at the same time as getting the commercial tents out of his storage barn.

She rose from the chair, feeling older than her years, and exited the town office. Down the block, Dot and Sharon worked tirelessly on the gardens, but that was her second stop. She got into her squad car and drove to the edge of town, slowing at the Gas-N-Go. Vince stood by his pumps with his son, Jimmy, drinking a beer. He dipped his baseball cap to her, and she waved in return, then stopped. "How are you?" she asked the duo.

"I'm at about a third of my supply. I'm doing what you ordered and only giving fuel to those on the list." He tapped the top page of the clipboard in Jimmy's grip. "Others are annoyed, but I told them those are the rules."

Judging by the glance from Jimmy, his dad was selling some on the side.

"How come your tanks are accessible? Weren't they cut off like the wells?" she asked.

Vince pointed behind them. "I never spent the money to upgrade these things. These are above-ground tanks from the Sixties. They hold it just fine, so why bother doing anything to 'em? But I did check, and the ground is deeper here too. Kind of how most of the homes kept their basements."

The left tank had diesel, the smaller of the three had propane, and the largest was clearly the unleaded stuff. "Thanks for listening to me." She almost drove off, but kept her foot on the brake. "Vince, do you mind if I borrow your kid for the afternoon? Kong needs more hands on deck."

"You want Jimmy?" Vince laughed, then wiped his lips with his forearm.

"Can I, Dad?"

"Sure, boy. What the hell."

Amelia exhaled in relief and opened the side door by stretching across the console. Jimmy hurried into the vehicle, probably before Vince could change his mind. "You okay?"

Jimmy still had the clipboard, and he blanched. "Should we bring this back?"

"I will later."

He put it on the floor and stared out the windshield. "You really need my help?"

"Yep." A bunch of trucks were parked by the open field. Mr. Tucker had swathed the long grass, making a space for their catchment system. Evan stood on a ladder using a hammer, while Kong shouted orders to his crew. There were five of them in total, including the Tuckers. Eldon steadied a piece of plywood, sliding it to Evan, while Katie handed the teenager more nails. Evan shoved them into his tool belt pouch and kept working.

Kong stopped what he was doing and told the guys to take a break. They ventured into the shade of the half-rotten barn, and Amelia set a palm on Jimmy's shoulder. "I figured he'd be more beneficial here than at the gas station."

Kong appraised the boy. "You ever used a hammer?"

"Yes, sir."

"You're hired. The tool belts are in my truck, and grab a pair of gloves too. We don't need you getting a splinter on this old particle board." Kong had an authority about him, and it didn't hurt that he was two-twenty and tattooed.

"It looks…"

"Like hell, I know." Kong observed the contraption. They'd built a large peak, spanning ten feet on both slopes. The gutters were attached to the edge of the makeshift roof, funneling water to a dozen caged tanks. In the rural parts of Carmichael, there were no pipes coming in from Jackson, so they relied on a water station ten miles out of town off the interstate. That made it simple to find the plastic bins. Around the field were twenty barrels, some old metal ones, others the kind a homeowner would keep under their gutter to spray their flowerbeds with after a storm.

"Will it work?" she asked.

"Yeah, it'll work."

"Can I see a demonstration?"

Kong's face split into a smile. "I've been waiting for this."

The crew exited their cover in the shade to watch with Amelia as Kong climbed the ladder, carrying a pail filled with murky pond water from a nearby slough. "The rain will hit the roof…" Kong drizzled it onto the top of the peak. It ran down the wood, landing in the gutters, spilling into the five spouts on this side, which led to a pair of tubs. Every container connected to the east drainage received a spattering of liquid.

"That's great." Amelia walked in a circle around the apparatus. "I see a couple of issues."

"By all means." Kong seemed irritated, and she wondered if she was overstepping her boundaries.

"You're having rain directly encounter the plywood. From my experience, it rots easily when left in the elements." Amelia recalled her neighborhood kids building a treehouse on her block in the woods in Jackson. The thing had only stood for a single year, and the walls had caved in after a particularly wet winter.

Kong stared at the peak. "Evan, can you grab fifty feet of tarp? We'll fasten it over the top and replace the gutters onto it."

"Won't we have to remove the eaves?" Eldon complained.

"We're doing this properly. Got a problem with that?" Kong asked the young man.

"No, sir." Evan began unscrewing the metal troughs.

"What's the other issue?" Kong asked her.

"Have you seen what happens in a deluge?"

Kong appeared to consider the question, then nodded.

"They overflow."

"I'd hate to waste good water because it comes too hard." Amelia wasn't certain of a solution, but she could already see the gears turning in Mr. Tucker's brain.

"We'll use more tarps. I got a whole pallet of 'em in my warehouse. If we connect them above the tubs, we can utilize the slope to funnel any runoff into those barrels," Mr. Tucker said.

Amelia backed up while they discussed the best way to solve the problem, and no one even noticed when she left. With this in place, all they needed was a magnificent storm or two, and they'd have supply to store for the duration of what passed for summer on Arcadia. Any drinking water would have to be saved. There were a thousand gallons of the stuff in Isla's base, but most of their population didn't know that. Water restriction was their top priority, along with food, until they could harvest the corn and garden vegetables.

The Gellers had livestock, and the Wickenhouses had chickens and pigs, but not enough to feed more than a few families through an entire season. Amelia dabbed her sweating brow, trying not to worry about tomorrow when they had so much transpiring today.

Someone had suggested they figure out how to hunt the Howlers for food, but Amelia wasn't sure it was such a good idea. If Caesar didn't return with Logan and find a way to Shift them home, anything would be on the table, but until then, she had to keep them in line.

The moment she entered the car, her radio chimed.

"Go ahead for Miller. Over."

The channel beeped, but no one spoke. "Miller here. Over."

Amelia pushed the receiver closer to her ear. Was that breathing? She pressed TALK. "If this is a sick game, you're wasting my time. Over."

The beep didn't come back, but Amelia guessed someone had been messing with her. Only a handful had the radios now, unless… No, Lillian Carson wouldn't bother with the childish tactic. She'd show up in the middle of the night with a gun.

She changed the frequency to the guard at Isla's base. "Chance? Over."

For an instant, she feared the worst. That Lillian had found the base and killed her sentry…

"You've got Chance. Over."

"Anything to report? Over?"

"Nothing but a corn maze and a barn. Karl's coming to replace me in an hour. That okay with you?"

Karl, Darcy Franklin's uncle, wasn't the most reliable sort, but he wasn't a screwup like his nephew. "That's fine. See something…"

"Say something," he finished. *"Over."*

Amelia turned the engine on and drove to her last planned stop. The daylight was dwindling, and she wished she could reach out to Caesar to check their progress. Was John near the Den?

The roads were quiet downtown, and the door to Dot's was jammed open. The woman stood in the shade under her awning, drinking what appeared to be lemonade. She smiled when Amelia parked in the same spot she'd been in when her tire was slashed that first night before the Shift.

"You caught me resting," Dot said.

"No one wants you to overheat." Amelia walked to the entrance, taking the key from her pocket. "Here, I forgot to give these to you yesterday."

"Thanks." Dot accepted it. "Lemonade?"

As much as Amelia knew they should conserve supplies, the idea of a sugary drink to keep her fueled was too promising to pass on. "Please."

Dot went in and returned with a tall glass. A couple of ice cubes clanged in the beverage. "Don't ask. It's my little secret." She gave a conspiring wink and sipped her own.

"It's so good." Amelia sat at the bistro set, enjoying the shade and the refreshing treat.

"Did you find the culprit from yesterday's burglaries?"

"Not yet, but we will."

"I believe you," Dot said.

They chatted about the weather and how the catchment system was coming, then Amelia crossed the street for a tour of the newly constructed garden.

"That row is nothing but yellow beans. Not my favorite, but we had a lot of seeds. Those are cucumbers." Dot pointed to the next section.

"Winter will come soon," Amelia said. "Jamal warned us of storms arriving in two to three weeks."

"We'll protect it. He said the snow doesn't stay long."

Sharon had a team of five women working in the sun, each wearing sunhats and tank tops. She stopped what she was doing and gazed up from her kneeling position at the corner of the field. "I don't see how it can be so hot then freezing in such a short period of time! Maybe Jamal was mistaken. The Den is farther out."

"That's true," Dot agreed.

Amelia didn't share their optimistic outlook. "We need to be prepared for anything. If they don't—"

"Find my son."

"Yes. We won't last by being optimistic, so let's be sensible instead."

"You're the boss." Dot grabbed a spade. "We're germinating seeds in the Wests' greenhouse, and we'll keep the most fragile produce in the barn to preserve them. Does that ease your mind?"

"A bit." Amelia wandered around, pausing near Sharon. "Dot seems…"

"Cranky?" Sharon used her hand like a visor against the sun. "Without those tents for shelter, we're baking out here. And tomorrow is her birthday…sixtieth."

"Really?" Amelia watched the woman tirelessly work the shovel.

"I thought we should celebrate, but she told me she didn't want any fanfare," Sharon said.

"Maybe this is just what we need. Let's arrange it at Kong's. Bring her there after the next workday, and I'll have it all set up." Amelia didn't know how to stage a surprise party, but Dot deserved the attention.

Sharon looked content while she planted more seeds, spreading them out with a ruler made from a cardboard cereal box.

Amelia returned to her car, glad the food issue was being worked on. Now she needed to discover who the resident burglar was, and plan a sixtieth party for a woman she barely knew.

2

"*Love…or get off the…*" She sang with the music pounding into the headphones and stopped when Wanda entered the tent. Summer removed them, and the song continued beating from the speakers.

"I know that one," Wanda said.

"You do?"

"I have a daughter a year younger than you," she said.

"Really? I assumed you lived in Harrison's closet." Summer thought it was funny until she saw Wanda's reaction. "Sorry, I was…"

"No, it's fine. Ainsley tells me the same thing." Wanda took a seat in Summer's tent, occupying the only chair besides her own. She showed Summer a picture of a cute girl, head tilted, posing for the camera.

"She looks fun," Summer said.

"She is."

Summer shut the music app off and tossed the headphones onto the cot. She'd been alone for hours, and even though they let her wander the area, there was nothing to do.

"Want to go for a walk?"

"Absolutely." Summer sipped a water bottle and glanced at the soldiers across the road from her tent holding guns. "What are they doing?"

"Patrols. Christine heard a Howler last night and is ensuring they don't try for the fences."

Summer had been indoors for so long, she hadn't realized it was dusk. How could they wait another four days before Shifting? She'd die of boredom in less than one.

The area was far less hectic since they'd completed the fence construction. Half of the military forces were gone, and the LTC employees nearly outnumbered the soldiers.

Wanda acted at ease, but Summer caught a nervous edge to the movements. She and Harrison didn't belong, but they were pretending for the sake of appearances.

The soldiers paired up in vehicles like golf carts and filed off, traveling around the perimeter where they'd cleared the corn stalks, until it was only Wanda and Summer on the main road. No one paid them any mind.

Wanda inhaled deeply and let the breath out slowly.

"What's that for?" Summer asked.

"Give it a go. It works wonders for anxiety."

Summer copied her actions and swallowed a bug. She coughed, and a second later, they were both laughing.

"You're making me miss Ainsley."

"The air hits different," Summer said.

"I'll never understand your generation's lingo."

"What do you mean?" Summer asked.

Wanda rolled her eyes. "This is why my parents always complained to me."

"It's the circle of life." The lights to the LTC lab were on, and Summer felt a slight rumbling beneath her feet. She almost expected Carmichael to magically appear, and was disappointed when it didn't.

They strolled on, keeping behind the tents but off the road. Summer heard a voice, and lifted a finger to her lips while creeping closer.

"…hasn't agreed, but I gave him to the end of the day."

"That's Christine," Wanda whispered.

"Yes, sir, but… okay."

Summer peered past a break in Christine's command central tent, and saw the woman set her phone down, then check her gun's magazine and chamber a round. Christine stood still for a moment, as if contemplating a major decision.

"Oh no. She'll kill Harrison if he doesn't accept the board position."

"How do you figure?" Wanda asked quietly.

"She was talking to the guy calling the shots. Why else would that conversation make her act like that?" Summer had watched countless action movies with Carly in her bedroom to know how things worked.

They hid behind the temporary structure as the floodlights snapped off. The sun had descended into the horizon, and the glowing orange insects rose from the woods beyond the chain-link fence.

"She's on the move." Wanda grabbed her arm, directing Summer to follow.

Harrison's tent was the second to last, and he shared it with his assistant. Two portable bathrooms stood between his and the largest residence, where the soldiers bunked.

Summer checked from around the corner, catching Christine blow a strand of hair from her face and absently touch the holstered gun beneath her power suit jacket. Summer couldn't picture Caesar with this cold-hearted witch.

"Harrison?" she called, and Summer heard the Velcro holding the door tear open.

"Can I do something for you?" he asked. Summer couldn't see him from her position.

Christine reached for her pocket, making Summer

nearly shout a warning, when a shiny chrome flask came out rather than a gun. Wanda hauled her back before she showed herself.

"I thought we could have a civilized conversation over a drink," she said.

The pause suggested Harrison was considering it. "Sure, why not?"

The pair vanished inside.

"What do we do?" Summer whispered.

Wanda had her phone out, and she typed a message. "His email doesn't chime, but he always checks it." She frowned. "*Harry, she's going to kill you if you say no. Just accept the position.* There, it's sent."

"What if he doesn't read it?" Summer asked.

"Then he'd better say yes on his own." Wanda's eyes widened.

"What now?" Summer blurted too loudly, then slapped a hand to her mouth.

Wanda swallowed but didn't speak.

"If Harrison's dead…they won't keep us alive either," she said, and moved closer to the front of the tent.

Summer viewed the fence, where the chain-link and wire at the top trembled with electricity. The floodlights were menacing, blaring a thousand watts of light into the perimeter. The Howlers would be wise to stay clear, but Summer expected them to gather their forces and attack once they realized they were trapped. They were smarter than Christine gave them credit for. So was Summer.

She neared the door flap, straining to hear the discussion.

"…not the finest vintage, but it's the best I could buy in Jackson," Christine said.

Summer glanced in, finding them drinking from coffee cups.

"I've had worse," he told her.

"We got off on the wrong foot," she said. "I know you hate me for what I did to Caesar, but aren't we doing this for money?"

Harrison grimaced and downed the rest. "Maybe you are, but I have a duty to my country…"

"Cut the crap, Harrison. Take the board seat. It comes with a million-dollar salary and an equity share," she said. "Fatina can have that beach house, and you can retire from HEO. Lydia won't ever want for anything. Imagine the generational wealth you'll pass down to your daughter and grandkids."

"How did you know my wife wants a beach house?" Harrison let her refill his cup.

"I do my research," she said. "Caesar told me how bright you were."

"Then what do you guess the odds are that I'd accept your offer?"

"Not high."

Harrison rose, walking with his back to Christine. He drank slowly while she stood, pulling the gun.

"I'm sorry to—"

Wanda burst in, holding her phone. "Harry, I've read over the contract, and everything's solid. You can agree to the job and sign the paperwork."

Harrison showed a moment of surprise, then nodded. "Great, thanks, Wanda."

"You're accepting?" Christine's gun was nowhere in sight.

Wanda passed Harry her cell, and a second later, Christine's beeped. "There you go. Fatina will be thrilled about the beach house."

Christine gazed at Summer, then the assistant. "Excellent. We'll talk in the morning."

The woman left them, and Summer fell into a chair, her adrenaline crashing after the spike.

Harrison rallied to the exit. "Was it that close?"

"She was about to…" Wanda mimed pulling a trigger.

"Then she still might." Harrison gestured at the cots. "How about we stay here tonight and take shifts?"

"Let me get my stuff," Summer said.

Harrison escorted her to her temporary home, and she grabbed the phone and headphones, along with her pillow. On the return trip, the howling began.

---

*A*nother duplicate night, then morning, and they were well on the way to the Den. John noticed Jamal's attitude change the closer they got. It put him at ease, and he loosened his tight grip on the steering wheel. The unit had half a tank of fuel, but they'd brought enough to fill it once.

He couldn't see past the rear window, since they'd crammed in a bunch of supplies found in the old mental hospital.

"I wonder what else has Shifted to Arcadia," John said.

"They're going to flip when they see this haul." Jamal held the necklace, dangling the large emerald. Neither knew if it was real, but John supposed that didn't really matter.

The plains went on for miles in all directions, and John couldn't view the forest from this position. It was why the Den had been situated there. The Howlers were rarely a bother this far from their habitat.

"Not bad. Three days…"

"For fifty miles," John said.

"The walk took me seven days, but I spent extra time

fishing, so I didn't go hungry."

"Which means it'll be a week back to Carmichael." John looked for the town. "We should beat the storm."

"That's the plan." Jamal moved and winced. He took out a bottle, shook it, and swallowed a pill. "There's only one more. I hope they'll prevent infection."

John had found medication in the hospital, but it was from decades ago, and stored in glass vials. They'd left it behind.

Jamal grew silent as they drove, but it was obvious his anxiety levels increased with each minute. The grassy plains moved in the wind, and he crested a slight rise, then slowed when he spotted the lake. Beyond it was the Den. Smoke drifted from several sources, and he recognized people wandering the streets. A man stood on the banks, holding a rod. When he noticed the incoming vehicle, he dropped it and began running.

Jamal reached over and honked three times in succession. "Let's go say hi!"

While he rounded the kidney-shaped body of water, the entire population greeted them at the town's entrance. Jamal hobbled from the vehicle, one hand on his injured stomach, and rushed for a woman. They embraced while John exited the JLTV, where he lingered, letting Jamal have his moment.

Friends surrounded Jamal, bombarding him with questions. He waved John to join them. "This is John Paulson."

"Hey, John," Maya said. She had short, dark hair, with burn marks on her right cheek and shoulder.

"Oh, this is for you." Jamal offered the jewelry, and Maya smiled ear to ear, holding it up to the sun. "Let me put it on."

She turned around, and he clasped it behind her neck.

"It's lovely. Now would you tell us what the hell you're doing here with a stranger and a military ride?" She investigated the back, where the gear they'd taken from the hospital sat in plain sight.

"Are you okay?" a bearded bear of a man asked.

"I think so, Ben." Jamal walked into town. "Let's sit around the fire and I'll explain."

John viewed the log cabins with thatched roofs. They had a water catchment patched together from various finds, some natural to Arcadia, others obviously from a Shift. It funnelled into a bathtub, and John wondered how they'd dragged it to the Den. And the logs for the homes must have been quite the feat to lug from the forest, unless there was a hidden cache of trees closer than the woods they'd avoided.

He counted ten cabins and a single tent that would have come with a resident when they'd Shifted. In the center of town was a giant stone firepit and a massive stack of chopped wood, protected from the elements by a patched tarp. A rotisserie held three fish and an animal he couldn't identity, and Ben walked over to rotate it.

The fire was mostly coals, since it was already hot. The meat sizzled evenly, hanging six feet over the pit. John's stomach growled at the scent of cooking fish.

Maya doted over Jamal, unbuttoning his shirt to assess his injury. After several minutes, she asked a woman named Louise to bring a poultice. John wasn't sure what that was, but Louise rushed off, returning with three bags. She began compiling various herbs and leaves into her palm, and they worked on Jamal while he told the story.

"I made it as far south as we go, ready to turn around and take the looping trail home, when I saw the smoke. I wanted to warn them about the Howlers in the forest."

A flurry of inquiries flew at him, but stopped when he

didn't respond.

"I found a house, and was so excited, I just ran up and banged on it." Jamal hung his head, glancing at the welts on his flesh while Maya tended to his torso with the fresh gauze they'd brought. "The guy shot me. He was trying to protect his wife. I can't blame him."

"Who?" Ben asked.

"My whole town was taken," John said. "Carmichael and a few miles in each direction were Shifted from rural Indiana to Arcadia."

"The town?" Louise whispered. "How?"

"This is the good part," Jamal said. "Depending on your views."

"There's a man named Logan Rutherford," John started.

"Logan from Shelter?" Maya asked.

"Have you met him?" John watched her reaction.

"Yes. Twice."

"He built a company called LTC, and discovered there were natural Shifts between Earth and other worlds, like Arcadia," Jamal said. "He went missing a decade earlier, and a lady from LTC took it upon herself to transport a couple of soldiers, military vehicles"—he pointed at the JLTV parked at the edge of their village— "and weapons to Arcadia to retrieve her business partner. Turns out some other people want to control our world."

Maya finished wrapping Jamal. "What are you saying?"

"Two trained soldiers are on their way to retrieve Logan so he can send Carmichael to Earth. And we're going with them," Jamal said.

The reactions were mixed. There was crying, cheering, and a few outright rants.

"I won't go," Ben told them promptly.

"Me either." Louise put an arm around the wilderness

expert.

"Sign me up!" an older man said. "I've been waiting to die out here, but not anymore. When do we leave?"

"Hold on, Peter." Maya watched John. "Can we have a moment?"

"He's cool," Jamal said.

"Please." Maya ignored her partner's comment.

"Sure." John glanced at the food, then walked away from the group, heading deeper into town. He was an outsider who'd shown up with a military vehicle, supplies, and a gun holstered on his chest, which he should have left in the car.

John strode to the nearest cabin, examining the interior. It was musty, with a sweet smell masking the odor. Wildflowers sat in murky water in a cracked vase on a homemade table. The beds had bits of grass jutting beneath the woven blankets. These people had done the miraculous and made a proper home in Arcadia, despite lacking any amenities or supplies. He touched the dried clay between the logs, finding it solid as a rock. He closed the door and strolled to the lake instead.

The fire continued to smoke from their town square, and the voices grew quieter as tempers simmered. The lake was smaller than the ones he'd visited with his dad. He doubted you could put a motorboat out here, but a fishing canoe would be manageable. The outer edge of the water was visible on all sides. He picked up the rod, finding a carved reel mounted to the base. "Incredible," he whispered, and set it back.

John sat on a bisected log as the water gently lapped on the rocky shore, until Jamal came to him. "Well?"

"We leave in two days," Jamal said.

"That's reasonable."

"I wanted to go tomorrow, but Maya suggested I take

an extra day to heal, and I can't argue with that woman."

"Maya's stubborn, isn't she? Reminds me of my sister."

"You look it up in the dictionary, and her picture will be there," Jamal said.

"Are you happy with this?"

"Not everyone's coming."

"Ben and Louise?"

Jamal nodded. "Only six of us will leave."

"Six?" John jumped to his feet. "Over forty of them are going to stay? Why?"

"It's been years, John. You don't understand."

"No, I guess I don't."

"Come on, let's unload the gear," Jamal said.

John followed him to the JLTV and went into it, backing the unit as far as he could. "This is ridiculous," he told Jamal.

Jamal met his gaze. "It's their decision, John. What if this doesn't even work? If we abandon the Den during the storm season, or during a major snowfall, the Wanderers will destroy our home. There'll be nothing to come back to."

"They can stay with us, or move to Shelter," he said.

"Now *you* sound ridiculous."

"Okay." John admitted defeat and considered things from their perspective. The Den was comfortable, if not utterly rustic. They'd learned to survive off the land, foraging and hunting for their meals, which his people would end up having to do if Caesar and Mr. Lawrence's mission failed.

With the help of some locals, they emptied the rear hatch out, with everyone admiring the finds. A young woman held the old shiny mirror, viewing her reflection. "That's what I look like?" she asked, stroking her bangs.

Maya rolled her eyes. "Gemma, you're doing fine."

John watched her, thinking his mission just got slightly more interesting. "Are you staying in the Den with the rest?"

"Me?" Gemma touched her own clavicle. "Nah. I like adventure. Nice to meet you, Earth boy."

"Earth boy?" John laughed. "Aren't we all from Earth?"

"I was born there, but I've been on Arcadia since I was seven."

"And how long ago was that?"

"Somewhere around thirteen or fourteen years?" Gemma shrugged. "But who knows for certain? Time seems to move differently."

With the JLTV emptied, Jamal closed it up and set a palm on it. "We'll leave the vehicle for them."

"Leave—"

"They can use it, and we can't fit everyone, not with the fuel cans, weapons, and our camping gear," Jamal said.

John had been hoping to drive back, traveling slowly enough for the convoy on foot to trail, even if he was hiking with them. The added protection of a sealed metal car in the wild gave him a sense of safety that being out in nature alone wouldn't offer.

"They'll run out of fuel," he reminded Jamal.

"So will Carmichael."

"Good point," John acknowledged.

"Gemma, do you want to give John the grand tour?"

"I'd love to." Gemma lifted her eyebrows and slowly spun. "This is the Den. That's it, tour over."

John liked her. "There must be more to it. Can you show me the gardens? How do you brush your teeth? I'm assuming there are bathrooms somewhere."

"Fine, you want the real tour. I can give you that." Gemma wandered off, and Jamal pointed after her.

"You'd better follow her, bud." Jamal leaned closer. "She's a bit of a wildcard."

"Are you coming, Earth boy?" Gemma asked from the log cabin.

"I see what you mean." He jogged down the worn path, passing a dark-haired resident who ignored John when he nodded at the guy.

3

*C*aesar used the brakes above the cliff face, getting out to examine the gorge.

"They weren't kidding about the inconvenience," Anders said. "It goes for miles, then butts up to the forest. According to Jamal, the woods are even denser there, with more Howlers and no room to maneuver the JLTV."

"We could make it with the bikes," Caesar said.

"Sure, but I don't feel like having Howlers dropping on me from the treetops, do you?"

Caesar involuntarily gazed to the sky, which was darkening with a coming storm. The canyon was spectacular, with rusty-orange rocks descending at a sharp slope to the bottom a mile down. A river snaked through the region, and vegetation grew along the banks. "Could we travel that way with the bikes?"

Anders stared at the panoramic view for a few minutes, assessing while Caesar did the same. "It would be dangerous. We can skim the perimeter for point of entry, but it might take some time."

"Nah, let's go around."

"North, then," Anders said.

"North it is." Caesar used his scope, observing the canyon. Strange horned creatures wandered the gorge's floor in herds. They reminded him of gazelles, but these, like all the animals of Arcadia, had three eyes. Their tails flicked at bugs like a horse's. He stowed the M4, returning to the JLTV. The fuel gauge indicated they were almost empty.

"Should we camp here?" The sun told him they had two hours before dark, and his hip ached from days of nothing but driving or sitting in the passenger seat.

"I'm down for that." Anders removed a red jerry can, adding it to the tank. "It'll be tight. I wasn't expecting the beast to guzzle this much diesel."

"We're not sailing on smooth pavement." Caesar emptied the second can, counting five more unused. "We might be taking the bikes on the way home."

"Then we can't bring more than Logan with us."

"I doubt he'll leave without his wife," Caesar said.

"Little Logan Rutherford, all grown up and married." Anders screwed the yellow cap on the empty can. "I'm shocked the kid from Dot's Diner is behind our predicament."

"It's quite impressive," Caesar reminded him. "Too bad someone misguided Isla."

"I can't wait to meet Senator Rutherford." Anders slapped a fist into his other palm. "I'm going to kick him right in the caucus."

Caesar laughed. "I'll be second in line."

Anders began to set up their camp. After a few nights on the road, they had a system in place. Despite Anders' claim that he wasn't in the kitchen much, he handled the cookstove, reheating canned goods. Ceasar did a perimeter check, ensuring there were no wild animal droppings in the area. He didn't want to be in the path of a predator they hadn't encountered yet.

Up here, the vegetation was sparse and rocky with no

water. Any wildlife would be in the canyon where leafy trees grew by the freshwater river, breathing nutrition into the region.

"Fire?" Caesar returned with a bunch of dried twigs.

"Why not? We're far from the Howlers."

Caesar watched as dusk came early, with dark clouds rolling along the horizon. They removed the trailer with the bikes and opened the JLTV, attaching a tarp to it, then pinned the ends to form a tent. They kept the fire on the far edge, in the opposite direction of the wind, so it would vent into the air. By the time they'd eaten, it was dark, and raindrops fell on their camp.

"We're about halfway there." Anders used soap, washing the bowls with yesterday's dishwater. Caesar dried them, then placed everything into the blue container, and they sat by the fire while the wind whipped the flames around.

"There had to be a canyon between us and Shelter." Caesar stretched his legs out, enjoying the reprieve.

"There's always a canyon."

Caesar understood the metaphor. "Your family will be okay."

"Lillian better not try anything while we're gone."

"Amelia's on alert."

"I have the feeling Lillian's not quite who she said," Anders told him. "She's cutthroat, killing the Wests, then the Benyuks, and Dr. Wickenhouse… that man was a pillar of the community. He helped save my dog years ago. Leftie attacked a porcupine, and a quill got embedded into his snout. I brought him to the doc, and he took such good care of my boy. Freddy was a kid then, and Joe was a baby."

Caesar sometimes forgot that this operative was from Carmichael, since he seemed so familiar.

"I've heard good things about you through the

grapevine over the years. Did you really blow that boat up and swim three miles to shore?"

Caesar rolled his aching shoulder, easing the muscles slightly. Their encounter in the maze was still fresh in his mind, and his body continued to endure the aftermath. "It was four miles, and yes, I blew it up. I was going to take down the target and leave the rest, but man, if you'd have seen those people… I ran around catering to those deplorable bastards for two hours before I had enough. Harrison ended up giving me a bonus, since it turned out one of the target's pals was also on the list."

"The list," Anders repeated. "Do you ever wonder who makes that?"

"Nope."

"Will you retire after this?"

Caesar considered the question before answering. "I've thought about it hundreds of times, mostly since losing Christine."

"I don't blame you."

"It's crazy, but I'm starting to forget her. Occasionally, I'll smell someone with her perfume and think she's there. Once in Manhattan, I thought I saw Christine in Times Square, but when I crossed the street, she was gone."

"That's not uncommon. I've seen a lot of dead people," Anders said.

"Yeah?"

"I'll find them in a crowd watching me. Then I blink, and they've vanished. My therapist says…"

"Therapist?" Caesar almost choked on his water. "You don't seem the type."

"That's why I need it the most. You've never talked to someone?"

"Only Harrison," he said.

"Caesar, that's not enough. If you bottle up this stuff,

it'll break you." Anders sipped his water.

"I'll take my chances. You miss the kids?" He changed the topic.

Anders shrugged. "Joe can handle himself. Candance fills Summer's head with the need to escape Carmichael, like it's diseased. It rubs off on Carly. Then I have to hear about how much she wants to get her education in New York or Los Angelas. Can you imagine?"

"You traveled the world," Caesar said. "Would it be so bad to have Carly experience the same?"

"Yes." Anders frowned; then it eased. "I'd have to be within range."

"So you're the shotgun on the porch kind of father, huh?" Caesar laughed, but Anders didn't.

"Try an assault rifle." He finally smiled.

The rain tapped on the tarp, some making it into the fire, where the drops sizzled and evaporated.

"Wanna call it? We can get up early," Caesar said.

Anders reached into the vehicle and unrolled a sleeping bag. "I've slept on worse." He touched the rocky surface. Caesar grabbed his own bag, not feeling like venturing into the rain. With the light off and the soft glow of the fire, Anders began snoring within minutes, leaving Caesar alone with his thoughts.

"Shhhh. She's coming," Sharon hissed, and Kong dimmed the lantern.

"I'm telling you, we have work to do tomorrow and…" Dot's comment carried through the dark bar as the door opened.

"Surprise!" the crowd harmonized, jumping from their

hiding spaces.

Amelia thought she genuinely seemed shocked, and Mr. Tucker, Dot's escort, winked at her. "Nice job," she told him.

"You guys didn't have to do this for little old me," Dot proclaimed, a palm on her chest. She wore a white blouse, as usual, covered in red dots, matching her hair color.

Dot hugged everyone, then reached Amelia. "Thank you," she whispered.

"It was a joint effort." Streamers from Sharon's garage clung to the roof, and they had a single cupcake, painstakingly baked with a gas cooktop by Belinda Wickenhouse. One candle rose from the center, tilting slightly to the side. Mr. Tucker lit it with his golden lighter and they sang off key. Dot blew out the flickering flame, lips moving without speaking her wish.

Amelia knew it would be about her son, praying for his safe return. They had fifty of Dot's closest friends crowded in, and everyone seemed happy despite the situation.

Kong stood behind his bar, looking as comfortable as a person could be in their own skin. He wore the bartender's uniform of dark jeans and a tight black t-shirt, complete with a white rag draped over a shoulder. "What'll it be?" he asked the guest of honor.

"I don't usually…" Dot glanced at the bar. "Is there any wine?"

"I have a couple reds," he said.

"That'll do."

"And you?"

"I'm good," Amelia answered.

Kong passed Dot a hearty serving of wine and slid a can of soda to Amelia, which she graciously accepted. She popped the top, and it fizzed like only a warm carbonated beverage could. She drank a mouthful, instantly perking up from the sugary caffeine.

Sharon clinked glasses with Dot, and the partygoers gathered at the front of the bar, while country music boomed from an old battery-powered CD player.

"Speech!" Daisy Geller called, and the others echoed the word until Dot drank half a glass and rose from her seat.

Dot sighed heavily, like the burden of the last week had overcome her, then smiled at her fellow townspeople. "I feel honored to celebrate my sixtieth with you lovely people." She gazed around the room. "I wish Isla were here with us. And my son, Logan, whom many of you know well…"

"He's coming," Sharon assured her.

Mr. Tucker raised a glass. "To Dot, may your kindness be reciprocated tenfold!"

"To Dot!" The group downed drinks, and Amelia drank more soda.

"Now let's party!" Faith called, and cranked the music.

Amelia sank to the bar, taking a seat on the stool near Kong. "This was a good idea. How did you stop the regulars from harassing you to keep this place running?"

Kong pointed to the rear exit, which was propped open. Five or six men were playing cards at a table, with a keg beside them. "It'll go bad anyhow. And they've worked hard these past few days."

"How's Chun?" Amelia asked after his wife.

"She thinks it's coming early," he said. "I don't know what we're going to do if that happens before we get home."

"You have a whole town at your disposal," she told him.

"That's what Chun's worried about." He laughed, and poured a refill of whiskey for Victoria, the motel owner.

She lit a cigarette, and Kong looked ready to intervene, but didn't bother.

The front entrance sprang wide, and Pastor Odell entered. For a second, everyone went silent. "Don't stop on my account. I just wanted to wish Ms. Hunter a happy birthday."

Dot set the wine down and shook his hand. "Thank you, Pastor. Would you care for a drink?"

"We have soda!" Kong called.

"Have anything without sugar?" The man of the cloth came to join Amelia, sitting next to her, and Kong gave him a seltzer. "You on duty?"

"Always. You?" Amelia asked him.

"God's work doesn't end at five P.M., much like law enforcement."

Something shattered, and Kong grabbed the broom, leaving his post.

Amelia and Odell sat in a comfortable silence while they watched folks dance to a classic western song. Mr. Tucker did a two-step with Faith, whisking her around the bar floor.

"There are times I wonder if I've missed out on the fun things of life," Odell said.

"Pastors can marry, correct?"

"Oh, yes. I haven't found the right woman, and I'm in my fifties. I think of my congregation as my children, in a sense. Every child baptized into the flock, leaves with something special, imparted by God through me."

"There's still time for love," Amelia said.

"And you?"

"Love?" She finished her soda and rotated the can slowly, not wanting to look at the pastor. "I don't know that I'm capable."

Odell clucked his tongue and stared at the dancing

folks. "No one knows what they're capable of until push comes to shove. Did you anticipate leading us in a crisis of this magnitude?"

"When you put it that way…"

"I bet when you woke up on Friday, you weren't expecting to be stuck in our little village."

"No. I was counting down the hours until I could take a shower and binge a TV show. I wanted to sleep in on my day off, walk to the Jackson market, and buy fresh flowers for my kitchen."

"Were you happy?"

Amelia took her time, pondering the very simple, yet impossibly deep question. "No. I'm not certain I ever have been. Maybe I've had pockets of happiness. How does someone know when they are?"

"Things will look different. You'll feel lighter from the weights of your existence, and life will flow smoother. People most often never realize they've had a shift until they're far into the new phase."

Amelia flinched at his word choice. They'd all felt the Shift to Arcadia. "I'm glad you're here."

"It's where I need to be," he said, and got off the stool. "I'd better head out."

"Have a good night."

Pastor Odell stopped at Dot's table, then left, while Kong returned with the broken shards in a dustpan.

"I think the wine has finally kicked in." Kong grinned at Dot and uncorked a bottle of Merlot.

"Cut her off. We all have to wake up early," Amelia said, aware of how lame she sounded.

"It's her sixtieth. Let her have fun."

Two hours later, Amelia guided a very drunk Dot to the parking lot and into her squad car.

"You're a peach," Dot slurred. Amelia reached over,

pulling the seatbelt down, and clicked it into place.

"Thank you, Dot."

"If my son wasn't married, I'd say you might be a good match." Dot rolled the window down, and for a second, Amelia thought she might throw up.

"I guess we'll never know."

Mr. Tucker had the others loaded on the school bus, and Kong waved at her from his truck. She started off, leaving the gravel parking lot behind.

"I was robbed," Dot said.

"You were?" Amelia wondered why she'd taken so long to say so.

"Of my son's life."

"Oh."

"He left me. I didn't get a wedding, a daughter-in-law…children. Does Logan have kids? Am I a grandmother?"

Amelia had never seen Dot like this. "We'll find out soon." She turned on Robson and headed past Dot's Diner a minute later.

"I love my diner."

"You'll be working there again in no time."

Amelia continued driving and found Dot's house shortly after. She pulled into the driveway and cut the engine, circling the car to help Dot out before she faceplanted in the rose bushes.

"This is my place. How did we get here?" Dot asked, attempting to walk. Amelia caught her and led the inebriated woman up the steps.

"Do you have your keys?"

Her purse fell to the porch. "In there."

Amelia guided Dot into the wooden swing and opened the bag, sifting through red lipstick tubes and dental floss to find the keyring. A moment later, it was unlocked, and she set the purse on the table before bringing Dot to her room.

She helped her change out of her outfit and escorted her to the bathroom. Amelia poured a glass of water for Dot, which she set beside the bed, along with an over-the-counter pill for the morning.

Once Dot was in bed, mumbling about Logan, Amelia closed the door and wandered down the hall. It was warm, and she slid the kitchen window wide, appreciating the breeze. With a check of the clock, she saw it was already midnight, meaning she'd have to wake up in six hours. Amelia probably should have brought them to the safety of their sanctuary across from the church, but hadn't wanted everyone to see Dot in this condition.

She listened for any signs of the Howlers, but the town was eerily quiet. No dogs barked, no music played from backyard firepits, just silence.

Amelia traversed the living room, eyeing the purse, then glanced at the locked door to the basement. She took the keychain and tried the various keys, not finding one that worked.

Next, she went to the office, which was stacked with old receipts and paperwork for the diner. After a brief search, she headed to the kitchen, checking the drawers. Amelia knew this was a blatant invasion of Dot's privacy, but she was drawn to the door and what secrets lay behind it. Why lock the passage to the basement? In her line of work, that red flag was almost as bright as Dot's hair.

Amelia climbed on an old wooden footstool, investigating the collection of cookie jars lining the top of her cabinets. Some had actual food in them, gone stale. Others were filled with rice, oats, and coffee. One at the end was stuffed full of cash in small denominations. On a quick guess, Amelia figured it must hold around two grand.

She put it all back and returned the ladder to its previous position.

A picture was slanted, and Amelia crossed to the wall of framed photographs, adjusting the crooked one. A key slid from behind it, landing on the hardwood floor. Her heart pounded in her chest, but her anxiety was probably wasted. She'd go into the basement, finding nothing but old mementos of Dot's son, carefully hidden so she didn't have to deal with the painful memories.

"Then why is your hand shaking so much?" she whispered to her inner voice.

Amelia used the key, pushing it into the handle, and it turned with a pop of the lock. She touched the metal, ready to investigate, when glass shattered from outside.

Amelia raced to the front step, finding a brick in her car's rear window. She cursed and pulled her handgun, running to the street, but the truck was gone. It was the same getaway vehicle she'd witnessed at the burglary the other day. Someone had to recognize it. There were only so many trucks in town. With a partial plate scrawled onto her notepad, Amelia had a lead.

4

John was restless on the wooden cot, and the tree boughs under him offered little comfort. He was in Jamal and Maya's place, on the spare bed used by a traveling scout when she was at the Den. No one had seen Wren for a month, which wasn't that unusual for the travelers, but her mission should have been completed by now.

John had listened to the locals discussing the possibility of another town up north, but none ventured far above the canyon separating the Den and Carmichael from Shelter in the west.

The cabins had no windows, since they couldn't block out the weather or bugs without glass or screens. The door had wooden hinges, and a sliver of moonlight crept past the cracks, landing on John's face. He turned, trying to get comfortable, but failed at every attempt.

It was fine. He'd suffer through two nights, then the group would head to Carmichael before the storm season hit the region. Hopefully, Logan would already be there with the operatives, and have the Shift prepared for departure when they rolled in.

John replayed the events of the past week, from ditching Katie on the side of the road to Darcy's house burning, then the Howler attack, and the news that his oldest friend was buried in a shallow grave at the town cemetery. And here he was, in a rustic village on an alien world, trying to convince people to leave with them so they could return to Earth.

While sleep evaded him, John pictured life at the Den if he stayed. Gemma was a catch, but John couldn't fall for any new girl he crossed paths with. He'd done it with Katie, and look where that got him.

Ben and Louise were skilled, so he didn't doubt they'd be able to teach him how to survive in this harsh world. No, that was too strong of a word. Arcadia wasn't only harsh. It was beautiful, a lush landscape filled with thriving creatures and untapped resources. No wonder Lillian's boss wanted to access the planet.

While the tech billionaires were reaching for the stars, here was an opportunity to visit planets like Arcadia with a device that Shifted you from one place to the other. If LTC had a monopoly on the technology, it would be invaluable—or disastrous.

Not all connections would be as vacant as Arcadia.

John's thoughts moved to his sister, and he tried to suppress his concern for her new position. Why had she volunteered to carry a rifle and wear a badge? For the same reason he'd left with Jamal, he supposed. They were linked by blood, both headstrong to a fault, a characteristic they'd inherited from their mother. Blaire Paulson had been a real piece of work. That was what his dad had called her, and he meant it in the most flattering way.

John glanced at Jamal and Maya on the other bed, her arms wrapped around his bandaged body, both sleeping soundly. The moonlight glinted off the necklace they'd found at the hospital.

The knock was so quiet, John barely heard it at first. When it happened again, he got up and walked through the compact cabin. He almost tripped on a stack of wood, but only grazed his toe. He peered down at his attire—boxers and a white undershirt—then shrugged and opened the door.

An object smashed him in the mouth, causing his vision to turn white.

"What in the…" Someone hauled John out and dragged him to the path. The rocks cut his knees, and John fought to gain control.

"This will be easier if you stop struggling," the man said. He got hit again, this time in the temple, and John crumpled to the ground. He blinked his eyes open, finding a cluster of incandescent insects floating above his assailant. He recognized the wild hair from earlier, then lost consciousness.

When John came to, he couldn't guess how long he'd been out.

"Hello?" Croaking one word made his head pound. The room was mostly dark, but John spied a fissure in the wall. He walked to it and checked his legs, finding dried blood. It appeared to be night. His hands weren't bound, and he poked at his teeth, hoping nothing was loose. They were intact, which surprised him, given the ferocity of the attack.

He sat on a homemade chair, attempting to think his way free of the predicament. As his eyesight acclimated to the dim space, he spied the room he'd been shown on the tour yesterday. On the far side was the Den's map of Arcadia, which really comprised the handful of landmarks and towns they were aware of.

John blearily assessed it now, finding Louise's carvings and artwork impressive. The canyon was sprawling, a lengthy gorge separating the land. They'd placed a question mark to the north, where they believed a town sat. With their new information, Louise had added the hospital and a temporary charcoal blotch for Carmichael.

Thankfully, John's headache subsided as he waited for his captor to show. It happened a couple of hours after he'd woken, and John braced for another strike when the guy entered, then locked the door behind him with a wooden plank.

"I was hoping I didn't kill you," he said.

"Why?"

"So I can do it my way."

"Who are you?"

"Van."

"Van, you're making a mistake."

Van was about John's age, with cagey eyes and a unibrow. His mouth was set in a constant sneer, which John had noticed earlier. Van carried a shafted weapon, with a sharp blade wrapped tightly on the top. It was stained red, and he held it like it was a third arm. "The only mistake was you coming to the Den, stranger."

"I'm not—"

The base of the spear swung before John could react, slamming into his cheek.

"Be quiet," Van said calmly.

John protested, then stopped.

"See, you can learn."

John touched his tender face.

"You're going to write a note." Van removed a piece of parchment from his shirt pocket, and a length of charcoal wrapped in animal hide.

"Why?"

"You'll tell them you've taken the war machine and gone back to your little town," Van said.

"I don't have the keys."

Van dangled them from a finger. "I do."

"You want me to go?"

"No. You misunderstand me, stranger. Write the note."

John took the sheet and staining stick and stared at them on the desk. "What if I don't?"

"You're dead either way."

He considered yelling for help, but that would get him a spear in the throat. He wasn't armed and had little to work with in the office. A dozen endings to a hand-to-hand combat filled his mind, and very few of them concluded with John's victory.

"At least tell me why—"

"We have something important here, and you've come to ruin it."

"Listen, I don't care what you think, you're wrong. I just want to get everyone to Earth."

"Earth," Van hissed. "We're misfits, stranger. I don't belong on your planet any more than you belong on mine." He paced the entrance, the spear point growing more menacing with each cycle.

"You don't decide for the rest."

"Gemma shouldn't have offered to leave."

John looked up, wondering if that was the true reason for Van's assault. "You love her."

"It doesn't matter what I want. She'll never see me if she leaves with you. I can't let our family be torn apart. Not again!" Van's movements grew jerkier, his mouth contorted with anger.

John sensed he didn't have long before he'd have to defend his own life. "I'll write the note. But why not give me the keys so I really can leave? You don't have to kill me."

Van appeared to consider the option, but only for a split second. "Okay, deal."

Judging by his body language, that was a blatant lie.

John used the charcoal, scribbling a brief message, and he finished by signing it with his initials, *JP*. "You happy?"

Van grinned and lashed out with the spear. John had been expecting it and dropped with all his weight into the chair. It shattered in pieces, and he snatched the broken leg, bringing it up to block the shaft.

Van screamed in fury, bashing at John from above, while John barely deflected each strike. His fingers were numb, clutching the whittled leg, but he held on, knowing he was dead if he faltered.

"John?" Jamal called from outside.

"In here! Van's trying to—" The spear grazed his shoulder, sticking into the dirt. It stuck, and Van's neck tendons bulged as he tried to pull it loose, like it was Excalibur and he was an unworthy commoner.

John rushed by him and raised the plank barring the door. Jamal jumped in with a shotgun raised.

Van stopped fighting and sank to his knees. "He was trying to kill me."

"It's not true," John proclaimed, suddenly unsure who they'd believe.

"John had no reason to attack you," Jamal said.

Dawn was upon the Den, and others were up, coming to investigate the commotion.

Ben gazed into the office, then at John. "What happened?"

John's explanation took a minute, and Ben scowled.

"We've warned you," Ben said.

Jamal's aim never wavered off the dark-haired man.

"He'll ruin us," Van stated.

Ben stared at his own feet while all the residents watched from the path. "By the governance of Arcadia, I have no choice but to call your life forfeit. I'm practicing

Themis."

John gaped at them, unsure how to react. "You're going to kill him?"

"He tried to murder you," Ben said.

"And it's not his first offense," Jamal added.

"I'll do it. It's my duty." Ben accepted the gun from Jamal, and walked behind Van, who surprisingly didn't object. He turned only once, to glare at John, before trudging away from the lake.

A few minutes later, the report of the shotgun echoed through the valley, and John felt sick to his stomach.

Maya kissed her husband lightly, then nodded.

"Change of plans," Jamal said. "We leave today."

––––––––

"*H*ow do you do it?" Harrison told Summer.

"Do what?"

"Wake up on that cot and not ache everywhere." Harrison stretched, and Wanda laughed.

"She's fifteen. My daughter can sleep like a log on my parents' ancient sofa bed. You know, the kind with the metal bar running…"

Harrison groaned. "I thought these days were over. I should be at the Carlton, not in this stinking tent in the middle of nowhere with Howlers on my doorstep."

Initially, Summer had found it weird sharing a room with the two strangers, but they already seemed familiar. "Maybe it's because you're so old." Summer knew it would get a rise out of him, and imagined Caesar liked to do the same.

"Old?" Harrison ran a hand through his thinning hair, and it stood on end. "Dammit, that's my problem."

"They didn't attack last night," Summer said, watching the fence from the doorway. Soldiers patrolled the border, looking bored. That would get them killed if they weren't careful, and put Summer in danger. She couldn't let a Howler battle distract her from returning to her family and Carly on Arcadia.

"No one's noticed the missing keycard yet," Wanda said.

The tent had its own bathroom out back, and it was far nicer than the regular plastic ones. It had running water and a flushing toilet. Summer used it and washed her face, then tried to comb her blonde hair into a semblance of normality, but it still fell limply over her shoulders.

There were three days before they stole the device and Shifted. So much could go wrong between now and then, but Summer had to hold tight to her faith in Harrison.

She ventured into the camp while Harrison and Wanda dressed. They let her have free rein, and rarely even looked in her direction as she strolled the road that ended at the fence. Summer watched the alien trees, trying to catch sight of a Howler, but none clung to the upper branches in the area.

"They pushed the northern border at around two in the morning." Christine's high heels were out of place as they clicked on the harsh road.

Summer assumed she wanted to be heard, or she'd have opted for a soft-soled shoe. "The Howlers?"

"About a hundred. The electric fence fried three, and they dragged the dead away with them," Christine said.

"Really? That's unusual, isn't it?" Summer asked.

"They might eat the others."

"Or bury them."

"Don't anthropomorphize the Howlers, Summer. They're animals."

"So are we," Summer countered. There was something about the woman that made her combative. It could have been the fact that she'd planned on cold-bloodedly murdering Harrison if he hadn't agreed to her terms. That meant Summer's own life was in jeopardy, yet she still couldn't stop herself.

"You're certain there are no humanoids on Arcadia?" Christine broke her gaze off the forest to watch Summer.

"You think I'm working for the aliens?"

Christine smiled, pulling her scar tighter. "I was just like you."

"Great, here we go…"

The operative grabbed her arm, tugging Summer close. "There's a time and place for defiance, but this isn't it, do you understand?"

Christine's nails dug into her wrist, and Summer held back tears. When she didn't respond, the grip grew tighter.

"Yes!" Summer finally relented, and the pressure vanished.

"This is bigger than a small-town girl's attitude problem."

"I just want my family."

Christine turned away. "You'll be with them soon enough." She didn't expand on the thought, just walked off when her phone rang.

The words sounded kind, but Summer recognized the threatening message. She'd be dead like her parents if Harrison didn't follow through with their plan.

The sky was overcast, and the woods holding the Howlers appeared darker than normal. She stayed there, observing the treetops, wondering how long before the animals came for the electric fences.

5

Caesar woke with a start to find his face covered in gunk. He wiped at it, clawing the goop from his brow, and realized the entire camp was coated in the stuff. "Anders!"

"I'm up." Anders had the same layer of clear, viscous slime on him. "The damned slugs were here."

The canyon had filled with mist, the dense fog rolling over the edge, creeping to the JLTV. Caesar couldn't see more than five feet. The fire had burned out, and the rain had dried up.

"Are they gone?" Caesar nearly slipped when he stood. He carefully treaded to the vehicle and winced when he checked under the hood. "We're screwed."

Anders cursed and tried to turn the engine. When it failed, he bashed a fist into the center of the steering wheel. "It's caked."

"We can try to clean it." Caesar began scraping the underside.

"Let's wait out the fog and search for a water source," Anders suggested.

It was an hour before the misty haze finally broke, providing a view of the gorge beyond the cliff. Slug trails carried from the ledge and on past the vehicle into the horizon.

"Did I mention I hate slugs?" Anders asked.

"I thought you hated snails," Caesar kidded.

"I despise all molluscs."

"Even oysters?"

"Especially oysters." Anders pointed at the tributary. "We either hike there, then carry buckets of freshwater up, or…"

"Take the bikes." Caesar set a hand on the motorbike mounted to the trailer.

Anders smiled and circled the vehicle. "It's better than trudging up a sharp slope with a pail of river water."

The vehicles were familiar to Caesar, used overseas by his squad in the 2000s. These models were exactly the same, even down to the desert camouflage. With full tanks, he expected to get four hundred miles under ideal circumstances, which Arcadia was not.

"What about the gear?" Anders patted the JLTV.

"I guess we leave most of the supplies. It'll be tougher on these, but we can still make it work. He can drive his wife," Caesar said.

"And we ride together?" Anders lifted an eyebrow. "Let's cross that bridge when we have to."

"Load as much as possible. Spare fuel, water, and food take priority." Caesar got to it, putting supplies into the bike's luggage attachment saddlebags. He strapped the tank on and added the first aid kit at the last moment, as well as enough ammunition to fight a minor war.

"Is that necessary?" Anders asked.

"You'll thank me when we need it." Caesar changed clothing, opting for a new pair of pants and a long-sleeve shirt, despite the early warmth. They left their old stuff in a pile next to the tactical vehicle and mounted the bikes.

"It's been a while."

"Just like riding a…bike." Caesar pulled the helmet on.

He stared at the handles, remembering how it worked slightly different from a regular street type. He turned the key, flipped the decompression switch, then had it running after a few seconds.

Anders attempted to start it, but it wouldn't kick into action.

"Want some help?" Caesar asked.

The other man went through the steps, and this time, it jumped. "Let's take the ridge and circle the whole canyon."

"Sounds good to me. Stay fifty yards from the edge, in case of a slide." Caesar revved it and hurried forward. He glanced back as Anders dropped his visor and chased after him.

It quickly became apparent that they had to exercise extreme caution. The land was too uneven, and the stone ground was slippery, probably from the horde of passing slugs. Caesar suspected it would dry as the morning heat baked the region.

He reduced his speed from thirty to twenty, eventually settling at a boring ten miles. Even then, the tires bobbed over the slalom-like hills. Occasionally, his front tire would lift, and the rear skidded until both were firmly on the ground. He'd expected to feel freer on the motorbike, but was quite the opposite.

An uneventful hour passed, then another, and Caesar began wondering how far the gorge stretched. It wasn't a surprise why none of the scouts like Jamal had gone this far north. A trip on foot would take ages, which was the exact reason a scout took the canyon to pass through to Shelter.

Anders waved him down, pointing inland. They stopped, and Anders removed his helmet, hanging it on the handles. "There's water."

"How do you know?"

"I see wildlife."

Caesar grabbed his assault rifle, using the scope, and recognized birds circling above. "Gotcha. Want to check it out?"

"We have the iodine tablets, so we may as well conserve our supply. Plus I wouldn't mind washing this slug mess off."

The lake was large, with spiky trees along the edge, positioned to face the sun. They offered a nice section of shade, and the men parked beneath the expansive boughs. Light reflected brightly from the rippling water, and Caesar could have been on Earth at any remote lagoon. He suddenly felt homesick for the first time since the Shift had occurred.

He stripped from his clothes down to his underwear, and motioned to Anders. "If something tries to kill me, do you mind shooting it?"

"No sweat." Anders leaned on the tree trunk, pulling a piece of fruit from his pack. He bit into the blotchy apple, surveying the landscape.

The water was tepid, and Caesar took the plunge. Once he swam past the shade, everything warmed, and he kicked his feet, floating on his back. He touched a finger to his tongue, confused. "It's salty."

"Guess we can't drink it." Anders shrugged. "We should have enough, and Jamal said the river is clean in the canyon if push comes to shove."

Caesar drifted deeper, watching the three-eyed birds flutter around, some diving into the lake. One rose with something stuck in its claws, and Caesar followed as it landed on the banks to claim its prize. "It's so familiar."

"But different." Anders held a two-pronged flower, both heads coming from the same stem.

"I wonder if any bipeds would have the triple eyes." Caesar pictured a Neanderthal with an extra eye, beating a Howler, then raising his club in triumph, while he scrubbed his cheeks and brow, then the rest of his body, until the last of the gunk had been washed clean.

"So far, they've all had them. You almost done?" Anders asked.

"Sorry, it's kind of nice in here."

"Don't get out on my account." Anders joined him, dipping into the water, and instantly dunked his head. He came up quickly, splashing his hair. "I needed that."

They took their time, and a half hour later, Caesar was on his bike, traveling north again. He'd mostly dried before donning the helmet, and when he looked at the sun, it barely seemed to have moved. Heatwaves distorted the rocky ground, indicating how hot the day was shaping up to be.

The land evened out, allowing them to pick up the pace, and Caesar risked going to twenty miles an hour.

He glanced into the canyon and hit the brakes, skidding. Caesar flipped the kickstand and jogged to the cliffside.

"What the hell was that?" Anders shouted. "You trying to kill us?" He stopped when he saw what Caesar had. "It's a building."

"No. It's a damned estate," he said, grabbing the gun. The structures were old, faded from years of exposure to the elements. It was a house and barn, and the ground between them differed from the rest of the region. "And it looks ancient."

Anders looked prepared to argue, then nodded. "That it does."

Caesar didn't love the idea of leaving his bike, but had little choice. They removed packs from the saddlebags, stowing enough water and supplies for one night. He brought the iodine tablets on the chance they were down there for longer.

Anders walked to the ledge, searching for a path to descend into the canyon. It took ten minutes before they both agreed on a route, and Caesar went first, carefully climbing over the cliff. He landed after a two-yard drop, and the rest of the way came easier. They maneuvered through loose rocks, and had to stop twice to alter their direction, then reached the bottom of the gorge. The sun was blocked from this angle, making the hike manageable.

Caesar forced them to take a quick break, drinking water and resting his legs, and they were off, marching toward the abandoned farmhouse. He neared the barn and checked inside, discovering old equipment.

"This stuff belongs in a museum," Anders said, picking up a rusted scythe from its iron mounts on the wall.

Caesar hefted a horseshoe and set it on the anvil. "What do you think? From the 1800s?"

"Probably." Anders exited. "Let's go to the house."

It would have been beautiful when it was built. The wraparound porch showed the age, and the weathervane remained on the peak, not spinning, since the cliff blocked most of the wind. He judged the metal had seized years earlier. The paint had all but peeled from the slats, but somehow, the porch held their combined weight as they ascended the stairs.

"Has anyone on Arcadia seen this?" Caesar asked.

"It's doubtful." Anders tested the door. The wood had swelled, but they managed to yank it open with some elbow grease.

They entered a living space that appeared to double as a dining room. The fireplace was huge, likely used to cook with. Utensils hung from hooks framing the mantel. Caesar counted four gas lanterns spread throughout the main floor. Everything creaked under his steps.

"They were fairly well off." Anders knocked on a grandfather clock that had long ago stopped ticking. A rodent scurried from a hole in the bottom and ran away, squeezing into the baseboards.

After a quick exploration, they found a set of bones in the bedroom. A rifle lay nearby.

Caesar walked to the yard and understood more of the story as they encountered three white crosses marked with names. "Mary-Belle, Elizabeth, and Joseph."

"A wife and kids?"

Anders rested a palm on the biggest grave marker. "This could have been me. I'd have ended up in that bedroom."

"Should we go back?" Caesar hadn't known what they'd find, but the realization that a family had Shifted from another age unnerved him.

"Let's stay the night. By the time we get up there, the sun'll almost be set."

"Good call, since we don't have the safety of the vehicle to resort to. Four walls are better than open air." Caesar thought about the skeleton. "He deserves a proper burial."

"I saw a shovel in the barn."

A short while later, Caesar lowered the bones into the grave, and Anders began dropping freshly dug soil into the opening. They crafted a similar cross, using materials from the shop, and Caesar found remnants of paperwork in the office. He carved the name Everett into the wood and used the shovel to hammer the spike into the ground beside the wife's.

"This proves Isla's theory," he said when they were done.

"Which one?"

"That the Shifts have been happening for a long time."

"I wonder what else we'll find on this journey?" Anders asked.

"Let's focus on the mission and get to Shelter so we can go home."

"If they don't stop us," Anders said.

Caesar smiled at his new friend. "I'd like to see them try."

6

"I've gone over the list twice, and it has to be Hector Doukas." Freddy tapped the resident list.

"I heard he died in the fire," Haley said.

Amelia didn't know the guy. "Who is he?"

"I haven't talked to him before, but I don't think he's too bad," Freddy said.

"He works for the Jackson County maintenance crew, doesn't he?" Haley asked.

"How do you know that?" Amelia stared at the name matching the registration in the town files.

"I did his cousin's hair a few times." Haley tugged on her own strands. "She loves it bleached."

Amelia reached out to Kong with the radio. "Have you heard of Hector Doukas? Over."

"Of course. He got rowdy one night a couple of weeks ago. Guess he was fired from his job. Over."

"Any idea where he lives? We can't find a fixed address. Over."

"Nah, I didn't ask. Over."

Amelia stared at the files on the desk, recalling the sensation as she'd stuck the key into Dot's basement lock. She'd forgotten the keys in the handle when her windshield was shattered. "What's the cousin's name?"

"Irene Doukas," Haley said. "She lives on Fir Street."

"Freddy, can you stop in at our sanctuary? Haley, with me." Amelia stormed through the town office, eager to find the man who'd been breaking into homes and had the nerve to throw a damned brick at her car.

Freddy stopped at his truck, resting a palm on the door. "Be careful, would ya?"

Amelia checked her magazine was full and nodded. "We'll be fine."

Haley stowed her rifle in the backseat, then hopped into the front. "Can we use the siren?" She reached for the dash, and Amelia gently swatted at her.

"No."

"The lights?"

"I don't want him to see us coming," she said. "From your experience, is he violent?"

"If he's like the rest of them, he might throw a few punches after drinking too much, but he wasn't out there beating on his old lady or anything. If he was, Irene would have told me. She's a gossip."

Fir Street was quiet, as most streets were since the Shift had left them stranded on Arcadia. Half of the town was at work tending crops, tilling gardens, and preparing for the storm Jamal promised was coming. The others took breaks at the sanctuary across from the church, where Odell continued to have two services a day.

Amelia scanned for the black truck, and it didn't take long to spot the tail end sticking from under a cheap carport. "That her house?"

"Yep."

Amelia parked behind the driveway, blocking any escape. "Stay close."

With her gun drawn, Amelia walked up the sidewalk to the steps, and banged on the screen door.

"What?" A woman opened it. She wore a pink tank top with a black bra beneath, and as previously mentioned, her hair was bleached white, with two months' worth of growth at the roots. Irene held a plastic kid's sippy cup, and Amelia heard the fussy child from inside. "Haley…"

"How's Caleb?"

"He's better off than us, because he doesn't understand what's happening." Irene pushed the door wide enough for them to enter, and Amelia lowered the gun. "If you're looking for my cousin, I don't think Hector's here."

"Where did he go?" Amelia asked.

"He's been acting strange since the Shift," she said. "Going out in the middle of the night, and coming home with…"

"Electronics?" she asked Irene, who nodded slowly. The interior of the place was charming, much nicer than she'd expected when pulling up. Books filled a small shelf, and the fireplace had an original painting over it, probably picked up at the Jackson art fair.

Caleb kicked his legs from a highchair, his chin covered in apple sauce. He reached for his water, making cooing noises.

"He's adorable," Amelia said, not feeling the same gush of excitement that some women did in the presence of children.

"Caleb, you're so handsome," Haley said. "Look at those big blue eyes."

"He takes after his father more than me."

Amelia didn't see any male touches in the place, and didn't ask about the dad. "Is Hector sleeping here?"

"Out back." Irene pointed to the kitchen window, and Amelia checked, finding an old Airstream in the yard.

"Mind if I…" Amelia was already out the door. The scent of blossoms filled the air, and the dozen various potted flower assortments were crispy from the heat and lack of water.

"Want me to come?" Haley asked.

"Cover me from the deck."

Haley hauled her rifle up.

"Is this really necessary? Hector's not that bad." Irene held Caleb, bobbing him up and down.

"Stay put," Amelia ordered, and jogged down the steps. The Airstream had a couple of lawn chairs by the entrance and an ashtray filled with cigarette butts. She knocked, prepared for Hector to bolt. "Hector, it's Deputy—Chief Miller. We need to talk."

The window was cracked, and she lifted to her toes, peering into the unit. She made out the silhouette of a man sprawled on the floor, his boots extended toward her.

Amelia opened the Airstream and lowered the weapon. She stepped out for a second to call to Haley. "He's dead!"

She didn't have to check for a pulse, since the linoleum was caked in his dried blood. Judging by how far it had congealed, she assumed this had happened shortly after he'd sped down the street by Dot's, tossing a brick at her squad car.

"Keep Irene in the house. I'm going to search the place."

Haley was pale, her gaze unable to break from the corpse.

Amelia touched her arm. "It's okay. We'll find out who did it. That's our job." But she already knew who the culprit was. A carving knife jutted from Hector's back, but it was obvious there were other cuts on his front side.

"I…"

"Just go."

Haley turned and threw up in the yard, dropping her rifle.

Amelia propped the door wide, and flies made their way into the camper. The sink was full, the table crammed with canned goods and prepackaged pastas. So he hadn't just been stealing electronics. She searched for evidence that he was working with Clive, but there was no drug paraphernalia, and only one empty six-pack of light beer. A few mismatched and unopened packs of cigarettes were piled by the bed.

She sifted through the cabinets and found an old revolver and a spattering of cartridges. A coffee can was overflowing with cash, and Amelia removed a stack, flipping the perfectly assorted collection of fifties.

"This is from the weapons deal," she whispered.

Amelia located Haley on the front porch with Irene, who was crying in her deputy's arms. "I'm sorry for your loss. You didn't hear anything?"

"No. Caleb woke me a few times in the night, and I saw the light on once. He told me he wasn't sticking around, so that's why I said he wasn't here," she managed.

Amelia strolled toward her car, wincing at the clear plastic covering her shattered window. "Freddy, come in."

"Sanctuary is secure, and the Repulsor is working like a charm. No sign of the Howlers since the last battle. Over."

"Good," she said, then lowered her voice. "Can you send Mr. Tucker out to Fir Street to Irene Doukas' house? Tell him to leave Evan at home. Over."

"Why?"

"Hector's dead. Tell them to bring him to the cemetery," she said. "Over."

"Roger that. Over."

Amelia walked up to the truck and peered into the box. A few errant cords from TVs and computers lay on the bed, but the rest of the material was gone. "What the hell is she doing with it?"

Haley had regained a bit of color. "Where are we off to?"

"To find Lillian Carson's hiding spot."

---

*J*ohn regretted leaving the vehicle behind after the first day of hiking. He'd barely escaped with his life, and his head rang from last night's attack. Van's fury had been clear, but the more he thought about it, the more he resented the entire situation. According to Ben, Van had a history of being abusive, which often ended in shouting matches and occasionally violence. It was obvious Gemma felt disdain for the guy, which John couldn't fault her for. It was something they both shared.

As they walked, John grew to despise Arcadia's ruthless sun. It burned hot, a constant presence in the blue sky. He used a stick to aid his journey, like the rest had done. Ben carried a homemade longbow, and his belt had five arrows clipped to it. He belonged in a post-apocalyptic movie, his beard hiding most of his features except the dark, calculating eyes.

Louise wore a leather hat to keep from burning. Jamal had a vest and shorts, his worn shoes repaired with various types of fabric. Maya marched efficiently, saying little, like she needed to conserve her words and strength.

The other man that came was named Peter, and his demeanor showed his distrust for everyone and everything surrounding him. He was probably only fifty, but could have passed for older after hard years on Arcadia, with skin so tanned, it resembled leather.

Gemma stayed at the rear of the pack, humming a tune. They'd taken two breaks in eight hours, and she seemed to have an unlimited resource of energy.

"Hey, Earth boy," she called, and John slowed. The term would almost be endearing, if she didn't say it with a hint of sarcasm.

"Yes, my liege," he answered.

Gemma smiled wider. "A girl could get used to that."

She'd been on Arcadia since she was seven years old, which would make her stunted in ways he couldn't even imagine. She was clearly intelligent, with a vivid imagination, and it drew John to her more than her optimism and undeniable attractiveness.

"What do you remember of Earth?"

"Not a lot."

"Where did you live?"

"A city…big one with a bell."

"The Liberty Bell? Was it Philadelphia?"

"I think so," she said. "I only saw the bell once. My parents brought me and my brother. I can't picture them. Isn't that sad?"

John viewed the landscape, which looked far different on foot than in the comfort of the military vehicle they'd left at the Den. "I lost my mom and dad a few years ago in a car crash."

"That's awful, but at least you know what happened to them," she said.

The comment stung, but he was sure Gemma had meant nothing by it.

"What was your brother's name?"

"John."

He suddenly understood why she referred to him by another title. "We're going to bring you home to them."

Gemma gazed at the sky. "A storm's brewing."

"It's clear as day," he said.

Ben stopped ahead. "Gemma, are you serious?"

She closed her eyes and slowly spun, arms outstretched. When she blinked them open, her smile was gone. "It'll reach us in two hours, from the south."

Ben gawked in that direction, and John could make out a hint of darkness on the horizon.

"How do you know?"

"I just do," she said.

"It's not that unusual," Ben told them. "Most villages around the world had someone that could detect an incoming storm. On Earth, we're bombarded by the weather network and television meteorologists. Out here, there's nothing to block our senses. Gemma's the best we have."

John figured it had something to do with a shift in the wind, or a heightened perception of barometric pressure fluctuations.

"Two hours?" Jamal sighed. "We're nowhere near the scout's cabin."

"We can make it if we push." Ben nodded at his partner. "How far is it?"

Louise used a cracked journal, scrawling notes with the nub of a pencil. "Seven miles."

"That's nothing." Peter rubbed his stubble-covered chin.

"Is there time?" Maya asked.

"It's a bit of a detour, but the terrain's pretty clear between us and the rest stop. The scout markers will guide us if we're hit before we arrive," Jamal said.

"What's a marker?" John hadn't seen such a thing.

"They're subtle, but we've left red pieces of fabric on trees, rocks, and whatever else keeps the scout on the proper path," he answered.

"Everyone ready?" Ben shouldered his pack, and John did the same, carrying the group's water supply.

They continued at a faster pace, and John tapped into his reserves. Even Gemma became somber while they attempted to beat the storm to their shelter.

From the urgency of the group, John surmised this was no regular storm like they had at home. His guess was confirmed a few minutes later when the south was filled with black clouds, lightning flashing sideways every second or two.

An hour into the final push, the air changed. John felt the electricity surrounding them, and his breaths seemed charged with the current. He glanced at his arm hair, finding it standing straight up.

"Is this normal?" he asked Gemma.

"It is on Arcadia." Gemma touched him, taking his wrist, and the contact sparked. "We're nearly there."

John spied a red marker on a skinny tree, then another a while later, resting under a small stone on a larger boulder. By the time they approached a log cabin, his back ached, and his legs burned from the day's tireless effort. He stripped the pack off and gazed at the storm while it struck the region.

Rain came in solid sheets, approaching their position. Jamal had the door open and ushered the ladies in before shoving John after them. The lightning crackled and hissed, followed by booming thunderclaps, which rattled the walls and shook the floor. Gemma sat on a cot, holding her hands over her ears.

Peter barrelled in, soaked from head to toe. "I needed a bath."

"Yeah, you did." Jamal laughed when he joined the rest of them.

The sounds of the storm dulled as the door sealed, but it continued to barrage the cabin. Ben opened a flue in the fireplace and prepared tinder in the hearth.

"What is this cabin?" John's mood improved as the flames sprang to life.

"Before I discovered there were others on Arcadia, I built this," Ben said. "I lived here for a year when Peter found me."

With the light, John recognized the layout was the same as the one at the Den. "How did you know how to do this?" He would be useless if he'd arrived here alone and afraid.

"I grew up off-grid. My parents didn't trust the government," Ben said.

"Who does?" Louise asked.

"They taught me to forage and live off the land before I could read."

"The Den would have been screwed without Ben," Jamal said.

John couldn't picture Ben and Louise ever abandoning Arcadia in favor of Earth, not after seeing what they'd accomplished. "You really won't leave?"

"I doubt it," Ben said.

John wanted to tell him they could have gotten to Carmichael with the JLTV much faster had the pair stayed behind, but didn't. "What if Logan helps us Shift before you can give them the option?"

"Then we'll have to live with that," Louise said.

Something cracked from the yard, making John jump.

"It's fine. We installed a lightning rod a hundred yards away for this purpose. It protects the cabin from burning down." Ben added a log to the fire. Even with the ventilation, a bit of smoke lingered in the air, and John wished he could open a window. "It'll improve when the wind tapers off."

"How long do these storms usually last?"

"Some are an hour, others take days," Gemma said.

"And this one?"

"Probably be over by the time we wake up, but the ground will be wet tomorrow." Gemma used her fingers to brush her hair.

John had the urge to relieve himself, and Ben directed him to the back of the cabin, where a wall separated him from the elements. It was poorly insulated, and water dripped in, but it offered privacy. The design carried the waste outside and funneled it on a slope, directed away from the structure. The rain would do the rest.

Once back, the group had broken bread, gathering at the table. He watched them, familiar with one another like a close-knit family. As he sat, he remembered the sound of the shotgun ending Van's life, and knew the courtesy of family only extended so far on Arcadia.

7

Caesar was grateful they'd finally located the corner of the canyon. It took much of the day, pushing the bikes to the limits, and he slowed and stepped a leg to the ground, pulling his helmet off. Anders did the same, and they stared at the canyon. "Shelter should be about two hundred miles that way." He pointed in that direction.

"We'd almost be there if not for this barrier," Caesar said. "We should make another hour or two."

"Let's sleep away from the cliff tonight. I don't want to encounter more of those slugs."

"Sure. What are you thinking?"

Anders used his gun scope, and Caesar joined him, scanning the landscape. "I'll be damned."

Caesar saw the tendrils of smoke as well, and his pulse raced faster. "Someone's nearby."

"It might be a scout from Shelter," Anders said.

"That would be advantageous." Caesar and Anders traveled slowly down the decline to where the camp appeared to be set. He gazed at the surroundings, suddenly aware that these trees were from Earth. They encircled a lake, with cattails like the kind he'd grown up around. The smoke came from an unattended fire, the coals burning hotly. A stack of broken sticks was piled near it, and Caesar tossed the driest on, wondering where its creator had bolted to.

A bag lay beside it, and Anders rifled through the meager possessions. He held up a sharpened rock, presumably wielded to gut fish. It was stained but clean. A leather strap and pair of scissors were next. Then a lighter, which didn't spark when Anders attempted to flick it. "A scout?"

"Probably." Caesar left his bike and used the rifle's scope, searching the region for signs of a lone human. "He must be off hunting."

Anders walked to the lake's edge and crouched, dipping a finger in. "This whole area is from Earth."

"Which means Arcadia Shifted to our planet," Caesar said. "Wouldn't we notice?"

"There's no vegetation out here, and it's mostly rocky desertscape. It would look like the lake dried up."

Caesar spotted something a few yards away and lifted a string connected to a stick jammed into the sand. "It's a gill net. The scouts must use this place to rest and fish when passing by."

"He'll be able to point us to Shelter," Anders said.

"We already know where it is."

"Or have a best guess." Caesar retrieved the LTC tablet, reading the last message from Logan.

Device 255889.33 LTC (Operator: Logan R)

The connection is weak. We might lose it during your trek. I'll keep the beacon on so you can see my location as you get nearer.

"I'm going to try to send a note to Logan," Caesar said.

Device 256615.21 (Operator Isla F)

We're north of the canyon and stopped at the scout's lake. Someone's here. We'll be at Shelter in two or three days. We lost the JLTV, so we'll only be able to take you and your wife.

It beeped and spewed out a rejection. *Link to device*

255889.33 failed.

"The beacon isn't even on." Anders tapped the screen.

"It's this way." Caesar gestured to their left.

"Who are you?" a voice called.

Caesar looked around, not finding the source. "Friends."

"Then why are you holding big-ass guns?"

Caesar motioned for Anders to lower his, after the operative did the opposite.

"You can come out. We're not going to hurt you."

A young man emerged from behind the trees. His shoes were worn through the toes, and he had a sleeveless sweatshirt on and tattered jeans two sizes too large for his diminutive frame. He had an animal caught in a snare, and Caesar noted the drooping ears and three eyes, reminding him of a rabbit.

"What's your name?" Anders asked defensively.

Caesar walked ahead of his counterpart, keeping his shoulders relaxed and doing his best not to be menacing. "I'm Caesar."

"I suppose that makes you Cleopátra?" The kid smirked.

Anders groaned. "I'm Anders."

"Duffy." He stepped forward, extending his hand.

Caesar shook, and the kid had a firm grip laced with thick calluses. "Nice to meet you, Duffy."

"Are you a scout?" Anders kept it formal.

Duffy hesitated a second, then smiled and nodded. "Sure. That's what I am."

"From Shelter?" Caesar asked.

Duffy lifted his prize catch. "Yeah, I'm heading there tomorrow." He almost dropped the food when he saw the bikes at his camp. "Those yours?"

"Yep." Caesar watched the man with caution. He'd

met plenty of shifty characters on the job, and this was no exception.

"How did you get them to Arcadia?"

"We were out for a cruise," Anders said.

"Are you two…" Duffy wiggled a finger between them.

"We're coworkers," Caesar quickly interjected.

"And the guns?"

"We found them a few days ago in an abandoned farmhouse."

That caught Duffy's attention. "The one in Milton's Canyon?"

"Could have been," Caesar said. "Who's Milton?"

Duffy laughed and started skinning the alien rabbit. "Milton is everything. He's the leader of Arcadia."

"Have you met Logan Rutherford?" Anders asked.

"Where did you hear that name?" He tossed the pile of guts into the fire and stuck the meat onto a spit.

"Everyone knows it." Caesar sat cross-legged, mirroring Duffy's position.

"How long ago did you say you came to Arcadia?"

"We didn't." Anders remained standing, and his presence couldn't help but be intimidating.

"What about you?" Caesar glared at Anders.

"Been around most of my days, I suppose. I'm from the swamps near Baton Rouge. Dad hunted gators and frogs, whatever put food on the table." The fresh kill dripped into the fire, and Duffy added more fuel. "Lived here ever since. Milton keeps me safe."

"You're not really from Shelter, are you?" he guessed.

Duffy spun the meat as it cooked. "What's with the interrogation? I said I was."

"Then we'll travel together," Anders told him.

"Fine by me. I've never ridden on one of them

motorized bikes. Will you teach me to drive?"

"No," Anders said.

"But I'll give you a ride," Caesar finished. "If you're telling the truth."

"In that case, I'll share my dinner." Duffy cracked his neck, and it audibly popped. "Milton says that when you break bread with people, you form a bond."

"Does he? What else does the great Milton say?" Anders inquired.

"He says a lot of wise things. It would be in your best interest not to insult him." Duffy's voice took on a dark tone.

Caesar watched him closely, sensing this Milton had powerful influence over the youth. "Milton runs Shelter?"

Duffy paused, probably deciding what lie to go with. At that moment, Caesar became aware they had a problem. "Yes, Milton is in charge of Arcadia."

"What about Logan?" Anders finally sat, but his M4 lay rested on his lap. The action didn't go unnoticed by their host.

Duffy's gaze settled on the weapon and he licked his lips, but not from the smell of roasting meat. "Logan works for him."

"What does he do for Milton?" Caesar continued the questioning, hoping to gain as much information as possible so they could eventually decipher the truth.

"Whatever Milton tells him to." Duffy looked to be about eighteen, but it was tough to gauge. He had bleached blond peach fuzz, and his skin was tanned and dirty in contrast to his hair.

"What do *you* do for Milton?" Anders asked.

Duffy tested a piece of meat and tore a chunk off, handing it to Caesar, then to Anders, with a slight hesitation. "I'm just a cog in the great machine." He sounded rehearsed, like a kid repeating something their father told them at the dinner table.

"The machine that's Arcadia." Caesar bit into it and wished they'd brought salt. It was gamey, but edible. If they ended up stuck across the Shift, he'd have to get used to this type of fare.

Anders ate as if it was his last meal. Caesar supposed the man always felt that way, after his near-death experiences.

"What if we told you we can bring you home?"

"To Shelter?"

"No, to Earth," Caesar said.

Duffy chewed his food, visibly pondering the news. "I'd call you a fraud. Milton says this is our home. Ain't nothing gonna change that."

Caesar turned the tablet on, showing the message from Logan. "Milton isn't at Shelter, is he?"

"I never said he was."

"You did," Anders blurted.

"No, I said he runs things on Arcadia."

"Have you ever been to Shelter?" Caesar asked, growing tired of the conversation.

Duffy finished his meal, tossing the bones into the fire. He broke the spit and did the same with it, watching the green stick hiss as it burned. "Are you accusing me of something?"

"Absolutely." Anders had far less patience than Caesar, and it was showing. He'd been out of the game for too long, and while he could handle himself in a fight, there was more to being an elite operative than shooting people.

Duffy rose, hands clenched. "You should leave."

"Settle down," Caesar said. "We meant no disrespect. We're strangers to Arcadia, and don't know the rules."

Duffy huffed and retook his seat. "You'd better go."

"Why?" Caesar peered at the dwindling sunlight.

"I'll tell Milton you were here, and what you said about going home. He won't like it."

Caesar waited for Duffy to explain.

"Milton says we're in Nirvana. There ain't no way he'll let anyone take us from Arcadia."

Anders hopped to his feet, moving to the bike. "Thanks for the meal, kid."

Duffy shrugged.

Caesar removed a protein bar from his saddlebag and tossed it to Duffy. "For the road."

"Cheers." He squinted at it, like he was trying to read the label but couldn't.

They rode away from the setting sun and stopped a couple of miles out.

"That was bizarre," Anders said. "I should go back and—"

"What? Kill him?"

"Milton sounds dangerous."

"I agree, but we are *not* shooting Duffy."

"Fine. I hope this decision doesn't bite us in the ass later." Anders flipped his visor down. "Let's get a bit more distance between us and his camp."

Caesar followed his partner, seeing Anders in a new light.

———————

Two days. Summer repeated it in her mind as she stared at the tent's ceiling. Harrison was awake, and rarely slept, not since learning how close he'd been to riding the River Styx. His words, not Summer's.

Wanda slept soundly, cradling her phone. She'd been

scrolling pictures of her kids, and Summer listened as the woman described each event. Seeing Wanda talk about her family made Summer miss her parents.

She checked the clock, finding it was three in the morning. Summer grabbed the cell they'd given her and opened a social media app. It failed without access to the internet, and she recalled how often she'd scrolled just purely out of boredom. After over a week without it, the urge had almost let go of her.

Summer put the device on the table and got up, walking to the exit.

"Where do you think you're going?" Harrison whispered. He was dressed in a suit, the tie draped on the back of his cot. A gun lay on his lap, and Summer wondered why Christine let him keep the weapon.

"I'm restless."

"Fair enough." Harrison joined her and opened the flap. The air had cooled substantially as they stepped out into the barren streets. The hum of the floodlights and electric fence was the only sound she could recognize. How many times had she taken this very road to and from Carmichael? On either side were cornfields, and beyond the sliced asphalt was alien terrain, fenced to keep the Howlers trapped within.

"We need to be in the barricade to Shift," Harrison said.

"Are you sure?"

"Reginald, my IT guy, has been working on the blueprints, and thinks the closer to Isla's base we are, the more likely the device will carry us to Arcadia." He showed her the phone, and the countdown had less than forty-eight hours remaining.

"Don't let Wanda come," she said.

"I won't." Harrison seemed like he was going to put a

hand on Summer's shoulder, then stopped himself.

"Thank you," she said.

"For what?"

"Coming with me to Arcadia."

"I'm going to warn Caesar."

"He'll be glad to see you," Summer said. "I miss my best friend too."

"Carly, right?"

"You do listen." Summer grinned.

"You talk a lot, like my daughter. I'm bound to retain something." The fence sparked; then a pink butterfly floated to the mossy ground, burned to a crisp. More of the insects landed, getting similarly fried.

They waited while a patrol drove around the boundary to the woodlands, their headlights casting shadows along the cornfields. When they were out of sight, Harrison began hiking the trail.

"Where are we going?"

"I'll need to scout it out. You should return to the tent…"

"No way." Summer jogged to join his long strides.

Harrison's watch buzzed, and he glanced in the direction of their camp, finding lights. "Take cover."

They rushed to the corn, while Summer tried to guess whose crops these were, and if they belonged to the Gellers. Their land stretched for miles, since they'd bought a lot of the fringe acres connected to their own property. The two soldiers slowly drove by on the cart, lazily holding weapons.

"They should pay more attention," Summer whispered as they passed.

"Three days, and they're already getting complacent. If this was my operation, I'd have a word with these guys." Harrison straightened his collar and reset the timer on his wrist. "Let's go."

They repeated the process twice more, hiding when the sentries came like clockwork. Eventually, Harrison walked to the fence, gazing up. "They've done a great job relaying power, but with a defensive position so vast, they've segmented the sources into clusters a mile long. All I need to do is cut the lines here—" He pointed to a box five feet up, attached to the chain link. Exposed wires rose from it to a metal tube he called an EMT conduit, whatever that meant.

Harrison snapped a photo with his cell and slid it to his pocket. "We'll cut this spot when the electricity is off and walk to the section of Arcadia that Isla built her base on. Reginald suggests our odds of actually linking with the LTC device double if we're there."

"We can really leave Earth?"

"Isn't that what you wanted?"

Summer nodded, though her inner voice warned her she might not return to her own planet again if she did. "Yes." Carly and her family were across, not to mention the dreamy Adam Iverson.

"I can't let them win. If Christine succeeds, they'll be wiped out once they have a connection to Arcadia. I won't allow that to happen."

"You sound like Caesar," Summer said, and her comment brought a smile to Harrison's face.

"Thank you." The watch vibrated again, and he pulled her from the path the military had cut through to give them a road along the fabricated border. "That was close." The cart rolled by with a third set of soldiers. From the looks of it, the passenger dozed beside the driver.

Summer heard the Howler before she saw three racing to the border. One jumped, landing atop the chain-link. It screeched in pain while its partners clawed up its back, circumventing their electrical defense.

The Howlers dropped directly in front of the cart, and the brakes slammed. Summer screamed as the sleeping soldier's throat was slashed. The Howlers were twitchy after the electrical fence voltage conducted through their friend.

The driver swung his gun up, but it was too late. The Howler grabbed hold of his leg with its tail and dragged him from the vehicle. Summer expected him to be killed, but Harrison intervened. His handgun popped three times, and the last living Howler took off at a gallop.

Summer ran to the cart as Harrison appraised the fallen woman. She was obviously dead, while the driver scrambled to his feet.

Harrison threw the radio closer to her. "Call it in!" And he was off. Summer clung to the handhold and forced herself up, while Harrison chased the escaped Howler.

"Where did it go?" Harrison hissed.

Summer scoured the area, trying to find the alien creature as it ran from them. "There!"

The stalks rustled, and Harrison cranked the wheel, nearly sending Summer reeling, but she held tight.

He sped between the rows of corn, using the maintenance path, and Summer continually caught glimpses of the Howler. It stopped, and he did the same, cutting the lights. The battery-powered engine ceased, and the region grew deathly silent.

Harrison rose, putting a finger to his lips, and held the gun, moving slowly and with intense care toward the halted beast. Summer watched from the cart, not wanting to fall victim to the lone enemy.

He returned a moment later with a look of resignation.

Summer noticed the stalks move. "Behind you!"

Harrison tumbled, taking the weight of the animal, and

his gun flew to the next row over.

Summer had to do something, but she froze while Caesar's boss attempted to defend himself. Teeth gnashed at him. She raced to the gun, picked it up, and pointed, her arms shaking so much, she kept sighting Harrison.

"Breathe," she repeated, recalling Kong's advice on the roof of the sanctuary. Summer shot the Howler in the third eye, and it flopped onto Harrison. For an instant, she believed he'd been killed. Then his hand jutted from under the Howler, and he struggled to roll out. Summer dropped the gun and helped him free. Harrison lay on his back, watching the stars, and laughed gruffly.

"What's so funny?"

"We want to march into Howler territory, and all I've been thinking was how to avoid Christine's detection. I'd all but forgotten the real threat was inside the fence," he said.

"But we're still doing it?" Summer had the urge to run away from her problems.

"Yes." Harrison rose, dusted off his pants, and kicked the dead Howler for good measure, then hauled the carcass onto the cart. "Thanks, by the way."

"You'd do the same for me," she said.

When they returned to the path, a dozen soldiers approached, red lights landing on Summer's and Harrison's chests.

"Stand down!" Harrison proclaimed. "Clean up this mess and double your sentries. And for the love of God, no more sleeping on the job, or it's your asses!"

Christine emerged from the last cart, acting amused. "Look who showed up." She gave a mock salute. "The general himself."

Harrison wiped a bead of blood from his lip. "Damn right. From now on, I'm directing our defenses."

Christine didn't argue, and relayed his earlier message to the newly arriving soldiers.

Summer got into the cart with Harrison, and they drove from the group to camp. Wanda waited at the tent, nervously pacing the street. She rushed Harrison into a quick embrace, then stepped back and frowned. "How dare you run off! Do you know how upset Fatina would be if I had to make that call? You're not an operative anymore, Harry!"

Summer tried to give them space, but she had limited options, and her energy was sapped.

"Phone Reggie. Bring him in."

Wanda opened her mouth, then nodded. "He's already coming."

"Good."

It was nearing five in the morning, and dawn was fresh on the eastern horizon.

"How about some coffee?" Summer asked.

Harrison closed the tent while Wanda moved to the brewer. "This had better work."

8

*A*melia woke with the sunrise, donned her uniform, and even took the hat she rarely wore from the squad car's trunk. She ran a finger over the brim and checked her reflection. She'd always thought it made her look younger, which wasn't a good thing as a female law enforcement agent in her late twenties. It had been a struggle to have anyone take her seriously, even before she got the badge.

A knock on the car window startled her, and there was Haley, wearing a metal badge they'd found in the town office. It was a fake, created for an old-timey western-themed fundraiser from years ago, but her deputies appreciated the symbolism. Haley carried two paper coffee cups and had her rifle, like always.

She set the drinks on the car and opened the door. "Thought you could use a caffeine shot this morning."

"We should conserve our supplies." Amelia still took the coffee. "But thank you."

"No worries." Haley sat and rolled her window open. The breeze was light and carried a hint of a weather change. They'd seen a giant storm off to the north last night, but it broke up before striking Carmichael. She suspected there would be more like it leading up to the massive event Jamal had predicted. "Where to first?"

"Isla's base."

Freddy waved from the fence, talking to Mr. Tucker and Evan. Vince and his son, Jimmy, nodded, listening to whatever they were being told. Dot slowed when she spotted Amelia, then averted her gaze.

"What's the matter with Dot?" Haley asked.

Amelia drove, not sticking around for a conversation with anyone. She had work to do. "She's embarrassed."

"About what?"

"Dot had a few too many at her birthday party, but it wasn't a big deal," Amelia said. She thought about the basement, and the click as the door unlocked. She'd tried to get Dot's attention yesterday, but the woman had been too busy.

"So what? If I got embarrassed every time I—" Haley stopped, then sipped her coffee. "She has nothing to worry about."

Amelia made it her habit to visit Isla's facility once a day. Kong guarded it after Eldon was summoned to help with an electrical issue at their sanctuary. The big man sat in the shade, directly at the barn's entrance, and rose when she exited the car.

"Hey, Chief."

"Kong. Quiet night?"

"I had to hide inside three times. The Howlers were on patrol, but I didn't have to engage. I don't think they like this place."

Amelia understood why. Below the ground, Isla had a giant room filled with a power source Amelia didn't comprehend. Even now, standing calmly, she recognized the slight vibration in her heels.

"It's good they aren't attacking the barn, but it obviously has them intrigued. Is your replacement coming?"

"I hope so. Chun's been feeling like the baby's ready."

"Isn't that early?" Haley asked.

"A little, but it's not as if she can hold off until we Shift home."

"Hank will show up soon. Why don't you go to your family?" Amelia suggested.

"Thanks, Chief. Anything else going on today?"

"We're still tracking Lillian."

"And you're sure it was her that killed Hector?"

"Had to be…he was stealing electronics for her. She was the only one that knew where the stash was stored," she said.

"I'll stop by the catchment and check on it. We were hoping the storm would hit Carmichael so we could test it," he told her.

"Be careful what you wish for," Haley muttered.

"Maybe it'll happen tonight." Amelia stepped aside while Kong got to his motorbike.

"See you two later." Kong put on his helmet and took off slowly.

"He's an asset to our team." Amelia undid the lock and entered Isla's staged barn.

"I'm glad you took a chance on Kong," Haley said.

"A chance?"

"Don't you know his story?" Haley closed up and flipped the bar over, sealing them in.

"No, I guess not." She'd seen the tattoos on his knuckles but hadn't asked.

"He was involved with a gang in Baltimore, and served ten years when he sold a gun to an undercover," Haley said. "After being on parole, the judge let him leave the state, and he came to Carmichael to open a bar. If you trust the rumors, he funded it with money he'd squirreled away from selling."

Amelia tried not to judge the man too harshly, considering actions spoke louder than words, and he'd done his time. "I only care what he does now. And he has a lot to lose."

"What'll happen when she gives birth? We don't even have Dr. Wickenhouse."

"But we have a load of grandmothers that have offered to help," Amelia said.

"There's a difference between baking cookies and catching a kid coming out of—"

A rumble on the floor interrupted their conversation. It continued as Amelia walked to the secreted hatch and propped open the panel. She used the keycard and tapped it to the sensor, gaining access to the underground bunker.

They lowered down the ladder, and Amelia ignored the main office, heading to the right. The machines kept humming with energy as lights flashed toward the central hub. That was a good sign. But why hadn't they gotten Carmichael to Earth at the last opportunity?

"Amelia…"

"Yeah?" she called.

"There's a new countdown," Haley said.

Amelia hastily returned, finding the monitor on. *38:17:06.* "Less than two days."

"We can go home?"

Amelia gazed at the equipment. "Unless you know how to connect this"—she gestured at the screen—"to that, we're staying on Arcadia." She marked the timeline, calculating when it would strike. "Just after dark tomorrow night."

"We should place people at the border."

"Lillian might have answers." Amelia took a last look at the timer and experienced a rising sense of panic. She'd been working on the assumption they had around two weeks before Caesar and Anders would return with Logan. If they left now, she'd be stranding Caesar on Arcadia.

When they got outside, Hank was by the barn holding a shotgun. "Chief," he said. "Deputy." He tipped his ball cap to them. "Lovely morning for guard duty."

"Just don't fall asleep. Kong's seen the Howlers nearby."

"Scout's honor." He made a sign of the cross, then lit a cigarette.

Amelia started her route, deciding to investigate every barn, hollow, shed, and home in the outer reaches of town.

They came upon an older property, and Amelia slowed in the driveway. "Are they accounted for?"

Haley flipped through her journal, nodding. "Mr. and Mrs. Ulrich. Seventy-one and sixty-eight. Both checked into the sanctuary."

"Good." Amelia didn't love that she had to trespass into so many people's homes, but the invasion of privacy was necessary to catch Lillian Dawson. The front doors were unlocked, which didn't surprise Amelia. These folks made burglary that much easier by their lack of foresight. She'd never liked the adage that locks only keep honest folks out. They also made a thief's job a hell of a lot tougher and forced them to make a racket should they decide to break in.

The layout was similar to other homes, with fluffy pink fabric drooped over the curtains. The sofas were out of the Eighties, and they still had an old television. A remote sat jammed into a reclining chair's side pocket, along with an issue of a popular magazine.

"What's this?" Haley held up a rocket-shaped toy.

"I've seen these." Amelia accepted the radio and adjusted the antenna, sliding the tip.

"What does it do?"

"It's a lo-fi radio, powered by a crystal," she said.

"No batteries?"

Amelia shook her head. "Nope."

"That doesn't seem possible."

There was no speaker, but it had a single bud that Amelia stuck into her ear. She slowly lifted the rod, knowing it would have nothing to pick up.

She froze when the slightest sound appeared. "How…"

Amelia listened, closing her eyes. "…*Milton Radio… threat to Nirvana… gather near Shelter.*"

As quickly as it came, the message vanished.

"Amelia, are you okay? You're pale as a ghost!"

"I think I just heard a communication from Arcadia."

"Aliens?"

"Very human," she said, catching the message's implication. Someone was planning on attacking Shelter.

———————

*T*he fields were wet in low-lying places, so their group kept to high ground. The storm had rocked the cabin relentlessly, and every time another bolt struck the rod outside, John had flinched. He even bit his tongue when he'd finally drifted off to sleep.

Now, long after departing, Jamal and Maya walked in the lead, with Ben and Louise taking the rear. Peter moved effortlessly, like he was used to taking fifty-mile hikes before breakfast, then another fifty after lunch.

Gemma kept her gaze on the sky, but had no predictions of incoming storms, which John was grateful for. The sun was high, suggesting they'd been on the march for four hours. They neared a lake, and the rocky ledges gave ample shade, so they opted to break.

"How far have we gone?" John asked while Ben unwrapped dried meat from his pack.

Louise checked her book, calculating their trajectory. "The cabin brought us off course, but we've done twenty miles."

"That's close to the hospital." John nodded, knowing they had thirty to go. Another day and a half, if they pushed it. He ate the meat and rolled his shoulders, feeling something pop. As they utilized the supplies, the bags grew slightly lighter, but it didn't make up for how sore his body was and how much he wanted to soak in a bathtub. These people were conditioned to the harsh environment, but John had only been without a roof over his head for a couple of days.

"Let's clean you up." Maya didn't give Jamal a chance to argue, and she stripped the bandages. "They're looking great."

Jamal smiled and pointed at the lake. "Why don't we rinse off?"

Maya removed her top and shorts within seconds. John averted his gaze and stared at the ground while they dashed into the water, cracking jokes.

"What about you, Earth boy?" Gemma removed her shirt, and John fought his instincts. Thankfully, she kept her bottoms on and ran in with a splash.

Ben laughed at John's obvious discomfort, which made him even more embarrassed. "You need a bath, John. Go ahead. It's good for the muscles."

With Ben and Louise joining the others, John had no choice, and he stripped to his underwear. Only Peter remained at the temporary camp, seeming disinterested in their recreation. The lake wasn't hot, but warm enough to find pleasant. "There isn't anything dangerous in here?" he asked.

"Not unless you count me." Gemma swam by.

They went deeper, until John had to tread water to keep his head above the surface, and Gemma floated off by herself, watching the clouds.

The jovial conversation ended when Gemma looked at the group with fear in her eyes. "Another storm is coming."

"So soon?" Louise asked.

"I don't think we have two weeks before the season changes." Gemma swam to the shore, and John did too, his clumsy strokes sending water everywhere.

They dressed hastily, still moderately wet as the clothing clung to their skin, and assembled the supplies.

"Where to?" Ben studied the horizon.

Blackness saturated the view to the east, filling John's chest with dread. "Is it bad?"

"Remember yesterday?" Gemma took the lead, darting up the naturally rocky path.

"Of course."

"This is far worse."

"We'll go to the hospital. John mentioned it's only a couple of miles from here."

"We shouldn't have left the JLTV," John complained.

"That's my fault." Jamal reached a fist out for John to bump. "I'll make it up to you."

"We're used to doing things our way," Ben added. "But you're right. The vehicle would have been more practical."

"I wish I'd have known the weather was changing earlier," Gemma said.

"That's okay." Ben put an arm around her shoulder as they walked.

"Do you think Carmichael is in its path?" John pictured Carmichael being hit with a massive tornado and moved faster.

"At this point? It might strike in two days." The moment the words escaped Gemma's lips, the wind gusted, sending dust flying. It was on their backs, so the debris didn't get into John's eyes.

The rain arrived within minutes, which shocked John, given the distance those clouds had to cover. The air seemed charged with electricity again, and the sensation disturbed him while they jogged toward the location Jamal had marked in his journal. He stopped at a high spot and pulled the book out, leaning over to keep the precipitation from soaking the pages. "This way!" he called.

Five minutes later, John spied the white spire and smiled. Lightning continually sparked above, creating deafening thunderclaps. His body shuddered with each, his heels vibrating as the surface rattled.

"Is it safe?" Gemma pointed at the spire, which took a lightning strike.

"Looks like they built it for that purpose," Ben said. "It's better than being stuck out here!"

John barely heard them, given the ferocity of the weather surrounding them. The Cadillac remained in the parking lot, and Peter set a hand to it. "My grandfather had—" A bolt struck it when they approached, throwing the man three feet back.

"Is he…" John stopped as Maya shoved past him, kneeling in the mud beside their fellow traveler.

"Don't touch him!" Ben warned.

Water hit Peter, evaporating from the heat. He flinched, gasped, then grew still.

No one moved for a solid minute, and John sensed the grief emanating from the Den residents.

Gemma was the first to break loose and rush into the cover of the awning near the building's entrance. Ben and

Jamal eventually confirmed Peter's death, and they carried him out of the rain, setting him atop the front steps.

Ben turned to face the storm, raising a fist in anger. "Damn you!"

Another bolt hit the car, this one shattering the windshield.

Louise dragged her partner to the doors, and John opened them, waiting until the rest were in before doing the same. He snuck a glance at Peter's corpse and wondered how many more would die on Arcadia before he made it home.

The walls shook, the furniture rattled, and the rod on the roof took a battering.

The storm was so loud, John thought it might tear the place apart. If he'd been scared last night in the cabin, he was petrified now.

"Is there a basement?" Ben asked.

"If there was, I don't think it came with the property when it Shifted." Jamal directed them from the foyer, past the gates they'd left wide.

"Our basements came with us, but the outer areas seemed to not go as deep," John told them.

"We've never encountered such a large area being Shifted, so I can't guess how it really works," Ben said.

They ended in the room with the fireplace, given the position within the structure. The beams were large and heavy in the ceiling, and Ben figured it might be the safest point.

John and Jamal cleared the three skeletons near the hearth, unceremoniously shoving them in the closet. Gemma sat in a dusty chair, her hands folded primly on her lap, and closed her eyes.

"Anything?"

"It'll break, but not for a while. I feel the pressure

shifting, heading south."

"Toward Carmichael," John whispered.

Thunder boomed, and the six of them clung to life, while Peter's body remained outside.

9

"We must be close," Anders said, using the tablet again.

Caesar nodded, and miraculously, the icon blinked onto the screen, displaying their position as well as Logan Rutherford's. "Hallelujah."

Anders tapped between the dots, and a distance appeared. "Seventeen miles."

"We're almost there." Caesar's feet were planted on either side of the bike, keeping it upright, and he scanned the horizon with his scope. "What I wouldn't give for a decent set of binoculars."

"I left them with the JLTV. It's tough packing light," Anders said.

The day was nearing its end, and they had a decision to make. "Camp?"

"Sure. We can get to Shelter by noon. Maybe Logan will feed us lunch." Anders offered a rare smile and gestured to a flat spot a short distance away. "I think we should have a fire tonight."

"We're far enough from the forest."

"I'm surprised that Duffy didn't attempt to kill us and take the bikes."

Caesar nodded. "I figure he would have, if he thought he could."

"I don't like the sounds of Milton."

"Then let's hope we don't run into him." Caesar was nearing Shelter, which meant Logan Rutherford. They'd use the last of their fuel and return to Carmichael with Dot's son, ensuring they'd travel to Earth on the next Shift. What would happen afterward wasn't in Caesar's hands, but he sure as hell wouldn't be sticking around town for long.

He thought about the deputy as they parked, turning the bikes off. Anders prepared the fire, while Caesar set up camp. He wished he could check in with Amelia and let her know they were okay.

Soon the flames shot up, the half-dried wood spattering as it popped and hissed. Anders added dried grass, helping the heat increase, and everything burned easier.

Caesar reached for the tablet and tried to send a message while Anders opened a can of tuna.

Device 256615.21 (Operator Isla F)
We're near Shelter. Arrival tomorrow morning.

Caesar stared impatiently at the device. "He's not responding."

"He said the connection would be spotty." Anders offered him half the can and a small fork.

"But the icons showed up, so we're coupled."

"It's dark. He might be sleeping," Anders said.

"I thought you were the devil's advocate?" Caesar laughed and took a bite. The salty protein hit the spot, but he'd prefer to eat it in a sandwich with mayonnaise and some pickle for crunch. What else would he miss about Earth if he couldn't go home?

"There's a time and place for naysaying, and this isn't one of them. I just want to get Logan and leave." Anders continually examined their surroundings, which wasn't easy to do given the brightness of their camp. "The fire was a bad idea."

"I was thinking the same." Caesar rose, finishing the tuna. He heard a *clunk* sound, but didn't understand what it was until he saw the arrow jutting from the saddlebags. "Get down!"

Anders didn't have to be told twice. He dove, then sprang up near his bike with the M4 in his grip. Caesar grabbed his own, using the night-vision scope. A dozen men approached their camp, carrying an assortment of weapons ranging from axes to baseball bats to a small bow. One had a revolver, and he held it clumsily.

They dressed in western clothing, leather vests with tassels, and cowboy hats. Caesar wanted to give them a chance to explain themselves, but Anders had something else in mind. He opened fire, hitting the front-runner. The man dropped, his hat flying off.

Caesar sighed and took down two before talking himself out of it. Another arrow was let loose, and it struck the bike behind him. They were fifty yards away, and Anders shot three, while Caesar's gun killed again.

The last five stopped in their tracks, and the leader put his arms high.

Caesar heard liquid falling and checked the bike, finding the arrow sticking straight into one of their reserve fuel cans. "Keep them honest," he told Anders, and grabbed something to plug the hole. He broke the shaft, shoving the tip in, then tilted the can so it no longer spilled out. Caesar set it to the ground and lifted the gun, aiming at the group.

"Why did you attack us?" he asked when it was clear Anders had no intention of making conversation.

"You're outsiders!" the man with the revolver said.

"What gives you the right to kill outsiders?"

The men looked at one another. "Them's the rules."

Caesar noticed how similar his mannerisms were to Duffy's. "Any of you named Milton?"

Revolver cackled a laugh. "Milton doesn't waste time wandering the desert. He has more important things to do."

"Why are you here?"

"We should ask you the same thing." The guy's smile revealed two missing teeth, and he spoke with a whistle.

"The biggest guns get to do the asking." Caesar glanced at Anders, seeing how close his finger hovered by the trigger.

"Then go ahead."

"Drop your weapons, and we can talk." Caesar lowered his assault rifle.

Two axes fell, then the bow, and the fourth guy released a knife. Only the leader with the revolver didn't relinquish his gun, but he didn't aim it at them.

"What's your name?" Caesar inquired.

"Braxton," he said.

"Where were you going?" Caesar had an idea, but wanted confirmation.

"Milton's done waiting for Shelter to agree to his terms, so we're moving in," Braxton said.

Anders shifted his feet, stepping closer. The men subsequently retreated.

Caesar recalled Duffy's comments about Milton overseeing Arcadia. "Where are you coming from?"

Braxton lifted the revolver. "Wouldn't you like to know?"

Anders didn't give him a chance to say more. He fired until all remaining five of Milton's crew were on the ground, blood soaking their western attire.

"Damn it, Anders. We could have gotten more

information."

Anders stood over the bodies, poking each with his gun. "Unless you were going to torture them, these guys weren't talking."

He picked up the revolver and spun the barrel. "This thing is ancient. It's a Colt from the late 1800s."

Caesar grimaced and crouched by one of the axe-wielding opponents. He checked the tag, reading a popular brand from that era. "Either someone Shifted to Arcadia with a load of second-hand clothing, or an old western town showed up years ago."

"Incredible." Anders took a fallen hat and set it on his head. "How does it look?"

"Tacky."

"You're right. It'll be better with matching boots." Anders walked around the bodies, sizing their feet up.

"What are you doing?" Caesar wasn't overly surprised by Ander's behavior.

"If these guys are moving for Shelter, don't you think we should look the part? How else are we going to blend in?" Anders tugged off someone's boots.

"I see your point." Caesar reluctantly searched for an outfit with the least amount of bloodstains. He buttoned up the shirt, threw the vest over the hole in the chest, and attached the hat to the bike.

"How much fuel did we lose?" Anders tore an arrow from his seat, and a bit of foam exited with the head.

Caesar hefted the can, shaking it. "About a gallon."

"Let's refill and ditch the cans."

They set about the task, and Anders dragged the bodies into a pile after rummaging through their pockets. He kept anything that might be of use, and Caesar felt like a graverobber. Things on Arcadia had become dark.

With the stack of Milton's gang near the fire, Anders

used a spattering of gas remaining in the cans and set the vessels on the leader's chest. He kicked a log from the pit, and it sparked as the flames caught.

"Come on, let's go to Shelter," Caesar said, donning his helmet.

He looked at the growing fire, then revved the engine and picked up speed.

---

*A*melia walked on the sanctuary's roof while the storm rolled in from the north. It started slowly, with a faint gust of wind. Rain followed, a drizzle at first, until it drove harder.

"Is the Repulsor okay?" she asked Eldon.

The young man nodded. "It seems to be working, but a generator gave up the ghost today at the fence. If we lose any more, or run out of fuel, we'll be at risk."

Amelia watched the clouds, uncomfortable with how low they were, and the shape of them. She'd seen funnel clouds forming in her life, but they'd never materialized.

The device Jamal had brought to Carmichael was small, and they'd connected it to a speaker from Pastor Odell's church, amplifying the range. The sound kept the Howlers at bay, and so far, they'd had no confrontations besides the odd attack near the boundaries. She had patrol volunteers constantly checking the perimeter, then relaying their findings to Faith on the radio. She had a makeshift office in the storage facility directly below Amelia's feet.

Three guards stayed on the rooftops, casually holding rifles.

"If the storm picks up, get into the building downstairs," Amelia ordered the trio.

Brent nodded and gave her a thumbs-up.

"And Eldon, whatever happens, you can't allow the Repulsor to break. Understood?"

Eldon saluted her. "You bet, Chief. I won't let—" He stopped talking as lightning forked sideways through the skies, temporarily blinding Amelia. Another blast shone brightly, and the area darkened as thunder followed.

She rushed to the main floor, finding most of the town's residents nervously waiting. The movie projector played an old reel from the abandoned theater, but only a few paid attention to the film.

"Are we going to die?" Mrs. Trefal asked.

"No one is dying. Stay put and don't go outside. It'll pass," Amelia said.

She stood at the exit, wondering if she should leave. The radio beeped. "You've got the chief. Over."

"I need help at the catchment. Can you bring a couple of guys? Over." Kong sounded worried.

This was their first chance at collecting water, and Amelia couldn't let it be squandered. Who knew when the next rainfall might come? "Give me ten! Over."

Mr. Tucker and his son were already on their feet, as if hearing her thoughts. "What can we do?" he asked.

Evan smiled, but it dropped when the building shook. "Kong's having issues with the catchment."

"Let's go." Mr. Tucker's ball cap flew off, and his kid ran to grab it.

They bolted to her squad car, with Evan taking the back seat, and she hit the gas. Pastor Odell was visible through the church window, holding a Bible. She waved, but he didn't see her.

There was no traffic between them and the field, so she made it quickly, with the wipers on high.

Kong hung on a ladder, gripping the edge of the tarp

as it flapped in the gale force winds. Evan arrived first and jumped, catching the opposite corner. Two water cisterns were toppled, and Amelia joined Mr. Tucker, righting them with great effort. She put all her strength into it and gasped as the rain dripped into her eyes.

Kong used a battery-powered nail gun, securing the tarp into place, and the moment he stepped off the ladder, it fell sideways, landing in the mud with a splash.

"We can't stay here!" she shouted.

"Where, then?" Mr. Tucker pointed at the barn, which was barely intact.

"Mrs. Lemar's old house is close!" Kong yelled. "It's our best bet. No one's lived there for a while."

"Show me the way!" Amelia had an idea how to find it, but in the storm, she was turned around. She made out Kong's taillights, and nearly lost him at an intersection in the gravel road.

"He went right!" Evan called.

Wind buffeted her car, and even with the wipers, the road could hardly be seen. A tense minute passed, and she recognized the red of Kong's brakes, parking at a house.

"By the grace of God, I hope those clouds pass by," Mr. Tucker prayed.

Evan made a noise as he fumbled with the door handle, then exited the car, darting after Kong.

Amelia stayed for a second, while the storm seemed to slow. The wind died, and the giant trees surrounding the Lemar property ceased their excessive sway. The wipers squeaked dry when the rain stopped. "Is it…?" A lightning show cut her off.

"Dear Lord, please protect us." Mr. Tucker wrung his hat nervously.

The clouds circled, making her fear the worst. A tornado was about to hit Carmichael for the first time in its long history. She chased Mr. Tucker to the front porch, where Kong was breaking in. He used the butt of his rifle, smashing the glass, and winced when the remnants cut his arm while he unlocked the door.

The wind resumed, rising in speed until Amelia had to block her eyes from floating debris. The house had been abandoned a few years ago, but nothing seemed out of place. Signs of Mrs. Lemar's belongings were everywhere, but Amelia didn't have time to investigate.

"Where's the basement?" Kong asked.

Mr. Tucker moved through the rooms grimly and returned. "She's got a crawl space." He opened the wooden hatch and gestured down. It was so dark, Amelia had to trust it was safe to go in. She felt the cool ground and was glad when Kong activated a flashlight. The beam shone over the plastic crates Mrs. Lemar had stored under there. Above them were the kitchen floorboards. Amelia crouched by a box of old Christmas ornaments with fake green mistletoe sticking from the top.

The sounds of the storm sent ice into her veins, and Mr. Tucker hugged his son, the muscles on his jaw protruding as he clenched for the coming assault.

Kong's gaze was distant, and she guessed he was thinking about his pregnant wife and kids at the sanctuary. Amelia's worry spread much further; she was responsible for the entire town.

She dipped lower, shielding her head with her hands, like ducking for cover under a desk during the Cold War era.

The destruction was evident as objects from outside slammed into the house. Glass shattered, and a whooshing sound sped into the cracks above. It was so loud, she wanted to plug her ears, but was afraid to move an inch. The wooden slats shuddered, and she risked a glance, finding the kitchen floorboards lifting one by one, the nails tugging loose from their resting place of the last hundred years.

Amelia thought this was the moment her life would end. Until the slats stopped tearing free, and something fell with a thump.

"It's passing us." Kong crawled out of the hole.

Amelia did so carefully, to not cut herself on the wreckage. She stood in what used to be a home, astonished to find all four walls gone. The stove was in the yard, the fridge toppled and open.

Mr. Tucker bent and picked up a picture of Mrs. Lemar and her family from thirty years ago, and dropped it. "We made it."

"But what about the rest of Carmichael?" Evan asked.

Amelia reached for her radio. "Come in… Dot, are you there? Over."

When she got no response, she switched channels. "Eldon, where are you with the Repulsor? Over."

Amelia's stomach flopped as the cyclone of wind approached the alien border. Three more tore through the region.

INTERLUDE

Logan

Shelter

D*evice 255889.33 LTC (Operator: Logan R)*

We might be under attack. Don't come or they'll take what you have, and likely kill you.

He sent the message, but the connection had faltered again. Since he'd dismantled the tower, the service had been hit or miss, mostly on the latter.

Logan had dealt with Milton's crew before, accommodating their demands for supplies and a share of their crop yield, but they'd never come with a force this size.

"What do we do?" Ruby asked. She was far too calm for the situation, which gave Logan a bout of confidence.

"We listen to them." Logan's people were outside, standing in a group, facing the incoming cluster of gunslinging bullies.

"Where did they get all those weapons on Arcadia?"

"I don't know." Logan assumed they'd stumbled on an old town that had Shifted years earlier. It was the only explanation.

The sky turned from ochre to black as the sun gave its final descent. The timing was impeccable, making the approaching army doubly ominous. He counted twenty, which wasn't bad, considering Shelter had a hundred, but these men and woman were armed, and they only had a spattering of weapons. Homemade bows and sharpened rocks were no defense against a crew with six-shooters.

His tablet beeped, indicating the connection was live.

Device 256615.21 (Operator Isla F)

We're here. Stall them and keep your heads down.

He showed Ruby. "Who do these guys think they are?" she asked.

Logan tried to picture Anders Lawrence, but struggled to recall his features. Caesar was a complete stranger. He wanted to tell them to stay out of it, or they'd get everyone killed, but refrained. If Milton had sent this many men to Shelter, it wasn't just for their supplies. He'd take it all.

The crew neared their town, each carelessly holding guns. The leader was a tall woman sporting a cowboy hat and a western vest, complete with bowler tie. He wondered why they chose to fight other humans, when they'd be so much stronger as an alliance.

"People will be people," he whispered, and Ruby nodded in agreement.

"Which one of you is Logan?" the tall woman called. Her voice was raspy, like her mouth was filled with sawdust.

Herald, the first person from the town on Arcadia, raised his hand. "I'm Logan."

The woman moved so fast, Logan didn't register the action until Herald clutched his stomach, dropping to the ground.

"Now, should I keep guessing, or will the real Logan step forward?"

Logan passed Ruby the tablet and thought about the message. *Stall them.*

He walked by Herald, who'd stopped squirming, blood

spilling from his mortal wound. Tears burned the edges of his eyes, but he fought the reaction, trying to stay tough for what was coming. "Who are you?" he demanded.

"You can call me Annie," she said.

He assumed it was a rip-off of the female Wild West gunslinger. "I'm Logan. Are you here for the crop yield? Because it's not ready yet."

Her laugh was throaty. "Where's the tower?"

"I've dismantled it."

"Why?" She came closer, and he smelled her body odor. The group leered at the townsfolk, like bulls trying to escape the starting gates at a rodeo.

He couldn't tell them about Carmichael, or the operatives approaching Shelter that very moment.

"Show me." She bumped his shoulder as she walked over the man she'd just killed in cold blood without so much as a glance.

Logan understood they were doomed. Milton, a man he'd never met, would take Shelter. He'd spent a decade on Arcadia, building a home for their residents, and it would all be stripped away because of a power-hungry lunatic from up north.

Two men followed Annie, and they shoved Logan forward when he slowed by Ruby. He met her gaze, then looked at the tablet, hoping she got the message.

Ruby put the device under her shirt.

"Where the hell is Braxton?" Annie asked her sidekicks.

"Shoulda been coming in from the west like you said," someone answered.

"Where's the tower?" Annie investigated the scattered pieces of electronics. Her eyes widened when she saw everything collected into a trailer. "Where were you bringing it?"

"Nowhere," Logan said. "I was moving it."

"What's its purpose?" Annie inquired.

"I wanted to set up a radio channel, so towns could communicate." Logan keeled over when a goon decked him in the gut. He fought for breath as the guy hauled him up by the collar.

"Try again." Spittle flecks hit Logan's face.

The locals made noises as the crew circled them. Someone had a torch taken from near the firepit, and he waved the fire threateningly to the residents, then touched it to the thatched roof of the closest building. The dried husk of grass spread the flames until the entire structure was ablaze, all within seconds.

Logan grimaced, prepared for a second strike when he spotted two silhouettes through the smoke from the edge of town. They wore the same western clothing, but they weren't holding revolvers. Annie's crew didn't seem to see the newcomers.

If they wanted Logan to stall, he would. "We were bringing it across Arcadia to another town. A new place."

Annie appeared genuinely shocked by the information. "Is that so?"

"On the other side of the chasm."

"Milton's Canyon," she corrected.

"Sure. Whatever you want to call it."

The crew neared his wife, and a man clutched Ruby's wrist. She pushed him and was slapped in return. Logan tried to get to her, but the duo with Annie firmly held him. "Point to it on a map, and we'll let you live."

"You'll leave us alone?" he asked.

Annie bared her yellowed teeth. "No, but you won't be shot. The town will burn, and we'll take everything worth bringing to Milton."

Ruby struggled with the guy, who clearly had ill intents

on his mind. Fury burned through Logan.

He recognized Anders and who he assumed was Caesar lifting their assault rifles, and locked gazes with the man from his past, even from fifty yards away. Anders gave him the slightest of nods, and Logan shouted, "Everyone down!" He dropped to his knees and saw Ruby kick her attacker in the crotch, then dive into their house as the bullets flew.

Logan lay flat on the ground, and Annie fell beside him, her cheek landing with a sickening thud. Her eyes glazed over, and she didn't flinch, even as she died.

INTERLUDE

Christine

Near the Arcadia Forest, Indiana

Gunther adjusted his glasses, explaining to Christine how the device worked. "It's only theoretical, since we've had no ability to test the Shift. It's based on Logan's schematics, and from what you're telling me, he used it to leave Colorado ten years ago."

Christine viewed the clock, finding it had twenty hours remaining before the energy fluctuations to Arcadia would optimize for a Shift.

"We have a problem, though," Gunther said.

"What's that?"

"It's better to show you." Gunther opened a laptop and accessed a file on the desktop. Christine saw a live feed of them standing in the LTC tent. She glanced at the corner of the space, then waved. Her arm moved on the screen. LTC has some seriously impressive surveillance gear. It was no wonder the man that hired her wanted control of the company.

Gunther clicked on the video and played it. Harrison entered the tent with his assistant and the kid from Carmichael. He opened the case with a keycard and presented the tablet to the pair.

"He knows," she said.

"Yep."

"How did he get the card?"

"One of my team, I guess. I'll have to investigate who is missing and—"

"Don't bother." Christine reached over his shoulder and powered the camera system off.

"Why did you do that?" Gunther turned, and she pulled a gun out, screwing on a silencer attachment.

She stepped back a few feet to avoid the spatter and watched Gunther slip to the tarp below him. The same tarp he didn't appear to notice as they'd arrived. That was the problem with tech guys. They were so detail-oriented with their projects, but were oblivious to the real world.

Christine rolled the body up and whistled shrilly. The soldier gazed at the covered LTC rep, then at her. "Dispose of this. Quietly."

"Yes, ma'am."

Christine held the device when he left. Senator Rutherford was getting too antsy, and Gustafsson hadn't responded to her last two messages. Christine was planning on traveling to Arcadia alone, so she could speed up the operation, but letting Harrison think he was in control would be better. It wouldn't hurt to have a man of his skill set across the Shift. She returned it to the black case, locked it up, and activated the cameras again, linking the feed to her phone.

Harrison could take it and try to escape. Christine would be there waiting.

PART THREE
CONSEQUENCES

1

Caesar was no longer used to battles of this magnitude. His missions tended to be smaller-scale these days. In and outs, with information gathered and as little bloodshed as possible.

Anders hadn't lost his touch at all. He mowed through the enemies without pause or deliberation. It was clear the man wouldn't leave any witnesses, and Caesar accepted that.

Logan had been smart to shout for them to duck, but only half did in the initial rush. Caesar carefully took down the lowest-hanging fruit, killing those at the fringe of the town. With the building burning, their position was blurred slightly, giving them the advantage. People screamed and shouted, clawing their way from Milton's crew.

He was glad their opponents opted to wear matching attire, because it made them much easier targets. Caesar wore his own shoes, while Anders had the pilfered cowboy boots. They both wore the hats they'd taken from Braxton and his pals. The disguises worked well, and saved Caesar from gunfire twice in the first two minutes. Both times, the gunslingers hesitated, believing he was on their side.

He met Anders near the fire, guns raised as they moved in unison. "How many?"

"Seven."

"I got eight."

"Leaving five." Anders waved at the residents of Shelter. "Get to the other side of town!"

A woman approached them, and a man limped in behind her, both holding revolvers they'd swiped from the dead. "I'm Logan, and this is Ruby."

"Take your friends and…" Caesar jumped in front of them when a shot was fired, and it grazed his hat. He gunned down the culprit and counted the kill. That left four.

"We're coming with you," Logan said unsteadily.

"Fine. But don't get in our way." Anders carried on, sighting the empty streets of Shelter while they searched for the last four. Caesar knew they couldn't leave any witnesses to return to Milton, or Shelter would be under attack again as soon as the guy could muster enough soldiers.

Caesar felt more at home with the smell of burning grass and an M4 in his grip than he had in ages. The bodies on the ground stank like body odor and iron.

Ruby and Logan stuck close, but Caesar kept in front of them. Even in the brief interaction, Caesar recognized Dot's features in her son's face.

Shelter was a sprawling village, far larger than he'd suspected, with multiple structures and a nearby lake. He wished he could have entered it in the daylight, being welcomed with open arms rather than fighting twenty equipped relics from the Wild West.

The area grew silent as they scoured for the remaining four. The crackling fire was the only sound. The population lingered across the village, and Caesar saw the bodies of the fallen. Their intervention was fast, but Milton's men had killed at least five locals before being stopped. Caesar told himself those were casualties of war, but he couldn't help but second-guess their decision to act so rashly.

The scene had been degenerating quickly. With the fire, and the men's bloodlust, things would have turned very bad within minutes. They'd done what was necessary, but he still couldn't shake the guilt at the sight of those innocent victims. It fueled his actions while they traversed the town. He spotted something to the right, and ran around the shed, finding a man panting his breaths, shakily clutching a revolver. Caesar didn't hesitate.

Three.

Anders' assault rifle snarled a few rounds, and another fell.

Two.

In the dark, Caesar noticed the hint of a moving silhouette. He shouldered the weapon, planting his feet, and exhaled with his finger hovering at the trigger. He touched it, and the runner grunted as they dropped.

One.

"Across the lake." Logan pointed, and Caesar used his nightscope to view the sprinting escapee.

"I'll go." Anders vanished from sight, and a minute later, the bike's engine roared to life, echoing through the silent village.

The noise grew quieter as he traveled farther, and silence followed a quick rattle of gunfire.

"We killed them all," Caesar assured Logan and his wife, who looked at the spreading flames. "Will he send more?"

"Milton hasn't been to Shelter by himself. He just sends representatives, usually five at a time. They come in, wave their guns around and take what they want, but they've never harmed us," Ruby said.

"Why the change?" Caesar asked.

"It was the tower. They'd heard rumors of it, and I think Milton wanted it for himself."

"What does it do?"

"I had hopes to recreate my Shift device on a larger scale, but didn't have enough power," Logan admitted. "I thought if we could tap into whatever Isla left in Carmichael, we might get home."

Caesar did his best to describe Isla's base, and Logan listened intently. "Then I don't need this. She's already done the heavy lifting."

"Why didn't we Shift when the countdown ended?"

"Because someone didn't want you to," Logan said.

Caesar hung back while Logan spoke to his people, trying to calm them. He was clearly a respected leader. The group stood somberly, mourning the loss of their friends.

Anders returned on the bike and shut it off, gesturing at the bodies. "Let's burn them while we have a fire."

They spent an awkward hour, with Ruby and Logan volunteering to help them strip the dead and take anything of value. They'd refused anyone else's help, claiming it was their duty to Shelter. Caesar was astonished to find small children among them, as well as a couple of elderly folks, and every decade accounted for in between.

Anders and Caesar dragged the bodies to the burning building and hauled the crew one at a time, adding more fuel from a woodpile to ensure the pyre turned the nightmare into ash before the sun rose. Other residents transferred supplies from the vicinity, mitigating the threat level of the fire.

When they finished, Caesar pulled off his hat, inspecting the hole in it. He'd been inches from dying. Caesar tossed it into the flames.

He glanced at the antiquated guns, the stacked ammunition, and piles of folded, bloodied clothing. "At least Shelter stands a chance next time."

"Let's make sure there isn't a next time," Anders said.

"We're not heading north to confront this Milton character." Caesar looked at the townsfolk in the darkness shrouding Shelter. "We're getting everyone to Carmichael and off this godforsaken planet."

"We can't drive them all."

"Then we walk."

"Three hundred miles?"

"Do you have a better idea?" Caesar asked.

"How about the river?" Logan had approached without Caesar noticing, suggesting he was too tired to be effective.

"What?" Anders rolled his shoulders.

"In the canyon—we'll save half the trip by using it. Actually, it goes underground and stops thirty miles from where Carmichael is," Dot's son said. Logan had shaggy, dirty blond hair and a matching beard. His eyes were a penetrating blue, and he looked spent after the altercation.

"You want to take a hundred people from here, hike into the canyon, then build enough boats to carry us through the gorge and underground for another fifty miles?" Caesar lifted his eyebrows in disbelief.

"That about sums it up."

"How do you know about the tunnel?" Anders asked.

"Because I scouted it before Shelter existed," Ruby said.

Caesar sighed heavily with exhaustion. "Can we decide

in the morning? I don't like to make decisions of this magnitude when I'm groggy."

"Sure. You can sleep in our bed," Ruby told him.

"Nah, I couldn't put you out."

"I'll keep watch." Anders reclaimed his assault rifle, gazing at the dark horizon. "What if Braxton wasn't the only secondary crew?"

"Annie mentioned Braxton, but not anyone else," Logan informed them.

"See?" Caesar patted Anders on the back. "We can't help them if we're sleeping at the wheel. You need rest."

"If you insist."

Logan stayed near the fire, and Ruby led them into their home.

Anders kicked off his boots and stole a blanket, spreading it on the floor. "You take that, I'll use this."

"Fine by me." Caesar lowered to the bed and was asleep before his head hit what passed for a pillow.

---

*E*vidence of the storm was everywhere as their group emerged from the mental hospital. The shutters were loose, tilted on the windows, but otherwise, it was intact. John supposed the building had been there for decades, and had surely endured a lot of inclement weather in that span.

They buried Peter now that the horror was finished, using tools from an old maintenance shed. No one spoke openly. Ben, Louise, Jamal, Maya, and Gemma just stared at the unmarked grave for a moment, and John left them to it.

Eventually, they strode by the car, and he shouldered

his bag, ready for the last leg of their trek. Carmichael was a mere ten miles down the plains, and after his recent few days, it felt attainable.

"That was as strong a storm as I've ever seen." Ben broke the silence.

"Is it over?" John noticed the temperature was lower. Usually, he'd already be sweating this early in the morning on Arcadia, but it had to be five degrees cooler.

Gemma shook her head. "No, but today is clear." She smiled faintly. "So far."

John didn't mind walking, but he'd never been much of a hiker. When he was younger, he'd enjoyed meandering around Carmichael, going as far as the Wests' place, then home. He liked the solitude and often ventured off alone, listening to music with earbuds.

That was different from journeying ten miles a day with a heavy pack through unforgiving terrain. His legs were tired, but he already sensed a difference in them. They were getting stronger, thicker at the thighs and calves.

Negotiating the prairies was tough, with the grass giving way below his feet. It made the steps spongy, adding to the effort required. In other stretches, the ground became harder, the waist-high fields growing sparser.

Ben pushed their pace, not willing to get stuck in between the hospital and Carmichael should a storm surprise their resident meteorologist, Gemma. She could sense them with uncanny ability, making John wonder just what her story was. Ben could claim that was a lost art, a skill gone with the ages, but it felt supernatural to John.

She was sullen today, not her usual grinning self, and John tried not to bother her, as much as he wanted to console her for losing Peter.

Jamal and Maya talked about what the future might hold, while Ben and Louise didn't add any commentary on the subject.

"My parents would be shocked to see me," Jamal said.

"Mom would flip," Maya told him.

"How long have you been gone?" John asked her.

"Thirteen years, I think."

John let out a whistle. "Where did you Shift from?"

Most of them didn't discuss that moment of their lives. They kept their stories close to their chest, likely trying to forget where they came from before Arcadia.

"I was a ranger at Yellowstone," she said. "We'd encountered a few dead wolves, and they sent me to investigate. They seemed to be poisoned, and we were concerned there was an issue with the groundwater. It was late December… two days from Christmas. I planned on going home the next morning. I had my bags packed, and gifts for my family in my suitcase." Maya beamed at the memories. "I never made it. I've always wondered if my sister and mom got their presents."

Tears fell down her cheeks, and she wiped them. "I don't even know how it happened. One step I was tracking wolf prints, the next I showed up a few miles west of this position."

John figured the discussion was over when Louise chimed in. "I came five years ago." She looked to be about forty, with wavy light brown hair. "I'd embarked on a journey of self-discovery." She watched the sky as they walked, her steps sure on the uneven grasslands. "I'd lost someone…a child."

Ben took her hand while she spoke. "I tried to cope. I did therapy, with and without my husband. After a year, I couldn't take it, and left him. So there I was, mourning my son on the Oregan coast…I walked into the ocean, determined to join him."

John's chest constricted.

"It wasn't meant to be. I opened my eyes and I was on Arcadia, in the middle of a field, surrounded by glowing insects. I thought it was heaven, and in some ways, it is."

"Peter found her less than a week after she arrived," Ben said, and glanced in the direction they'd come from.

John counted himself lucky that he'd Shifted with his town. He doubted he was strong enough to survive an entire week without supplies or companionship.

The group didn't speak for a while as they marched toward Carmichael. Ben only slowed the pace when they reached the edge of the forest. "This is where things get tricky."

"Do you have another Repulsor?" John asked him.

"No. Jamal had it. We have little need for it at the Den, since the Howlers don't venture that far." Ben eyed the woods, then the sky. "If we go quickly, we can get to the town's border by dusk."

"Do the Howlers attack during the day?"

"They will, but only if you stumble into their territory. They're mostly nocturnal, so I'm hoping they're asleep," he said.

John was glad to have a revolver, and Jamal still carried a rifle. It might not do much if they encountered a group of predators, but having the weapon gave him confidence to enter the treeline.

The moment his foot stepped in, a howl carried from somewhere in the distance.

2

"*I*t's gone," Amelia whispered. She walked along Carmichael's main street, viewing the destruction. The garden Dot and Sharon had worked tirelessly to create was torn up, the soil spread around the park.

"It's not salvageable," Dot said. "We'll have to restart."

"Don't bother now. If we're about to get snow, let's wait it out." Dozens of residents wandered aimlessly, examining the devastation the tornadoes had unleashed on their homes.

Dot glanced toward her diner. "All this destruction, and the storm spared my diner."

The burned factory down the street was in shambles, ripped to shreds. Isla's flower shop remained standing too, but most of the other buildings had been devastated.

Her deputies were on the road, scouring every square mile of Carmichael in case someone needed help. Their only saving grace was that ninety percent of their population slept at the storage facility at the edge of town.

She'd never examined Isla's shop, and she left Dot when Sharon arrived, holding a checklist of things they needed to do.

Amelia tried the front, which was locked, and moved to the alley, seeking the delivery door. The handle turned, and she pulled it open. The back of Isla's store had three fridges, with clear glass showcasing her flowers. They were bundled in groups of similar colors. An unfinished bouquet sat on her workbench, the petals wilted. In the salesroom, everything had died, and the fragrant floral scent had a hint of decay to it.

"What was your plan?" she asked Isla, wishing the woman had survived the horror she'd endured. Isla had spent a decade getting Carmichael to Shift. She'd assembled a collection of weapons, bringing soldiers…and then was killed before she could travel to find Logan, her co-founder.

Isla had been so kind to her that first night at poker. It didn't make sense that she could be behind the transportation of this many people. Every death they'd experienced was on her, but that didn't matter, because Isla was dead too.

Amelia sat on a chair and lowered her head. She was so tired.

Yesterday, she'd been hopeful they could keep it together for a couple of weeks until Logan showed up. Now she wasn't so certain. If Caesar's pal Harrison was on the job, were they trying to move Carmichael home? Why hadn't anything happened yet?

Amelia stayed put for a few minutes, her mind reeling with unanswered questions.

She thought about Dot's house and the locked basement, and wondered why it bothered her so much. Amelia stood to view the red-haired woman across the street.

"Chief, can you come to the sanctuary? Over." Haley was only supposed to contact her in case of an emergency.

"I'll be right there," she said. Amelia unlocked the place and went out to the sidewalk where her squad car was parked. Luckily, the toppled tree beside it at Mrs. Lemar's had just taken off the passenger mirror. With the broken rear window, her ride was in rough shape.

Pastor Odell was outside the fence surrounding their home base, holding a Bible and speaking with Candice Dawson, Summer's mom.

"Good afternoon," Amelia said.

"Our house is gone," the woman grumbled. "We were a year from paying it off. I doubt my insurance covers storms on another planet." She laughed hysterically, and it quickly morphed into a sob. "What are we supposed to do?"

Others met up, and Amelia heard similar stories. From an early count, a quarter of the homes in Carmichael had been totaled last night. Even if they were on Earth, a rebuild would take ages.

She stuck around, trying to reassure them, but nothing could console the group.

Amelia thought about the timer at Isla's base, and guessed they had a measly five hours before it reached zero. Would it give them a second chance to escape Carmichael near the border?

She realized why Haley had called her there once she climbed to the rooftop. Eldon held the Repulsor with shaky hands.

"It must have fried." Eldon offered her the small electronic device. "I've tried everything since it stopped emitting the frequency an hour ago."

Amelia accepted it and flipped the apparatus over. It didn't look like much, but she was no expert. She passed it to Eldon, then grabbed his shoulders, staring him in the eyes. "We need you to fix this. Do whatever you can."

"I'll keep at it."

"Eldon, if the Repulsor fails and the Howlers come…"

Amelia left the rest unsaid. The town was in disarray from the night before, and she doubted they could muster much of a defense.

Haley waited for her at the steps, and they returned to the main room. The townspeople looked at Amelia as if expecting instructions. She cleared her throat, observing the people she'd barely known a week ago. "We're going to be okay."

It was obvious they wanted more. Amelia absently set her palm on her holstered handgun, stepping closer. The movie projector was off, and Klein prepared dinner near the open bay doors. The aromatic scent of garlic and onions wafted to her position.

"Carmichael got hit with a terrible storm, and many of you lost your homes," she said. "We need volunteers to sift through the wreckage and safely take anything of value to the town, or of personal importance to you. Do I have…"

Nearly everyone raised their hands.

"Okay." Amelia scanned the crowd, her gaze settling on Helen Lawrence and her daughter. "Helen and Carly can lead the job, and Mr. Tucker will ensure you have safety gear like goggles, gloves, and hardhats."

Mr. Tucker nodded. She'd have to apologize for demanding so much of him, but he'd proven such a reliable asset.

Vince cleared his throat. "I have some equipment at the gas station I can lend out."

"Thank you, Vince."

He stood taller, and his son shone with pride.

"Has anyone checked on Clive?" Amelia inquired.

When they confirmed no one had gone out to the Raddison farm, she mentally added it to her list.

"Are the Howlers coming?" Karl asked.

Rumors spread quickly in Carmichael. "Eldon's going

to fix the Repulsor."

"What if he can't?" Hank coughed and took a cigarette from a pack in his pocket. He moved to light it, but Faith slapped his arm, stopping him.

"He will," she half-heartedly assured them.

Haley tapped Amelia and whispered in her ear, "Do we mention the Shift?"

Amelia shook her head. "I don't want to worry them."

"Are we ever going home?" Mrs. Henderson asked.

"Yes, because my son's coming with Anders." Dot came from the entrance. The sun cast a long shadow onto the floor. "We've experienced something traumatic, and that storm is the least of it. Keep close to your neighbors tonight and hold your heads high, because no matter what's occurred on Arcadia, we'll rebuild this town stronger and better than before."

The speech from their matriarchal leader appeared to bolster spirits, and they scurried away as Klein advised them dinner was being served.

"That went well," Haley said.

"Where's Freddy?" Amelia hadn't heard from the deputy in a few hours.

"He was checking on Kong."

"Let's go."

Fifteen minutes later, they parked by the field with the catchment system. Miraculously, the series of containers remained upright, and Kong perked up when he spotted them approaching. "It worked!"

Amelia viewed the white plastic cubes, finding water sitting halfway up a few of them. Others were nearly empty, and Kong explained the funnel system had failed on part of the contraption.

"I figure we collected nearly seventy gallons."

"That's a heck of a storm." Amelia had been so

distracted by the spinning tornadoes, she'd forgotten about the downpour that followed. It had rained for hours, all the way until sunrise, which she'd thought might never arrive.

Haley searched the grounds. "Is Freddy here?"

"He was, but he left to check on his parents' place. Belinda was there with the animals."

"Can you bring Haley into town?"

"Sure, but where are you going?" Kong asked.

"I have a detour." Amelia took a last glance at the water. "Nice job, Kong. I mean it."

"Thanks," he said. They watched her leave, climb into the car, and drive away.

She pulled over on the gravel road, rolled her window down, and stared at the cornfields. Only a fraction of the fields were destroyed by the storm, which was a blessing. She'd rather the crops be decimated than the houses, but the weather gods had other ideas.

Images of her time in Carmichael flashed through her mind, and she gritted her teeth. The flat tire outside of Dot's. The woman lending her a car. Finding Summer Dawson and Carly Lawrence in Caesar's motel room after Gus and his goons chased them. So many things had happened in a week, and she'd processed none of it. She closed her eyes, seeing the dead from the initial fire and Howler attack. Mayor Vivian's bright yellow shirt, covered in bloodstains...

"Ahhhhhhhh!" Amelia screamed, clutching the steering wheel. She hit it with her palms, and the horn sounded. "This is who you always were. You just didn't know it yet."

Caesar saw something in her, and the people of Carmichael now looked to her for guidance. It was her destiny to lead them home to Earth.

Amelia took another few minutes to watch the field

sway in the wind before returning to reality. As she drove, her breaths were calm, her focus on the upcoming tasks. There were only four hours before the timer once again hit zero, and Amelia wanted to be prepared for anything.

Belinda waved as she entered the property. Freddy's lovely wife had a cluster of hay, and fed it over a fence to a pair of white-speckled horses. The scene reminded her of an old painting.

She parked and strode to the pasture. The area was untouched by the storm, and Amelia was grateful for it, given the tragedy the Wickenhouses had already endured with the veterinarian's murder.

"How are the animals?" Amelia asked.

"They're rambunctious. The dogs were terrified last night, and rightfully so." Belinda smiled as the horses took the remaining hay. "Want to see them?"

"Sure." Amelia had thought about getting a dog, then remembered how demanding her shifts were. They walked the fence line and ended at the barn. A cacophony of barks escaped through the door, some playful, others somber.

They entered and were immediately accosted by a cocker spaniel. Her tail thrummed like a conductor at the crescendo of a sonata. "Who's this?" Amelia knelt and got licked on the nose.

"That's Buttercup." Belinda scratched another dog behind the ear. "She belongs to Faith, but with everything going on, most took us up on the offer to house their pets until we return home."

They had an assortment of kennels across the barn of varying sizes. A door had been propped open on the side, leading to a fenced yard for the animals to roam. Amelia watched as the animals played. Some drank water; others slept, the activity from last night exhausting them. She wished she could curl up and do the same. At a quick guess, the Wickenhouses had twenty-five dogs.

"They don't fight?"

"There are a couple of tougher ones that we're keeping in the shed," Belinda said. "I let them out most of the day, and they stalk the perimeter. I think they're keeping the Howlers away. They come when I call for dinner. Thankfully, the town came through on those supplies. People don't have much stored up for themselves, but they sure had ample food for their pets."

"Mind if I take Freddy?" She finished a belly rub on Buttercup. The dog met her gaze when she stopped the contact, as if demanding more.

"Go ahead. We finished dinner early." Belinda led her to the house, and Freddy exited.

"Hey, Chief," he said.

"Should we go to the sanctuary tonight?" Belinda asked.

Amelia didn't know. "Maybe it's safer here, since you have a patrol. The Repulsor's not working."

"Damn," Freddy said. "Lock up the dogs before sunset and bring the pigs in. Leave Rusty and Hammer out."

"Okay." Belinda pecked her husband on the cheek. "I'll stay indoors with your mother. She's been antsy for a puzzle."

"I love you," he said, and Amelia gave them space.

Freddy halted at his truck a minute later. "Where to?"

"Dot's," she said without further explanation.

3

Summer nervously paced the tent, unable to stop the rapid beating of her heart.

"Where's Reggie?" Harrison had his dress shirt off and wore a sleeveless undershirt. She caught sight of the tattoo on his arm.

"He'll be here," Wanda assured him.

"What's the tattoo?" Summer asked, hoping to distract herself with mundane conversation.

"Huh?" Harrison glanced at it. "I always forget it's there."

"He did it to trick Caesar," Wanda said.

"That's not why—"

There were three vertical lines, each slightly embellished with an artist's flourish.

"It's the three pillars. There are countless takes on the theory. Caesar and I both got them when I convinced him to work for me."

"You embedded a tracking device into him," Wanda said.

"Isn't that like, illegal or something?" Summer asked.

"It's for his own protection." Harrison donned another shirt, and instead of his usual business attire, he opted for a black crewneck t-shirt and put on his shoulder holster, then slipped a light jacket over it that could have easily said *FBI* on the back. "It's time to leave, Wanda."

"But…"

"The moment they realize we stole the Shift device and entered the alien woods, they'll bring you in for interrogation. You don't want to be on the brunt end of Christine's methods, believe me."

Wanda looked around the room like she had to pack, but no one had any possessions besides their phones. She clutched it to her chest, then hugged Harrison, holding on for a while. "Be careful, Harry."

"I will."

"What do I tell Fatina?"

"Escort her to the safehouse. My daughter too. Say Caesar needs my help. She'll understand," he said.

"Take good care of this girl." Wanda hugged Summer next.

Harrison exited and returned with Sheriff Lyle. He tipped his hat to Summer and motioned for Wanda to follow him. "I'll get her situated, and to the airport in the morning," Lyle said.

"Thanks for the help," Harrison told him while they shook.

Wanda gave them a pleading look, then left the tent.

"Will they let Wanda leave?" Summer asked.

"Christine hasn't been seen all afternoon, and the soldiers are getting jumpy. Word is there's been a Howler cluster spotted on the east side of the fence, which makes our lives easier."

"What are the Howlers doing?"

Harrison grinned and stared at the road to the south. "I think someone may have headed that way earlier and dumped a bunch of raw meat."

Summer had wondered where he'd gone a few hours

ago. "Convenient."

"Very." He checked his phone, showing her the display. *1:17:01.*

"Great, just when I was vibing." Summer walked outside, surprised to find how dark it had gotten. Stars shone brightly, and she viewed the light pollution from Jackson on her right.

A hundred yards away was the border to the forest, with the floodlights humming along with the electric fence. A few soldiers lingered near Christine's personal tent, but they didn't seem concerned. Chatter emerged from their residence, and Summer strolled over, finding ten of them sitting at a table, playing poker. She didn't let them see her and returned to Harrison.

"When do we go?" Summer eyed the LTC tent.

"I wanted Reggie here."

A pair of headlights shone from the direction of the interstate, and a military four-wheeler braked at the start of their camp. A female soldier guided a man from the passenger seat, keeping a gun pointed at his back.

"This man was caught trespassing on foot," she said. "He claims you asked him to come, and that Ms. Hawkstone approved of his presence. Is that accurate?"

Harrison nodded. "Yes."

"I've tried to contact Ms. Hawkstone, but can't. I trust you're telling the truth," the woman said. "I'm leaving him in your custody." She drove off, and only when she was out of sight did Harrison approach him.

"Reggie!" he proclaimed, and Summer got a good look at the IT guy. He was tall and thin, with wavy dark hair and a pronounced nose. Reggie smiled at his boss, but it seemed forced. He had a green Martian giving a 'thumbs-up' on his t-shirt.

"What is this place?" Reggie stared at the fence. "You

said it was alien, but damn…those trees." He must have noticed Summer, because he gave a slight head tilt. "Hey, I'm Reginald, but you can call me Reggie."

"Summer."

"Like the season," he said.

"Right."

"Enough with the pleasantries. We have work to do," Harrison said.

They rushed into the tent, and Reggie removed his backpack, pulling a laptop out. "Okay, I've gone through the files you sent, and that was some wild stuff. Logan's old theories were radical, but since you claim he actually went to this other planet, I had to take it all seriously."

"How so?" Harrison asked.

"He thought it might be possible to Shift to ten different worlds, with Arcadia being the best option because of its similarities to Earth. He was only going based on what he called temporal frequency mirroring." Reggie had a graph open, but Summer couldn't understand what any of the data points implied. "Tracking down where the TFM would operate was a struggle, but he chose a location in Colorado to test it, given that the altitude made the connection crisper."

"Then why can we Shift from Carmichael?"

"His co-founder, Isla, took these files and built something…a powerful device that might have raised some red flags from a"—Reggie glanced at the door and spoke lower— "nuclear fission standpoint."

"She's using nuclear energy?" Harrison blurted.

"In a sense. Where she bought some of this stuff, I couldn't tell. She worked in secret without the board knowing, and the files were mostly hidden," he said, typing quickly. "But I found this in Logan's database, and I believe that's what she created."

The detailed image showed a series of towers linked to a central sphere. "She built this in Carmichael?" Summer asked.

"That's what I'm assuming," Reggie answered.

"What was Logan's reason for this?" Harrison gestured at the screen.

"He wanted to create a permanent link. With one of those on Arcadia, and a matching one here on Earth, you could hypothetically pass through a field at any given moment," he said.

"A connecting tunnel between resource-rich planets and Earth, right in our own backyard," Harrison said.

"Would the base need to be on ground level with Carmichael?"

"No. According to his notes, Logan hypothesized the pair of Shift apparatuses could be up to a thousand miles apart," Reggie said.

Harrison sighed. "I know what Christine's job is."

"What?" Summer peered at the entrance as if saying the woman's name might summon her from thin air.

"She's supposed to bring Logan in so he can build a matching structure at an offsite facility. They're going to manipulate him by threatening to kill everyone in the town if he doesn't comply." Harrison flexed his fingers. "And when he's done, they'll do it anyhow."

Summer gasped, realizing her family and friends were going to die unless someone stopped these bastards. "Can't you help?"

"I'll do my best," Harrison assured her. "Do we have any idea where they'd put the laboratory?"

"I haven't gotten that far."

"Reggie." Harrison grabbed his pack of antacids and chewed two of them. "You'll stay and figure out where LTC is constructing the second location. I need you to do it quietly, because I have a feeling that Christine's boss will shoot first and ask questions later."

"I just got here," Reggie said. "You sure you don't want me coming to Arcadia?"

Harrison appeared to contemplate the option. "No, head south on foot, and stay off the road until the interstate. Then hitchhike to Jackson and contact Sheriff Lyle." Harrison handed him a business card.

"Hitchhike?" Reggie was dumbfounded.

"Go now!" Harrison ordered.

Reggie closed the laptop, pausing at the exit. "I won't fail you." And he was off.

Summer understood Harrison's theory, and when she saw the soldiers drive by in a cart, she couldn't help but feel like a prisoner once again.

"Grab a jacket." Harrison opened a case under his cot and stuck his cell phone in it. He took the one they'd given Summer and dropped another metal device inside. Caesar's boss pressed his index finger on it, and it beeped before smoke billowed from a vent.

"What's that?"

"I don't want anyone tracking us," he said. When he checked inside the black case, only ash remained. He slid it back under the cot and motioned to the street. "It's time."

The LTC tent was being guarded by a single man, and the moment they approached, he took a call on the radio and ventured away. "That was easy," Harrison whispered.

Without turning on any lights, he pushed in, and using the glow of the computer screens to guide him, took the box containing the portable Shift device. The monitor ticked below one hour before the optimal TFM, or whatever Reggie had called it.

Harrison used the keycard to access the container and retrieve the apparatus. He put it into his jacket pocket with no deliberation and led Summer toward the fence. Instead of walking the path that would have soldiers patrolling on carts every ten minutes, they took to the corn. Summer inhaled the heady scent, wondering how many more times she'd be forced into the crops before this adventure was over.

Her shoes were caked with dirt when Harrison stopped, and Summer plucked pieces of cornstalks from her borrowed black jacket.

"Where did I put it?"

The night was dark, but the floodlights gave enough ambiance to see by, even though they were pointed at the fence and forest beyond.

Harrison knelt and dug a sack free, dumping the contents to the soil. He picked up a set of tin snips and tested them, clicking the beak together. They lingered at the edge of the corn, and when the next patrol circled by, he counted to ten and hurried to the barricade they'd been at the other day. She saw the same frayed wire by the electrical box, and Harrison didn't waste time cutting it. The section of fence stopped humming.

"Won't it still be charged?" she asked. "It's all metal."

Harrison pulled out gloves with rubber tips and put them on. "When the power is severed, the segments should stop conducting. It's a safety feature, but better to be careful just in case." He set to the task, cutting chain link after chain link. Since nothing sparked, Summer supposed he was correct.

"It's harder than it looks," he grunted. By the time he had it pried apart, Summer estimated they had above fifteen minutes left. She went in first, and Harrison tried to follow, but got snagged. "Crap." He slid from the jacket, which held the Shift device, and carefully pulled it loose from the sharp metal. The fabric had a tear, leaving a piece of black behind.

"They're coming," she whispered from within the forest.

The sound of the approaching patrol made Summer panic. Harrison motioned behind a tree, and they ran, hiding as the cart passed. She was certain they'd spot the cut fence or notice the loose wires, but the vehicle didn't slow.

"Thank goodness." Harrison wiped a bead of sweat off his brow. "We're low on time. Can we make it?"

Summer hadn't been to Isla's base, but she'd heard it was behind the corn maze in Carmichael. She tried to picture the town and where they'd entered from, and pointed forward. "It's a mile or so this way."

"Then we'd better hurry." Harrison kept hold of the device as they ran, and Summer prayed the Howlers stuck to themselves.

4

*I*t had become more difficult to see beneath the protection of the dense forest. The sun was nearly gone for the day when John guessed they were approaching the Carmichael border.

Ben's gaze was wary as he searched the trees for signs of the Howlers. John's own palm was sweaty where he clasped the revolver, and Jamal kept his rifle up.

"What's this?" Gemma walked into a clearing. She looked both ways, and John stepped closer.

"Oh, my God." The woods were torn apart in a straight line, heading directly for his hometown. A short distance off, a second path had been sliced into the forest. "The storm did a number on them." John stated the obvious.

"It was terrible out here," Louise said.

John jogged forward, fearing the worst: that his home and everyone he cared about had been destroyed in the disaster.

"Stop where you are!" Ben called.

Leaves rustled, causing John to discover two Howlers watching them from up high. They dangled from fingered tails, three eyes following each movement of the humans below.

"These are sentries," Ben whispered, pointing deeper in. "They have a nest nearby."

The light dimmed while the sun set, and John recognized a dozen more animals by the reflection of their eyes. He'd gotten as far as the Den, survived extreme storms, and was so close to home, he could smell the cornfields, and now he'd die before knowing if Haley had survived.

"Keep walking," Louise said, taking the lead.

John did, trying not to let fear overwhelm him. They'd fought plenty of the creatures, but from a rooftop with ample ammunition. There was no advantage here for their group.

Gemma ran when the first Howler dropped from its hiding space. The rest followed in quick succession, traipsing through the forest beyond the shredded trees. Bits of bark and leaves were everywhere, left in the tornado's wake. Maya tripped on part of a lingering trunk, and Jamal caught her, dropping the rifle.

The Howler took the opportunity, lunging for Jamal's partner. John intervened as the animal clawed at her stomach, shooting it in the hindquarters. The beast roared and changed focus, while the rest surrounded them.

Jamal re-gripped the rifle, muttering his thanks, and they backed up into one another, facing the enemy in a circle.

"What do we do?" Gemma asked.

"We fight." Ben wielded a hatchet, but otherwise, all they had were walking sticks.

Some animals kept to the shadows as others stalked into the clearing. He'd be lucky to kill three of them before his bullets were spent, and those would have to be expert shots.

Light shone from the north, and it took him a second

to realize it was a truck. The driver honked repeatedly and went as far as crashing into a pair of Howlers before braking. A woman stuck her upper body out of the window and sat on the door, aiming an assault rifle at the Howlers. She continued to honk, using her knee while firing.

The animals ran at breakneck speed, fleeing to their nest in the woods.

John relaxed until he recognized who had saved them. Lillian Carson didn't lower her weapon, just shifted the focus to them.

"Put it away. They're gone," Ben said.

"You." Jamal protectively stepped in front of Maya.

"You're still alive?" Lillian asked. "Impressive."

"Who's this?" Maya asked.

"She's the one that killed the Benyuks and Freddy's dad," John said.

"Drop the guns."

"I don't think so." John pondered why she'd save them from certain death, only to kill them. "You won't hurt us."

Lillian sighed with resignation, then dropped the barrel. She left the truck running and stood at the door. "Hop in."

"How did you know we were here?" John asked.

"I didn't. Just lucky, I guess." Lillian gestured to the truck's box. "Get inside."

Ben and Louise hesitated, but the howls returned, making the decision.

Lillian pointed at John. "Up front."

He waited until Gemma had gotten into the box and did as Lillian demanded.

"Pass that to me." She nodded at his gun.

John relinquished it to her. "Is Carmichael…"

"It's fine. Some homes are trashed, but it could have been far worse." Lillian's brow had a streak of black grease.

"Any deaths?" he asked.

"How should I know? I'm not subscribed to the newsletter, okay?"

She checked behind them, confirming the guests were seated, and turned around, driving toward town. "I admit I killed some people."

He tensed, letting her talk.

"We couldn't find Isla's base, so Jamal was the only way I could locate him."

"Why is that so important to you?"

Lillian stared at the bumpy path as she slowly crept over the carnage. It eased as she exited the forest's border and entered farmland. "I doubt you'd understand."

"You'd already murdered them."

Lillian flinched and finally glanced at him. "I'm going to tell you something, and you decide what to do with it."

John's heart rate picked up. "I'm listening."

"Caesar's wife is alive, and she's running an operation to connect Earth with Arcadia. Her boss is—"

"The senator?"

"No. Yes, he's part of it, but..." Lillian seemed unsure how to explain the situation. "There are five major organizations, like the ones Anders Montrave and Caesar Hawkstone operate under. Christine joined someone on the outside. He's bad news."

"How do you know?"

"Because he's my boss too." Lillian got to the road, and the ride became smoother. "Mr. Gustafsson wants Logan, but won't allow Carmichael to return."

"He's going to leave us here?" John asked.

Lillian blinked slowly. "In a sense."

"He'll kill us."

"Yes. I've done things I'm not proud of, John, but Isla wasn't as innocent as she claimed. She knew his plan was to have the town Shift back to Earth, only to be slaughtered. I couldn't allow that."

"Suddenly you're altruistic?"

"There are no rights and wrongs in my line of work. We keep the power balance steady, meaning we live in the gray zone. What I did was justified in my mind. People like Anders and Christine would understand, but maybe not Caesar. He's a self-righteous son of a bitch, and doesn't color outside the lines."

"So having my friend murder Isla is okay with you?"

"It saved the lives of everyone you know and love."

John swallowed a lump in his throat. "It doesn't matter if I'm glad we're alive, you still—"

"Jamal was supposed to lead me to Logan so I could warn him. If they bring Logan back and use the Shift, you'll all die, and Mr. Gustafsson will have access to Arcadia. He's already constructing a matching power source to Isla's, creating a permanent bridge between worlds. This venture is worth a fortune, and he believes there are other planets reachable."

"And I'm supposed to trust that you actually want to help us? Why?"

Lillian Carson slowed to turn down a narrow gravel road, then halted. "Because someone reminded me there were other options in life."

"Caesar?"

She nodded. "And Amelia. I don't know what happened to me, but damn…I used to stand for something."

"But you killed the Wests…"

Lillian frowned. "Where did you get that idea?"

"Caesar said—"

"I did nothing of the sort. Mr. West was half-deaf, and his wife was no better. They got up at the crack of four

A.M., so I figured their place was as good as any for the deal," she explained.

"If you didn't shoot them," he said, "who did?"

---

*A*melia watched Dot's place, considering if she should just go up to the door and knock. The diner owner was home, her sedan parked in the driveway.

The red-haired woman paced in her living room, a dark shadow behind the curtains. She hadn't opened them in the hour since Amelia had arrived across the street.

"Are we going in?" Freddy asked.

She checked the time and reached for the radio. "Haley, come in. Over."

"*Deputy Paulson in position at the border. Over.*"

"The Shift is supposed to occur in a few minutes. Let me know if you see anything. Over."

"*Will do, Chief. Over.*"

Amelia was in a constant state of anxiety. The Repulsor hadn't been fixed, and the countdown from Isla's base was nearing completion. She couldn't figure out how to connect the computer system to the frequency, so she expected it to falter again. It was better to keep them in the relative safety of their sanctuary, with fences and armed guards on the rooftop in case of a Howler attack.

"We haven't finished our search for Lillian," Amelia said. "Why am I wasting my time worrying about Dot's basement?"

Freddy shrugged and knocked on the dash. "Let's go."

"All right." Amelia felt lost at sea without a lifejacket. The town was in disarray after the storm had displaced them. "Where's the nearest border?"

Freddy pointed east. "Toward Jackson."

Carmichael seemed different today as she drove. Darker. Colder.

Lightning flashed repeatedly. Freddy frowned deeply. "Is that another storm?"

"I hope not." Amelia doubted they could take another hit like last night's and survive.

She kept on moving, checking the clock to estimate the time remaining. They parked at the boundary with two minutes to the end of the countdown and exited the squad car. Freddy held the rifle, and Amelia instinctively carried her handgun. She reached for her hat and put it on, then adjusted her badge.

The air grew heavy, and the trees blew with the increased speed of the wind. Her fingertips tingled, and the ground below her feet vibrated subtly. She suspected the closer you were to Isla's base, the stronger the reaction.

The rustling leaves began changing.

5

"Here we are…" Harrison touched the device once the countdown on his app showed zeroes.

"Why haven't we Shifted yet?" Summer asked.

"Are you certain this is the right spot?" Harrison tapped the screen.

"You'd better hurry," a woman said. Christine emerged from the trees, carrying a pack and holding an assault rifle.

"What are you doing here?" Harrison demanded.

"Going to Arcadia."

"I don't think so," Caesar's boss quipped.

Christine approached with caution. "You have about thirty seconds to use that to connect with the TFM, or you're staying on Earth."

Summer wished she knew what to do. They couldn't bring Christine. The woman was a nightmare.

"Fine. Get us to Arcadia, then explain yourself," Harrison said.

Christine took the device and flipped a small switch on the side. "Was that so—"

The air shimmered, and Summer's breath caught in her lungs. One instant she was in the alien forest; the next they were beside a barn.

Kong rose from a lawn chair by the entrance, jumping in surprise. His gun lifted, as did Harrison's. Kong hesitated on who to target, so Summer nudged him in the proper direction. "Point it at her!"

Christine just held her weapon in a resting position. "Stop screwing around, Harrison. You wanted to get to Arcadia. Here you are."

Summer inhaled the familiar scent and rushed to Kong, hugging the bartender. She didn't know him well, but he was a family man, a safe, sturdy figure from Carmichael. It only took her a second to notice the fallen trees by the corn maze, and the hole torn into the edge of the landmark.

"Tell me why you came with us," Harrison said. "And how you knew we had it."

Christine smiled, tightening one side of her mouth thanks to her scar. "I have to expedite the mission. Mr. Gustafsson is worried that your operative will fail, and we can't allow that to happen. Isla wasn't supposed to die. This place should have brought them back last week, and we'd finish the connection on Earth, but clearly, someone messed up. If only I'd come myself rather than leave the job to Lillian…"

Summer recalled the woman who'd turned out to be a traitor. "*You* sent her? Lillian's a murderer!"

"It's part of the gig, right, Harrison?"

Summer gaped at the man aiming a gun at his counterpart. "Is that true?"

Harrison cleared his throat.

"A three-star general has more blood on his hands than Lillian and I combined," Christine said. "Now lower that gun before I take it personally."

Harrison relented and nodded at Kong. "Who are you?"

Kong glanced at Summer. "Kong, sir." He patted the shiny chrome star on his chest. "I'm a deputy."

"By whose order?"

"Chief Miller's," Kong said.

"I guess things have changed," Summer murmured. "Did anyone hear from Carly's dad yet?"

"Nothing, but we weren't expecting to for another week."

Harrison knocked on the barn doors. "Do you have the key?"

Christine was champing at the bit to get in, and that told Summer all she needed to know. They couldn't let her into Isla's base.

"Nope. Only the chief has the keycard," Kong said.

Christine had the portable Shift apparatus, and she dropped it, stomping on the electronic panel.

"What did you do that for?" Harrison argued.

"I don't want anyone getting any ideas." Christine peered around the field. "We need your truck."

Lightning flashed in the distance.

"What happened here since I left?" Summer asked Kong.

"John departed with Jamal for the Den, and no one's seen Lillian. The storm nearly tore this place in half, but we made it mostly unscathed. Your house was destroyed," he said, and Summer's heart sank.

"My parents?"

"They're fine. Almost everyone was okay, since they were at the sanctuary."

"Carly…"

"Don't worry, your friend's good."

"Isn't that touching?" Christine held her palm out. "Keys."

Kong dug into his pocket and offered them to the armed woman without further prompting.

Summer noticed his radio when it clicked.

"Border is normal toward the interstate. I saw the tents and a

couple of soldiers; then they were gone. Over." The voice sounded like Haley Paulson's.

"Same on the east edge of town. Over." That was Amelia. *"The weather's getting worse again. I suggest we all reconvene, in case the Repulsor can't be repaired."*

Christine gestured at the truck. "Kong, do you want to drive?"

"I can't leave my posting," he said.

"What about the storm?" Summer asked.

"I'll be okay." Kong grinned at her. When Christine wandered off, with Harrison trailing her, Summer leaned in. "Radio Amelia and let her know who showed up. Her people will kill everyone in town when they retrieve Logan."

Kong grimaced but gave a nod of understanding. "I'm on it."

Summer climbed into the backseat and scooted to the middle of the bench while Christine started it. Harrison looked nervously at Summer, as if trying to decide what to do.

She was back on Arcadia, and as the sky filled with bright flashes, followed by loud booms, Summer realized she'd made a mistake.

———————

*I*t had taken half a day to pack the town of Shelter's supplies, and the first few miles were excruciatingly slow. With nearly a hundred residents joining their expedition, Caesar knew what to expect. Three hundred miles at this pace would see them all dead of old age before getting across the chasm to Carmichael, but they'd picked up the pace. The largest and fittest people took turns dragging the wheeled carts filled with survival gear.

Anders rode ahead on his bike, with a trailer clipped on. It contained the weapons they'd confiscated from Annie and her misfits, along with a few integral pieces of electronics Logan couldn't bear to part ways with.

Caesar let others take turns with the motorbike, hoping it gave some of them reprieve as the elderly or youngest members of the group rode double.

"How far have we gone?" he asked Logan's wife, Ruby, when the sun had descended.

"Seven miles." She marked numbers in a journal, and returned her pen to a pocket. "I can see you're disappointed at the speed, but we can't leave our people at Shelter after the ambush. Milton will eventually learn what you did and retaliate. He's not a forgiving man."

"What *we* did?" Caesar grumbled. "Would you rather we hadn't intervened?"

Ruby took a moment, then sighed. "That's not what I meant."

"Annie and her friend Braxton didn't seem like the type to go easy on you," he said.

Ruby squinted at her husband a few rows ahead, talking with an older man. "The first time they visited, the prospect of extending our reach excited us. We'd already been trading with the Den, Freeport, and Water's Edge, so why not this new village up north?"

Caesar filed the names away, realizing how widespread Arcadia was.

"When the representative from Tombstone came, we thought it would be the usual business. Logan asked him for electronics, as was his custom, and we offered to give them food and water. There are five members of our group that manufacture clothing from the pelts of the animals we hunt, which usually draws the best prices for trading among our communities. The scout asked for a tour, and we naively gave it to him. I showed him our stocked lake, the tools we'd constructed and found on our endless scouting missions, and he recorded everything in a journal."

"What happened next?" Caesar asked. Someone slipped on his bike near the front of their progression, but held on before spilling to the ground. The driver shot Caesar an apologetic look and continued.

"He left in the middle of the night without a word."

"What was his name?"

"That was Braxton," she said.

"Well, he's dead. How long ago was this encounter?"

"Four years after Logan arrived. They didn't return for two years. We'd considered sending a scout north, but Logan's instincts were right. They were dangerous. Word flowed down from the folks in Water's Edge that a man had risen to the head of Tombstone, a cutthroat bastard named Milton. An entire town had transported from the Wild West era in rural Arizona, along with countless old revolvers, outfits, and ammunition. Apparently, one of them figured out how to use the ancient billet press machines, and they're running a tight operation."

Caesar glanced at the collection of guns they'd stolen from Milton's dead companions. "How many are there?"

"Rumors suggest anywhere between fifty and two hundred, but if they sent twenty-something to Shelter, it might be higher." Ruby's shorn, dirty blonde hair appeared gray in the moonlight, and her dense clusters of freckles shadowed her face as she appraised the marching folks. "Do you really think we can leave?"

"Yes." Caesar had seen the room below the barn floor at Isla's base and sensed the dormant power thrumming through the computer network. "Barring unforeseen circumstances, of course."

"That region is prone to storms," Ruby said.

"We've heard."

"Hopefully, they can hold on until we get there. Logan gave up on being rescued years ago."

"Isla seemed like a decent woman," he said.

"Logan thought so." Ruby slowed while Anders stopped at his lead position on his bike. They caught up to him and viewed the landscape as the valley spread out below them. The prairie grass rippled in the breeze, reflecting the moon's crisp white glow. A forest lingered to the right, but the trees were taller and spikier, different than the ones surrounding Carmichael.

"Do the Howlers hang out here?" Anders asked Logan.

"No, but there are other dangers."

"Like what?" Caesar inquired.

Logan motioned to his scope. "Check the sky just above the treeline."

Anders did, and flinched. Caesar slipped his own gun off his shoulder and used the night vision, finding huge, winged creatures skimming the tops. "Are those bats?"

"A variation, only with an eight-foot wingspan," Logan said.

"Do they travel far?"

Ruby nodded. "Wait a moment."

Caesar viewed the five giant bats floating in circles. They moved above the woods to the prairies, descending toward the ground in long, looping turns. One dove; then the other four followed. He heard the hint of a screech in the wind, and they were off, flapping as they took their prizes to their nests.

"What are they eating?" Anders asked.

"We call them grubs. Basically a knee-high burrowing

animal, similar to the gopher but without any teeth. They feed on insects in the grasslands. We don't use them for anything. Their blood reeks, and you can't get it off your skin if you touch it," Logan said. "With the Flitters on the hunt, it's best if we rest for the night."

Word spread like wildfire, and the group began setting up camp. Their five scouts directed the population, and within ten minutes, the place was set up, with a guarded border and a roaring fire. Without the Howlers to think about, Logan figured a fire would bolster their spirits, since they'd upended their lives at Shelter. It was the only home many of them had known following their arrivals on Arcadia, some as far back as two decades ago.

Caesar had walked away from a few things in his life, and could imagine the worry occupying their minds as they sat around the flames, wondering what tomorrow might bring.

They hadn't traveled a great distance, leaving an awful lot remaining. He watched the specks flying through the sky to the south, thinking about Milton. He sounded like every target Caesar ever had on the job.

His primary mission was to see everyone safely to Carmichael and help Shift them, with Logan's aid. But the anxious voice in the back of his mind told Caesar he needed to kill Milton.

6

*T*he walls were closing in around Amelia. The Shift had lasted for mere seconds, then they were back on Arcadia. Even though she'd expected that result, a tiny part of her had hoped the Shift would be permanent and they'd be home, regardless of leaving Caesar, Anders, and John behind.

"We should go." Freddy tapped her shoulder.

She'd been standing like a mannequin, watching the cornfields for five minutes. The stalks swayed dramatically while the wind increased speed. She shivered when a drop of rain landed on her nose. "Do you feel that?"

Freddy rubbed his palms together. "It's getting cold."

"How can it change so fast?" Amelia got to the squad car and cranked the heat on.

"Jamal said that winter would come after the storms." Freddy's door slammed behind him.

She flipped the wipers on as rain pelted the windshield. "I'll take this over another flurry of tornadoes."

"Definitely," he agreed.

Amelia turned around, struggling to see the roads as the intensity of the deluge increased. It shifted from fat drops to balls of hail clinking off her hood and roof. They tore through the bag covering the rear window, making it even colder within the car.

She clutched the wheel with one hand and used the radio with the other. "What's the status, Eldon? Over."

"Chief, it's Kong. Over."

She sat upright. He sounded anxious. "Go ahead. Over."

"I'm at Isla's, and the strangest thing happened…"

Amelia and Freddy shared a worried glance.

"Summer Dawson appeared from thin air." He paused, and Amelia's heart raced. *"A guy named Harrison came with her, and a woman called Christine. Summer asked me to warn you. She said they would kill us once they find Logan."*

Amelia's worst fears grabbed her by the throat and squeezed. "They want to kill us? Who does? Over."

"Christine and whoever she's working for, I assume. Isla, Lillian, this lady, and the senator, I suppose. Over."

"How are things at the base?"

"The ground stopped shaking, but it seems fine otherwise. I should have brought a jacket, because it's snowing. Can you believe it? Over."

"Good work." She flipped to Eldon's frequency. "Eldon, report! Over."

When they didn't get a response from the rooftop at their sanctuary, she pushed the gas pedal harder. "Try Haley."

Freddy did, and after the second attempt, her voice carried through, sounding like she was running.

"…Howlers…dead…fence…"

Amelia balked and raced to town, nearly sliding into the ditch at the sharp turn near the railroad tracks. She recovered, and Freddy almost bashed his head. "Sorry about that."

The lights were off at the storage facility. Their fence remained intact, and gunfire occasionally blasted from the rooftop. The church doors were closed, and Amelia took stock of the situation as calmly as she was able.

Howlers patrolled the street, and she detected a break in the barrier, where the creatures casually meandered through, clawing to the building. The human defenses were weaker tonight, but the guards on the roof still fired, killing the few that entered the property. They hadn't been expecting a full assault, not after last night's storms and the incoming weather system.

"There are too many," Freddy said.

Amelia tried to formulate a plan, but couldn't decide how to react. If the Howlers broke into the building, the people of Carmichael would die.

Ahead, one floodlight kicked on, and Amelia saw Buck Iverson jabbing at a beast with an iron spear while Mr. Tucker fixed the generator. More men and woman approached, among them Haley, firing her rifle to clear a path to the second generator.

With no time to consider a better alternative, Amelia started forward. A truck flew past her, barreling into a cluster of Howlers. It honked loudly, and two figures emerged from the cab, moving to the roof of Kong's vehicle. They opened fire, cutting down row after row of Howlers, until the pack fled the scene.

A second later, the rest of the floodlights snapped on, casting a protective glow over the entire parking lot.

Amelia drove closer and exited, rushing to the truck as Summer climbed from the back. She jumped at Amelia, hugging her. "Are you okay?"

Summer looked older from her recent experiences, and she nodded with tears falling.

"Who's in charge?" a woman demanded, hopping off the hood to the street. She tapped a dead Howler with her boot, then met Amelia's gaze.

"I am," she said, trying to be firm. "Chief Amelia Miller."

"You're the deputy in over her head."

"I'm not—"

"Fix that fence," she ordered. "And someone clear out these bodies. Maybe a few Howlers on stakes will keep them away until I repair the Repulsor."

Amelia watched as the woman strode off with more confidence than she'd ever felt in her life. "Who is that?"

Summer stared. "That's Christine… Hawkstone."

Amelia's jaw dropped. "You mean…"

"Caesar's wife isn't dead," Summer said.

"Jeez," Freddy managed, gazing at the man. "What about you? Caesar's long-lost father?"

"Funny. Name's Harrison Gregory." He offered his hand to Amelia first.

"Caesar's boss," Amelia said.

Harrison reached into his pocket, and she flinched, thinking it might be a handgun, but he removed a tin of antacids, and popped two straight into his mouth. "Someone better repair that fence."

Christine stormed indoors.

"What's this about someone trying to kill us?" Amelia quietly asked.

"We won't let anything happen, mark my word," Harrison assured her, without answering the question.

"Caesar thought his wife was dead—or was that another lie?"

Harrison shook his head. "We all did. Anders and Christine were on a team years ago, and things went south. She was supposedly killed in the line of duty, chasing a biotech weapon, and he ended up in prison trying to save her."

"Then why is she in Carmichael, pretending she's

running our operation?" Amelia asked.

"Because everything was a lie. She took the money and is working for my nemesis, Mr. Gustafsson. He's seeking to build a Shift device to link to Arcadia on Earth, so he doesn't want witnesses. My guess is they take Logan home, and…"

"Leave us here?" Freddy chanced.

"Guess again." Harrison walked toward the fence.

Amelia caught up with him. "What do we do with Christine?"

"Let her think she's in charge until we figure out how to stop them," he said, as if it were that simple.

John added a log to the fire while Gemma hummed an unfamiliar song. Lillian sought refuge in an abandoned cabin near the border. It once belonged to a family who'd sold the property to the Gellers when the father died, and the kids had opted out from the corn business. It was three miles from the Gellers' primary residence, with nothing but remote cornfields in between, making it an ideal place to hide.

It didn't surprise him that Amelia hadn't discovered it yet. There were no roads leading to it, just a slight break in the crops that offered enough space for the truck to wind through.

After days of hiking and restless nights waiting out storms, John was beat. Ben and Louise lay on the floor, arms wrapped around one another as they slept. Maya used fresh bandages to change Jamal's dressing, thanks to supplies provided by Lillian, and they were at the table, trying to remember how to play cribbage on an old board and a deck of cards with the ace of hearts missing.

The cabin wasn't entirely sealed, and a chilly breeze entered from a crack in the roof, but the fireplace worked wonders. John poked at a log, and the flames rose higher as the bark on the opposite side caught.

Lillian stood at the window as the hail turned to snow. "First the tornadoes, and now this." She huffed a breath and sat in a rocking chair near the hearth.

Gemma stopped humming. "The season is two weeks early."

"Is that unusual?" Lillian asked.

"Weather is often unpredictable on Arcadia," Gemma explained. "The patterns seem quite consistent, but we've only been tracking them for a few years, so there are hiccups. When your lives depend on accurate predictions to stay alive, you put a lot of focus on it."

John rarely worried about the weather on Earth. They had snow in the winter, but it rarely lasted more than a week before the sun's glow melted the thin layer from the ground. If it got too bad, the buses would stop running, and he'd call in to the hardware store.

It made him think about a particular day when he was twelve. It dropped two feet in a night, and they'd woken to discover Carmichael blanketed in white. Haley loved it, and the first thing she did was rush outside in her pajamas to make a snow angel.

Their mom had been upset, but soon all four of them were in the yard with boots, jackets, and gloves, throwing snowballs. No one went to work or school. Instead, they drank hot chocolate with pink marshmallows, and watched their favorite movies for hours.

He remembered how disappointed Haley was the next morning, when the streets had melted enough for the bus to use. She'd cried as the brakes squealed to a halt by their house. He'd squeezed her hand, promising another storm like that would come, but it never had. Until now.

John rose, and Gemma joined him at the window. He used his sleeve, wiping a layer of grime from the glass, and they viewed the snow accumulating in the yard. He gave up and saw stacks of electronics behind them, most of it already disassembled.

"What are you doing with this stuff?" John finally asked.

"I had someone fetching things for me," Lillian said. "I'm guessing he must have been caught. He just stopped coming by."

"Who?" John noticed how she dodged his question.

"I was hoping to contact Logan, but I don't think I can," Lillian told him.

She had fragments of radios, computer boards, and televisions strewn out on the bedroom floor, some connected to screens. Lillian had a generator outside, but opted to leave it off, trusting their light and heat to the fire.

"They won't let you back into town," John warned her.

"Talk to the deputy on my behalf," Lillian said. "In the morning, you'll drive to them and assure her I'm a friend."

"It's not that simple."

Jamal shifted in his seat, setting the cards down. "Isn't it?"

"How so?" John asked.

"Look, she killed a couple of people trying to save your town. Ben shot Van. They call it Themis. We do what's necessary to survive. This is Arcadia, not Earth. We're governed by different rules here, all leading to our survival," Jamal said.

"Themis?"

"Greek goddess of justice. That's what we call the death penalty."

John wondered how Jamal could be at peace with this woman. "You saw her murder them, then abduct you."

Jamal shrugged and shuffled the cards. "All I'm saying is we might need her help. They'd be foolish not to hear her out."

"Jamal's right," Gemma added. "Don't you want to go home, Earth boy?"

John rubbed his knuckles, then lowered his chin in resolve. "Yes."

"Then go talk to Amelia. I can't keep hiding in these crops like a hermit, not with the fate of Carmichael looming over my head," she said.

"Okay."

"Yeah?"

"Yeah." John pointed at the others. "We'll all go."

"I'd rather you left a couple of them," Lillian said.

He'd expected a negotiation. People like Lillian rarely gave in to demands, especially when their own lives were on the line. "You want to keep hostages?"

"That's not…" Lillian exhaled. "If you all leave, what's stopping them from coming out here and gunning me down? The Wickenhouse son might take benefit of my solitude and seek revenge."

John tried to imagine what he'd do to someone if they'd killed his father, leaving the mother crawling away. "We'll do it your way, but don't expect others to be so generous."

Ben watched them, probably thinking about their own laws at the Den.

"I deserve that." Lillian pulled a bottle from the cabin's wooden cupboards and offered it to John. He sipped the booze and passed it to Gemma, who sniffed the contents, then drank a mouthful. She gasped, wrinkled her nose, and handed it to Jamal. They wordlessly took turns until it circled back to Lillian, who gulped a serving and resealed it. "The pact is complete. Now, let me show you how to play, because you're driving me nuts."

Jamal moved the chair out, making room for Lillian at the table. "You mean it's not two points when you get sixteen?"

"It's fifteen."

John blocked out the chatter, trying to think how Amelia and the rest would react to Lillian waving the white flag.

Gemma smiled at him, then hummed a new song while the snow continued to fall.

7

Summer thought returning to Carmichael would fill her with relief, even if they were on another planet, but it did the opposite. The air was thick with the scent of Howler blood and gunpowder. She stepped over the fallen beasts tentatively, keeping her gaze on the ground.

"Summer!" Carly shouted from beyond the barrier protecting their sleeping quarters. She couldn't see her best friend, but she hurried through the group, eager to reunite with Carly.

They crashed into each other, hugging tightly. Carly let go and laughed nervously. "I thought I'd lost you."

"Not even a Shift can keep us apart," Summer joked. Carly's cheeks were concave and her skin sallow, like she hadn't been eating or sleeping well.

The mood differed from before. Then it had been hopeful, the residents believing they'd travel to Earth on the same morning Summer disappeared. Summer's last few days in the LTC camp were boring, but she hadn't gone without, despite living in a tent.

Buck Iverson dragged a Howler onto a tarp, and Summer noticed his son, Adam, helping the cleanup efforts.

Carly was more important than a boy she'd just met.

"How have you been doing?"

"Your parents…"

Candice and Steve Dawson rushed from the entrance, her mother's movements clipped and tense. Her dad reached her first, burying his face in her neck, and muttering that he loved her over and over. Her mom's eyes had a familiar filmy visage, indicating she'd recently taken a pill to 'relax.'

When it was her turn, she took Summer's hands with clammy fingers. "You shouldn't have come back."

Summer fought her emotions, not wanting to be upset. "You were safe. My sister…"

"Mom, they wouldn't let me go."

"What?" Steve asked after composing himself. "That's preposterous. Next time, call a taxi, and—"

"Listen up!" Christine shouted from the front doors. "Everyone who isn't working on the fence or burning the animals, inside. Carmichael is now under a mandatory curfew of dusk, and you cannot leave these premises until after dawn. Understood?" She peered at the gathered crowd, who didn't respond. "Good." She left.

"Who's that?" Carly murmured.

"Caesar's wife." Summer rubbed her elbow while staring at the incoming snowflakes. They fell lazily, drifting to the parking lot. Soon more had accumulated, with the temperature quickly dropping.

"His *wife*?" Carly blurted. "That's crazy. She's so…"

"In her evil villain era," Summer finished. "Right down to the scar and her cringy leather jacket."

"I don't like the sounds of that, Steve," Candice muttered.

"Villain…" Her dad balked at them.

"Let's go in." Summer guided her parents to the entry, where Haley Paulson held the door. Her rifle remained in her grip, and she nodded at Summer while she passed by.

"Does anyone know we've disappeared?" the young woman asked her quietly.

Summer shook her head. "Nope."

Haley pursed her lips. "Then we'll have to do this ourselves."

Summer searched for Harrison or Amelia in the busy building, but couldn't find either. Instead, Dot and Sharon hurried from the makeshift kitchen, fussing over Summer. Katie joined them, bringing a bowl of soup.

"Hungry?" Katie asked.

Summer almost declined, then smelled the salty brine. "Sure, thanks."

The room had a few hundred locals crammed onto cots and air mattresses. Their fear was palpable after the Repulsor's failure and subsequent Howler attack. Christine's arrival added an extra element of uncertainty to their situation. Caesar took charge without acting like it, but his wife was his opposite. Summer wondered if that had drawn them to one another in the first place.

"Our house is gone," her dad said as she spooned a serving of soup. "The storm destroyed half our block."

"Don't worry, you guys will stay with us until…" Carly didn't finish, since their future was up in the air

Summer's memory of the sanctuary had been skewed. She'd thought it was a safe space, playing movies and giving respite to the town. Tonight, it felt cold, the weather from outside creeping through the concrete exterior walls. The film projector remained off, and only a handful of lanterns were lit, since no open flames had been allowed given what had happened downtown on the night of the initial Howler assault.

Summer ate, and eventually her parents wandered off, telling her where they were sleeping and that they had a blanket and pillow set aside.

"It must have been wild?" Summer asked Carly.

"The worst. You should have heard the storm. I thought the roof would blow off, and that a twister would pull me out of bed," Carly said. "I guess a snowstorm isn't so bad."

Summer's eyelids felt heavy as the town prepared for sleep. She leaned her head onto Carly's shoulder and sighed. "I won't allow them to kill us."

"Who's killing who?"

"Never mind." They had enough to do.

She spotted Harrison leaving the office with Amelia, and the new chief headed to the stairs leading to the roof.

---

*H*arrison had said all the right things, but Amelia couldn't let her guard down around the older agent. He claimed to know precious little about LTC, and that he'd only come to Carmichael after tracking Caesar, using a GPS link he'd given his operative years earlier.

Christine was the one to watch.

Amelia found the woman at the roof, under a white canopied sun shelter they'd finally gotten Clive to loan them for a fee.

"I can't let you have—" Eldon clutched the Repulsor, and stopped speaking when Amelia arrived. "Chief, she's trying to mess with it."

"It's okay," Amelia said. "Can you really fix the device?"

"I can fix anything." Christine's scar jutted out, and she frowned, taking the Repulsor from Eldon.

For an instant, Amelia feared the woman would drop

the device and stomp it to bits, but she didn't.

"Where's the tools?"

Eldon grabbed something from the table. "That's all I have."

"Soldering…" Christine picked up the handheld kit. "Perfect. Now give me some space, kid."

Eldon looked to Amelia for guidance, and she nodded once, letting him leave.

Two guards watched the streets through their rifle scopes, not breaking their gazes.

While Christine operated on the panel, Amelia contemplated the odd weather. In her mind, they were still in the heart of summer on Earth, and the fact that it had been stiflingly hot for the first few days on Arcadia did little to ease the confusion at the sudden change.

She walked from under the canvas canopy, and Harrison joined her, moving out of earshot.

"We can't trust her," Harrison said.

"What about you?"

Harrison seemed surprised by the comment. "Chief Miller, I promise you on my wife and daughter that I will never knowingly harm anyone under your charge." He put a palm to his heart.

Amelia briefly wondered if the man beside her was even married, or if he was making it up. Caesar had randomly spoken about his boss, and it was obvious *he* trusted the guy.

"I hear you worked with Caesar," Harrison said.

She questioned where he'd gotten that information, then remembered that Summer would have briefed him on everything that transpired between Shifts. "We did."

Harrison ran a hand over his balding head, wiping accumulating snow off his skin. "He'll be upset when he sees her. I'm worried his emotions will blind him. We all believed she'd been killed in action, making him a widower. He struggled to recover from the loss. I swear, the man hasn't so much as gone on a date in a decade. Even Fatina, my wife, thinks he's overreacting, and she believes in the one soulmate theory."

Amelia thought about their goodbye, and the warmth of Caesar's touch. Christine's arrival likely killed any chance that they'd had.

"Chief, the Howlers are returning. Over."

Amelia checked the other ledge, finding Freddy with Haley at the fence with their weapons ready.

"Should we handle this?" Harrison called to Christine twenty yards away.

"We don't need to." She smiled and pressed the Repulsor on. A light blinked; then the screen activated. "Would someone get the generator running, or is everyone in this godforsaken town worthless?"

"I don't like her," Amelia whispered.

"You haven't seen anything yet." Harrison stepped aside while Vince came with Jimmy on his heels. They started the diesel gennie with ease, and the Gas-N-Go owner shot Christine a leering glance, which she quickly countered by touching the assault rifle leaning nearby.

"Who are they?" Harrison asked her.

"Vince and his son, Jimmy."

"The gas station creep."

"Summer really filled you in on everything. Did you make notes?"

Harrison tapped his temple. "Like a steel trap. Unless it's for when garbage day is, or my anniversary, apparently."

The Repulsor began to operate properly, and soon the frequency emitted from the church's speaker, sending the signal out in a few miles' radius. The Howlers that had braved the streets now scattered with reckless abandon, leaving them at peace for another night.

"That should do it." Christine cleaned up her job site, sliding the tools into their proper places before marching over to Amelia's position. "Show me Isla's base."

Amelia felt the keycard pressing into her chest beneath her uniform's top. She'd strung it on a leather strap, not wanting to lose what might be the most valuable key in the whole town. "No."

Christine's gaze narrowed. "This isn't a negotiation."

With a single glimpse, Vince plucked the weapon from its resting spot, blocking the roof's exit.

"The way I see it, you don't have the power, Mrs. Hawkstone," Amelia said. "This is our town. Not yours, not some half-rate senator's, and certainly not this Mr. Gustafsson you're working for." Her pulse ran hot, but she kept her composure, needing to show the intruder that she wasn't in charge. That title belonged to Amelia.

Christine shrugged and looked at Harrison. "She doesn't know that I could kill everyone on this roof within twenty seconds, does she?"

"Probably not," Harrison said solemnly. "But with me around, it might be harder than you think, and from what I've heard, the chief's no slouch."

Christine slowly nodded, as if conceding. She walked by Vince, stopping inches from his face. "If you so much as breathe near me again, I'll use that gun to beat you to death."

Vince stood his ground, but her unrelenting stare made him retreat a foot.

"We'll go to the base in the morning," Christine said before disappearing down the rungs to the stairwell.

Everyone seemed to breathe easier with her departure. Amelia brushed the snow off her shoulders and strolled to the exit. "Thanks, Vince."

"Any time, Chief."

Amelia motioned to Eldon. "Don't let the Repulsor out of your sight. I'll have someone bring a jacket and blanket."

It was still cooling, and Amelia worried the weather would grow unbearable before long.

"Jimmy and I will get it for him. Then we'll stand guard, if that's okay," Vince said.

Harrison followed her from the roof and stopped at the bottom of the stairs. "The people really respect you," he said. "Word of advice?"

"I'm listening."

"Don't push Christine too much. I'm pretty sure she was about to execute me a few nights ago, if Summer and my assistant hadn't intervened. It's not blood in that one; she has coolant in her veins."

"I appreciate the warning." Amelia spied Christine with Dot, getting a bowl of soup. "Can you stick around here?"

"Certainly." Harrison crossed his arms. "Where are you off to?"

"Finishing something I started." Amelia made sure Dot didn't see her departure and snuck out the side doors and into the snow. She got to the car, but quickly realized she'd been blocked in. Amelia considered borrowing someone else's vehicle, then let the bumper push against the smaller hatchback and carefully nudged it.

Her tires slid, and she eased off the gas, taking it slower. It wouldn't do her any good getting stuck or crashing on the way to Dot's house. The locked basement had been playing through her head for days now. She imagined Sheriff Lyle reminding her to follow her gut, because half of police work was instinct.

The streets were empty due to the blizzard and Christine's lockdown, but it still took her fifteen minutes to arrive at her destination. Frost crept on the edges of the windshield, and the busted glass made her wish she'd borrowed another car.

She killed the engine and grabbed the spare key she'd kept.

As she walked up the sidewalk, she glanced back, realizing her tracks would be covered within minutes. Amelia reached the door, and hesitated before unlocking Dot's place. It was warm inside, with the house sealed from the elements. If the temperatures continued to drop, it wouldn't stay comfortable.

Amelia found the basement key in the same hiding spot she'd returned it to the other night. It slid into the handle with a slight jiggle, and the back clicked open with a turn.

With a flashlight on and her gun raised, Amelia descended the stairs.

8

Caesar woke.

The image of his wife's smiling face vanished from his dreams, and he returned to the present. He slept on the flattened grasslands, staring at the cloudless night sky. Anders was out cold a few feet away. Logan and Ruby were next in line, sharing a homespun blanket.

The traveling town slept, and Caesar guessed only a couple of hours had passed since they'd gone to bed. He nearly closed his eyes when he noticed a glimmer in the distance.

He soundlessly slipped from the bag and carefully trod to the outer edge of camp with his assault rifle. Using the scope, he investigated the source, finding a person moving back and forth, as if pacing. From this far out, and in the dark, he thought it was either a woman or perhaps a lean man.

Caesar considered waking Anders, but didn't want to cause alarm, so he went off on foot, glad he'd kept his boots on. He rarely stripped out of his clothing when sleeping outdoors on the job, and it had saved his life more than once.

The land tilted downward toward the valley they were planning on traversing at first light, and that was where he marched, occasionally checking the scope to ensure the target hadn't vanished. He could now see it was a woman scrawling notes into a book. She stopped every few minutes and tapped a finger on the pages. She was at the edge of an abrupt drop twenty feet into a rocky crevasse, and mist rose from the opening.

He came upon her a few minutes later and watched from a section of bushes blocking him from her sightlines. The woman muttered letters out and kept writing. This continued for a while before Caesar lost patience.

He stepped clear, holding the weapon up but not directly threatening her. "What are you doing?"

She dropped the book, revealing something in her other hand. "How did—"

"Answer me."

He'd initially thought she'd be around twenty, but up close, she was actually closer to forty. She was rail-thin, and even in the dark, her skin had a weathered texture. He'd seen her on the trek that day, but didn't know her name.

"I'm…" She snatched the discarded journal and held it to her chest defensively. Tears formed in her eyes.

Caesar squinted and viewed the contraption in her hand. "That's a telegraph for Morse code."

"It's harmless. I'm practicing. We're hoping to build a network in all the towns so we can communicate," she said.

"Who are you?"

"Becka."

"Becka, give me the notepad."

She shook her head. "It's mine."

He outstretched a palm. "Now."

Becka looked as though she might bolt. He didn't feel like chasing someone around the uneven ground at night. A rock bounced into the hole behind her as she slowly backed up.

"Let's not do this. Give it to me, and return to camp. We'll sleep, and be on the way in the morning," he promised.

"It wasn't my idea!"

"What wasn't?"

"Milton will want to know what happened at Shelter," she said.

The sound of the mysterious leader's name gave him pause. "And you're sending him messages in Morse code? Don't you require radio waves or something?"

The contraption wasn't the run-of-the-mill telegrapher he'd seen in museums. It had a light on the underside, suggesting there was a power source.

"I don't know how it works, only that it does. I send updates on Shelter, and they keep my brother alive," she said.

"He's a captive?" Caesar asked, and she nodded.

"We're from a village up north. Bruce and I came together about twelve years ago," she said. The device clicked, sending her a response.

"Mark it down," he ordered, and she did, ticking off the incoming telegraph. "What's it say?"

"To get the location of Carmichael," she admitted after a slight delay.

Becka gave away her plan to escape before he started moving. He lunged, trying to reach her, but could only grasp her sleeve as she fell into the narrow fissure. He looked into her fearful eyes. "You're going to be all right." Caesar let go of his gun and dropped to his stomach. He stretched his fingers, but the fabric tore.

Becka dropped, bouncing off the rock walls, and landed with a thud, her body contorted in a horrific angle. In the dark, he made out her frame and heard nothing but distant insects chirping.

"You okay?"

Caesar retrieved the gun as he rolled to his back, aiming at the newcomer. When he saw Anders, he lowered the barrel. "I could have shot you."

"Nah," Anders said dismissively. "I was watching the whole thing."

Caesar got to his feet and gazed into the opening. "We have to retrieve the journal."

"Is that a telegraph?" Anders pointed at the device, lying sideways on the dirt.

"It is."

"Milton?"

"The one and only," Caesar said.

"We'll have to deal with him." It wasn't the first time Anders had mentioned this, and Caesar doubted it would be the last.

"Let's put a pin in that." Caesar motioned to the crack in the ground. "You want to do the honors?"

Anders shook his head. "You started the mess, you finish it."

Caesar laughed, almost countering that Anders slip down there since he was smaller, but bit his tongue. "Stay ready in case I get stuck."

"Always." Anders used his scope, sweeping in a slow circle before relaxing. "Just be quick. There's still a few hours of sleep I could get."

Caesar grabbed hold of the ledge, lowering himself, and found a foothold, then something to grip. The twenty feet took a couple of minutes to descend, and he was grateful Anders' flashlight beam didn't settle on Becka. Blood spilled from her lips, and her neck was bent in the wrong direction. He collected the journal and placed it into his pocket before scaling the height. He propped himself up by spreading his feet on either side, moving far slower on the ascent.

When he crested the top, Anders helped him, and Caesar grabbed for the notebook. He flipped through the pages, finding dozens of transcribed messages, each with a series of dots and dashes above the scribbled handwriting.

"She's been feeding Milton details about Shelter for years," Caesar said.

"If he's got someone at Shelter, he might have infiltrated the Den as well." Anders reached for the device, which had turned off. "What are the chances we can keep the charade going?"

"Give Milton a false location?"

"That's a good plan," Anders admitted.

"Only if we had an army."

Anders appeared thoughtful, then shrugged. "Fair point. Let's get some shuteye. I think we've had enough action for a night."

"What about her?" Caesar gestured at the corpse.

"Leave her. She's a traitor, and deserves to be treated as such." Anders started off on foot.

"Milton captured her brother. Becka didn't have a choice."

Anders faced him. "Choices are all we have."

---

*A*melia descended the stairs with an abnormal amount of trepidation. The hair on her arms was on end, and the flashlight wavered more than it should have. *Breathe.* She paused near the bottom, wishing the power was on. Amelia had never liked basements. Her own had been filled with remnants of another era, junk her mother had collected for decades.

Once, when she was seven, her mom asked her to gather something from an old box, and when she'd gone, the door had slammed in behind her. She tried it, but it was locked.

After banging on it relentlessly, she gave up, and heard a man's voice after the doorbell rang. Amelia had mustered the courage to go all the way down and amble through the overstuffed boxes to the dusty sofa. She cleared a space to sit, found a dog-eared mystery novel, and read until footsteps clicked on the hardwood, and the front door closed.

Only then did her mother call for Amelia. *Dinner's in an hour. You'd better peel the potatoes.*

Amelia now strove to ignore her childhood fear, and entered the basement, finding another door. Luckily, it wasn't locked.

The second she saw what Dot had been hiding, she reached for her radio, but she'd forgotten it in the car.

Printed photos filled the east wall. The heading *LTC* was labeled over a series of candid shots of Isla. At the flower shop through the window, preparing an arrangement, then walking down the street with a cup of coffee. Amelia flinched when she saw the blurry one with Isla standing at the barn, peering behind her suspiciously.

"Dot knew," Amelia whispered.

The next set was of Lillian Carson. Lillian in Jackson, meeting with Reagan. In a black SUV, wearing sunglasses as she scoped out the West farm. Lillian talking with a man in a limousine in what looked to be Manhattan.

Then Lieutenant Reagan, her coworker. Amelia appeared in two of the shots, but clearly, she wasn't the target. Sheriff Lyle stood apart, giving his daily assignments to the team. Amelia had never particularly liked Reagan. He was pompous, and he lacked self control, but she hadn't wanted him dead.

Amelia considered the basement, but refrained from touching anything, like this was a crime scene that forensics would come and comb for prints. The flashlight beam focused on the north wall, which had a map of Carmichael. It was blown up and slightly pixelated, with the date 2013 in the corner.

Isla's house was marked, along with the flower shop and the base. There were notes written in the margins, but in some kind of code Amelia couldn't quickly decipher.

Her gaze drifted to the Wests' farm, which was denoted with a sharp red X. She recalled Reese's comments about Dot coming to visit before they were killed, and that she'd heard a woman's voice on the night of their murders. They'd assumed it was Lillian, because Occam's Razor suggested that the most obvious answer is usually right.

"What did you do, Dot?" she asked.

Was Dot aware of Isla's plan? Clearly, she'd suspected Isla's involvement for some reason, along with Lillian and Reagan.

Amelia found a tablet and prayed the battery wasn't dead. She powered it on, and it had three percent life remaining. She checked the web browser first, but the history was clear. Next, in the email application, she located the answer.

Senator Rutherford, Dot's brother-in-law. He was working with Lillian to bring Logan home, so he must have somehow tipped Dot off.

Amelia opened the email and read it.

Dorothy, I'm sorry about your financial troubles. My brother shouldn't have left you with that debt. It was reckless, and unfair.

Amelia didn't know anything about Logan's father, or Dot's relationship with him.

What if I told you there was a way to pay it off and get your son back?

Amelia scrolled to the response.

Why would you ever dare say such a thing, Bucky? I'd love not to worry about my bills every day, but Logan's gone, your brother's dead, and I'm alone.

Either explain yourself or lose my contact information. I won't be harassed like this.

The messages continued.

Dot, this will be difficult, but Logan was working on something important with LTC. What I'm about to tell you is…

The battery icon flashed, replacing the email, and the screen turned dark.

She froze, hearing something from upstairs. Amelia drew her gun, racing up the steps, to find she'd been locked in.

"Dot, let me out!"

No answer.

"Dot! I can help you. We'll make sure you're reunited with Logan!" Amelia banged a flat palm on the door, noticing now that the frame had added metal bars to prevent the latch from being kicked in. The fact that the slab swung inward made it worse, since it would be nearly impossible to break it from this side.

Her flashlight flickered, then cut off, and Amelia found herself alone, in the dark, and in her worst nightmare. Trapped in a basement.

Suddenly, she was that scared seven-year-old girl again.

"It'll be better this way." Dot's voice finally responded. "I won't let you stop me from getting Logan." The words held power, and Amelia called for her as the footsteps clunked loudly. Then the front door creaked open, and slammed closed.

9

John was getting used to sleeping in uncomfortable positions. The cabin was crowded with all of them piled into tight quarters, but they'd made it work. This morning, he'd be reunited with his sister, and everything would return to normal. Or what passed for normal routine on Arcadia.

He shivered and noticed flecks of frost creeping from the cracks in the outer walls. The window was completely caked in ice, reminding him of the countless times his father read him a story about Jack Frost. He stared at the fern-shaped tendrils while Gemma stretched nearby.

For a second, he thought Lillian might have run during the night, but she emerged from a stack of old clothing, rubbing her eyes.

Jamal and Maya were in the tiny kitchen, using the gas cooktop to make coffee. "You have no idea what a luxury this is. We've tried to duplicate the beans, but nothing on Arcadia comes close to a match."

Maya stuck her tongue out. "It all ends up tasting like someone's old socks steeped in hot water."

"But we still drink it," Louise added.

"That we do," Ben said.

"Who's going into town?" John had given up on the

conversation yesterday when they couldn't come to a consensus. The people from the Den yielded to Ben's decisions, since he was in charge of their town, so John's opinion held little sway.

"You decide." Ben nodded his chin and accepted a cup of instant coffee from Jamal.

John surveyed the group. "Gemma and Jamal will join me."

"So it shall be," Ben said with finality. John figured Gemma's positive energy would help when he proposed the plan.

Lillian had the fire going in minutes, which had burned down to orange coals. The wood caught with a small amount of persuasion, and John warmed up quickly. The heat caused ice to melt, and it dripped on the floor near the exit.

"I'll be right back."

"The outhouse is behind us," Lillian said.

John had done enough fishing and hunting trips when he was young to be used to a bathroom without plumbing. That was all the people of Arcadia had, and he wondered what other luxuries he wouldn't have again if they failed to get home.

The door didn't budge when he first attempted to push it, and he saw why. A drift rose three feet up the cabin, blocking them in. Maya came to help, and they had freedom. And nowhere to go.

The air had a bite to it, and John ignored the complaints from the others while he scanned the terrain.

"It's bad," he said.

"No kidding," Jamal replied from the cabin. "Can you keep the winter out there?"

"What did you say about those snow animals?" John had all but forgotten that early conversation on their drive to the Den.

"Wanderers," three of them said as one.

Ben sipped his coffee, euphoria spreading across his expression. "God, I missed this stuff. Would the Wanderers show so quickly?"

"Not a chance," Jamal said. "We don't know where they live, but they usually arrive three days after the first snowfall."

"But they will come?" John imagined the fox-sized creatures with snouts like anteaters, burrowing through the fluffy white land, gnawing on their houses.

"I'm not sure," Ben admitted. "It depends if this melts in time."

"We'll be safe at the sanctuary." John slipped into his boots and threw a fleece jacket on. He took a step, and the snow settled above his knee. After closing the door, he rounded the building, moving to the wooden outhouse.

A terrible thought passed through him. The crops might be ruined. They'd had bad weather before harvest, but the sheer weight of snow would be enough to break half the stalks, especially the newer fields.

John viewed the area, sensing how quiet it was. Usually in winter, sounds carried from miles away. He could hear the train running alongside the interstate if he was out of town, but on Arcadia, the silence was deafening.

He dug the outhouse free and quickly used it, his teeth chattering by the time he marched back to the cabin. The scene was beautiful, and it filled him with nostalgia for an era he'd never lived in. He appreciated the smoke rising from a chimney, and a home built off the land with your own two hands. It was no wonder some of the Den residents would hesitate to abandon this lifestyle, rather than returning to the hustle and bustle of the real world.

It was the ultimate life off-grid, that few could ever

experience with such intensity. There were no bills, no trading your time for a paycheck, just doing what was necessary each day to survive. A primal part of John desired that path. The realistic side hoped they were close to solving the Shift, so he could take a hot shower and use his favorite streaming services.

It wasn't long before John, Gemma, and Jamal were in the truck, with Lillian standing near his cracked window. "Remember, I'm on Carmichael's team. They will kill you. With them, there is no getting home. Ever. I can help."

John nodded and drove off, checking the rearview mirror to see Lillian in the snow, watching their departure.

"Do you trust her?" Gemma asked.

"No," he said.

"What about you, Jamal?" Gemma glanced at him in the backseat.

"Hell no. She killed people right in front of me, but…I believe her story."

"So do I. If anyone learned what kind of lush land we've stumbled upon, they'd be lining up to get control of it. Carmichael's population returning would be disastrous for them. If Lillian's telling the truth, we're dead."

"How can she stop them?" Jamal pondered.

"She can't alone, but between her, Caesar, Anders, and our deputy, there's a chance," John said.

"Four people against an army? I don't think so."

"Maybe they'll help us with Milton," Gemma said.

John frowned, driving through a bank of snow to hit the side roads. "Who's Milton?"

Gemma tensed, and Jamal shifted positions from the back. "Sorry."

"For what?" John demanded. "Who is Milton?"

"A bad dude," Gemma whispered.

"Bad like Van?"

Jamal laughed, but it sounded nervous. "Nothing like Van. He was a predictable threat. Milton's…"

"Unpredictable," Gemma finished.

John waited for them to expand on it, but they didn't offer much. "Where does Milton live? Shelter?"

"It's called Tombstone," Jamal finally blurted.

"There's another town?"

"Yeah, up north a way. No one's seen it," he said.

"None have visited there and come back," Gemma corrected.

"And why is this the first time you're mentioning it?" The tires slipped, and he bounced into the ditch. "Damn it." He tried to escape, but the rear end fishtailed.

John got out and grabbed two pieces of wood from the box. They were jammed under a foot of snow and a collection of ruined electronics.

"What are you doing?" Gemma asked.

"I need to grip something solid." He crouched in the cold, shoving them under the rear tires.

Jamal helped push as he rocked the truck back and forth until it shot forward onto the road. He gathered the wood in case it happened again, leaving the vehicle running. The cornfields looked okay in these parts. Most of the snow had fallen from the stalks, and bright green leaves contrasted the otherwise pristine white landscape. The view gave him hope of an eventual harvest.

But they had bigger things to worry about, like being executed by a brigade of soldiers should they Shift to Earth.

John saw the storm damage and detoured to drive on his street. The homes on this side of town seemed intact, and a few broken tree limbs were all they had to show for the tornado striking Carmichael. As he neared downtown, the destruction was abundantly clear. Dot's diner and Isla's place still stood, but the rest had been destroyed.

"I can't believe there's an entire town," Gemma whispered in awe. "We could move here and help them rebuild."

"I'd rather go to Earth," Jamal said. "Maya's supporting that decision now. We can get married…with our families present."

Gemma winced at the mention of family. She'd been so young that they were probably a blurry memory.

John directed the truck to the edge of town, and relief flooded him when he saw the storage facility remained standing. The fence had held, and the lights were off in the daytime. Snow had started to melt in the growing morning warmth. It dripped off the parked vehicles, and he noticed movement coming from the church. People were hanging around, some entering the foyer.

He stopped and turned the key. "Let's find Amelia and tell her what we know. Stay close."

Gemma took his meaning literally as they approached the guards at the fence. She had her arm looped into his, and Jamal stuck behind him.

"Is that you, Paulson?" Brent asked. Haley's ex-boyfriend had grown his beard out, as most of the men had, including John. With a baseball cap on, he looked rougher than usual.

"Hey, Brent," he said.

Brent pulled him into an embrace and patted his back aggressively. "I'll be damned. I just lost five bucks."

"Why?"

"I bet you'd never…forget it. Your sister's gonna be thrilled."

"Is Haley here?" he asked, and Brent pointed to the roof, then whistled with two fingers in his mouth.

John peered up, finding Haley with her rifle. She wore

a pink knitted hat with a pompom on top. "John?" she shouted, then vanished.

Before they got to the entrance, Haley flew out the front doors and bashed into him. "Johnny, you made it."

"I promised, didn't I?" he asked.

"And there's no breaking a Paulson family promise." Haley let go and gazed at Jamal, then Gemma. "Hi, I'm Haley."

"Gemma." Her eyes were bright as she looked at the vast structure. "Is this where you live?"

More folks exited the building, and soon a crowd had gathered around John and his visiting friends.

"Where's Amelia?" he asked.

Kong shook his head. "We haven't heard from her since last night."

"Is that strange?" John furrowed his brow, searching the group.

"She's been running herself ragged," Kong said. "I figure she's sleeping in. Freddy just took over for me at the base."

"Can you try her?"

Haley clutched the handheld and attempted contact. "Come in, Chief. Over."

Radio silence.

"I'm sure Kong's right. She's sleeping." Haley cleared her throat when Katie arrived from the building.

She rushed toward John, giving him an awkward hug, then eyed Gemma. They seemed to appraise one another, with Gemma probably unsure why.

"This is Katie."

"Are you Earth boy's girl?"

"'Earth boy'?" Katie asked, and John pointed to himself.

"That's me."

"No, John is free to do as he wishes."

"What are you doing here? Where's the rest of the Den?" Haley checked.

"I…" John's gaze fell on the exit, where Summer Dawson came from. "You're…" An unfamiliar man was behind her, and John sensed something had seriously changed.

Summer smiled at him, then at Gemma and Jamal. "You made it."

"Uhm, who's this?"

"It's Caesar's boss, Harrison."

"How…"

"It's a long story," Harrison said. "What news do you have?"

"We bring a message from Lillian. She's safe in the woods with some of our friends."

Dot joined them, her eyes puffy with dark bags beneath them. A woman with a scar on her face came with the diner's owner, and walked through the melting snow.

"I guess I missed something," he murmured.

"Did you say you know where Lillian Carson is?" the woman asked.

"I'd rather talk to Amelia—"

She laughed and grabbed his collar, dragging him closer. "Tell me where the traitor is. Unless you'd rather I beat it out of you."

INTERLUDE

Reggie

Jackson, Indiana

*E*very noise coming from the motel parking lot had Reggie on edge. He'd done as Harrison recommended and snuck to the interstate. It took two hours for someone to pick him up, and that came as no surprise. He wouldn't have stopped for a hitchhiker, especially one that was covered in dirt and bits of cornstalks. He'd showered twice since then, and still stank like vegetation.

Sheriff Lyle had brought him to the motel, using his own credit card to purchase the room. That didn't ease Reggie's paranoia that some operative would bust down his door and give him two to the chest and one in the brain at any moment. Why would the sheriff stay at this seedy dump in the middle of the week? If someone was watching the players involved, surely they'd notice the discrepancy in the algorithm.

To Reggie, everything was an algorithm. That was how things worked. To most, it was a buzz word used by tech companies to inflate their stock price, but Reginald, IT aficionado, knew better. Every decision, every action, and every reaction could be documented in cyberspace, but there was also an immeasurable stroke of luck. An anomaly that gave him hope for the future, because life was more than a simple pattern.

Reggie knew for certain their boss, this guy that hired Christine Hawkstone, would have all the bases covered. It also helped that LTC was the leading designer on temporal subroutines in the world. When he'd first learned about the exponential developments their team had created, he'd considered resigning from Harrison's crew to apply with LTC.

In the end, he preferred working behind the curtain like the wizard himself, never showing his face.

Reggie used his laptop, hacking into the motel's cheap closed-circuit TV network. The five cameras surrounding the building were positioned poorly. One had a spider web blocking the view, and another pointed at a garbage can, overflowing with trash bags.

After he'd watched for an hour, a car pulled up to the front, and a guy in a suit exited, then entered the office. It was ten in the morning, not even close to what a normal place would call check-in time.

He flipped to the indoor feed, and a middle-aged woman placed her glasses on, nodding when the guy spoke. She held up three fingers, and Reggie glanced at the receipt on the desk next to his laptop. Room Three.

Panic made him freeze. He wasn't an agent like Caesar or even Harrison. He was no soldier, and didn't know how to shoot a gun unless you counted using a video game controller, because then he was an expert.

This was no game.

The guy slid a twenty onto the counter and left. He walked by the other camera, directly to Reggie's room.

Reggie gathered his few belongings, stowing the computer into his pack, and rushed to the rear window. It protested, but opened after a good shove. Reggie tried to figure out how to remove the screen and ended up punching it with a grunt.

A knock sounded from the door. As he climbed out, the knocking grew louder, more relentless.

Sirens rang mercilessly, and for an instant, he thought they might be coming for him. Instead, the stream of firetrucks and emergency vehicles headed west toward the interstate.

Reggie left the room's window open and bolted. The motel butted up to a gas station and a grimy diner where four semis with trailers were parked along the access road. He tried the first trailer, but it was locked. The second slid up, and he rolled in with his pack and closed it from the inside.

He sat there panting, fearing the man would find him.

Two minutes, then five. When twenty passed, he finally calmed. Reggie was about to leave when the wooden base under his seat shook, then continued to vibrate as the truck lurched forward.

He contemplated escaping, then figured his odds were better if he stayed put and let the driver take him out of Jackson.

Reggie removed his phone when it buzzed in his pocket, and he saw a web alert had been triggered.

He read the headline twice to make sure he'd gotten it right.

Entire town is destroyed in a wildfire. Crews arrived on the scene too late. Carmichael, Indiana, is gone.

Reggie clicked the link, finding images of a massive fire. He doubted anyone else recognized the alien trees burning amidst the border of cornfields.

INTERLUDE

Trent

Freeport, Arcadia

Trent stretched his arms overhead, feeling a pop in his spine. He grabbed an axe, carefully sharpening the blade with a dull stone, and set to the task. He quartered the logs, then broke them into smaller piles before chopping the individual sections. It was tough, back-breaking work, but he relished in the movements.

Sweat covered his bare chest, dripping down his spine as he labored. He'd come to Arcadia seven years ago, in what he considered to be the worst era of his life. Poor. Jobless. Living in his car. This… He paused the effort, wiping his brow with a rag. This was the dream. No one could take it from him.

Trent smiled at the others, setting about their daily routines. Freeport was his favorite village, and he'd settled here after roaming for his first four years. The Den was too remote, and Ben had some strange ideologies, particularly when it came to respecting the land. Shelter, while more advanced than his home, was too much of a target, given Logan's notoriety.

Water's Edge had the nicest location, with access to fresh water and the ocean, but that was only if you could handle the random weather bombarding the coastline without warning. Trent preferred the sacredness of Freeport. The valley below was vibrant, with fruit trees and warm lakes. Up here on the hillside, you could see for miles in all directions, giving you notice of incoming scouts—or enemies.

Thankfully, the renegades that bothered the other villages were yet to test Freeport. Maybe that Milton character hadn't heard about them, but Trent doubted it. They were on a constant watch for invaders, but today, like every other, the valley view remained peaceful.

Trees held a certain importance, considering how hard it was to process them. These woods were devoid of the Hangers that the folks to the northwest had to deal with, but the forest still had its challenges. Like dragging the felled logs up a thirty-degree slope for two miles. Trent had come to Arcadia weak and unmotivated, and things had changed for the better.

He finished the section he was on and placed the wood in neat piles. Trent didn't like jagged lines. He began the bottom row with nine pieces, and incrementally lowered that number as the stack grew.

The sound of a motorized bicycle floated on the breeze, catching his ear, and he stopped what he was doing, resting the axe. Others from the village halted, observing the incoming plume of dust as Bailer rolled closer on the edge of the ridge.

Freeport had other modes of transportation, ranging from a horse-drawn carriage to pedal bikes, but nothing allowed their scouts to move from region to region with as much efficiency as the solar-powered unit. Bailer had left two weeks ago, with directions to visit Shelter and ask for a trade. It was said they'd gathered a bounty of seeds for a particular berry bush that had run low in the valley. Seeds had become currency, but food trumped all other requirements. Fresh water might be on top of that list, but each of their towns had ample supply, so it became second nature.

"Why's he in such a hurry?" Pintar asked.

Most of their population gathered in the town square, which was just a communal firepit they often converged at each night. The mood was somber when they realized the trailer on the back of Bailer's bike wasn't attached. That meant he was coming home empty-handed and had wasted two weeks.

Bailer screeched to a halt, and he wiped his dry, dirty face, brushing debris loose. When he opened his mouth, there was grime on his teeth.

"What happened to you?" Trent asked the returned scout.

"I got to Shelter," he said, then, "Water. I need water."

Evangeline scooped a serving from the nearby barrel, and he gulped it ravenously until it was empty, and motioned for more. Only when the second glass was consumed did Bailer seem to breathe easier. Trent waited impatiently, hoping the guy had a good excuse for leaving their trailer behind.

"You went to Shelter…" Trent made a 'get on with it' gesture.

"They're gone."

"Gone?" Pintar asked. "As in…" He slid a finger across his throat.

"I'm not positive. They had what appeared to be a pyre, and a handful of skulls didn't incinerate with the rest." Bailer looked terrible. "I arrived two days ago. Maybe a day and a half, I dunno. I came straight home."

"Did they leave supplies?" someone asked.

"Where did they go?"

"Was Logan there?"

"Can I borrow the bike, since you're back?"

Trent's vision narrowed as he thought about the burned bodies. "Everyone give him space!"

The incessant questioning ceased.

"Thanks, Trent." Bailer made a noise, like he'd recalled something important. "There was a note." He pulled it from his pocket and passed it over.

Trent unfolded it, finding a string of numbers. "It's a coded message."

The code had been Logan's design. Something for the scouts to carry with them in case the leaders of their villages needed to pass confidential information.

Of their eighty-seven people, only Trent could decipher it. If anything happened to him, the knowledge would be passed on to his eventual successor. It wasn't a perfect system, and they rarely had to implement such drastic measures, but clearly, this was one of those times.

Trent took it into his cabin and closed the door. Tiny black flies buzzed at the roofline, and he noticed a break in the boughs protecting his roof. He made a mental note to remedy that as soon as he was done.

He sat on what passed for his bed and scanned the missive, flipping it upside down. From there, he used the numbering system to count forward, then backward from the center of the alphabet to determine the letters. Since there were two middles, they'd gone with the M for middle, rather than N.

It took a few minutes to read the entire page. He wrote nothing down, just remembered and transcribed the next number until he had the message.

Milton moved in. We defended. Shelter is abandoned. Going home.

After that, a quick set of coordinates, labeled reversely in letters, based on the quadrants they'd created as a community. Trent assumed the crew from Tombstone understood this system.

There was a knock on the door, and Trent balled the paper up. "What?"

It was Peg, and she looked upset. "We found something."

Trent only wanted to finish cutting wood, but the universe had other ideas today. "Show me."

Peg pulled a device from a bag, along with a journal. "Darren started asking too many questions, and Pintar got suspicious. They raided his quarters."

"Without my approval?" Trent really didn't mind. He was tired of them passing every minor detail through his desk.

"You're going to want to see it." Peg flipped the book open, where dashes and dots filled the pages.

"What's this?"

"Morse code."

"Can we read it?"

"I can't."

Trent sighed and thumbed through the journal, finding dates on the top corners. "He's been communicating with someone for two years?"

"We're assuming it's Milton."

"Damn it." Exhaustion crept into Trent's shoulders as the weight of his position sank in.

"Are you going to exercise…"

"Themis," he said, remembering Logan's reasoning for the title. Themis was the Greek goddess of justice, law, and order. "You and Darren were…"

"Sometimes." Peg stared out the door. "Just do it quickly, would you?"

"Does he deserve that?"

"Not for him. For me."

Trent nodded grimly, then rose. He felt a knot in his tense muscles and exited the cabin. *Going home.* He wondered what that meant to Logan, and grabbed his axe.

PART FOUR
HOMECOMING

1

*T*he group's mood altered after Caesar explained what happened to Becka. No one returned to her rocky grave for a proper burial. Logan was disgusted with her and reprimanded himself for not realizing they'd permitted Milton's spy to stay with them for so long. "No wonder they knew about the tower," he muttered.

Ruby pushed the people's pace, as if their personal failure was something to be punished and the rest of the town must suffer for it.

Caesar didn't care how they spurred the villagers on, since he wanted to get to Carmichael as quickly as possible. He doubted their ability to move everyone in an underground waterway, but Logan's confidence bolstered his own. Logan struck him as the type to never worry he couldn't finish a goal. If he put his energy to it, it would be done. There was no preamble or deliberation, just action.

Anders gave his bike to another man, who doubled with an older woman, and walked with Caesar in relative silence, only occasionally commenting on the terrain or timeline.

Caesar was content to march in peace, his mind not focusing on any particular thing. Too much of his life had been devoted to intense concentration and problem solving. He enjoyed the moments where he could release those notions and purely exist.

He had Becka's book, and they'd gotten the gist of the communications between her and Tombstone. Milton wanted Carmichael's location. Who'd told them of its existence? How did they possibly hear about it, when it took ages to travel around this godforsaken land?

The march continued endlessly. The few younger children didn't complain, because they were used to hardships living on Arcadia. They didn't know better, and wouldn't be able to imagine sitting in front of a television watching colorful characters sing mindless songs to entertain them. Out here, the kids had to pull their own weight.

The sun had changed since they'd Shifted. It was still bright and larger than Earth's, but it came in at an altered angle, the ferocity of its temperature less oppressive with each passing day. Caesar had never loved the heat, particularly being overseas with the Marines: sweat constantly dampening your fatigues, the skin somehow simultaneously feeling cracked and wet. He'd done his duty and had expected a normal job after his service.

He wondered what his life might have been like if he'd neglected to go for dinner with Harrison that fateful winter night.

Caesar had been out of the Corps for six months, taking his time to decide his next steps. But working security for a private firm wasn't very stimulating. He'd stood by a metal detector, repeating the same phrases over and over, observing weary employees scanning their ID badges. It was an endless cycle of assistants with overfilled trays of coffee and executives talking loudly on their phones, as if they were the only ones in the foyer.

The job was so fruitless, he felt the seconds ticking by, each day punctuated by short breaks before finally being released to the world at six in the evening when the building closed. He did the work for two months, and considered the banality of the menial task. Caesar had been prepared to go to HR and quit when Harrison entered the building.

The general had grinned at him, hands on hips from ten feet away. "Dinner?" he'd asked.

"I'm on the clock."

Harrison showed his watch as the minute hand moved. "Not anymore."

A bank of lights shut off behind him, and Caesar flipped the metal detector off, then locked the gate. "Okay. Dinner."

He'd been hesitant because he had no interest in being reinstated. Caesar wasn't getting any younger, and the dream of a family and house in the suburbs remained far in the distance. When he'd learned that Harrison had gone private and promised important but relatively low-risk jobs, his mind was made up.

The excitement he'd felt reminiscing with Harrison had sold him on the new future. He'd make significant money, while being able to have a home base.

Now, stalking through the alien terrain, trying to escort a hundred civilians of another planet to Carmichael, he guessed the expensive whiskey and twelve-ounce Wagyu steak had aided his decision. It was done by the end of that night, contract signed, his life in Harrison's hands.

The first job was simple. Track a network of

information leaked from the Pentagon to Miami, where the physical copies were being sent offshore. It only took Caesar three days to determine which staffer had been bought, and a week to trail the shipment to a Caribbean island.

Everything had to be done beyond the law, which complicated matters. After a few jobs, he'd determined what he'd get away with, and what he wouldn't. Often Harrison ended up apologizing to some foreign dignitary or another about the mess left behind by Caesar, but that was the boss' duty. Caesar saved lives. Harrison bailed him out.

Anders Montrave was a legend in the field, responsible for stopping two terrorist threats on US soil, and one in Paris. That mission was with Christine, though she'd never speak of it. Besides the time they'd collaborated in Istanbul, she wouldn't join him in shop talk. He figured it would be easier that way when they both retired.

After four months of being married, and deep into their second bottle of Malbec on the coast of Argentina, they decided to open a consulting firm. Christine would handle the operations, and Caesar would manage the staff as the face of the company, because in her words, 'People respect a buff military type to have their back.'

He'd been unable to argue, and they'd clinked glasses, sealing the plan that never happened.

Caesar returned to the present and watched the residents of Shelter marching tirelessly across the plains. The two bikes revved ahead, then slowed as they approached the edge.

"We made it already?" Anders asked.

Ruby smiled. "The canyon spreads out in the west, then south an extra fourteen miles. The river's closer to this section." She pointed at the gap, but Caesar had to trust her word for it, since he couldn't see the body of water.

It took ten minutes to reach the cliffside, and their group stared in awe. Most of Shelter hadn't been this far from their town before, and the children displayed a healthy mixture of excitement and fear at the expansive view. Birds flew overhead, and a handful of large land animals wandered the deep gorge.

"Is there an easy way down?" Caesar used the scope, searching for a trail. As he spotted the switchback, Logan identified it.

"I spent a week out here with Trent from Freeport making this. We figured it might help us one day."

"Help you do what?" Anders inquired.

"Escape." Logan led the people single file, holding his hand out to an older woman.

Caesar waited with Anders until they were at the pack's rear. "Milton's a bigger threat than they're even letting on."

"No kidding," Anders said.

The sky had turned gray toward Carmichael, and he hoped they weren't too late.

_____

"I'm not saying a damned word until Amelia gets here," John said.

"We can't find her," Harrison told him.

They were in Dot's Diner, a private place that they could speak freely in. John's sister watched the street with her rifle in hand, while Dot whipped up something in the kitchen. John was suddenly starving. It had been a couple of hours since he'd arrived that morning, and half of the snow in town had melted. The roads were damp, the sidewalks slushy, but the precipitation clung to the grassy areas.

"Why did you transport Christine in the Shift?" He glanced outside, expecting the woman to show up for the second time.

"It's complicated," Harrison said.

"How? She's clearly insane." John rubbed his neck, where she'd almost strangled him for Lillian's location.

Harrison's fingers wrapped around a cup of coffee. "I believe you about Lillian Carson."

"You do?"

"I'd never heard of her until recently, but there have been talks about Gustafsson bringing in an operative. I guessed it was Christine once I saw her with the LTC tents and Senator Rutherford." He lowered his voice when he mentioned Dot's brother-in-law. "But it's obvious he sent her in to ensure things went according to plan. What I don't trust is her assurance that she's turned tables after a bout of inspiration. The deputy doesn't like Lillian either."

"Chief Miller," Haley corrected.

"Whatever." Harrison sipped the steaming beverage.

"Then talk to her," John said.

"I would, if you'd give us her location." Harrison sat upright when Dot entered carrying three plates of breakfast, despite the late hour. How she'd managed to keep hash browns, toast, and eggs this long was beyond John, but he dug right in.

"I'm worried about Amelia." Haley joined them at the table, picking up a fork. "Thanks, Dot."

The diner owner sat but didn't partake in the meal. "You're welcome, darling. I love to feed people."

"Where did she go? Is it possible she froze?" John asked.

"Don't even say that!" Haley proclaimed. "It's not *that*

cold."

"Unless she got stuck in the elements overnight," Harrison countered, receiving a glare John was familiar with from his sister.

"We'll start a search," Harrison relented. "Get volunteers and comb the streets. If anyone spots her squad car, have them bring the information to one of your deputies. Does that work?"

"Yes, sir." Haley bolted for the exit with her food mostly untouched.

"Sis! Don't forget…"

She ran back and scooped the eggs and took the toast for the road.

"I'll take my street!" Dot called to Haley. "I have to grab something from my house anyhow."

"Okay, I'll mark it as checked!" Haley left in someone's borrowed truck.

"Can you put the plates in the kitchen?" Dot asked from the exit.

"Sure thing." Harrison gave her a smile, and John was alone with Caesar's boss. "There's no one listening now, son."

"I'd still rather wait until Amelia—"

"We might not have time. Christine was going to kill me if I didn't accept their position with LTC. I'll be the scapegoat for some crisis on Earth, and they're probably coming for my team. I've already convinced my assistant to relocate my family to a safehouse in Boston. My IT guy was sent on a mission far above his skillset, and Lillian Carson could be the key to our survival. Bring me to her right now, and let me, not Christine, decide what to do with her information."

John considered it, and finished his plate, then Haley's. "Let's go." He scraped them clean in the kitchen and set them in the sink, pausing at the wall before leaving. John picked up a framed photo and squinted. There were twenty people in a group, all wearing dresses and suits, and a banner hung in the ballroom. *Rutherford Reunion 2007*. Dot was there, appearing much the same, but almost two decades younger. Her hair was bright red, her dress spotted with polka dots. "Is that…"

Harrison snatched it and paled. "It's Christine." She stood beside Logan, and with the man that would become a senator.

"Is she related to them?" John realized the issue. "Dot knows Christine?"

Harrison stared at the photo. "It can't be. Wouldn't they have recognized each other?"

John pointed at the SUV, and looked both ways when exiting. "Damn it. We have to get to Dot's."

2

Amelia was used to solitude. Even on the job, there were countless lonesome hours in the squad car. The only time she spoke to anyone was on a call, or for her daily meetings at the station. But after a day in Dot's basement, she figured she was pushing the edge of sanity.

She'd sat by the door, atop the stairs, for the first two hours, hoping someone would make themselves known so Amelia could plead for them to release her. Then she'd explored every square inch of that disturbing basement. The longer she lingered there, the more certain she was that Dot Hunter wasn't the charming woman she portrayed herself as.

The notes became rambling; the letters to her son were over the top. Grief came in many facets—Amelia understood that—but it was obvious when a grieving mother became something else. An obsessed fanatic. It all changed when Senator Rutherford told her Logan might be alive.

His constant communication spurred her on. Since the tablet battery had died, Amelia had to go by what Dot's erratic journaling described, as she read in the dim light. She'd be paid enormous sums to help guarantee Logan got home to her. The people of Carmichael wouldn't make it, but the coverup would be simple and straightforward. Dot herself would undergo a name change and be allowed to spend her days near her son, who'd be overseeing the Shift project for the company he'd founded with Isla.

Isla… Dot's best friend, the person she was instructed to grow close to, so they could ensure the Shifts happened at the precise moment. But that hadn't occurred, because Lillian Carson had intervened. Amelia was now confident Lillian would have shot Isla herself if time permitted.

What was Lillian's motivation? Why kill someone that was obviously working on behalf of Senator Rutherford? They should have all been on the same page. Dot. Isla. Lillian. Striving for the goal of getting Carmichael to Shift with Logan so LTC could access Arcadia. That left the residents to deal with, implying they were as good as dead. Amelia guessed a fire was the best option, given their remote location. No one would question it, especially with the senator's influence.

So what changed things?

Amelia swallowed when the creak of the front door sounded, and footsteps clipped on the floorboards above.

"I'll open it, but you have to be on the bottom of the steps, with your gun at the top!" Dot called.

Amelia held her gun up, aimed in the center of the door.

She recalled the woman at her sixtieth birthday party, the kind words she'd said drunkenly on the way home. *You'd make a great daughter-in-law, Amelia.* Had she been less inebriated than she'd let on? Did she know Amelia had been searching her home for a key to the basement?

The door handle clicked, and Dot filled the shadowy exit. It was even later than Amelia had guessed. She knew she should tap the trigger, trying to shoot her through the wooden door, but she couldn't bring herself to do it.

The shotgun barrels aimed at Amelia's chest. "You've given me no choice."

"Dot, you don't have to do this." Her own handgun pressed into her palm.

Dot came down one step. "Why couldn't you let it go? I wanted to work with you."

"We still can. No one has to know about your involvement," she assured Dot.

Dot made a mocking face. "If only I could believe that. But I can't, because you're too honorable."

"I wasn't even supposed to be here."

"I called the department," Dot said.

"Lyle sent me to the burglar call, but it was you…" Amelia was putting the pieces of the puzzle together, and the picture they formed was bleak. "The flat tire."

Dot raised one hand, then returned it to the shotgun. "I couldn't have you trying to leave too early."

"You loaned me your car."

"Just like I made friends with Isla, who wasn't supposed to die. Lillian will pay for what she did."

"Darcy killed her," Amelia reminded Dot.

"Lillian wrote her death sentence."

"Like you did for the rest of Carmichael?" Amelia's anger fueled the comments. "You watched these people grow up. You'd let them all die so a corporation can control Arcadia?"

The shotgun shook in Dot's grip as she continued to descend the steps. "I didn't have a choice. Logan's alive, and if there was a shred of hope I could be reunited with him, I had to take it. He's all I have."

Amelia exhaled as the shotgun aimed at the green carpet rather than her.

"And here we are," Amelia whispered, bringing Dot's full attention to her once again. "Do you really believe they'll let you live when they kill the rest of us?"

Dot nodded. "I'm family."

"How did your husband die?"

The question seemed to throw Dot off kilter. "A boat accident."

"Convenient," Amelia said.

"You think it was all a setup?"

"Let me go, Dot. I need to protect the residents of *your* town. Do you understand?"

"Perfectly." Amelia sensed the instant Dot's decision was made. It was in her posture and how she widened her stance, bracing for the recoil.

She lifted her own weapon, preparing to fire, when something banged and Dot's eyes widened. She dropped the shotgun and stumbled down the last two stairs, landing awkwardly.

"It's me!" a man shouted. "Don't shoot!"

Harrison rushed into the basement, stopping above Dot's dead body. They met gazes, and he holstered his gun. John Paulson was behind him, and Amelia realized she'd missed a lot in a short amount of time.

"When did you get here?" Amelia checked Dot for a pulse but found none. The kill was clean and precise, obviously done by a trained professional.

"We made it to Carmichael last night," John said.

Amelia watched Dot. "You didn't have to—"

"I think I did," Harrison told her, and she nodded sadly in agreement.

"Dot killed the Wests. She's the reason I was in town before the Shift, and Dot knew of the plan to retrieve her son for a while," she said.

"I guess Themis really does work." John rubbed his knuckles.

Amelia took the tablet from the desk while Harrison

examined the photos on the wall. "Explain."

"Themis is the Greek goddess of law, order, and justice. When someone in the community puts the others at risk, or commits a treasonous act, the leader is responsible for ending the threat."

"Ending it?" Amelia knew what he was implying, and the notion didn't sit well.

"Like Harrison just did." John gazed at Dot. "I used to adore this woman."

"So did everyone else," Amelia said. "How do we describe her death to the town?"

"We don't," Harrison suggested. "Not yet. Let's lock that door and tell them she's sick."

"They'll come looking." John removed the shotgun, taking it with him.

"John's friend Gemma thinks the snow will return tonight with a vengeance and stick around for a while before it melts. Let's keep everyone busy in the meantime."

Amelia considered this. "Are any of the crops ready?"

"Part of the Gellers' crop is matured. I bet if we push, there's enough light to get some of it harvested," John said.

"I'll see if they're willing to start." Amelia stopped when Harrison blocked her path.

"Ask one of your deputies to handle that. You and I have somewhere to be."

From the look in his eyes, Amelia was going from one dangerous situation to another. "If you don't mind, I'd like to freshen up."

He stepped back, and Amelia rushed from the basement that had held her captive all night and day. She hurried into the bathroom and flung the curtains aside, letting a glimmer of light into the room. Amelia turned on the tap, hoping for a bit of water, and only a few drops escaped the faucet. She used it to wash her face and stared at her reflection, telling herself that Dot's death was for the best.

How was any of this real? Could she really act like Themis, a Greek heroine of justice, when pushed?

"Yes, you can," she said.

When she emerged, Harrison was at the exit, the key to Dot's basement looped on his finger. He tossed it to her, and Amelia locked up.

Amelia scanned for her squad car. "Where is it?"

"Dot overheard Haley trying to organize a search, and she put it in the garage." Harrison manually lifted the door, revealing her vehicle.

"Let's take Dot's instead. I'm sick of the cold seeping through my busted window," she said. A minute later, she drove toward the Gellers' property in a dead woman's car.

3

Summer never wanted to let Carly go. They held hands as they walked along the roads, wearing winter boots borrowed from Carly's place. She'd gone to her own house to check what had survived the storm, but it was trashed. They'd salvaged an old sweater and her jewelry box, filled with plastic trinkets from her youth. She left it in the snow, done with being a child. The situation surrounding them demanded that she grow up, and Summer was determined to do just that.

"You sure we can manage this?" Freddy asked Mr. Tucker. Five harvesters were lined up, their exhaust melting the snow remaining in their wake.

Mr. Tucker removed an earplug and leaned out of the tractor. "Son, anything below twenty-eight Fahrenheit means trouble. We've been hovering at thirty-five all day, but if the weather continues, it'll drop to around twenty overnight. If we want to recoup any of the harvest, it has to be done now."

Summer stepped aside while the giant machines rolled into the cornstalks. These were the ripest, planted ahead of schedule by Daisy Geller and her husband. Some of the more seasoned farmers opted to plant early each year, hoping to have a larger and earlier yield. Daisy suggested it changed the taste, but Summer figured corn was corn.

The silos and barns loomed at the edge of the field. Summer watched while the stalk stompers pushed in deeper. The five combines moved through the stalks, cobs breaking free and sorting into the machines.

"How have I never seen this before?" she asked Carly.

"Because your mom made you study Latin instead?" Carly joked.

The air filled with a sweet scent that inspired a good feeling in Summer. Maybe they'd make it after all.

Carly let go of her grip. "What was it like?"

"Earth?"

"Yeah."

"I think you remember," she said.

"Come on, we might be stuck here forever. Did you see any TV? What about new music? Did we miss anything? Weren't the fashion awards on?"

Summer shrugged. "I didn't have access to anything."

"That's pretty boring."

"I was trying not to die," Summer said.

Carly hugged her. "I'm sorry."

"What about you? It must have been scary."

Jimmy arrived with his father, and the boy waved at them before joining Vince in the fields where a combine had stopped.

"I guess you were distracted," Summer said. "You and Jimmy?"

"He's got some work to do, but I think he's cute."

Down the road, Summer spied Adam Iverson with Buck as they talked with Evan and Kong. A familiar knot tied in her stomach at the sight of the boy. He wore a thick black jacket, and had already matched them in height.

"How are you and Adam?"

"I haven't spoken to him since I returned," Summer

said.

"What are you waiting for?"

Adam broke off with his father and started in her direction.

The temporarily paused harvest machine was back on the move, kicking up a cloud of exhaust. Summer caught up to Adam. "Hey."

"Hey," he said.

"I…"

Adam leaned in and kissed her on the lips, right in front of everyone. The workers were busy, either in the field or discussing how they could harvest as much as possible before the incoming clouds unleashed another foot of snow.

Summer stood still, unsure what to do, and Adam did it again. "I missed you."

"You did?" she asked.

"I thought you were gone for good."

"I had unfinished business." Summer didn't know where those words came from. He was about to say something when they were interrupted.

"Adam, we need a hand!" Buck called from the second stalled-out combine. He jabbed a pitchfork into an opening on the side, while Mr. Tucker shouted for them to turn the engines off.

"Sorry, duty calls."

"Will you be at the sanctuary later?" she asked while he jogged from the road.

"I'll try, but they think this'll run until the snow comes harder!" Adam entered the area of the field where the stalks were cleared of cobs, splashing mud onto his boots.

"I saw that." Carly pursed her lips. "Who'd have thought that a kid with no electronics could be so…"

"So what?" Summer asked innocently.

"Hot. The boy is hot. Don't make me say it again." They both laughed.

Summer glanced at the darkening sky, sensing an alteration in the air. She breathed out deeply, finding a plume of mist. "It's getting cold."

"Let's go back," Carly said. "They don't need us out here, and I think Reeve was looking for volunteers to read stories to the little ones."

"Since when do you volunteer for anything?"

Jimmy approached them, hat squished in his grip. "Are we reading again tonight?"

Summer sighed. "I'll catch up."

"You sure?"

"Yeah, I could use the air."

Vince remained behind while Jimmy took his father's truck, and he traveled slowly, staying on the road as more snow fell. The harvesters seemed to take a long time, but Summer assumed they were being cautious. They usually had one or two per field, not five, and it wasn't very common to have snow to contend with. At least, that was what Mr. Tucker had said during their initial meeting before the work started.

No one noticed her walking down the street. It was only a two-mile hike, and she didn't mind the stretch after spending a week captive in a tent. Summer removed the earbuds and a solar-charged cellphone from her belt bag, choosing a saved playlist.

She shivered and threw on the knitted hat, which was now a valuable artifact from her past. A year ago, she'd have avoided it at all costs, but this was part of the new, mature Summer Dawson. She was in her growth era.

After a mile, she could barely hear the sounds of harvesting. The town came into view a minute later, and she ached at the sight. Pieces of the road were torn up, the light posts toppled and cleared to the side. The old tire shop was rubble.

Summer walked by the next business, astounded by how a twister could seem so random in its choosing. It didn't seem fair.

Flakes drifted in as the clouds filled her view, and Summer hurried to the storage facility. Carmichael no longer felt safe, even with the Repulsor sending out a frequency to keep the Howlers away. She jogged the last half mile, glad to see the fenced building at the end of the road.

A lantern shone from the church's window, drawing Summer closer. She kicked snow off her boots at the entrance and pushed open the heavy wooden door. "Hello? Pastor Odell?"

"In here, Summer," he said.

Pastor Odell sat on the front pew, a Bible folded over his lap. She traveled through the spacious aisle with socked feet so she didn't drag a mess into the place of worship. Summer removed her jacket and draped it on the adjacent pew, then took a seat next to him.

He ran a finger down the page, finding the proper passage. "*In order to not fear the unknown, you must have the fear of God in you.*"

"Why is God so scary?"

"He isn't."

"Then why does the Bible tell us to fear him?" she asked.

"You're a smart girl, Summer. Most people just take the sermons with a grain of salt and move on with their lives. Not enough of us are curious. It's important to ask questions."

"Like why we were all sent to Arcadia?"

"Maybe it's a test," he said.

"Like Job? We're being tested on our faith?"

"No, I don't think so. But this is a good time for reflection." Pastor Odell closed the book gently and set it aside. "I've heard rumors."

Summer waited for him to explain.

"Are they true?"

"Depends."

"That there's no intention of sending Carmichael to Earth," he said.

Summer kicked her feet, her toes brushing the floor. "Yeah."

"Then we'll have to fight," Odell said.

"I guess."

The pastor placed a palm on his Bible. "Corinthians says that the weapons we fight with are not the weapons of the world. But I won't stand by while my congregation is slaughtered."

"Me either." Summer thought about that night, chasing Howlers with a shotgun.

"Then we're on the same page." Odell rose, his knees creaking with the motion. "It's getting dark. That woman decreed a curfew, and I don't want you to be punished."

"She's not in charge," Summer said.

"A person like that always gets what she wants. Keep your eyes on her."

"I will." Summer could sense she was being dismissed, so she extended her hand, shaking his for some reason, and plodded back in her socks to the exit. Before leaving, she looked to find the pastor kneeling before the cross on the stage, his head bowed in prayer.

———

John directed Amelia to the hidden cabin, and they nearly got stuck twice along the way.

"Who built this?" Amelia asked.

"It's pretty damned old." John closed his eyes, imagining finding everyone from the Den murdered, with Lillian gone, but as they approached, smoke rose from the stack, and he noticed more than one shadow moving within the structure.

Harrison gripped his gun, and Amelia touched it, lowering the weapon. "No guns. Not yet."

"But she's…"

"Let's hear what she has to say. If what John's telling us is half-true, we'll need someone of her…*level* to help fight Christine and her employer's forces," Amelia said. "Plus, we had a decent rapport before."

"Fine, but the second I get an itch, I'm—"

"Pulling the trigger," she said.

Harrison reached into his pocket and brought a tin of antacids out. He popped two and shook the container. "Damn near empty."

John got out and went ahead. "Lillian, it's me!"

The door opened, and the phony DOD agent stepped into the snow, waving frantically. "What took you so long?"

"Christine caused a ruckus," Harrison said, and Lillian's gaze snapped at him.

"She's here?" It was the first time John recognized tangible fear in Lillian's expression.

"In the flesh." Harrison had taken charge. It was obvious a man of his stature wasn't used to sitting back. "What do you want?"

John spotted Louise, Ben, and Maya as they emerged from the warmth and into the cooling evening. Ben nodded, as if checking on him. John gave a thumbs-up, then quickly dropped his arm, feeling foolish.

"To help," Lillian said.

"You killed respected members of this town, and because of your choice in locations, the Wests were murdered," Amelia interjected. "How can we possibly trust you?"

"Like I told John, I wasn't responsible for their deaths."

"It was Dot," John blurted.

Lillian looked shocked. "The diner woman?"

John nodded.

"That's impossible."

"I was locked in her basement all day," Amelia said. "Part of the reason no one returned to this cabin yet was because she trapped me there and John wanted to find me. Which I'm eternally grateful for."

"Where is she?" Lillian asked.

"Dead," Harrison answered coldly.

"She had photos all over her walls, some of you. The senator was feeding her information, riling her up," Amelia told Lillian.

"They'll do anything to ensure Logan's return, and to keep a passage to Arcadia. That's what I needed to tell you. I prevented the town from Shifting completely when the countdown ended," she said.

"Why?" Amelia had her hand resting on her holstered gun.

"If I hadn't, the townspeople would be dead, including you." She looked at Caesar's boss. "I'm guessing you're Harrison?"

He nodded.

"Did she have soldiers on the other side?"

"About a hundred," he said.

"Armed?"

"Very," he agreed.

"If Carmichael returned to Earth, the witnesses were to be murdered. Then they were planning on burning the entire place in a twenty-mile radius. I bet you were part of that plan too. Possibly me. I never felt indispensable with Mr. Gustafsson," she said. "I just bought us time. I knew once I acted, no one would believe me, so I grabbed Jamal and decided to find Logan. Only…I was intercepted."

John thought she sounded remorseful, but he didn't think he'd ever trust her, not after how she'd so easily killed Dr. Wickenhouse. Gray area or not, the kindly old veterinarian hadn't deserved that ending.

Harrison took a step closer to the cabin. "Let's say we're willing to bring you in. What's your plan? How can we stop your employer from ever thinking about Arcadia again?"

Lillian tossed her weapon into the snow and strode into the yard. "I kill Christine and relocate the Shift. If we transport Carmichael to its regular location, none will survive."

Amelia laughed, and John had to join her at the pure absurdity. "You're going to help us Shift to Earth, but not to Indiana?"

"Precisely," she said.

"How?"

"That's where Logan comes in."

Harrison looked at John, then Amelia, who seemed to telepathically send him a message. "Okay, Lillian Carson. You get one chance, and if you fail us, it's…"

"Themis," Amelia finished.

Lillian didn't ask for them to explain. She must have gathered they'd kill her by the context.

"You'd better contact your deputies and have them

contain Christine. The moment she sees me, she'll flip," Lillian warned.

Amelia used the radio, pressing talk. *"Anyone have eyes on our new friend? Over."*

"Negative." Kong's feed had a lot of noise, suggesting he was still working on the harvest.

"Negative," Freddy said.

"Affirmative. What do you want me to do? Over." It was Haley.

"It's too dangerous. Christine won't think twice about shooting John's sister."

"Here's what we're going to do," Amelia said, laying out their plan.

4

"We should stop for the night," Logan suggested.

"Ruby, how far until the underground river entrance?" Caesar asked Logan's wife. He hated to part with the bikes, but they couldn't risk losing them in the water, so two volunteers were meeting them across the canyon.

She shook the flashlight, charging it, then retrieved the mapping journal. "About two miles."

He looked at Anders. "What do you figure?"

"Let's get to there." Anders nodded and kept a steady pace.

The people were dead on their feet, zombies sloughing their way forward. Children slept in their parents' arms, and a couple of old ladies were being carried by friends. Everyone's bodies ached, their patched-up shoes and boots not prepared for such a journey.

More than once, Caesar wished he'd convinced them to drop these folks off and return for them later, but Logan demanded they stick together, and Caesar couldn't fault him for that. They were a close-knit community, though Ruby seemed more cautious after learning about Becka's involvement with the enemy.

It was too dark to see well, especially with the clouds blocking the usually intense moon. A fog had settled near their ankles, rising to their knees minutes later.

At the bottom of the canyon, the terrain was much different from the prairies above. There was a dense patch of grass, though he couldn't tell the color at the moment. His boots depressed slightly with each step, and evidence of moisture was everywhere. Trees with thick leaves rose toward the sky, and flowering bushes lined their path.

Anders crouched at the rear of the crowd and gestured at something. Caesar looked, finding a large pile of animal scat. Anders poked it with a stick, and the end sank in. "It's fresh," he said.

Caesar scanned the gorge, but failed to see past a hundred yards in the dimness. From his present position, the front of the group was lost in the growing mist.

He listened for sounds of the creature that made this, and pictured the large, antlered beasts he'd seen below before. Three eyes and matted dark brown fur, with a flinching tail. They appeared to be herbivores, like a moose on Earth, but nothing was for certain. Just because Caesar ate the odd salad didn't mean he wouldn't go for a steak occasionally.

"Logan!" Ruby called.

Anders took off, with Caesar trailing. Both had weapons at the ready when they approached the front lines and gawked at the out-of-place structure. Mist rolled up the gray brick walls, and for a second, Caesar thought it was abandoned.

A flashlight shone in a window of a three-story brownstone. Caesar counted four units, one of them sliced in half.

"Someone's inside," Logan whispered.

The light traveled from the top window, coming down a floor, then to the entrance. A woman ran out, clutching a bathrobe around her. "Can you help us?"

Caesar took a wary step, lowering the weapon. "We're friends! How did you get here?"

As he neared her, he saw how diminutive the lady was. She had big plastic glasses and wavy gray hair, her bony knuckles grasping the flashlight. "I went to bed last night, and we woke up here."

"We?" Anders asked.

Caesar caught sight of movement in the adjacent townhouse, and soon two more residents emerged.

"This is impossible," Logan said. "The Shift shouldn't have taken them."

"We found a farmhouse. How much of the things you built Shelter with came from Arcadia?" Caesar asked.

"Okay, so it can happen, but usually, it's remote, not..." Logan neared the complex. "Where are you from?"

"Seventy-third Street and Columbus," a man said. "Manhattan."

"We're breaking for the night!" Ruby told the group, who seemed delighted by the news. The teams started competently setting up camp, and within minutes, a fire was sparked.

They met with the strangers, hoping to settle their nerves. "I'm Caesar, this is Logan, and that's his wife, Ruby. He's Anders."

"Pleasure." Anders tipped the cowboy hat he'd worn to keep the sun from burning him.

"Talia," the first woman said.

"Greg." The guy was heavyset, with a handlebar mustache and a buzz cut.

"Emma." The woman swayed as if she'd had a few cocktails.

"Where are we?" Talia asked.

"Arcadia."

"Like the place with the video games?" Emma sat on

the front steps.

"Not the arcade. It's a Greek reference for utopia," Logan said.

"Oh." Emma cried, and Ruby joined her at the stairs, putting a protective arm around the woman's shoulders.

"It'll be okay. We were all scared initially."

"How long have you been here?" Greg asked.

Logan and his wife shared a look. "A while. But we're working on returning to Earth."

"We're not on Earth?" Greg shouted and paced the grass. "This isn't happening. Wake up, Greg! Bernadette's going to be so upset when I don't come for dinner with her parents!"

"Did you feel a rumbling?" Logan asked.

Only Talia nodded. "Yes, faintly, but I thought it was an issue in the subway. I'd been in bed for a couple of hours. I like my mornings. I get a bagel at Zabar's, then walk to the museum and feed the pigeons."

"Bernadette called saying she had to work late, so I was listening to records when the power went out."

They all looked at Emma. "I was in the bath. I slipped when I got out and almost cracked my head open." She winced and parted the hair, revealing a bump.

"Is it just you three?" Anders asked.

Talia shook her head. "Sebastian took off. He was going for help."

"When?" Logan inquired.

"This morning. We settled for the night. I was hoping to wake up from this nightmare," she said.

"It's very real. Do you mind if we share your space tonight?" Ruby pointed at the doors.

Emma hesitated but ended up shrugging. "Sure. What's mine is yours."

Ruby set to it, bringing the most frail into the

brownstone. Talia, a retired nurse, had an assortment of first aid equipment in her place, and offered her assistance.

"I worked on the Upper East Side for thirty-five years," she said proudly.

"Then you'll come in handy." Caesar thought about Carmichael losing their only medical professional when the local veterinarian was killed. "Thanks for the hospitality."

Talia smiled at him in the darkness, and she touched his bearded face. "You remind me of my son." She turned when she entered. "Please don't disappoint me like he did."

Caesar stood there, unsure what to say, and decided to investigate their camp. "What if this is happening more frequently?"

Anders lingered by the edge, watching the scene, and grunted. "Do you think it's natural or caused by a Shift device?"

"These three don't look like the type to work for LTC, do they?"

"Nope, but maybe their friend Sebastian did. You heard the bit about the ground shaking." Anders gazed in the direction they'd been traveling. "I'll check the surroundings, then scope out the cave entrance."

Caesar figured it was a good idea, despite the ache in his hip and shoulder. "Let's go."

Five minutes later, the duo strode away, searching for clues of the guy's path. When they didn't find any, they walked toward the cave, using the faint outline of the moon through the clouds to guide them.

The grass grew sparser when Caesar stopped by a stone fissure. It rose a hundred feet high, blocking their passage unless they went around the mountain.

"Sebastian could have easily found this in the daylight." Anders gestured at the twenty-foot-wide hole leading to the cavern below.

Caesar wasn't interested in exploring it tonight, not without the proper gear and Ruby, who'd been down there.

"Help!" The voice was barely discernable.

Caesar ran to the cave.

"Help!"

Anders flicked on a flashlight and let out a breath. "It's a good thing we came."

"He needs our help." Caesar opened the pack he'd been carrying, retrieving a rope. He tied it to a gnarled tree, then looped it around his waist. "Let's hope he's no deeper than this is long."

"I'm right behind you." Anders held the flashlight high, keeping the beam above Caesar as he entered the hole. Loose rubble made him slide, but he caught himself on the wall and stayed upright.

"We're coming!" Caesar shouted.

"Thank God! I'm stuck!" The voice was stronger, and bounced from around the corner. The cavern was tight, and Caesar had to turn sideways to squeeze through.

A young man was pinned under a beam. His foot had disappeared into a crack, and blood stained the rocks by his ankle. His jeans were torn, and his skin was sticky with sweat, his color drained to a ghostly white.

"Are you Sebastian?" Anders asked.

"Yes. How did you—"

Caesar lifted a hand, and he stopped talking. "Is it broken?"

"I don't—"

Caesar crouched, feeling into the fractured stone, and shifted some debris. "Okay, I think I can free you, but it might hurt."

"How much?"

Caesar didn't wait; he just twisted the leg when he'd created enough space. Anders hauled the man up, and he was no longer trapped. Sebastian wailed in pain as they set him on the ground.

Caesar appraised the wound and asked Sebastian to move the foot, which he did. "Good news is, it's not busted, but it'll swell up. Keep the shoe on, and we'll bring you to the brownstone."

Anders grabbed Caesar by the arm, moving him away to speak privately. "Did you see his jacket?"

He read the three letters on the chest. "You work for LTC?"

The man blanched. "Yes. How can you tell?"

He noticed the bag, and Caesar unzipped it, pulling free a tablet, which also had the stamped LTC logo. "You made them Shift."

"I swear I didn't know what I was doing. We opened a new building, and I was curious about what this contraption did. Don't let them fire me," Sebastian pleaded.

Caesar powered it on, and lights shone brightly. "We need to show this to Logan."

Sebastian grimaced as he tried to stand. "Logan?"

"Rutherford."

"Logan Rutherford is *here*?"

"What about it?" Anders asked.

"That's what our building is named… the Logan Rutherford Center."

"How inspiring," Caesar said. "Come on, Sebastian. We're going to introduce you to your company's founder."

"But he died like ten years ago," the man said. Caesar figured Sebastian had been in middle school when that happened.

"He didn't die. He's just been hanging out on Arcadia."

5

*B*ringing Lillian to the base was risky, but Amelia had little choice. Caesar was a few days or more from returning with Logan, and she didn't know if they'd ever show up. She recalled the message over the radio waves in that ancient toy, speaking about moving on Shelter. It was possible Logan was already dead, and her allies were walking straight into a trap.

Freddy had a fire going near the barn, and used one of the white canopy tents they'd borrowed from Clive as protection from the increasing snowfall. He jumped up when they arrived and looked hesitantly at Lillian as she trailed behind with Harrison.

"Chief, are you in danger?" he whispered.

"No. Maybe, but time will tell. Anything to report?"

"It's been quiet as a mouse." Freddy stared at the wall of corn across the yard. "I heard some Howlers rustling in there earlier, but they never came out."

"Be careful, and call in for backup if necessary."

"What are you doing with her?" Freddy frowned, and Amelia couldn't blame him. She'd killed his father and nearly his mom in the process. "Don't tell me…"

"We need her help."

"Amelia…" Anguish filled Freddy's expression. "You

can't trust her."

Lillian was within earshot, and she stepped closer.

"Get away from me!" Freddy's rifle snapped up.

"I'm sorry about your parents," she told him. Lillian wasn't armed. It was a concession she'd fought, but Amelia wouldn't agree to bring her to the base otherwise. "There's always collateral damage with missions."

"They are *not* collateral damage!" He looked ready to fire, but Harrison grabbed the barrel, pushing it aside.

"We'll have time for justice when everyone's home, okay?" Harrison's voice was commanding but calm. It had the desired effect, and Freddy relented, resting the gun against the barn.

"You shouldn't let her inside," he said.

"Noted." Harrison nodded at Amelia, who opened the doors.

Lillian gazed around as they walked to the middle, where the secret access hatch remained locked. Amelia used the keycard Isla had given Caesar on her deathbed.

Harrison descended the rungs first, then Lillian, followed by Amelia.

Lights flashed on from their movement, and the computer screens turned on. The previous countdown showed *00:00:00*, but the second Amelia touched the keyboard, it recalibrated. *95:22:59*.

"I'll be damned," Harrison said. "There's another opportunity to Shift in four days."

"Logan probably won't be here yet," Amelia said.

"It's possible. If they drove directly to Shelter on the JLTV and back, they might show in a day or two." Lillian examined the room, then quickly investigated the power core space. The lights flashed between towers, toward the central unit.

"You knew how to stop the Shift, so how do we start

it?" Harrison asked her.

"I broke something outside." She used her phone and zoomed on a photo, then indicated a panel on the exterior wall. The fracture was only visible when you looked up close. "I don't have the tools or understanding to fix it."

"And you did this to prevent us from being gunned down," Amelia said.

"Correct."

"Logan will be able to connect with another location, and Shift Carmichael?"

"Yes. I've read everything he's ever written on the subject. It's the same theory that Mr. Gustafsson is working with at the remote laboratory. Connecting to ground zero isn't necessary, if Logan's calculations were correct, and from what I can see, he's rarely wrong."

Harrison coughed. "Except for the time he traveled to Arcadia alone and couldn't return."

"A temporary lapse of judgment."

"He was too eager to test his revolutionary Shift," Amelia said.

They exited the Shift device's underground power source room, and Amelia walked through the supply bay Isla had built. "We're running low on food and water. It's time we brought this to town."

With the produce and bread depleted at the grocery store, and staples being consumed faster than they'd expected, the people of Carmichael could use a win.

The pair of JLTVs were gone, but Isla had other vehicles in storage. Amelia began filling a trailer with cases of water while Harrison gathered crates of canned goods. Lillian added bags of rice and packages of ramen to the mix. In an hour, they had both trailers stacked full and connected to the ATVs they'd kept behind.

Amelia used the ramp and opened the hatch leading to

the outdoors. Snow fell into the bay, and they took turns driving their supplies into the night air, while the other guarded Lillian.

She parked the ATV and waited while Lillian walked down the ramp, coming to join her. Harrison drove the vehicle with ease and slowed near them, watching the sky. "It's getting worse."

Amelia went the long way to close the bay. She climbed up the rungs, sealed the hatch, and returned to the front doors, clasping the lock.

"Freddy, I'm sorry about your parents, but Lillian is here to stay."

He rubbed his hands by the flickering fire, but didn't look at her. "If she hurts anyone else, it's on you."

Amelia swore she wouldn't let that happen. She left Freddy without another word and gave Lillian the keys to Dot's car. "Stay at the cabin for the night. There's no sense in creating a commotion."

"Can you imagine the look on Christine's face if we showed up with you?" Harrison asked.

Lillian had the door wide, and she paused before getting in. "Please don't doubt that I'm on your side."

She drove off, and Harrison stared at the car plowing through the drifts. "Until it doesn't suit her. I've seen a lot of double agents in my days, and if they change teams, it's only a matter of time until they turn back."

Amelia watched Harrison, wondering if he'd ever flipped sides.

———————

*S*ummer woke with the sun. She'd always hated the beeping alarm clock that used to rouse her from dreamland each morning. The incessant noise was something she'd thought she'd never miss, but at this point, she did.

Summer's home had been destroyed in segments, first by the Howler attack, then by a flurry of tornadoes. Now the town was covered in a deep blanket of snow, which might have excited her a year earlier.

Today, she felt the creeping cold and pulled her blankets higher. Her mom and dad shared a mattress beside her, Steve's arms wrapped around Candice. They rarely displayed this level of affection, and she wondered if it would last. One day soon, her mom's happy pills would disappear, and Summer was afraid of what might happen next. She'd been taking them for years.

Carly and Joe shared another double mattress, and their mom had a cot with a couple of jackets draped over her instead of a blanket, which were in short supply now that a chill had snuck into their evenings.

She sat up and saw bursts of her breath in the air.

Amelia had shown up late last night with trailers of food and water, proclaiming they'd found a secret storage compartment at Isla's base.

Klein, Dot's cook, was already in the kitchen, wearing an apron. A few others spoke quietly near the communal living space they'd assembled. Without running water, they'd dragged a few portable bathrooms from around town, and Summer dressed with all of her layers, risking the cold.

The plastic door banged hard since it was frozen, and she used it as fast as humanly possible. When she exited, Kong stood by the fence, looking panicked.

"What's the matter?" Summer asked.

"It's my wife," he stammered.

"Is she…" Summer feared the worst.

"No, Chun's having our baby!"

Summer looked for Kong's wife, but realized she hadn't seen the woman in days. "Where did you leave her?"

"At the bar. I have it fortified and heated, but…" Kong paced. "Dot was supposed to help me, but I can't find her."

"What about Sharon? My mom might be able to do something."

"Can you check?" Kong tried starting the truck on the street, and the engine finally took after a few attempts.

Summer rushed in, finding more residents awake. She hurried to her mom and shook her shoulder. "Mom!"

"What is it?" Candice bolted upright.

"Kong's wife is having the baby, and I thought you could help."

"Why me?" She patted her own hair.

"You had a kid, so…"

"Your mother was doped up and doesn't remember—"

"Steve!" she reprimanded her husband.

"I'll join you," Mrs. Lawrence said, already dressing. "I spent a few months' training to be a doula, but didn't end up liking it. Too many bodily fluids."

"Ew, Mom," Carly complained. "I'm totally coming too."

Her brother rolled over, yanking the blankets higher. "I'll be here if you need anything."

Sharon stood in the kitchen, boiling water in a kettle. She looked up when Summer arrived, and beamed. "Good morning, Sunshine."

"Chun's having the baby."

Her expression grew stoic, and she turned the kettle off. "I'll get Dot."

"Have you seen her?" Sharon asked Klein, who was stirring the pot of oatmeal.

"Not since yesterday."

"Okay." Sharon sighed and grabbed her jacket. "Let's go."

It was a tight squeeze into Kong's truck, but they made do. Kong drove too fast around the corners. The snow was fluffy, falling in fragments, not like last night when it had endlessly bombarded Carmichael. The truck slid, barely gaining traction as he came to a stop before starting forward again.

"*Kong, where are you?*" A handheld radio sat in the cupholder, and Kong reached for it, nearly going into the ditch. Summer snatched it from the backseat.

"We're almost there!" Summer told the pregnant woman.

"I was really hoping she'd wait until we were on Earth," Kong said.

"Chun didn't have a choice," Sharon advocated.

"My second one flew out of me like a fastball," Mrs. Lawrence joked. "This is Chun's third, so we probably don't have much time."

Kong just about crashed into the bar, but braked, sliding into a concrete barrier protecting his building. He left the truck running, and didn't even close his door.

Carly and Summer were squished into the middle, and exited last, with Summer cutting the engine and pocketing the keys he left behind.

She'd never been in any bar before, and walked through with curiosity. It smelled funny, and everything was decorated with dark wood. It had certainly been designed by men for men, and could use a few sparkles to brighten the mood.

"It's warm," Carly said.

The generator growled from behind the building, its hum vibrating the windowpanes. Inside were four electric heaters. Summer noticed a couple of fire extinguishers on the tables, suggesting Kong didn't trust the cheap imported devices.

Cassie barreled into her dad, and the little one, Bo, lifted his arms up, wanting to be held.

Chun was in a booth, propped up by blankets when they arrived.

"Come on, kids, let's go do some coloring," Carly said, grabbing Cassie's hand.

"I want to see the baby!" Bo cried.

Summer didn't mind kids, but Carly was always better at handling them.

Sharon and Mrs. Lawrence took charge, barking orders at Kong, who rushed off to do whatever they asked of him.

Summer walked behind the bar, not wanting to get in the way, and opened a can of warm soda. It fizzed, and she swallowed the sugary drink. In the back was an office, with paperwork stacked on a messy desk. A safe was bolted to the wall, and a rifle leaned in the corner beside Kong's swivel chair.

A few kegs of beer sat in the next room, and she stared out the window, hoping it didn't get any colder. Ice stuck to the glass, but she still saw the alley behind Bullseye.

Summer noticed movement and squinted, trying for a better view. She grabbed the rifle in case it was a Howler. The generator grumbled loudly, and she guessed it needed to be refilled. She knew they had to turn it off to add fuel, so she ignored it, lifting the gun to use the scope.

Whatever she'd spotted…

The snow bulged in a straight line, like something burrowed under it. She recalled what John Paulson's friend, Jamal, had said about the Wanderers. Summer spied more lumps aimed at the bar, and she waited at the door while one popped its head above the cover. The snout was long and light gray, reminding her of an anteater. It peered directly at her and opened its mouth. Through the scope, she could tell the teeth were extremely sharp.

She rushed in and heard the cries of a newborn echoing in the main bar.

Kong smiled proudly, clutching a tiny baby to his chest. It was swaddled in a towel, and she paused, wondering if her own father had been that delighted when she was born. "Meet Athena."

"She's super cute, but we have a problem."

6

"*T*his is your house?" Gemma wandered into the front, spreading snow on the floor.

John left his boots on and moved aside while Haley entered, with Jamal and Maya behind.

"Yep. Home sweet home." He pointed at the sign that said the same message. His mom had crocheted it when she took a class years ago, and had never made another one. She'd said it was a collector item and deserved to be on display. Haley thought it was hideous, but he didn't have the heart to take it down.

The place was freezing, and John went to the back, firing the generator on. After a few tries, it finally thundered to life, and he quickly plugged in the boxy electric heater they had books piled on in the living room.

"What's this?" Gemma pointed to Haley's salon station.

"That's my workspace."

"Work?" Gemma asked.

"You know, a job to make money," Haley said.

"We don't have money on Arcadia."

"But we trade things," Jamal said. "And everyone takes on certain tasks."

"I help harvest the crops, and gather berries, and

predict the weather," Gemma told John's sister.

"It would be better if you could change the weather," Haley told them.

Gemma closed her eyes and wrinkled her nose, uttering a strange sound. "I tried, but it didn't work."

Jamal and Maya laughed. "She made a joke."

"Come on, Earth boy, I thought you'd have a sense of humor." Gemma touched his arm, and Haley's gaze followed the contact, making her grin.

"I'll get the fire started." John rarely used the hearth, and hoped the flue wasn't packed with soot. His dad always had it cleaned by an old guy from Jackson each summer, but John didn't bother.

In ten minutes, the fireplace was crackling, and for a second, it seemed like they were just a group of friends gathering on a weekend afternoon. He didn't have much to offer them, but found the remnants of Darcy's beer collection in the kitchen sink. They weren't quite frozen, but were damned cold. Jamal looked at the can as if he'd struck gold. "I haven't had a beer in years."

John's fingertips warmed, and his earlobes finally melted. He sat on the couch next to Gemma, grateful his house remained intact when so many others hadn't.

"This is nice," Maya said. "It's a proper home."

"We have a real home." Jamal sounded defensive.

"I know, honey, but there are doors, and rooms… a roof that doesn't leak."

"I was going to fix it, but I've been scouting."

"Did you hear that?" Haley was at the window, looking at the snowy landscape out front.

"Nope." Jamal took a sip of beer, smacking his lips in appreciation.

"It's probably the generator." John sank into the cushions, savoring his own beverage.

Gemma rose and sat in Haley's salon chair. "Could you do my hair?"

"Sure."

Gemma's was dirty blonde, cut at irregular angles, and parts extended past her shoulders. The bangs were erratic, but the effect was charming.

Haley set her rifle aside, which John had noticed she rarely did, and her demeanor loosened as she changed into stylist mode. She ran her fingers through Gemma's hair, lifting sections and making faces while she pondered the best course of action.

It wasn't long before the comb and scissors were moving. He hadn't watched Haley operate in ages, since she was usually finished by the time he returned from the hardware store.

In the last couple of weeks, he hadn't given that life a thought. For some reason, he assumed they'd never return home, that their fate was sealed. He supposed it was what the self-help books he'd once read all described as 'living in the moment.'

John pictured his old job and wondered what Mr. Holmes would say if he showed up next week, explaining that he'd been unable to come in because of an unforeseen Shift.

If what he'd overheard was true, someone wanted all of them dead. He didn't doubt Amelia and Harrison's plan, but a lot of their hopes hinged on Logan Rutherford. Dot was dead too. Would that change Logan's motivation to help them, or would he side with Christine, as she'd so arrogantly assumed?

John enjoyed working at the hardware store, but couldn't imagine doing it again. Stocking shelves, helping customers find the proper P-trap for under their sink, trying to match the thread on a #8 metal screw. There were other planets, liveable ones like Arcadia, and they had the ability to travel to them.

"Do you think there are more?" John asked out of the blue, breaking a moment of silence.

"More what?" Jamal rotated the beer can.

"Worlds we could Shift to," John said.

"Probably." Maya burped lightly. "Excuse me."

"I just want to Shift home." Haley continued, cutting slowly. Gemma stared into the mirror with wide eyes.

John added wood to the fire and spied something strange in the front yard. It took him a moment to understand what was out of place.

"Jamal...you mentioned the Wanderers coming in the snow," he said.

The man jumped from his seat, hurrying to the window. "Damn it."

Five lines burrowed below the surface, all speeding directly for John's house. "They can't get through a foundation, can they?" he asked.

Haley had finished, and she was brushing Gemma's hair. "What's a Wanderer?"

"They destroy our cabins and eat our bedding, blankets, whatever they can. They're a pest, and an unwelcome one," Maya advised.

Haley set the scissors down. "How do we stop them?"

"With great difficulty." Jamal flinched when the first creature slammed into the outer walls.

---

*A*melia looked at the street from her temporary space at the town office building. "Say again. Over."

"They're surrounding the house. Jamal calls them Wanderers.

They're not aggressive unless cornered, but they'll destroy everything in sight. Over." Her deputy, Haley Paulson, sounded scared.

"Same here, Chief. Chun had the baby, and we're all okay, but these things are gnawing at the doors. Over," Kong said.

Amelia would have laughed if she wasn't so tired. "Of course there are monsters trying to eat our insulation."

Christine tapped her foot at the office entrance. "Give me access to the base, and I'll Shift us home."

Christine had miraculously agreed to be chaperoned, but only by Amelia, who was certain it related to the keycard in her pocket.

"I thought we needed Logan for that," she said.

Christine laughed airily, and for a second, Amelia saw why Caesar had fallen for her. If you took away the constant frown and forgot about the pink scar running down her face, she had a natural charm that enveloped the room. "I have many skills, Deputy."

"Chief," she corrected.

"Sure. Make up all the titles you want, but what are you going to do when they ship you back home? Go work for Lyle? His entire department has been paid off for years."

Amelia watched her, trying to see if she was lying, but doubted it, since Lillian had already confirmed the same information.

"Bring me there, and we'll let everyone go. I have the power to change the plans."

"The countdown says we have four days until it's a match," Amelia said.

It must have been news to Christine, because she gave away her surprise. "So the traitor didn't shut it off after all."

"I don't have time for this. We're under attack by something called Wanderers, we have a Repulsor keeping the Howlers off our asses, and the latest snowfall is unprecedented. The crops are basically ruined, other than what they could harvest last night, and my deputy just had a baby, but he's now trapped in the bar with his family."

"It won't matter in four days. Even if Logan doesn't show, I'll give you safe passage home," Christine said.

"Why don't I believe you?"

"Because you're working on the assumption that Harrison Gregory is telling you the truth," she said. "You have no idea what kind of man he is. If I told you the things he's done, you'd never sleep again."

Amelia yawned at the mention of the word. "How about you go ahead, then? And while you're at it, tell me why you let Caesar think you died."

Christine adjusted her jacket, which was slightly too large for her frame. She would have frozen to death if she hadn't borrowed one. "You've fallen for him."

"I have not," Amelia hissed.

"Caesar has that effect on women. Believe me, I was his ultimate victim. It wasn't just those rugged good looks, but that didn't hurt. I nearly got fired for accepting his help on that mission in Istanbul, but I would have walked to hell and back for Caesar."

Amelia listened, hoping she'd elaborate, and Christine did after a brief contemplative pause. "The first year was heaven. We both loved our independence, so time apart was natural. When we reconvened in Paris, Lake Como, or Denpasar, the encounters were filled with passion. Then Caesar told me he wanted to retire and start a consulting company, and everything changed. The more he pushed to move in together, the longer I stayed away. It didn't matter how handsome or determined he was, I couldn't be what he needed. I'm fractured, Amelia." She smiled at her own comment and touched her scar. "When Mr. Gustafsson offered me a position, I jumped at the chance. It was the truth, really. The woman Caesar had fallen in love with *did* die in Chile."

"Tell me about Harrison," Amelia said.

He emerged from the hall. "What about me?"

"I didn't hear you come in," she told him.

"I'm stealthy." Harrison glared at Christine. "Been spreading lies again?"

"What can I say, I've always liked being a storyteller," Christine said.

"Can we cut the crap? Let me guess, you're painting me in a negative light and begging Amelia to give you the key to the base?"

"Something like that."

"Amelia's too smart."

"We were having a nice conversation until you showed up," she said.

Amelia watched Christine, trying to gauge if this would work or not. "Harrison, I actually think we should bring her."

Christine shot him a cocky stare. "I won't do anything to hurt the people of Carmichael."

"You promise to transport us when the countdown is over?" Amelia asked.

"Yes." Christine made the sign of the cross and kissed her thumb.

Amelia had too much to do, but this was their first step to freedom. While the Wanderers were dangerous, Christine was a bigger threat than the snow-covered rodents.

"I'll drive," Harrison grumbled. "Someone needs to have a level head here."

The snow had stopped falling when they reached the edge of town, and a few sets of tire tracks ran to the Raddison farm.

"This is the wrong way," Christine said.

"No. The barn you saw wasn't the real base. It's where she built the power core, but not the controls," Harrison said.

"Smart," Christine said from the back seat. She was buying it.

Clive and a couple of his friends were outside when they entered the Raddison farm driveway. He had a fire going in a rusted barrel, and they circled it, palms lowered for warmth. Clive tossed a cigarette when they approached and leaned in, like Amelia might roll the window down. She didn't.

"These are the guys you chose to guard the Shift?" Christine asked.

"Looks can be deceiving," Amelia said. "Clive's ex-army, and these two are scrappers."

In the car, hot air blew on her face, keeping her warm, but she quickly regretted not wearing a hat and gloves when they exited.

"Clive," she said with a nod. He had to act cool, or they'd lose any advantage.

"Chief." Clive's tattoos showed beneath his scarf, and Amelia noticed Christine looking at them.

"Where did you serve?" she asked Clive.

He fidgeted, grabbing another smoke, and lit it. "I served with the 4th."

"That's not what I asked you," she said.

"I don't want to talk about it unless you're with the VA, because I've been asking them for help for years."

Amelia appreciated Clive's quick mind, which a shock, considering the business he was in and the fact that he partook of his supplies.

Christine turned toward the barns. "Show me the control room."

Harrison gestured to the pair of snowmobiles Clive

had prepared for them, and Christine got on behind Caesar's friend. Amelia didn't know how to operate it, so Clive drove the old clunky unit. When Harrison took off, she leaned closer. "Where did you get these?"

"Are you asking as a friend, or a cop?" He laughed and flicked the butt.

"Never mind. Is it all set?"

"There's only one way to escape the freezer, and it's from the exterior."

The plan had been perfected when she spoke to Clive last night. He confirmed that his ancestors once had a meat processing plant on the property. His grandfather would butcher all hunting season, then store the kills in a giant fridge in the barn.

He revved the engine, and the vehicle rattled, exhuming a cloud of black exhaust. "Why don't you just kill her?"

"Collateral," she said. They'd discussed that at length last night, but even Harrison seemed hesitant to outright murder Caesar's supposed deceased wife before giving him a chance to see her again. He deserved an explanation from the horse's mouth.

Amelia realized Christine was right. She had started to fall for the operative by the time he'd left Carmichael with Anders. It could have been the pressure of their situation, or that she hadn't had a decent date in forever.

The wind and velocity blew snow in her face, and she closed her eyes, praying this wouldn't go sour. Amelia glanced at the second barn's roof, finding Brent there with a rifle. He was a good shot, and she didn't want to ask Haley to take the position. Amelia hated that she'd rather risk this man than her deputy, but it was the truth.

He wore white, blending in with the snow-covered peaks. Amelia's heart sped up as they slowed near the trap.

Clive discreetly passed Amelia a key. "Almost forgot this."

She thanked him and strode through the accumulated snow to the entrance.

"I will get you home," Christine promised. "In four days, when the frequency matches, we'll transport you to Earth."

And be greeted by machine guns, Amelia thought. *I don't think so.* "Right this way."

She unlocked the padlock, and they entered the old butcher shop. Meat hooks hung from chains on the rafters, and even though it hadn't been used for decades, the walls seemed to hold the scent of blood in their pores.

Harrison lunged, unclipping Christine's handgun with practiced efficiency. In one swoop, he had the magazine ejected and tossed it to Clive outside. They both pointed 9MM pistols at her. "In the fridge."

Christine began laughing. She bent at the waist, slapping her thigh, until tears formed. "You two really thought I was such easy prey?"

Amelia and Harrison exchanged a nervous glance.

"Clive, ex-army, hey?"

Brent walked in, holding the rifle. Clive picked up the magazine, clipping it into the Sig Sauer. Katie, the diner waitress, stepped out of the fridge, holding a shotgun.

Amelia thought about Dot and how she'd hired Katie a few months earlier. They were all in on this together.

"Clive, you said I could trust you," she whispered.

He winced, scratching at his neck. "I'm already going to hell. I may as well get some cash."

Amelia felt the weight of the moment, and shunned it. "No," she whispered.

"No?" Christine stalked over like a tiger, unafraid of the pair of guns on her.

There was no way this woman would let them live. Adrenaline coursed through Amelia's veins. Fight or flight. She glanced at the exit. Harrison hadn't budged, but the tendons in his hands were pronounced.

"Give me the guns, and you won't feel a thing," Christine said.

Katie swallowed but didn't move the shotgun. Brent had the door covered, and Clive shakily held up a weapon.

"How could you?" Amelia asked the girl.

She didn't respond.

"Drop them!" Christine shouted.

Amelia shifted on her feet, unsure what to do.

In the end, Harrison acted first. He fired at Clive, aiming straight at his forehead. The shotgun blasted when Amelia tackled Katie, and Brent grunted when he was struck. In the span of ten seconds, all three of them were incapacitated.

She held Katie's wrists while the girl fought, and Harrison tried to catch Christine as she bolted. The snowmobile cranked on, and Amelia heard gunfire.

He returned a moment later, chin hung in resignation. "She got away."

Brent writhed on the floor. He clutched his bleeding stomach, and Amelia didn't think he had long. Clive was clearly dead, lying in his own blood.

"Why didn't you go after her?" Amelia panted.

"I couldn't leave you here with them." Harrison kicked the door wide. "Damn it. We should have seen this coming. People like Christine anticipate risks."

"Are you going to kill me?" Katie staggered to her feet as Amelia hauled her up.

Harrison glared at the woman. "Not if you tell us everything."

Amelia saw the moment Brent died. Haley had dated

this man, and he'd teamed with the enemy. She had a lot of bad news to break to the town.

Once outside, she took a long inhale of cold air, trying to calm herself. She instinctively reached for the lanyard around her neck, and found the keycard to Isla's base was missing.

7

*P*assage through the tunnels was difficult initially, but the walls widened as the ceiling height rose. Caesar had lost track of time hours earlier, but none of that mattered. Getting to Carmichael did.

Talia, Greg, Emma, and Sebastian had all fought them on leaving their brownstone townhouses, as if they had a future at the base of the canyon without food or power. Emma moved as if she was in a dream until they'd reached the underground corridors. Then she broke out in tears.

Transporting a hundred people a few miles below the surface wasn't a simple task, especially in the pitch black. Their solar-powered flashlights only held a charge for so long, and they were asked to alternate, preserving what little light they had. At the moment, two were lit up: Anders' military-grade version at the front of the line, and Caesar's at the rear.

Logan strode ahead of him, clutching the tablet. "I can't believe we found someone from LTC."

"Do you really think it's a coincidence?" Caesar asked. "You don't?"

Sebastian had seemed truthful in his proclamations that he'd stolen the device from the lab. "Stranger things have happened."

"I screwed up back then. I had my version harnessed to the magnetic fields and shortsightedly assumed the same would be true on Arcadia."

Caesar figured Harrison would understand what Logan meant, but he didn't. "Okay."

"If there's a way to reprogram this to recognize another source, it might be possible to use the tablet to send someone to Earth," Logan said.

"To a random location?"

"Yes."

"Who would go?" Caesar asked.

"That's a good question." Logan slowed as the line of people stopped. "What's the holdup?" he called over the chatter.

"We've reached the water!" someone shouted.

"This plan better work." Caesar pictured them floating on the river to Carmichael.

The line trudged along, and it took ten minutes before they filed into the cavernous room. Caesar flicked his light off. The sunlight poured in from a hole in the ceiling that continued for what had to be a mile to the canyon's surface. It brightly reflected off the water, which flowed at a steady pace, coming from below their feet. The cave reeked of sulphur, and Caesar hoped the exposure wouldn't harm anyone's lungs.

Ruby commanded the residents of Shelter, directing them to assemble the crafts. Caesar had seen the supplies they'd been hauling from their home as individual pieces of junk, but these folks had clearly practiced this task before. He supposed there was ample downtime without books, social media, or televisions.

While they constructed two rafts, Logan walked the outer banks, using the tablet. Sebastian trailed after him, and Caesar joined them, not trusting Logan alone with anyone at this point. Only Logan could get them home, meaning Caesar was his bodyguard until that day.

"You're a genius," Sebastian said.

"Where's the lab?" Logan asked.

"In the Adirondacks."

"Big, empty space no one will ever miss."

"That was the idea. I was off for the weekend. The commute is doing all sorts of gnarly things to my car."

"Have you met Senator Kevin Rutherford?" Caesar asked.

"Me?" Sebastian pointed at his chest. "No, but we got some kind of company-wide email stating that he'd taken over the board. We thought that was strange, considering he's in office."

"My uncle is an ambitious man." Logan had led them a hundred yards on the riverbank to a narrow ledge. The water flowed fast two feet lower, and Caesar picked up a twig, dropping it in. The branch floated out of sight in seconds.

Caesar walked around them, finding a sparkling stone hidden in the cave's wall. He scratched at the rock surrounding it, and bits flecked off, revealing more of the crystal. It was shiny and smooth-surfaced, like the stuff they'd discovered below the cemetery in Carmichael.

Logan touched it, and the tablet in his pack made an alert. He retrieved it, and his eyes grew wide. "It's connected."

"To what?" Caesar asked.

"To…it's actually linked to Arcadia." He showed Caesar the screen, where a countdown appeared. *27:14:02.*

"You mean we could stay here for a day and use this to go home?" Caesar glanced at their group. "But the radius is limited, right?"

"It was big enough to bring the brownstone building,"

Logan said.

Sebastian motioned for the tablet, and Logan gave it to him. "We've made a few alterations since your original version. It was rough around the edges…no offense."

"None taken. That was a prototype."

"You can adjust the span, but this connection isn't strong." Sebastian peered up. "The link is weak, and you'd be lucky to have an entire person Shift."

"Is there a chance someone would be split in two?" Caesar asked.

Logan stared at the device. "Yes."

"Then we'll find more stones to power it, but for now, let's focus so we can leave together," he said.

Logan seemed prepared to argue, but he powered the tablet off and returned it into his pack.

Anders approached as Logan hurried to the aid of his wife, with Sebastian once again following the founder of LTC.

"Anything interesting?" Anders asked.

"The tablet links to these rocks, and with a larger source, we could utilize the power and Shift."

Anders gruffly laughed. "No kidding. I didn't think they'd be capable of producing boats so quickly, but I have to give them credit. They're not messing around."

The sections were ten feet long, linked with straps and tied at every three beams. Two of the men were already in the water, bobbing beside it as they joined more sections.

"We'll see how they work when we load fifty people on each."

"Why are they so narrow?" Anders asked.

Ruby glanced up from her journal. "The river gets tight in a few spots, and this was the only way to ensure safe passage."

Caesar now understood their strategy. Pieces of the raft

were strapped together like train cars, able to make bends as the river snaked below ground.

In an hour, it was completed, and the Shelter residents proudly viewed their accomplishment. The kids jumped up and down, while the older members gathered the remaining gear.

Soon they were loaded onto the floating rafts. Water splashed between the logs, but that was the price to pay for expedience. The group from the brownstones huddled close while Anders hung at the rear raft, nodding at Caesar as they released the boat ties keeping them harnessed to the bank.

"Hold on. We're in for a bumpy ride!" Ruby called.

If it went according to plan, they'd be just outside Carmichael in a couple of days, and they could put this nightmare behind them.

Caesar crouched while the raft took off. The window to the sky vanished, sending them into the dark. One flashlight stayed in place, mounted to the craft's nose. It dipped and narrowly illuminated the river ahead as they rushed in the direction of Caesar's temporary home.

---

*T*he children screamed, and Summer wanted to join them. Only Kong's presence kept her from shouting alongside his kids.

Mrs. Lawrence clutched a broom, prepared to bash the Wanderers if they breached the outer walls.

Chun held her baby, breastfeeding the infant. It was so new.

"*All hands on deck. Christine has stolen my keycard and is likely heading to Isla's. We have to prevent her from doing any damage.*" Amelia's voice crackled on the radio. "*This is not a drill. Shoot on sight. Over.*"

Summer flinched at the news. Amelia was asking her deputies to kill without question.

Kong grumbled as the Wanderers gnawed on his walls. "Amelia, are you sure she's dangerous? Over."

"*Our plan failed. She had Clive, Katie, and Brent helping her. Clive and Brent are dead,*" she said.

Sharon put an arm around Summer, pulling tight.

To everyone's surprise, Chun smiled sadly. "Kong, go. They need you."

"What about the Wanderers?" he asked.

"We'll leave from the roof!" Cassie proclaimed.

"What do you know about the roof?" Kong asked his daughter.

She shrugged. "I do my homework there sometimes. It has a ladder leading to the alley."

"Can you do it?" Kong asked his wife.

"Yes."

Kong passed Summer a rifle. "Helen, the keys are inside the van."

Summer gave Kong the keys he'd left in the truck, suddenly feeling younger than her years.

"Don't let anything happen to them."

She'd faced a lot, but having Kong ask her to protect his children was different. It was terrifying.

"I won't," she said, regardless of her doubts.

Kong used the radio. "I'm on my way. Over."

"*We're busy at my place, but we'll do our best. Over,*" Haley said, sounding stressed.

"*Freddy? Come in. Over.*" Amelia sounded distant.

Kong sighed. "He's on watch at the base. If Christine harmed him, I'll…"

"Just go!" Summer yelled. Kong kissed his wife, then

the new baby, and ran to the roof, not trusting the front doors where the Wanderers chewed.

Everyone donned their jackets, and Carly made sure the kids had gloves on. She stopped Bo near the roof entrance in the office and tied his laces for him, while Chun wrapped the baby into her winter coat.

They bolted up the stairs, and Summer reached it first. Kong had left the hatch open, and she saw him taking off in the truck. The snow wasn't falling, but the air was freezing as they climbed to the top of the bar. The gravel crunched beneath her steps while she crossed to the ladder. Below, the Wanderers were no longer hidden by the snow. She counted seven at the entrance and found more breaching the bar. Summer waved their group forward, grabbing the rungs.

"Careful, they might be slippery," she warned, and Carly started her descent.

It took a few minutes, especially with Chun holding a newborn, but they made it to the ground level. Luckily, the creatures were indoors, having penetrated the walls. Summer wondered if Carmichael would ever recover from the devastation of being on Arcadia for only two weeks.

She stood guard, holding the rifle while everyone piled into the van. When she reached it, she realized there was no room for her.

Mrs. Lawrence started to get out, but Summer shook her head. "Leave. I'll be fine!"

Carly protested loudly, but the door slid closed, and they spun off.

Summer considered her options and decided the main road would be her best bet. She could head into town or wave down someone to help her.

The snow might have stopped falling, but the drifts alone were nearly impossible to break through. Summer took to the edge of the cornfields, where the crop helped block the accumulation. Her teeth chattered, and she realized this had been a terrible idea.

A vehicle approached from the north. The truck careened, and Summer recognized the driver. She ran to the street, and they stopped a few feet short of hitting her.

"Take me with you!"

Lillian Carson reached over and opened the door, letting Summer in. "At least you have a gun."

"*Freddy, come in!*" Amelia called through the radio.

"I have some business to attend to," Lillian said, with a handgun in her lap.

Summer nearly asked to be let out, but kept silent as the truck sped into danger.

8

*J*ohn thought they had it bad with the Howlers, but at least they weren't hellbent on property damage. He tried not to worry about the place he'd called home for his whole life, and focused on escaping in one piece.

The yard was filled with lines from the burrowing monsters, and he paced the living room, determining the best course of action.

"How do you prevent them from coming into the cabins?" John asked.

"Rock walls, but there's no time for that." Jamal swung the rifle up. "But we usually don't have guns to blow their heads off."

"I have to get to the base!" Haley had a foot out the door, and John hauled her by the arm, slamming it closed. Bits of snow clung to her shoe.

"Sis, these are trained operatives you're talking about. Christine might have killed Freddy!" John reminded her.

"I don't care. This is what I signed up for."

John noticed Donovan in his front yard. "Damn it."

The neighbor kid had always been a pain in the butt, and today was no different. Four burrow marks reached the boy, and he stood frozen as his blue puffer jacket flapped with the wind.

"If we leave the house, they'll find a way in," Maya assured him.

John sighed resolutely as he took a last look at the living room. "Come on."

He ran down the steps and across the yard. There was movement as the Wanderers scaled the foundation and clung to the siding. A rodent was half buried into the dryer exhaust vent, and it disappeared into the cavity.

"Donovan!" he called.

The boy seemed to be in a trance.

John stopped on the next lawn, and the Wanderers lifted from their hiding spots below the soft snow. They turned to face John with their snouts defensively raised. "Do you have any firecrackers?"

Donovan nodded.

"Of course you do," he said. "Light them and run to me. Got it?"

Donovan licked his lips and removed a cluster of red firecrackers. He had a pink plastic lighter, and he tried to flick it with a mitten on.

"Pull the glove off!" John called.

Haley had the vehicle running, and Jamal covered Gemma and Maya as they jumped over a couple of Wanderers.

"Don, you have to hurry."

The boy fumbled with the mitt, and the lighter fell into the snow. He looked up with red cheeks and tears in his eyes. The Wanderers were closer, their body language threatening. They were the size of a fox, but their stature didn't make them any less fearsome. Their teeth were long and pointed, used to tear through fabric, wood, and apparently, vinyl siding, so John had no doubt what they'd do to human flesh.

John stepped, and one stayed to challenge him. At this

distance, John didn't believe he was a good enough shot with a revolver to hit it, so he didn't draw the weapon yet. "Pick it up and try again."

Donovan snatched it, blew on the lighter, and slid his thumb, making a flame. His tears stopped when he touched the fire to the fuse. He held it, staring at John.

"Get over here!" John opened his arms.

The first cracker burst, and the noise startled the animals. As it continued, they dove below the snow, rushing to the street. Even the ones from his house had vanished at the popping sounds.

Donovan jumped at him, and he almost fell at the kid's weight. "You're getting big," he said. "Where are your parents?"

"With everyone else."

"Why are you here alone?"

"I wanted to make a snowman."

John saw the half-formed attempt in the front yard. "Hop in."

Donovan didn't have to be told twice. Jamal waited until John was in the vehicle, and he climbed in, slamming the door.

Haley took off in the driver's seat. "Hold on!"

"We can't bring the kid to Isla's base," John said.

"Sure we can. Just keep him hidden." Haley tore through the streets, tires sloshing in the sloppy mess. The air was cool, but parts of the road had melted to the asphalt as the clouds broke off.

She sped past the corn maze and up the service trail they needed to circumvent the area. Isla had done an admirable job of staying out of sight, so good that it had taken them ages to discover where she'd been operating the Shift from. Most of the townspeople still didn't know its location, and Amelia intended to keep it that way.

A truck pulled in when they arrived, and it braked beside an unoccupied snowmobile. John recognized it as Clive's ride. Freddy's vehicle was there, but he saw no sign of the man.

His sister barely parked before hopping out, and she rushed toward Amelia and Lillian.

"Summer, stay behind with them," Amelia told the Dawson girl.

"You get in more trouble than me," John said.

"I guess we're just lucky," Summer quipped.

"Can you make sure nothing happens to Donovan or our guests?" John asked.

Summer looked ready to argue, then nodded, doing as he'd asked.

Jamal and John had weapons drawn, and he wondered how much longer he'd be living in this nightmare.

———————

*A*melia checked behind her, finding John Paulson and Jamal, the guy who'd been shot at the Benyuks'. She wanted to tell them to stay outside, but they needed reinforcements if this was going to end well. Lillian moved quickly, her gun gripped with two hands, and calmly pointed at the high peaked ceiling.

"Hold here," she ordered the pair of men. "No one gets out unless it's us, understood?"

"Yes, Chief," John said purposefully.

"Haley, go with Harrison."

She glanced at the snow-covered ground. "Roger that."

Harrison had circled around to the far side, where the ramp rose from the basement base, in case Christine attempted an escape.

Haley expected to find Freddy lying face down in a pool of his own blood, but he wasn't in the room.

Lillian reached the hatch first, and it lay wide open. The floors vibrated from the power source below. Amelia couldn't begin to guess Christine's reasoning. She needed the Shift to connect to Earth and bring Logan Rutherford home, so she wouldn't be there to destroy it.

Lillian peered into the opening. "It's dangerous to dive headfirst. Christine could shoot on sight."

Amelia thought about Freddy, the volunteer who'd recently lost his father, and had a wife to think about. "I'll go." Before Lillian could comment, Amelia descended the rungs. When she landed in Isla's secreted base, Christine wasn't visible.

The ramp doors were secured, and the few supplies they'd left behind remained stacked near the exit. A screen was on, meaning Christine's passage had triggered it. The countdown ticked, the big numbers spanning the entire monitor.

Lillian brushed Amelia's shoulder on the way by, her gun aimed at the entrance to the power source. "She's in there. I can hear her."

They approached the room, and Amelia saw Christine in the center, standing at the crux of the network. The lights blinked as the towers passed energy through the system. She recalled someone mentioning nuclear power, and made a silent prayer that Christine wouldn't dare blow anything up.

"Hands up!" Lillian shouted, and Christine slowly turned. Freddy stepped out of cover with his fingers intertwined behind his head. His left eye was swollen, growing worse as she watched it.

"Stay where you are!" Christine ordered. She held a tablet and had a weapon aimed at Freddy's back.

"What are you doing?" Amelia stowed her sidearm into the holster, signaling she was willing to negotiate.

"Going home," Christine said.

"The countdown—"

Christine's face twisted as she sneered. "The countdown is irrelevant. We've improved Logan's theories in the time since he vanished. Getting to Arcadia is a challenge, but leaving is simpler. Unless you have to transport a large footprint, like Carmichael."

She keyed something into the tablet. The floor buzzed with latent energy, and Amelia could sense a pivotal event was about to transpire.

Lillian looked lost, like she was trapped between two worlds and didn't know which path to choose. "I thought that was only a prototype."

Christine snapped her gaze up. "How did you even hear about it?"

"Mr. Gustafsson—"

Christine flinched at the name. "I'm the agent-in-charge, and he gave me this in case I needed a quick departure."

Lillian pulled a cell phone out. "I have the same technology linked to this. He said I was the agent-in-charge."

Christine laughed, the noise muted among the dozens of humming computer towers. "Then I guess we're at odds."

"Gustafsson doesn't care who secures Arcadia for him, so long as he has it. What are you going to do? Leave for Earth and return with an army, to kill the people of Carmichael?"

"By now, Carmichael has been wiped from the world, the land purified by fire. Funerals are being arranged by out-of-state family members. Who will miss you, Amelia?

Lillian?"

Amelia took in the words. "They've already burned the alien forest?"

"It was planned after my departure. I ensured the soldiers would follow my orders. And none of it matters, because you're not getting to Earth." Christine removed a device from her jacket pocket and connected it to the central tower. "In three minutes, this base will explode and Carmichael will forever be stuck to Arcadia."

Amelia watched in horror as the device blinked. It was the size of a pack of cigarettes, but she didn't doubt the chain reaction it might spark, particularly if there was plutonium or something present.

"You'll die with us," Lillian spat.

"No." Christine shoved Freddy forward, and he landed on his knees. She holstered her gun and hit a button on the tablet. The room pulsed brightly, and Amelia stumbled as the ground rocked.

Lillian fired at the other agent, but was thrown sideways, bashing into a tower. Light enveloped Christine, and when it dissipated, she was gone.

The device continued to beep gently while Amelia ran to it, seeking to pry it off. "It's really on there."

"It's a fast-drying cement. You'd need a jackhammer to remove it!" Lillian grasped Freddy's arm, helping him up. "If she's telling the truth, we have two minutes."

Amelia hadn't sprinted so quickly in her life. She sped up the rungs, thinking only about self-preservation and saving those around her. "Harrison! Haley!" she shouted at the top of her lungs when they hurried through the barn. "Run!"

John and Jamal must have understood the urgency, because they were already at the vehicles. Freddy fumbled for his keys and started his vehicle remotely.

Amelia took the truck they'd come in and raced around the property, with Lillian clinging to the door. She honked and motioned to the truck bed while not coming to a stop. Harrison basically threw Haley into the box and jumped on, while she tore through the snow into the corn crops.

She could almost hear the ticking of the explosive, counting down the seconds until detonation. Cornstalks bashed the windshield, and it made her push the gas pedal harder.

The eruption was catastrophic, and the fields were torn up as the explosion rocked Carmichael. It came at her in a wave, rushing underneath the tires. She kept moving, even as the earth grew unsteady. Amelia didn't stop until she reached the alien border, and finally peered toward Isla's base. Smoke rose high, a deadly signal that the barn and the base were eradicated.

Harrison knocked on the rear window, and she opened it. Haley stumbled to her feet, and Harrison tapped his watch. "I've got a built-in Geiger counter. I'm picking up minor traces of radiation. Let's get out of here and put the region off limits."

Amelia barely heard his comments. "Our way home is destroyed."

Haley's breaths came in ragged, misty exhales. "We're never leaving Arcadia."

"What about the phone? You told Christine—"

"It was a bluff," Lillian admitted. "I was grasping at straws."

"Then we really are stuck," Amelia said.

"Want me to drive?" Harrison asked.

She stayed parked. "Did you get out?" she asked into the radio.

"*Roger that,*" Freddy said. "*John and the rest are ahead of me.*"

Amelia slid to the middle of the bench, stuffed in with Lillian. "Take the wheel," she told Harrison, and he did so without hesitation.

"Maybe Logan will have an idea," Lillian said.

Amelia's thoughts turned morbid. Perhaps Caesar and Anders were dead, and Logan Rutherford hadn't survived at Shelter after all. Her mind kept repeating the message she'd overheard. *Milton Radio... threat to Nirvana... gather near Shelter.*

9

Caesar held tightly as the river thrust them forward, directing their raft down a five-foot drop. The logs landed with a thump, splashing water everywhere. He'd been soaked for an entire night, though in the darkness underground, he couldn't tell the time.

With the glow of the sole flashlight pointed ahead, it was difficult to see his surroundings, but he made out the shape of Logan holding his wife near the stern. He inched his way closer, not wanting to lose balance and fly off their mode of transportation. He'd doubted the effectiveness of their plan initially, but now he thought they'd overshoot their timeline and get to Carmichael even sooner.

"How are we looking?" he asked the duo.

Ruby had a crude drawing of the tunnel system as she remembered it, and cradled the book, trying to protect the pages from being drenched. "We'll ultimately end up in a vast basin, and that'll mark the halfway point."

Caesar settled in for the ride, attempting to meditate as he'd once done in the field while waiting for mission commands. He figured three hours had passed before the rafts began slowing. A few lanterns flashed on, illuminating the cavernous space.

More of the blue crystals lined the walls. They reflected

the glow of lights, making it brighter as the boats drifted by. They all but came to a stop, and someone tied them together. Anders walked along the uneven base, joining Caesar at the lead raft. "That wasn't fun."

"Did you expect it to be?" Caesar asked.

"They could have offered us complimentary peanuts. What I wouldn't give for a coffee and a towel to dry off with." Anders stretched his back, making his spine crack. Caesar rose, doing the same.

"Ruby says we're halfway there."

"I'm going to kiss the ground when we land," Anders said.

Caesar scanned the hollow section of tunnel and pointed to the right. "What's that?"

"Probably just a rock." Logan dismissed the concern, talking with his wife as they leaned over her map.

Caesar grabbed the light mounted at the front of the raft and relocated the beam onto the object. "That's no rock."

Everyone paused what they were doing, and Ruby had to warn the people to spread out so they didn't topple the craft. It bobbed unsteadily while drifting through the corridor.

Whatever was down there with them was rounded, with a glistening surface.

"Is it metal?" Anders asked.

"Only one way to find out." Caesar jumped in the water and kicked his feet, swimming to the mysterious object.

He set a palm on it, treading lightly, and his hand depressed slightly. A scaled being moved, sinking below. A limb smashed into Caesar, throwing him deeper. He held his breath, finding the enormous creature unraveling. Caesar dove toward the others, hearing the cries of the passengers. Logan had a pole, like a rowing oar in a gondola, and he used it to push the raft faster.

Caesar sensed it was swimming when the waves tossed him aside. He arrived under their boat and fought for air between the logs before carrying on to the far edge. Anders clasped his wrist, hauling Caesar from the basin.

"Nice job. You woke it up," Anders said.

"Hurry!" Logan urged the rafts forward. Water gushed loudly ahead, suggesting they were approaching a ledge. "Hold tight!"

They dropped down the falls, nearly throwing Caesar off, but he held the ropes. Someone flailed by him, landing in the water. The giant eel slithered through the lake, snatching the man. He screamed; then blood floated up behind the raft as they picked up speed.

"It's following us!" Anders called. He had his assault rifle out and fired at the unsuspecting monster.

"Save your bullets," Caesar warned when the beast dipped from sight.

"I have to undo the rafts," Logan said. "If something happens to—"

The eel slammed into them, hurling another person overboard. It had to be twenty feet long and three wide. Caesar suspected it had a solid core consisting of dense muscle and bone, considering how cold the water was.

They needed to stop it. "Do you have a knife?" he asked.

"A knife?" Ruby was bewildered, her face ashen.

Caesar mimed a stabbing motion. "Yes! A blade!" He nearly stumbled when the eel hit again.

Logan was at the stern, severing the rope tethering the pair of rafts. When they broke apart, he shoved the tool at Caesar. "Take this!"

It was part of a long saw, with a pointed end and sharp

teeth.

"What are you thinking?" Anders asked.

"We won't survive with *that* attacking us for the next day!"

Anders took a coil of rope, made a lazy noose, and looped it at the ankle. "Don't let go," he said, and took the tool from Caesar. When he jumped, Caesar grabbed the other end of the rope, cinching it to the log under his feet. He tied it and added his weight by spinning it to tighten on his waist.

Anders shot straight at the eel, wrapping an arm around it, and stabbed with the saw. When it didn't penetrate the hide, he changed tactics, slicing at it with the teeth instead. Caesar looked away as he disemboweled the eel, flinging entrails behind them. The rope had pulled taut, and Anders released his grip on the underwater opponent when it floated to the surface, dead.

Caesar hauled the nylon length, getting Anders onto the raft as the bow dipped, reaching another waterfall. The rapids carried them faster, but Anders was on board, lying on his back and laughing.

He dropped the saw. "Did I really just do that?"

"If you mean jump into the river while chopping a giant eel in half, then yes," Caesar said.

"How many did we lose?" Anders asked Logan and Ruby.

The Shelter leaders looked shocked by the events. "Four."

Caesar examined the water, ensuring the eel didn't have friends. "I'm sorry."

"It wasn't your fault. I don't have any doubt that it was waiting patiently for us to pass before it attacked," Logan said.

"Now what?" Anders took off his shirt, wringing it out.

"We wait." Ruby clutched her journal and marked their location on the map as treacherous.

"Is that it?" Summer walked across the street from their sanctuary. The pools of melted snow splashed under her feet.

"Jamal thinks so," John Paulson said. His sister patrolled with them, her wary gaze settling on everything at once.

"The snow will melt, and the storm season might be finished with, but we have a disaster on our hands," Haley said.

Summer had watched Isla's base explode late yesterday afternoon. It was a full day later, and she'd barely come to grips with their reality. Until now, they'd been banking on using the Shift when Logan returned to send them home.

It was gone, along with any sense of hope Summer had clung to.

Pastor Odell greeted people, carrying his Bible. Summer thought even the Good Book couldn't help them today.

Carly jogged over, dangling keys on her finger. "Wanna go for a ride?"

"Why?" Summer kept walking.

"My mom says I can take the van."

"Great."

Carly grabbed her wrist. "What's the matter?"

"We can't leave Arcadia."

"So what?"

Summer let John and his sister continue their search for Wanderers and faced her best friend. "Carly, don't you get it? You're never going to school again."

"Good, I hate school."

"What about traveling? We had plans to see the world after graduation," she said.

"I've barely ever left Carmichael. What am I missing?" Carly's smile was infectious, and Summer laughed.

"How do you keep such a vibe?"

"We have each other," she said. "Plus, apparently, my dad's not just a boring old guy with a consulting firm. He's a secret agent, and he'll bring Logan here."

"Logan's been stuck on Arcadia for a decade, so why would he be able to help us?"

"Let the adults figure that stuff out, Sum. We're kids, or did you forget?"

Summer peered at the storage facility where her mom was talking to Mrs. Lawrence. "I didn't expect those two to become friends."

"Me either," Carly admitted.

"Why do I find it kind of ick to see them together?"

"Because it throws the space-time continuum out of balance."

Summer took Carly's hand. "I've missed you."

"I haven't gone anywhere."

"But I have," Summer said. "I promise to stop ending up in the middle of stuff."

"Oh, please. You love drama. Only nothing ever happened until a few weeks ago."

The alleys had snow, but the Wanderers seemed to have disappeared from town. They left destruction in their wake. Combined with the Howlers' attacks, and the twisters that tore through Carmichael, their home was a disaster. But Carly was right. They had each other.

A car pulled up and idled beside them. Adam sat in the driver's seat with the window down, despite the chilly air.

"You ladies want to go for a ride? My dad is giving me time off."

Buck Iverson remained at the fence, checking the base for any flaws since the Wanderers tried eating it.

Carly and Summer looked at one another. "Sure," they echoed.

"But I thought you wanted to take the van?" Summer pointed at the keys Carly carried.

Carly put them away. "This is more fun."

"Do you mind if Jimmy comes?" Carly asked, and Adam shrugged.

"Not at all."

Carly found the teenage boy near the church with his father. "Can Jimmy leave for a bit?"

Vince gazed somberly at Adam's car. "That Buck's kid?"

Carly nodded.

"Go for it, but stay cautious." Vince returned to his conversation with Pastor Odell.

They piled into the pristine relic, and Adam put an arm around Summer's seat, looking into the back. "Where do you guys want to head?"

"Can we just cruise?" Summer wanted so badly to feel a sense of normality.

"Of course." Adam started downtown.

They passed the mayor's old office, and she noticed Dot's car and Freddy's trucks out front. She ignored them, knowing it wasn't her business. Summer decided then to live in the moment and be a teenager.

At least for a night.

10

"*W*here's Dot?" Katie sat in the chair across the town office boardroom table, giving the impression Amelia was running a budgetary meeting rather than an interrogation. Harrison was at the end, fingers steepled, indicating he was deep in thought. With his eyes closed, Amelia figured he might actually be sleeping, but he replied before she did.

"That's none of your business," Harrison said.

Katie was uncomfortable. Amelia wasn't usually the one to conduct questioning, not after the perp was brought in, but the woman gave off all kinds of signals she was guilty. The way her foot bounced up and down. Her shifting gaze.

Amelia viewed the sunset, finding half the snow in the yard melted. It had been a big storm, but the group from the Den suggested it might be past the region already, given how far south they were.

She kept quiet for another minute, drinking water. "Want some?" she asked Katie.

"Yes, please."

"Then talk." Amelia set a bottle on the table, out of reach. It wasn't a kind ploy, but necessary.

Katie adjusted a loose strand of hair. "When I signed up for the team, I had no idea what it was pertaining to.

They hired me…"

"Who?" Harrison interjected.

"I'd done a few jobs in the past, and went to the marketplace after the last one finished."

"Marketplace?" Amelia asked.

Katie exhaled, as if they were clearly dense. "Have you heard of the dark web?"

"Of course," Amelia said, though she'd never actually seen it.

"People need all kinds of favors. I've acted as a student's teacher to keep them from being sent to one of those military schools. I even posed as a wife so a guy could get the trust fund his overseas parents promised him. Plus a few other jobs."

"Okay, so you're on the marketplace, seeking…employment." Harrison drew air quotes around the word. "What does the ad say?"

"It was basic. Just the payment, and what they were looking for. Woman. Twenty to thirty. Serving experience beneficial."

"How much?"

"Fifty grand upfront on acceptance, and another hundred on completion," Katie said. "Sounded fair, right? Rents were cheap here, and it was simple enough. I came into town, and I got the job. When I tried to breach it with Dot, she acted oblivious."

"They offered you a hundred and fifty thousand dollars to do what, exactly?" Amelia finally sat.

"Move to Carmichael, Indiana, and work at Dot's Diner. The instructions specified that I'd be contacted once certain thresholds were reached. I didn't push them, since I was being paid so well."

"Is John Paulson part of the network?" Harrison asked.

Amelia doubted it, but given their situation, it was a good question.

Katie laughed. "John? No. He's a townie I ended up dating because I was bored. I built a whole backstory about being married to some loser before." She showed her ring finger. "I used tanner on my hand while wearing a plastic toy ring."

"Who else is lying?" Harrison kept going, but Amelia didn't mind. He had more experience than her.

Katie looked pointedly at him. "In this town? Good question. I didn't even know Isla wasn't from here. It wasn't until Lillian came that I was given further instructions."

"Who gave them to you?" Amelia asked.

"Lillian. At least I think it was her."

"And what did it say?"

"I don't remember." Katie averted her gaze, staring at her fidgeting hands.

Harrison slammed a palm on the table. "Tell us now."

Amelia guessed it was her job to play good cop. "Katie, the rules have changed. We don't have a jail here. These people are talking about Themis. If you break the law, you die on Arcadia. Is that what you want?"

"I didn't do anything!"

"You came to Carmichael to act as a server at a small-town diner for over six figures. What did you expect the job entailed?" she asked.

"When I heard Dot's connection to the guy missing from the tech company, I figured it was related to that. Then she mentioned her brother-in-law being a senator, and I knew it was connected."

"You assume the senator wanted you to keep his dead brother's wife company?" Harrison said glibly.

"No…maybe."

"Did you really hurt yourself the night of the Shift?"

"Yes. I decided to blow off steam and get out of Carmichael for the weekend. I planned on driving to Jackson to stay in a hotel, order room service, and enjoy some of that money."

"But you crashed," Amelia said.

"I did."

"When did you receive the instructions?"

"After the first Howler attack."

"Lillian was still pretending to be with the Department of Defense at that point," Amelia told Harrison.

"When can I go?" Katie asked. "I seriously did nothing wrong."

"You helped Christine escape and pointed a gun at us," Amelia said. "How did that happen?"

"The ad in the marketplace had an image on it. It was a circle with a dash in the center."

"So?"

"Christine has the same tattoo on her wrist."

Amelia thought about where she'd seen that before, and recalled Anders Lawrence had it on his wrist. "Harrison, could it be the mark of their old team?"

"That's the symbol for the Greek letter theta. It's not uncommon for operatives to have identical tattoos marking their team," he said. "Caesar and I have matching ones."

"I recognized it at breakfast and asked if she'd ever been to the marketplace. That's when she pulled me aside and demanded my help. She ordered me to bring someone else in, and Brent was wrapped around my finger, so it was an easy sell."

"Thanks to you, he's dead," Amelia said.

"Actually, it's thanks to you. If you weren't trying to trap Christine, none of this would have happened."

"Nice deflection, but it won't hold up in the court of Arcadia," Harrison told her.

"You're not seriously going to murder me, are you?"

"Murder's a strong word. Themis is a punishment, not an act of passion," he said.

Katie rose, knocking the chair back. "I didn't know about the Shifting, I swear! I wish I'd never come to Carmichael!"

"You and me both," Amelia said calmly. "Sit."

Katie obeyed, then let out an anguished cry.

"Tell us about Dot."

"Dot?"

"Yes."

"She's... well, you've spent a lot of time with her. She's a nice woman."

"We didn't really know her," Amelia whispered.

"Didn't..." Realization struck. "Dot's...dead?"

"Themis," Harrison repeated. If he wanted to scare the prisoner, it was working.

"What did Dot do?"

"You really have no idea?" Amelia asked.

Katie shook her head dramatically.

"Dot killed the Wests."

Katie's jaw dropped, and unless she was a talented actress, which Amelia doubted, this was news. "But she's so..."

"Dead," Harrison said coldly.

"If you hold this strong moral code, why is Lillian Carson free?" Katie wiped her tears.

"Because even though she's screwed up a lot, she prevented these people from being executed," Harrison advised. "And because of you, Clive and Brent aren't breathing, and Christine left Arcadia, blowing our chance of going home."

Katie's composure fractured again, and she rested her brow on the table.

"What else did Christine tell you?" Amelia asked.

Katie stayed still for a moment, then gazed up. "That Anders worked with her. That's it, I swear to God."

Amelia froze and looked at Harrison, who lifted a finger. "Thank you, Katie," he said, and escorted her to the door, where Freddy waited.

"Cuff her and bring her to the file room," Harrison told the deputy. Freddy snapped the handcuffs on Katie, and they wandered down the hall, leaving the pair alone in Mayor Vivian's old office. Harrison plunked onto his seat and intertwined his fingers behind his head. "It's a lie."

"Are you sure?" Amelia tried to recall every memory she had of the family man. He'd fought alongside Caesar in the Minotaur corn maze, determined to locate Isla's base—which someone like Lillian or Christine would try to do as well.

"No, I'm not sure. I never in a million years would have suspected Caesar's dead wife to be leading the charge on an alien planet."

"Where do you think she went?"

"Back to Earth to figure out their next steps. For now, they have nothing to worry about, because we can't transport home. The Shift is busted, and we're stuck on Arcadia." Harrison opened his antacids and dropped the last two into his palm. He took one and pocketed the remaining pill. "I should have retired when Fatina told me to."

"Christine said the town site is burned. No one will miss us," she said.

"They'll miss me," Harrison said.

"And the soldiers…won't someone talk?"

"Probably not."

"Who's looking for you?" Amelia asked.

Harrison smiled. "Wanda, my assistant, isn't just a schedule organizer. And Reggie hides behind a computer, but he's got the skills to figure this out. I told him to locate the new LTC facility."

"Can he target specific areas of Arcadia?"

"I don't believe so. Just like Isla couldn't send Carmichael to Logan's location. They don't have the knowledge yet."

"That's a positive. Maybe they'll leave us alone," Amelia said, picturing living her days out this way.

"They won't."

Amelia remembered the mission Caesar vanished on. "Because of Logan Rutherford."

"Precisely."

"It's getting late," she said. "We've had a big day."

Harrison yawned on command. "It's your call. Keep Katie confined for now?"

She nodded. "I'm not ready to live by Arcadian law. Not yet."

"Understood." Harrison reached out, and she shook with him. "You're doing a great job."

"Thank you."

"I met your boss, Sheriff Lyle."

"Dot told me he was involved like the rest."

Harrison sighed. "I sent Reggie to find him."

"Then…"

"Reggie will be okay." Harrison grimaced. "But Wanda was supposed to contact him too. If she was intercepted, then my wife and daughter might not have made it to the safehouse."

"I'm sorry. Want a lift?" Amelia asked.

"Don't worry about Anders. Christine thrives in the chaos. She wanted to leave us with doubts," he told her.

"I agree." Amelia hated guessing who she could trust.

———————

Light shone in the distance, suggesting an end to their perilous journey. Caesar hadn't been dry in two days, and his fingers were wrinkled like prunes. They traveled the second half with minimal interference, primarily because the river widened while speeding up.

Anders hadn't spoken in hours, but that wasn't unusual. Logan and Ruby talked while using her journal, and it was obvious they were in love.

The Shelter leaders put the book away and faced the group. Everyone crouched on the rafts, some sleeping in the middle despite the steady spraying from below.

"We're at the end!" Logan called. "Time to prepare!"

Word spread quickly.

"Does the river slow?" Anders asked in a gruff voice.

"No," Ruby answered. "It continues below the rock, probably to an outlying ocean."

"Meaning we're about to crash into a shoreline at twenty miles an hour," Caesar said.

"That sums it up." Logan didn't seem fazed by the threat of impact.

"What are we doing about it?" Caesar inspected the front of the lead raft.

"Jump."

"Jump?" Anders repeated.

"We'll escape off the raft and climb up the slope to the path above," Logan said.

"That's insane!" Caesar shouted over the river noise. It grew louder as they neared the end of the visible flowing water.

Logan patted him on the back. "At least there are no more gigantic eels to contend with."

"This plan is nuts," Anders muttered.

Logan and Ruby split up, moving across the rafts to explain the plan to their people. The four recent transplants from the brownstone came to Caesar. "They're not serious, are they?" Greg asked. "I can barely swim. I never passed the third level when I was a kid."

"Talia, what about you?" Caesar asked the older woman.

"If this is how I die, then that's His plan," she said.

"Sebastian, you're in charge of helping Talia. Emma, can you swim?"

She stared at the rocky edge coming up fast.

"Emma!" he shouted, and she snapped to attention.

"Yes, I was all-state in college."

"Bring Greg up there." He pointed at the slope on the left of the riverbank.

She looked dazed, then nodded. "If I have to."

"I'm sorry I called the landlord on you," Greg said, and Caesar walked away, leaving them to it.

Logan tossed some crates from the back and unfurled a net, with stones weighing the corners.

"Everyone ready?" he shouted.

No one seemed excited as they began leaping from the rear edge of the rafts, splashing into the running water.

"Caesar, can you keep this end?" Logan thrust the corner of the woven net to him. "I'll go to the right, and you head to the opposite."

"And what are you trying to catch?" he asked.

"The crates, and anyone that can't swim to the shore."

"No pressure," Caesar said under his breath.

Ruby was already off, with Anders on her tail.

All that remained were the two of them, and the cliff

was coming up fast. The rocks looked sharp and jagged, the bottom worn smooth from the constant stream rushing by.

"If you're caught under, you won't have air for miles," Logan called.

They perched on the wooden log, and Logan counted down from three.

When he reached the end, the front raft smashed into the barrier, crumpling loudly. Caesar submerged in the river, instantly losing his orientation. He swam toward a beam of light aimed from the shore, where some of the population had already arrived safely. Others called out, but all he could focus on was helping Logan with the net. The second raft crashed more softly, given the errant logs slowing it. They bobbed around, nearly striking Caesar in the chest. The wood brushed his shirt, tearing the fabric, but he stayed afloat. Caesar hit the barrier, grabbing hold of it with one hand while fastening the net to a sharp protrusion. He dropped the rope, and it sank with the weight of the rock.

Logan did the same on the far end, and it worked as he'd intended. Some of their supplies were caught by the net. Logan swam to the collection, fighting the angry current while clutching the cliff. He shoved them to Caesar, who moved the crates to the shore, where Anders and Ruby hauled them up.

"Where's Talia?" someone called.

Caesar found the New Yorker clinging to a log, her glasses dangling from the string on her neck. With Logan's efforts, they dragged her along, and he put an arm under her, lifting the thin woman while he staggered from the water. She coughed a lungful of liquid and gasped while Caesar sat on a boulder.

"We did it," Logan said.

The logs continued to bash into the wall while water flowed beneath. Light shone from an opening in the ceiling, giving hope to the soaked Shelter population.

Ruby pulled the journal from a plastic bag, which had kept it surprisingly dry, and made a note. "Let's reach the surface, so we only have thirty miles remaining."

The hike up was exhausting, given the ordeal they'd gone through, but the inhabitants of Arcadia rarely complained. Even the children stayed quiet, resolutely marching up the gravel incline.

"This will be a couple of miles," Anders said.

"I guess we have to come up higher than the base of the canyon."

"I want an evening at home with my family. I'd love a serving of my wife's lasagne right now."

"And a glass of 2008 Bordeaux from Harrison's collection," Caesar added.

"I don't know anything about wine, but I'd take an old Scotch."

They emerged, and the brightness almost blinded Caesar after two and a half days in the dark. The sun had altered positions, and it hung lower on the horizon. The air was colder, and snowflakes fell from the sky.

"We're too late," Logan said.

"For what?"

"The storm already happened, if there's snow," Ruby answered for him.

"Do you mean…"

"Carmichael might have gone through the season change," Logan finished. "Let's walk a few miles before we camp. It'll be a struggle with these frigid temperatures."

"Thirty miles is quite a hike."

"It's worse in snow," Ruby said.

The group began marching in the direction of

Carmichael without complaint, and Caesar glanced to the right, where the alien forest lingered. Within those woods were the Howlers, but he suspected they were far enough away not to be an immediate threat.

They reached high ground before the sun set completely, and he saw the snow-covered valley between them and Carmichael.

Anders stared at it with him, and he knew what the man was thinking.

"Don't worry. Your family will be okay."

The duo, who'd left with the bikes, revved the engines and rolled forward, removing their helmets.

"Any trouble?" Caesar asked.

"Not a soul to be seen," Doug said.

Without another word, they started setting up camp for what Caesar prayed was the last time.

11

Gemma pulled the blanket, and John shivered as the cool air hit his skin. He blinked and examined the storage facility in the dark. He didn't remember her climbing into bed with him, but she had chosen a cot directly beside his. Nothing had happened, or he'd definitely have a memory of it. He viewed her breathing softly, then noticed movement across the room.

Hundreds of locals were sound asleep. Not even the cook, Klein, was up yet, which meant it was around three or four in the morning. John lifted his arm, checking the old leather-strapped watch that once belonged to his father, and saw it was twenty after four.

Maya, Ben, and Louise were sleeping, but Jamal's spot near his wife was vacant.

John heard a door softly latching at the exit and slid from the bed. He had the sudden urge to relieve himself, and guessed that was where Jamal had gone.

His bare feet plodded along the cold concrete floor, and he went straight for his shoes. Once they were tied, he went to the portable bathrooms. He regretted not throwing a sweater on as he jogged to the bathrooms. They were all vacant.

John used it, squeezed sanitizer, and returned to the

parking lot while wiping the substance into his palms.

The generators' noise was constant near the fence, keeping the defensive floodlights activated. He glanced at the rooftop, finding his sister holding a rifle and staring into the distance. He waved, but she must not have seen him. Instead of calling to her, he searched for Jamal.

His shoes got wet as he splashed in the melting snow. Parts had frozen to ice in the night, but the temperatures were already increasing with the threat of dawn, which wouldn't happen for a couple more hours.

He found Jamal near the large trash bins in the back, and something about his posture kept John from giving away his position. Jamal crouched to retrieve a bag. Before reaching in, he glanced around, making John duck.

When John checked again, Jamal had a set of keys dangling from a finger. He almost intervened, but stayed hidden, his gut telling him to remain a silent observer.

They circled the rear of the building, and Jamal unhinged part of the fence, leaving the barricade. John watched as he got into an old van and tried to remember who it belonged to. It was the Benyuks'.

Instead of pursuing Jamal, he bolted to the front, finding Buck Iverson on guard as his son dozed in a folding chair.

"I need out." John pointed to the street.

"The Howlers were active a few hours ago," Buck said, opening the gate.

"I'll be careful." John headed to the busted-up SUV they'd borrowed from the Gellers and flipped the visor, making sure the electronic key was there. He waited to start it until the Benyuks' van had passed by. "What are you doing, Jamal?"

John trailed him at a distance. He didn't have to worry about the lights, since the front end was smashed and they hadn't been replaced. It made skulking through Carmichael easier.

The moon was low and bright from its position in space. John had given little thought to where the planet Arcadia was in relation to Earth. How far had they Shifted? Were they even in the Milky Way? He suddenly grew queasy at the notion.

Jamal accessed a gravel driveway, and John gazed at the familiar spruce-lined road. "The Benyuks." Jamal had been shot here by the homeowner when he'd shown up in the dark. Lillian later killed three people here, taking Jamal captive. What purpose would he have sneaking to their house at this hour?

John parked by the trees and got out. The snow hadn't melted in the shade created by the evergreens, and he traipsed in it, jogging toward the farmhouse.

Jamal neared the front of the home and entered without checking behind him. John hurried, wishing he'd brought his gun. His new friend had to have a good reason for his actions, but John couldn't think of what that might be.

John crept up the steps, listening. When he was greeted by silence, he walked in, detecting movement from a bedroom down the hall. He nearly warned Jamal of his presence when he heard the clicking sound. It was brief, a constant clacking, like someone typing on a keyboard but hitting the same two letters over and over.

A floorboard groaned under his weight, and John froze when the clicking ceased. He refused to breathe, and when it began again, he exhaled and continued.

Jamal was on the bed, facing the window with a device on his lap. His lips moved in the moonlit space, forming unperceivable words. His finger wagged, pressing the lever with the knob. John had seen something like this in a textbook. A light glowed from the bottom.

It was time to ask the question.

John stepped into the room. "What are you doing?"

Jamal attempted to hide the telegraph key. "Nothing. I left some stuff here."

"And that?" John pointed at the device beside his leg.

Jamal breathed slowly, the deep, resounding sigh that usually preceded bad news. "You shouldn't have followed me."

"If this was so innocent, why do it at five in the morning, and not just walk through the guarded gate?"

Jamal frowned and rose. He held a snub-nosed revolver aimed at John. "Seriously, dude. You didn't have to come. I like you."

"And I *liked* you until you waved a gun in my face," John told him.

"You want to know what this is?" Jamal asked.

John nodded, but really wanted the guy to drop the weapon.

"I'm a scout, and I've seen a decent amount of Arcadia. I was on the road two years ago, minding my business. As a scout, it's my job to retrieve anything of value. So much junk appears through random Shifts, and we decide whether to use what we find, or trade it with the other communities. There I was, peacefully sitting at a fire, when a man showed up."

John weighed his options while Jamal spoke. He could turn and run, which might be the best choice, because the gun's range wasn't great, especially in the dark. Or he could tackle Jamal and fight it off. "Who was it?"

"His name's Milton. He gave me something like whiskey and a cigar. Then, after we shared a meal, he came close, like right up to me, and spoke quietly into my ear. I'll never forget it."

"What did he say?" John asked.

"*I own you. If you whisper a word to your village, I will kill them all, starting with your wife. Take this. Use it. You're mine, Jamal. Everyone on Arcadia is mine.*"

The revolver lowered.

"There wasn't a choice, man. I'd spent an hour telling him everything about our village. About Ben and Louise, and my relationship with Maya, and he'd listened amiably. I didn't suspect someone on Arcadia could be so evil."

"Have you met humans?" John asked.

"Sure. But this is a new world. I thought it would be different."

"What did he ask you to do?"

"He gave me this." Jamal picked up the device used to send Morse code. "Gave me instructions and told me to keep him informed with details, like how many people we have, et cetera. Any time I found something on a scouting mission, I had to report it."

John understood the implications. "He knows."

Jamal's chin dropped. "Yeah, I gave him Carmichael's location." The gun was still in his grip, but it pointed at the ground.

"Are you going to kill me?"

"Kill?" Jamal looked at the revolver and tossed it to the bed. "No way, man. I…I just want this to be over. I'll come clean. I got so used to reporting in that I figured if I didn't send him a message, he'd move for the Den while we're gone."

"How does it work? We don't have telephone lines on Arcadia."

Jamal flipped it and showed him the power source. "Arcadia's full of these stones, and he's connected to them. Don't ask me how."

John lunged, picking up the gun without any resistance.

He put it into his pocket and motioned to the telegraph unit. "I'm sorry, Jamal, but we have to bring you to Amelia and tell her everything."

"I know." Jamal shoved it into his bag and walked by John, drifting through the house. "If it helps, I never wanted to do it."

"Then why did you? You could have gone home and told Ben what happened."

"You didn't meet Milton," Jamal said.

They trudged in the snow with Jamal in front, getting to the SUV. Jamal got in without comment, and John kept the gun close by.

The lights to the town office were off, save one. He spotted Amelia in the foyer, pacing back and forth, even though the sun hadn't risen yet. She stopped when Jamal and John approached the entrance, and he guessed she could tell the news was bad when she saw their expressions.

"What is it?" Amelia held the door, letting in a cool morning breeze.

"Jamal?" John urged.

Milton's reluctant spy began talking.

"*W*hat are we going to do?" Amelia asked the group around the boardroom table.

She looked at each of them. John Paulson and his sister Haley were present, with Kong and Freddy, still swollen-eyed, beside them. Next was Harrison, along with Mr. Tucker and Vince. They'd elected to invite Lillian, despite her precarious position within the town hierarchy. Ben and Louise had joined, given this involved their village and one of their people. Sharon rounded out the group, and she seemed distracted since being woken an hour ago.

"Can we start at the beginning?" Freddy asked. "This is a lot to process at seven AM."

Amelia eyed the carafe of coffee and poured more into her cup. She walked to the whiteboard and removed the marker's top. "Before I begin, I have news. Dot Hunter is dead."

Sharon started to cry, and Haley took her hand. "How?"

Amelia gazed at Harrison, who answered for her. "Dot wasn't who you thought. She captured the chief and was about to kill her. She knew about the Shift, and was willing to let you all get killed by this Mr. Gustafsson in exchange for a clean break with her son."

"That's not possible!" Sharon bellowed.

"It's the truth," Amelia confirmed. "I'm lucky John and Harrison came, or I'd be the one buried in her basement."

"Then Christine Shifted from Arcadia and blew up the base. Harrison's checking the Geiger counter twice daily, and so far, it's not emitting heavy signs of radiation."

The mood in the room grew more somber with the news, even though they'd already known these details. Being reminded they couldn't go home dampened their already low spirits.

When no one interjected, she wrote the word *Milton* on the board, and Ben sat upright.

"What do you know about the guy?" she asked.

"Just rumors," Ben admitted. "There's been talks of a place up north called Tombstone."

"Jamal is working for him," Amelia said.

"What? No way." Louise looked at John. "What's she telling us?"

384

"They met on the road a couple of years ago, and Milton threatened him, saying he'd come to the Den if Jamal didn't comply."

"Which leads me to the next issue," Amelia said. "Jamal gave him our location before John interrupted." The room exploded in conversation. She let them vent for a minute before raising a hand. "Given the size of Arcadia, Milton won't arrive before Caesar."

"We don't know that he's ever coming," Sharon said.

"Caesar's never failed a mission," Harrison stated bluntly. "And he won't start now, especially with Anders Montrave on his team."

"Montrave?" Sharon asked.

"Sorry, Anders Lawrence."

"Unless he's working for the other team," Amelia added.

"Why would Anders betray us?" John asked.

"He and Christine have the same tattoo... a theta symbol."

"All the old teams did it." Lillian loosened the button at the end of her sleeve and rolled it up, revealing an owl inked on her skin. "I know, not my first choice either."

"That eases my mind a bit," Amelia said. "We have a big dilemma. Christine informed us Carmichael no longer exists on Earth. They've burned the alien forest that replaced your homes, so if we Shift there, we'd likely be killed on site. Our best chance is to stay on Arcadia and figure out a plan when Logan shows."

"His mom and co-founder are dead," Lillian said. "It might be difficult to convince him of anything at this point."

Amelia sipped the coffee, hoping the jolt of caffeine would distract her from the creeping sensation they were too late. "Lillian, what are your thoughts?"

"When we had the base intact, I'd anticipated sending the town to the remote Colorado mountains, where Logan vanished a decade ago. Mr. Gustafsson wouldn't know, and we could escape back to civilization."

"Then what?" Haley asked. "Go our separate ways, and pray a trained assassin doesn't eventually come knocking?"

"I figured Harrison here would have a suggestion," Lillian said.

"I have another idea." Harrison tapped the table, and everyone got closer. "I go to Earth, find Mr. Gustafsson, and kill the bastard. I'll use his laboratory to connect with this planet and bring everyone home."

Amelia hadn't considered the option. "Even if that works, we're still trapped on Arcadia. Half the town is gone, we're running low on supplies, and a psychopath wearing a cowboy hat is coming for us."

Louise nudged Ben in the arm. "Tell them."

"What is it?" Amelia asked.

Ben cleared his throat and combed his beard with his hand. "There's a town."

"Where?"

"Ten miles south," he said.

"Why haven't you mentioned it before?"

"It didn't seem relevant."

"Who lives there?" Harrison asked.

"That's the kicker. No one. It's empty. I came across it in the early years, but figured it was too close to the forest, considering that's in Howler territory. We eventually got the Repulsor, which worked for scouts, but not for an entire village. You've extended the Repulsor's reach, and it would probably cover the total distance."

Mr. Tucker spoke for the first time. "You're forgetting something."

"What's that?" Ben asked.

"It's ten miles through alien forest."

Vince scratched his nose. "Not to mention the effort of dragging out a generator, and the fuel needed to keep it running."

"It's an option," Amelia said. "How big is this place?"

"It's an old settlement from the 1800s," Ben told her. "There's a water tower, shops, houses. It's nowhere near as large as Carmichael, so you'd have to expand. I can help with that."

"What do you mean?" Louise asked. "We're leaving the Den?"

"Did you hear what they said? Jamal gave us away to Milton. If he comes for Carmichael, do you think he won't venture out to the Den too?"

"Which means more mouths to feed," Sharon added.

"We can fend for ourselves," Louise told her.

Amelia didn't like the plan. "Moving everyone from Carmichael to an abandoned town through Howler-infested territories sounds challenging."

"It's that or face Milton when he shows up," Harrison said. "We have trained soldiers, and if Caesar arrives with Anders, that ups our chances."

"Either option puts our people at risk." Amelia weighed the choices. "We wait until Logan's here, then decide."

Ben rose. "In the meantime, I have to exercise the Themis with Jamal."

Amelia's arm hair stood on end. "You want to kill him?"

"He betrayed us. That is an offense worth death on Arcadia." Ben moved for the door. "I suggest you do the same with the woman you have trapped in the other room."

"Katie?" Amelia intercepted Ben at the exit. "No."

"No?" Ben set his hands on his hips. "This isn't the States. We have our own laws."

"I'm running things in Carmichael, and I refuse to allow you to murder Jamal or Katie, no matter their crimes."

"You shot Dot," Sharon exclaimed.

Harrison furrowed his brow. "I support the chief. It's her town. If you want to kill your own people outside the borders, go ahead."

"Jamal loves you guys. Milton's the problem," John said.

"And this Gustafsson." Amelia sighed. "We have enemies in every direction. The elements, Howlers, Tombstone, and Christine Hawkstone's team."

Ben's neck cords tensed, but he relaxed when Louise touched him. "It's okay. It's time we change our rules. Arcadia's growing," his partner said.

"We'll see," Ben murmured.

"Thanks for meeting with us. Please keep everything said to yourselves. Clearly, we can't trust our own population," Amelia advised. "Caesar will be here soon."

She sank into the chair while they exited and stopped Kong before he left. "How's Athena?"

"Pink and fussy," he said.

"Can you make sure no one bothers our prisoners? Put Vince on it."

"You bet, Chief."

"Then go spend the day with your family. They need their father."

Kong smiled and marched down the hall.

Lillian and Harrison remained in the boardroom, and Amelia picked up her coffee cup. "I don't like any of these options."

"It's time to put two heads on a platter," Harrison said.

"One on Earth, and one on Arcadia."

"Easier said than done."

Lillian laughed. "This is what we do."

12

"*W*hy are we doing this?" Carly shuffled her feet as they approached the Franklins' home.

"Because they asked us to," Summer said.

Adam's car hauled a trailer, and they moved from house to house, essentially breaking in when necessary. "Are we abandoning Carmichael?" he asked.

"Looks that way." Summer read the handwritten list. They were instructed to take any batteries, food, water, blankets, and jackets with them, as well as gas cans, guns, and ammunition.

"All the essentials," Carly said. "They forgot to add camping gear to the list."

Summer reread it and nodded, doing just that. They'd visited three places so far and hadn't found much of value. She checked the keyring and took the one with the Franklins' house number on it. Some residents couldn't bear the thought of stripping their homes or supplies, and gladly relinquished the duty to the road teams.

Jimmy was across the street with Evan, and they waved.

"I'll be right back." Carly left before Summer reminded her they were on a time crunch.

"Guess it's you and me." Adam smiled and held the

screen wide to unlock the door.

The room was stuffy, so Summer moved to the kitchen window, cracking it open. They began the slow process of rifling through the drawers. She pocketed any batteries and took a heavy flashlight, as well as the handful of dog food she found in the pantry. The animals at the Wickenhouse farm would need it. "What are they going to do with the dogs and cows when we leave?"

Adam wouldn't look at her.

"What's the matter?"

"My dad said we aren't going anywhere."

"Seriously? What about Milton?"

"Summer, he never changes his mind."

"But…"

Adam touched her cheek. "What if Milton doesn't come, and you can stay too?"

Summer had heard the rumors. The news of a dangerous group from up north had spread through town. She didn't see how they could linger when an armed militia was heading in their direction. Summer also wasn't a fan of heading to a vacant town, site unseen.

Adam leaned down and kissed her.

Summer forgot about the snowfall, the twisters, and the rubble where her own family home had been, and let herself go.

"I leave you for two minutes, and you're making out." Carly's interruption stopped them, and Adam bolted to the hall.

"You didn't have to do that," Summer chided her friend.

"Who knew that farm boy would get so embarrassed?"

"Come on, let's keep searching." Summer descended into the basement, where she uncovered a box of camping essentials, still new in the original packaging. In the garage, they discovered a half-filled jerry can of gas and two rifles, along with five cases of ammo.

Once everything was loaded, they returned to the street and kept on to the next property. The house was already broken into, and the television was notably missing from the wall brackets above the fireplace.

"Only losers resort to vandalism," Carly said.

"It could have been a lot worse." Summer repeated something she overheard the adults saying earlier.

"We're not really going, are we?" Carly pouted, sticking her lower lip out.

"What choice do we have?"

"I can't believe Caesar married that witch." Carly lifted a pack of cookies triumphantly. "Score."

Life on Arcadia would be a far cry from the comforts of Earth. Summer had spent years thinking about her future, and now she had nothing to look forward to.

She told herself that the grownups would handle things, but the older she got, the more she realized they weren't that different. Everyone was afraid.

Carly moved slowly, like her energy was sapped. Summer walked up to her when they reached the end of the block, their trailer three-quarters full of supplies. More people converged at the crosswalk, and despite the uncertain circumstances, the folks she'd been surrounded by her whole life seemed optimistic. She put an arm around Carly's waist and smiled when Adam and Jimmy arrived with a pair of baseball gloves, a softball, and a bat.

"Wanna hit the park?" Jimmy asked.

She caught her mother's gaze while she talked with Mrs. Lawrence and Mrs. Trefal across the intersection. She wasn't allowed to spend time unsupervised with boys, but her mom nodded, giving the approval she'd sought for years.

"Last one there's a Howler's dinner!" Carly shouted and took off.

"They sure did a number on your bar," Amelia said.

Kong picked up a section of torn felt from the pool table. "Hungry little bastards."

"Where do they go?" Harrison wondered. "Damn things must be hanging around underground, waiting for snowfall."

Lillian Carson grabbed a pool cue and hung it on the wall. "Can you remind me which booth your wife gave birth in, so I can avoid it?"

Kong shot her a glare. "Sit up there."

He walked behind it, kicking an upended trashcan. "I spent years dreaming of owning my own business, and here it is, taken away."

Amelia didn't quite empathize, since she'd owned nothing in her life. Her car was a lease from the dealership in Jackson. Her apartment was rented one year at a time, to give her the freedom to leave at any given moment. She'd lived there for five years.

"I met Chun shortly after I was released," he said. "God, she was so beautiful. Chun worked in property management in Baltimore, and without her help, I'd have been homeless. She forged some paperwork, since no one wants a convict in their building. Six months later, we were moving to Carmichael. I literally used a map and chose Jackson at random. She had hopes of a lateral movement with her company, because they were spread across the region. But before we got there, we found out she was pregnant with Cassie. We stopped in Carmichael on the way to Jackson, and…I saw this place for lease."

Amelia imagined herself taking such a chance, and struggled to. She sat at the bar with Harrison between her and Lillian. Kong took his usual position on the other side, unconsciously buffing the surface with a cloth.

"And that decision got you to Arcadia," Harrison said.

"Wouldn't have changed a thing. We have three incredible children, and I've been happier in Carmichael than at any other point in my life. Chun too. We love the open skies, the air, the people…when they're not fighting over tables and betting on darts." Kong eyed the bar, where the Wanderers had decimated some of the leather seats. "What'll it be?"

Harrison went first. "Anything strong. Make me remember why I don't drink the hard stuff."

"I'll have a double," Lillian said.

"Same." Amelia smiled with little joy, since she had to leave Carmichael to venture into the alien woods.

Kong poured four servings into three ounce shot glasses and passed them out. "To…"

"Those we lost, and protecting those we haven't," Amelia said, and they clinked the glasses together before downing the contents.

Amelia didn't visibly react when the liquor burned, and accepted a second serving. Lillian drank it straight away.

"I never expected it to play out like this." Lillian played with a coaster, spinning it on the bar.

"This isn't the end," Harrison said.

Amelia sensed their chances of ever getting to Earth had depleted. Now they needed to survive on this harsh planet and tend to a thousand people. If anyone could do it, it was the residents of Carmichael.

Kong set to his task, filling a box with booze. "Don't tell a soul about this, or they'll come for me."

Harrison nodded. "As long as you share, we won't have a problem."

They walked out of the bar, and Kong hesitated at the exit. He flipped the sign to CLOSED and sighed as the door shut slowly. He left it unlocked, and they got to their vehicles.

"I'd better check on the family," Kong said.

"Thanks for the drink." Amelia went into Dot's car, feeling slightly uneasy about driving the dead woman's vehicle. She escorted the pair to their staging facility at the church. The pews had been moved, making way for the supplies to be sorted.

Outside in the parking lot, five trailers were being unloaded. They'd stripped the town's houses and businesses of anything they might require long-term if they decided to leave Carmichael. Amelia already decided it wasn't smart to go through the forest without scouting it first, and she was leaving soon with Ben and Louise.

Milton couldn't travel quickly, and that would give Caesar time to return with Logan. Whatever good that would do.

She watched as the Paulson siblings hauled a crate from a trailer, joking with one another. Pastor Odell gave orders, helping carry boxes when necessary. Sharon noticed her and smiled, but it never reached her eyes. No matter the reasoning, Amelia felt slightly responsible for every death that had transpired since the Shift.

"You don't have to go." The words startled her, and she turned to find Summer Dawson. The girl's eyes were bright.

"Thanks, but someone does."

"At least take this." Summer handed her something.

Amelia looked at the cell with a Princess Diamond sticker on the back. "What's this?"

"My old phone. The playlist is pretty tight." She passed Amelia a solar charger for it. "I think you'll like the first song."

Amelia held the device as Summer rejoined her friends. She put the earbuds in and tapped the screen.

"Love… or get off the…" Amelia listened to the sound of a younger generation and glanced at the sky, finding the day coming to a denouement.

———————

"*I*t's dark. Should we go on?" Logan asked Caesar. They'd long since given up taking charge, conceding their decisions to him, and Caesar wouldn't have minded, if not for the constant glares from the people of Shelter.

Everyone was damp, tired, and incredibly annoyed at the relentless pace he'd set. The adults basically dragged the children, the oldest alternating on bikes. Caesar's shoes were practical, but after the events of the last couple of weeks, even those were beginning to wear. The ordeal had the group on edge, but he wouldn't stop when they were so close to the goal.

"Ruby, how far?" he asked, probably for the fifth time since lunch.

"Two miles to the border," she said.

"Then what?" Anders asked. "We march into Howler territory, exhausted and weak?"

Caesar almost smelled the sweet cornfields. He needed to see Amelia and know that they were alive. He also wanted to get Logan to his co-founder's base so he could begin working on a way home.

He gazed at the crowd. Greg hugged himself, and two women from Shelter swayed on their feet. "Break time."

"No fires," Logan warned them. "The Howlers are too close."

Caesar motioned to the bikes. "I'm going."

"What?" Anders asked.

"I can't stay here. Look at this. It's obvious a massive storm already hit them, and there's snow and ice near the forest." He passed the scope to Anders, who nodded when he saw it.

"Fine."

This surprised Caesar. "No argument?"

"I'll protect them. You make sure my family's okay." Anders put a hand on his shoulder. Caesar glanced at the tattoo on his wrist.

"That'll be my first stop." Caesar got onto the motorbike, which had a nearly empty fuel tank. He tested the other, discovering even less gas. With his assault rifle strapped around his back and a full magazine in his 9MM, he said his goodbyes and rode slowly down the harsh terrain, nearing the alien forest. A couple miles deeper was the relative safety of the boundary.

He glanced at the people of Shelter setting up camp and felt a sense of dread. Caesar stopped, lowering his feet, and contemplated if it was worth the trouble.

After two minutes, he continued driving toward the treeline.

He entered the woods with trepidation. The Howlers would be drawn to the noise of the bike, and on uneven ground, they'd have the advantage, especially in the dark.

He made it the first half mile without incident, the tires jostling on the forest bed. The engine struggled, and he checked the gauge, finding it completely empty. "Come on, just another mile."

It didn't obey. The exhaust rumbled, and the gauges dropped. Caesar let the bike fall to the ground, and he surveyed the boughs above. With the rifle out, he used the night-vison scope, searching for Howlers.

When he didn't see any, he ran, heading straight for the border. Caesar's legs were already exhausted after a full twenty-four hours of hiking with minimal breaks, but he pushed himself, eager to learn the fate of the town he'd become intertwined with.

The second he spotted the edge of the Gellers' cornfield, he remembered the radio tucked into his pack. He released the bag, rummaging through it. Caesar drank the last of the water in the canteen and grabbed the walkie, pressing talk. "HQ, this is Caesar. Over."

"Caesar?" It was Amelia.

The first Howler fell from the tree, and it was soon surrounded by a dozen more.

13

*A*melia drove to his location. *Caesar's here.* The thought repeated constantly, urging her to move faster.

Harrison and Lillian were almost out of the doors before she hit the brakes in the corner of the Gellers' property. The agents sprinted to the whereabouts he'd given her on the radio.

Twenty of the animals howled and screeched, surrounding a person. A bunch were already dead, but the rest didn't seem to notice.

Harrison opened fire, shouting for Caesar to stay down. Lillian killed another three without delay, and Amelia used her sidearm, shooting repeatedly, until all twenty were dead. Caesar lay on the grass, motionless.

For a second, she was sure he'd been mauled. Amelia choked back a sob and knelt at his side, setting a palm on his neck. He groaned while rolling over.

"What took you so long?" His face was dirty, and his pants were torn at the shin. He smiled, showing blood on his teeth. Caesar coughed, then noticed who had accompanied Amelia to rescue him. His handgun flew up, aiming at Lillian.

"It's okay, Caesar," Harrison said.

His gaze flicked to his boss, then his expression grew

even more confused.

"It's a long story, and I don't think we should do this here." Harrison offered his hand. "How about we go into town and discuss it?"

"Where's Logan?" Lillian asked.

"Can we just…" Harrison started away.

Lillian shook her head. "Is he alive?"

Amelia sensed the desperation in her voice.

Caesar glanced between them. "Anders is with him. They're two miles past the border. We've pushed them too much, and it was too dangerous to cross the forest at night."

"Thank God." Lillian folded at the waist, breathing deeply.

Harrison and Lillian walked ahead, and Amelia hung back with Caesar as he limped toward the truck.

He reached for her hand. "Are you okay?"

Amelia laughed at the incredulous question. Here he was, nearly ripped to shreds by a cluster of Howlers, and he had the audacity to ask how *she* was doing? "I am now." She slipped her fingers into his, and Caesar's warmth enveloped her.

If only she didn't have to tell him that his wife was very much alive and determined to kill every last person in Carmichael.

———

*C*aesar had wanted to get straight to business, but Harrison demanded he follow orders, which included a cold shower, fresh clothes, a cup of coffee, and something to eat.

Caesar felt like a new man as he traversed the town

office halls. Two of the doors were closed, and Vince stood between the rooms, holding a rifle.

"Vince," he said.

"Caesar."

"What are you doing?"

"Guarding the prisoners," Vince answered.

"Who…"

Harrison pointed to the boardroom. "We'll fill you in."

Caesar gratefully accepted a second cup of coffee, knowing the luxury would soon be in short supply. He hoped Logan could tap into the power source below Isla's barn and send them to Earth before they ran out of staples.

Amelia entered, her uniform replaced with a pair of jeans and a white knitted sweatshirt. He'd never seen her in anything but a uniform, and he imagined her on a day off, doing simple chores like grocery shopping.

Lillian joined them, and Caesar gritted his teeth. "Would someone tell me what the hell happened while I was gone?"

"Can you fill us in first?" Harrison asked.

Caesar took a drink of coffee and noticed they'd closed the door behind them for privacy. The room had come straight out of the Eighties. There was even a tube TV on a rolling tray, like his audiovisual club had in high school.

He listed off the various stops he and Anders made. When he mentioned Duffy discussing Milton as though he was a cult leader, their postures changed. He understood they were aware of the man from Tombstone.

He glossed over some details of their river trek and ended with his journey into the forest mere hours earlier.

"I'll be damned," Harrison said. "You and Anders have quite the body count."

"You'd rather I let them take over Shelter?"

"There's something you need to know." It was bizarre

seeing his boss on Arcadia. Two worlds collided as he sat with Amelia and Lillian.

"What?" Caesar's patience had come to an end. "Just say it already."

"The base is destroyed," Amelia blurted.

He released the coffee cup, staring at her. "Excuse me?"

"Summer and I didn't Shift here alone. Christine was the agent in charge of the LTC operation," Harrison told him.

Caesar's pulse quickened with the news. "Wait… what? *My* Christine?"

Amelia frowned at the possessive comment.

"She didn't die in Chile, Caesar. It was a setup." Harrison reached into his pocket and removed a tin, but nothing was inside when he shook it.

"Anders…"

"As far as we know, he's clean," his boss said.

"Christine isn't dead?" He'd lived with the fact that he'd lost his wife for years, and had even grown to accept it after a time. What he couldn't grasp was why she'd do this to him.

"I'm afraid not. And she's—"

"A bitch," Lillian commented.

Caesar watched the traitorous murderer. "You're the expert." Lillian didn't take the bait, and he was glad, because he wasn't in the mood to argue.

"Where is she?" Caesar rose. "In one of those rooms?"

"Do you think we'd leave Vince to guard her?" Amelia asked. "No. She left."

"Left?"

"She Shifted before destroying the base."

"So…"

"We're stranded on Arcadia." Amelia seemed oddly

calm.

"What else?"

"You know who Milton is already. You mentioned a spy from Shelter, with the telegraph? Well, Jamal had one too. He gave Milton our location," Harrison said.

Caesar processed the information. "You're saying my wife's alive, running a mission to murder the population of Carmichael and secure a link to Arcadia for…"

"Mr. Gustafsson."

"Also, a dictator from a place called Tombstone is coming for us, and we have no way to travel to Earth."

"Right."

"There's more," Amelia said. "Ben found a town ten miles south. We're going to scout it and bring everyone there."

"Then set a trap for Milton in Carmichael," he said.

"Exactly."

"Lillian, have you touched the weapons?"

"What weapons?" Harrison asked.

"I'd almost forgot about those," she said. "No, they're still at the Raddison farm, unless Amelia moved them."

Amelia shook her head.

"What kind of gear are we talking about?" Harrison leaned his elbows on the table.

"RPGs. Frag grenades. More assault rifles," Caesar listed.

"Enough to stop a bunch of cowboys?"

"Enough to stop Christine's army," Lillian added.

They discussed it for a while longer, but Caesar barely heard them. Christine wasn't dead.

Harrison lingered at the exit when the others departed. "If I'd have known, I would have told you."

"Thanks." Caesar dizzily got up. "I'll feel better in the morning."

He walked with his old friend outside, where the cool air brushed against his cheeks. Amelia gazed at Dot's Diner, and he joined her while Harrison drove off with Lillian. That was a duo he'd never expected to see.

"Dot's going to be happy to see her son," Caesar said.

"I guess we forgot to mention something else." Amelia looked pale.

Caesar listened, barely able to believe his ears.

Nearly everyone in Carmichael was present, waiting for the arrival of the incoming guests. Ben and Louise stayed with Gemma, and Maya stood behind them, clearly distraught to learn her husband was a spy for Milton. She claimed not to know, and John believed her, for whatever that was worth.

The snow had completely melted in the crops, and Mr. Tucker thought they might still salvage some corn if the weather improved.

"What do you think, Gemma?" John asked.

She glanced up, smiling. "The worst is over for now."

John sensed a different kind of storm on the horizon, but didn't mention that.

"There they are!" Donovan shouted. He smirked at John and pulled a firecracker out of his pocket, raising his eyebrows.

"Not now, kid," he said, and the neighbor boy nodded confidently, stowing it for later.

Caesar emerged from the forest, guiding the others. Anders must have run out of fuel too, because he came on foot. The group looked exhausted, their skin pale and drooping with malnourishment.

John understood they'd be sacrificing supplies for the one hundred strangers, but supposed he'd hope for a similar treatment should the roles be reversed. Ben rushed forward, meeting a man with long blond hair and a bushy beard. He was thin but appeared strong beneath the leather clothing. The woman with him had to be Ruby, and both Louise and Ben spoke well of the couple from Shelter.

The Arcadians embraced, and Caesar talked to Logan while he searched the crowd. John saw the moment he was told about his mother and Isla. Logan shoved past the agent, his movements frantic. Ruby reached for him, but he broke away.

"He'll heal. Time is the ultimate medicine," Gemma said.

John got that as well as anyone. "He'll never be the same."

"That's true." Gemma held hands with Maya, and they walked to the incoming crowd.

Haley approached, staring at the reunion. Anders hugged his kids, then his wife, and Helen cried while she touched her husband's dirty cheek. "I don't want to leave," John's sister said.

"Neither do I, but we have to warn the Den."

Haley gave a surprised look. "Does that mean you're going with Ben?"

"Ben's offered to show Amelia where the town is."

"Meaning…"

"I'm traveling with Jamal and Maya."

"I thought Jamal…"

"What Jamal did was a gray area…it's about survival."

"He gave up our town to a bad guy," Haley said.

"To protect his friends and family."

"I wouldn't have done it," she added.

"What if Milton was holding a gun to your head?"

"Don't say that!" Haley slapped his arm. "Did Amelia approve it?"

"Yes. Ben wasn't pleased, but I don't think he could have executed the Themis rights to his best friend," John said.

"What if he's still working for Milton and you're being tricked?"

"Then I'll deal with it." John watched Maya with the others.

"Make way while I load everyone up!" Mr. Tucker called from the bus when he opened the door. The tires sank in the muddy passageway between the cornstalks, and the air brakes hissed.

The residents of Shelter slowly entered the vehicle, acting bewildered by their surroundings. Logan and his wife got on last, with Ben trailing in behind them. Caesar stayed on the ground with Anders while Mr. Tucker drove them to town.

"Now what?" Haley asked.

"We celebrate being alive."

———————

*A*melia walked through the cemetery, recoiling at the number of freshly dug graves they'd added since the Shift. Each was marked with white crosses, the name of the deceased carved into the wood. She stopped at Vivian's and crouched, touching the marker. The mayor had been a colorful character, as bright as the clothing she wore. Amelia couldn't fill those shoes, but she'd do her best to keep the people safe.

Caesar stalked the area with Anders and Harrison. She watched them, seeing how similar the trio were. Lillian was behind with Logan Rutherford.

"I don't believe my uncle would kill anyone," Logan said.

"I'm not asking you to, but these are facts."

Logan's gaze burned into Amelia's eyes. "They're all gone. Isla…my mom."

It had been a full day, and he didn't seem any closer to acceptance.

He held a tablet they'd taken from an LTC employee. She'd listened to the story about encountering the brownstone with Sebastian and the Shift device, and it didn't feel like a coincidence he'd appeared directly in their path. But maybe she was reading into it. Anything could seem too convenient if you tried hard enough.

Amelia joined them near the backhoe, where they'd dug up more of the blue stone. The tablet's screen shone when Logan approached the quarry, and he confirmed there was a link. The countdown showed 00:12:01.

"How does this work?" Harrison asked.

"It'll take longer than we have to explain," Logan said.

"But I can use it to go home?" Caesar's boss asked.

"From what I understand, I have three options." Logan typed on the tablet. "We could travel to the spot where Carmichael once sat in Indiana, to the facility my uncle's built in the Adirondack mountains, or to rural Colorado. I can only connect there because I know the coordinates."

"What's this *we* talk?" Caesar spoke up.

"I thought I'd go reason with my uncle—"

"No way." Caesar took the tablet from him. "Mr. Gustafsson is calling the shots, and he'd just as soon shoot your uncle the moment he becomes a liability."

"But everyone said they want me back." Logan looked at Lillian for support. "Maybe they'll leave you guys alone.

I'm willing to sacrifice—"

"Sure, what a sacrifice. You get to leave to Earth and run the company you abandoned ten years ago because you were too careless," Anders said. "While we're here being attacked by cowboys."

Logan fumed, but to his credit, kept his composure. "What would you suggest?"

"I'll go." Harrison lifted a hand. "Send me to Colorado. My family should be in our safehouse. I'll reach out to Reggie and find the building in the Adirondacks. Sebastian already gave us the rough location. How hard could it be?"

"Then what?" Amelia asked him.

"I storm it, then bring you all home," he said with confidence.

"Good plan," Caesar said. "I should—"

Amelia's heart sank. "No. They need you, and I think you know that."

Caesar met her gaze and nodded. "I won't let Milton or…or Christine harm anyone."

She breathed easier and checked the timer, finding there were only seven minutes remaining.

"So it's you?" Lillian gestured at Harrison.

"Unless you want to join me?"

Lillian seemed to contemplate it, then shrugged. "I can't leave Logan here."

"I'm coming." The comment from Anders shocked the entire group. "I talked to Helen already, and she agreed. We'll take their organization down and transport everyone home."

Harrison pursed his lips, deep in thought, and gave in with a sigh. "I'm not doing this because I want anyone to have revenge. I'm doing it because I'm not as young as I once was."

"Don't sell yourself short," Caesar said. "You never

were that fast."

Amelia smiled at their exchange, and could tell Caesar would miss having his friend on Arcadia.

"It's nearly ready." Logan glanced around. "I didn't expect to find my hometown again, especially not on Arcadia. It's barely changed."

"Unless you count the tornado damage," Amelia said. She wondered if the others were wishing they could travel through the Shift to Earth. If Amelia did, she had nowhere to go. Surely Mr. Gustafsson would be alerted if she tried using a credit card or, God forbid, went to work like nothing had happened.

Caesar and Anders acted like brothers heading to conflicting wars. They shook hands and separated while Harrison stood by Amelia.

"These are good people, Chief, and there's no one better to lead them. Keep it up, and everything will be fine." He leaned closer to whisper, "And when the time comes, let Caesar do his thing. And don't judge him too harshly for it. This is what I built him for."

Amelia nodded, but the words affected her more than she showed.

"Be ready." Logan held the tablet out to Harrison. "I wish we could keep it here, but it's better this way. I'll try to duplicate the tower and harness the stone's energy to give you a beacon from the lab."

Anders and Harrison strode off, lingering among the rocks.

One second, they were there; the next, they vanished, with only a shimmer of the air.

"He won't fail us," Caesar said. "Come on. There's a war to prep for."

"I'll need to contact the other towns. Water's Edge, Trent at Freeport, the Den… What do we call Carmichael?

It's the antithesis of an Arcadian village name," Logan told them.

Amelia tried not to overthink the coming battles. "Let's call it Lost Town."

"Lost Town," Caesar repeated. "That's perfect."

They got into separate vehicles, and Amelia viewed the cemetery from the side mirror as they drove off, wondering how many more would end up buried on Arcadia before this was finished.

EPILOGUE

Christine

Remote Adirondacks, LTC Laboratory

The helicopter's rotors were loud, breaking the near silence of the mountain range. Christine waved a cluster of gnats from her face and inhaled the fresh air. She hated it here, much preferring the sounds and smells of the city.

Her orders had been precise. *Get to the facility. Now.*

No comments about her performance, no responses to the encoded message describing her experience on Arcadia. None of this surprised her, because Mr. Gustafsson wasn't overly verbose in their few interactions.

"I have important things to do," Senator Kevin Rutherford complained.

"Settle down, Bucky."

"Just because you—"

"Cut it out. Your complaining is tiresome." Christine watched the black helicopter lower to a parking pad, where the senator's car waited patiently. They'd already spent an hour outside, anticipating her employer's arrival. Clearly, he wasn't as punctual as he expected them to be.

She thought about the mission, and how she'd missed seeing both Caesar and Anders. That was for the best. She was sure of her skills, but those were dangerous agents, particularly when wronged. She didn't want to admit to herself that she'd fled because she couldn't face Caesar, but it was the truth.

"Have you met him?" she asked Kevin.

"No."

The single-word response worried her. Christine had done jobs blindly before, but not for this many years. Despite the assurances to herself, she couldn't fight the seeping dread as the copter landed.

Two black-clad armored soldiers emerged, facemasks covering their heads.

It was a solid minute before the man exited. The wind blew his long hair to the side, and he wore an open collar with a white blazer and blue pants. He looked like he belonged on a yacht, not in the wilderness of upstate New York. The second she laid eyes on him, she understood just how dangerous he was.

The soldiers flanked him, their guns unfamiliar to her.

Gustafsson removed his expensive sunglasses and dropped them into his breast pocket when he was in the shade of the lobby entrance.

Kevin moved first, extending a hand.

The soldier shot him in the chest so quickly that not even Christine could react. He gurgled blood from his mouth, gasping for air.

Gustafsson stepped over him, motioning for Christine to join him. She glanced at the senator, watching him die.

"You did well," he said. "But we need to expedite things. The team is coming in two weeks. We've cleaned up the mess in Carmichael, so we have nothing to worry from the locals. Can you lead the team to Arcadia?" Mr. Gustafsson had a Scandinavian accent, perhaps from Norway or possibly Finland. She hadn't spent enough time in those countries to be certain.

"Yes, I can lead them." She swallowed, assuming her

fate would mirror the senator's if she faltered.

"Excellent."

"What's so special about Arcadia?" she chanced.

"It's not Arcadia I'm interested in." He stopped at the door while his soldiers opened it.

"Then what?"

"It's what lies beyond Arcadia."

They entered the building, and Christine had a feeling her life was about to change forever.

———————

Milton

Rural Arcadia

*M*ilton crouched at the ledge, seeing the farmhouse below. "They had to have come from this direction."

Duffy nodded, but that was to be expected. The kid agreed with anything he said, and Milton liked that.

"They were on motorized bikes?" Milton asked.

"Yes, sir. Never seen something like them before."

Neither had Milton, but he'd heard the stories.

Milton was one of the few members of Tombstone to have been born and raised on Arcadia. It gave him a certain connection to the land the others couldn't fathom. He'd done well to downplay their size to these insignificant villages, but it was the time to strike.

They'd avoided assimilation to this point only because he'd allowed it, but it was time to be united.

Duffy and Milton followed the trail and eventually encountered something alien to the land. He set a palm on the hood and wondered what this was called. It was obviously designed for military purposes. He examined the interior, finding supplies loaded in the back. A few guns, the style different from the revolvers dangling at his hips, along with matching ammunition.

Duffy touched one, and he urged the boy away.

The keys were in the ignition, and Milton tried turning it. The engine clicked but didn't start, so he found a way to release the hood, and investigated. "Sliders came and gunked it."

"We need water," Duffy said, and Milton nodded, gesturing to the canyon.

"You know where to find it."

Duffy knew better than to argue, so he didn't. It took nearly an hour before he reappeared from the cliffside, carrying a bucket he'd brought from the transport. Water sloshed from the edges as he walked, and more spilled when he set it down.

"Scrub it," Milton ordered, and watched the boy clean the engine.

Milton let it dry, then cranked the key again. It caught, and he celebrated with a nip from his flask.

"Where are we going?" Duffy asked.

"To Shelter."

"Why?"

"Annie and Braxton haven't checked in."

"Are you worried?"

"Never." Milton hadn't driven before, but neither had the kid. He understood the basic principles of it. When he was younger, he'd spent hours in a rusted old chassis of a Shifted farm truck, pretending to be a race car driver from Earth. The planet sounded so incredible, but he knew it was only a temptation, for Arcadia was their Nirvana. This was heaven, and he feared the devil had arrived. The devil had to be tamed, and Milton was up to the task.

It was a bumpy start, with Milton nearly driving into the canyon named after him. He guided it away from the gorge to the prairies.

"You can get around so much faster," Duffy said.

Milton didn't like relying on this level of technology, because they had no fuel and no means to repair it. But for now, he'd take the advantage.

They found Shelter before dusk, and he observed it from afar, not seeing movement. He left the vehicle and grabbed his guns, hiking to the town.

"They're gone." Duffy rubbed his chin.

Milton's imagination took hold when he saw the spent cartridges on the ground. He picked one up. "It looks like your friends met Annie." He noticed a pile of hats near a burned pyre and cursed under his breath.

"They ain't my friends," Duffy quickly retorted.

These were his top soldiers. Dead.

Milton returned to the vehicle and gripped the steering wheel tightly. "Send word to Tombstone. It's time to prepare."

"For what?"

"The reckoning." Milton put it into drive and sped north as the sun set on Arcadia.

THE END

Of
Shelter: Lost Town Book Two

Continue the story with
Fracture: Lost Town Book Three

ABOUT THE AUTHOR

Nathan Hystad is an author from Sherwood Park, Alberta, Canada.

Keep up to date with his new releases by signing up for his newsletter at www.nathanhystad.com

Made in United States
Troutdale, OR
09/05/2025

34288241R00245